GUARDIAN OF THE DROWNED EMPIRE

FRANKIE DIANE MALLIS

SEVEN QUEENS PRESS

Cover Designer: Stefanie Saw

Character Art: Tony Viento

Map Art: K.C. Hayes

ISBN 978-1-957014-03-6 (Hardback)

ISBN 978-1-957014-04-3 (Paperback)

❀ Created with Vellum

For the First Novels Club: Donna, Janine, and Sara. Okay, yeah, technically this is my second novel. Though it used to be part of the first. But more importantly, I never would have gotten here without you three.

GREY VILLA

V E R T A V I A

CRESTHAVEN

TOWN OF
SERATION

URTAVIAN WOODS

SHADOW
STRONGHOLD

TEMPLE
OF DAWN

U R T A V

KATU

B A M A R I A N   D E S E R T

ARKTURIO
TOWNHOM

GREAT LIBRARY

S C H O L A R ' S
H A R B O R

MUSEION

D R Y   W A V E   C L I F F S

LUMERIAN OCEAN

N

SOTURION
APARTMENTS

GRYPHON
ISLAND

GUARDIAN
OF BAMARIA

SEA TOWER

BAMARIA

LUMERIAN OCEAN

N

AMARAN ISLANDS

LETHEA

GRYPHON ISLAND

...RIA

...MERIAN EMPIRE
...ERIA NUTAVIA

DAUGHTER OF THE DROWNED EMPIRE

PREVIOUSLY...

On the night of Lady Lyriana Batavia's seventeenth birthday, she finally begins a courtship with Lord Tristan Grey, a wealthy and politically important nobleman. But her celebrations are paused while she attends the Revelation Ceremony for her eldest sister, Lady Meera, the Heir Apparent destined to rule their country, Bamaria, as High Lady one day. Her cousin and best friend, Lady Julianna, will also participate.

While Lyr and Tristan share secret looks and touches, the ceremony comes to an abrupt halt as Jules steps onto the dais. The Revelation Ceremony reveals a Lumerian's magic—bound after birth. This is done so that when the magic is revealed, the Senate can easily spot a vorakh, or forbidden power. Jules immediately begins to show she has one—visions. To Lyr's horror, her cousin is arrested right before her eyes by the Imperator—the Emperor's nephew, and she must sit and watch calmly as she loses her cousin. Everyone in the ceremony has turned on Jules, including Tristan whose Ka hunts vorakh. Lyr cannot show emotion or there's a chance the rest of her family could be implicated and harmed. Another ruling family, Ka Azria, were all killed by the Emperor for this reason. When Meera's turn comes, her magic appears weak and strange, but not enough to worry Lyr who is convinced she can save Jules. She dismisses Tristan, tries to gain assistance from her bodyguard Markan, but ends up drugged and returned to her Ka's fortress of Cresthaven.

Lyr's father, the Arkasva and ruler of Bamaria reveals that Meera does in fact have visions, but he covered it up, and now he expects Lyr, Meera, and their middle sister Morgana to swear a blood oath. No one can know about Meera's condition or their father's role in covering it up. Breaking the oath means death, but Lyr swears.

Two years later, Lyr is turning nineteen and will participate in the Revelation Ceremony. But the past two years have taken their toll. Morgana developed the second vorakh, mind-reading. And now Lyr must not only keep both sisters' secrets, but also takes charge of most of their care since vorakh is debilitating for them. Though warned not to venture into the city after a recent akadim attack, Lyr ventures out with Tristan who has no idea of the secrets she's keeping, or that she's using their relationship as a shield to hide her Ka's secrets. In the city, Lyr acquires a priceless heirloom from a half-Afeyan jeweler who is also a librarian. And Tristan discovers and arrests another vorakh. Lyr notices the Imperator's men, foreign soldiers are all over the streets—their presence has been growing for a long time since the rebellion that took place when her father came into power. The soldiers are attacking a young man in the streets. Rhyan Hart, a forsworn soturion in exile from his country, and Lyr's first love, and first kiss. She stops the fight and brings Rhyan back to Cresthaven much to Tristan's annoyance. At home, Meera reveals her latest vision showed Lyr turning into a black seraphim. Lyr saw the image twice earlier that day, but doesn't know what it means, only that it's associated with the phrase "*Shekar Arkasva*" hinting her father is not the true ruler of Bamaria.

At the ceremony, Lyr is unbound and to her horror, reveals no magic at all. Believing she is hiding vorakh, the Imperator has her arrested and imprisoned until they can determine what vorakh she is hiding. That night, Rhyan guards her cell and helps comfort her. When the test is finally administered, it is revealed that Lyr has no magic. She's expelled from the Mage Academy. But she is given the chance to avoid exile by becoming a soturion. She will have seven months to prove herself capable and be tested by the Emperor.

Lyr is bound to Rhyan with kashonim, blood magic that will allow her to call upon Rhyan's strength in battle, but will also forbid a relationship between them. Lyr tries to discover more about Lumerians who have no power, but her only source material appears to be a scroll about the Goddess Asherah that Mercurial, an immortal ambassador is borrowing. Not believing herself capable of surviving the brutal warrior training along with frequent attacks and harassment from her classmates, Lyr decides to skip training to try and press her engagement to Lord Tristan, hoping if she fails the Emperor's test, at least Tristan's Ka might protect her.

But Tristan's grandmother, the head of his Ka refuses. She informs Lyr that the rebels who tried to unseat her father have returned and are planning another attack. They are using the black seraphim as their symbol.

Lyr trains for a month, fighting her growing attraction to Rhyan while trying to care for her sisters, keep Tristan happy, and discover more about the Emartis. But when they attack the Soturion Academy, Lyr learns that Rhyan isn't just training her to be a soturion, he is also her bodyguard. Because the attack happened over the academy, the Imperator is informed, and will return to Bamaria.

Lyr is scheduled for combat training that night in the academy's arena, but before she can attend, she learns Meera is having a vision. Lyr races home to help her sister, and sustains several injuries. Late for the training, she rushes back before she can clean herself up, and Rhyan sees her and realizes she's hurt. Knowing she can't fight in her weakened condition, nor can she sit out with the Imperator observing, he makes her call on kashonim, giving her his strength. But when the fight is over, the Imperator reveals that he knows she skipped training, thus breaking their bargain. He removes three months of her time to prepare for her test and sentences her to four lashes.

Injured, Lyr is cared for all night by Rhyan who reveals that he still has feelings for her, but will not act on them because of the oaths they swore to be apart. It is the first time in two years Lyr has ever allowed anyone to care for her cuts and bruises, fearing that they may reveal Meera's secret. The next morning, Mercurial, the immortal approaches Lyr again, attempting to lure her into a bargain. He will grant her her magic power, the thing she needs to survive and protect her family, but Lyr refuses. She knows deals with the Afeya can be deadly.

Rhyan reveals that he was beaten by his father, and kept from touching his own magic and power during training. He believes he can train her to survive, outside the academy in secret. Still injured, Lyr is sent home to consider his proposal, knowing it will be extra work, and force her to be with him even more—something becoming more difficult as their friendship and attraction deepens.

At home she discovers her classmate Tani is a member of the rebel group that attacked her and her father. Lyr fights Tani, realizing now that maybe she does have strength to survive. Before the fight ends, Tani reveals she knows something is happening between Rhyan and Lyr, and that she illegally used kashonim. Lyr's Aunt Arianna breaks up the fight, and the following morning, Lyr decides: she's ready to train with Rhyan. But just as she makes her choice, Mercurial appears and hints that he will force her into a bargain one day, and that she has more power than she knows.

THE FIRST SCROLL: BLOOD OATH

CHAPTER
ONE

(Two years earlier)

A month. A month had passed since I'd seen Jules. Since the Bastardmaker had taken her. Since the Imperator had ordered her arrest.

I squeezed my eyes shut, willing the sun to reverse course, to stop shining so fucking brightly through the glass of my window. How could it be day again? How could it be light and beautiful outside? How were the sounds of waves crashing against the shore and birds singing with the ocean breeze allowed to continue when Jules was…Jules was….

I rolled over in my bed, burying my face between two pillows. As if I could suffocate my thoughts, my memories. As if I could stop time.

A sob wracked my chest, but there were no tears in my eyes. My cheeks and my pillows were dry and had been for days. I'd run out of tears.

My older sister Morgana stomped down the hall, the exasperated cadence of her footsteps giving her away. She paused outside my door. A moment passed before there was a knock. I sank deeper into my pillows, clutching my belly. I needed to eat. My stomach was aching, and nausea roiled inside of me I was so hungry. But the thought of leaving my bed, putting food in my mouth, chewing, tasting, swallowing...that left me feeling sicker.

Morgana's knocks came louder, more urgent, until her fist was pounding the door with an unrelenting force.

"I'm asleep!" I yelled—or, at least, I tried to yell. My voice was raw and muffled, cracked from days of crying and disuse.

"You've been asleep half the week." The door burst open. The hinges creaked sharply before coming to an abrupt stop. My door couldn't open all the way—not with the barrier of clothes strewn in piles across my floor. "Fucking Moriel."

I didn't move, didn't look up. I didn't want to. I didn't want anything. Just Jules. Just for Jules to be...to be....

Here.

But she wasn't. She never would be again. We'd gotten official word. She'd reached Lethea, the place where they took criminals, the place where they took those with vorakh, forbidden magic. Lethea was the place where those Lumerians were stripped—had their magic taken away. It was a procedure that killed. And we'd been informed the procedure was complete. Jules was gone.

"It smells like gryphon-shit in here," Morgana said. Her sandaled foot landed with a slap against a free space of carpet. Cursing under her breath, she paused before there was another slapping step and another as she awkwardly weaved her way through the labyrinth of the mess my bedroom had accumulated.

"Lyr? Lyr!"

My mattress shifted with Morgana's weight. Incense clung to her skin, the scent wafting toward me. It was perhaps the first pleasant scent that had been in my room in days.

"You have to get up." There was no gentleness in my sister's voice.

"Get out," I said, my own voice hollow.

"Tristan sent word for you this morning."

I groaned. "Already?" Tristan and I had been courting for the past month. After a season of flirtation, we'd finally become official —on the same night Jules had been arrested and taken.

I wasn't up to it today, to seeing the wealthy nobleman whose Ka hated vorakh so much they tracked, hunted, and arrested them. Every Lumerian Tristan caught with forbidden magic was handed over to the Imperator, the nephew to the Emperor, the overseer of half the Lumerian Empire—and a monster.

Seeing Tristan was draining me. I'd had to pretend for a month, a whole fucking month, that things were fine, that I was myself and not remotely sad at all, like I'd forgotten Jules had even existed. It was the only way for my family—my Ka—to survive.

I'd preened in front of Lumerians when we were out and smiled for the nobles who attended the parties at Grey Villa while I hung on Tristan's arm so I could shift public opinion of Ka Batavia back to a favorable light. I had to show that despite having a family member with vorakh, we fully and completely repudiated and rejected our cousin. After all, the youngest Heir to the Arkasva—me —was dating the most prominent member of a Ka known for hating vorakh—Lord Tristan Grey. His grandmother, Lady Romula, a powerful member of the Bamarian Council, had even released an official statement blessing our new and fragile union.

I could handle the fake smiles, the waving, the dancing, the sitting still and looking pretty. I'd been born to move through life with eyes on me, with scrutiny and gossip following my every move. I was Heir to the Arkasva; it was in my blood.

But playing my role in private was harder. I'd had to pretend for Tristan that I'd wanted his touches and kisses as much as I had before—before he'd turned on Jules.

Another noble Ka, Ka Azria, had had vorakh in their family. They'd ruled the neighboring country of Elyria for years. When their secret had been discovered, the Emperor had obliterated them —every last child had been killed.

Both my public smiles and my private kisses were to keep us from that same fate. But today, my body and my heart just didn't seem to care.

"Lyr," Morgana snapped. One of the pillows over my head was snatched away. "It's noon! Which you'd know if you saw which direction the sun was shining in through the windows. You don't hear the timekeeper having a Godsdamned concert every hour? How many pillows are on your head?"

"What do you care?" I asked.

"Auriel's bane." She pulled my blanket, making a noise of disgust as the fabric pooled around my ankles. My whole body shivered as cool air hit my skin. "Seriously, Lyr, when was your last bath? Never mind. I don't want to know." She tugged on another pillow. "Gods, I can't wait until my fucking Revelation. Then I can use a stave instead of touching this shit."

A memory flashed through my mind: Jules's stave. She'd been so excited, choosing the path of mage, remaining so still and brave when Arkmage Kolaya had cut her wrist to begin the process. Her stave had been produced, a beautiful twisting of moon and sun wood with her name magically carved into its side. It was supposed to have been a sacred moment, the first showing of the magic that had been bound inside her body since she was born.

But the only magic Jules had ever performed was forbidden— vorakh. She'd immediately fallen into a vision, fear and terror gripping her as she'd seen something none of us ever could or would see. The stave had fallen from her hand and rolled onto the floor. I'd been so embarrassed when she'd first dropped it, not having any idea at the time what it had meant. And then she had been arrested, taken away, and was now gone from my life forever.

The tears were back. How was it I could cry until I was all dried up, and then out of nowhere, one simple question, one comment, one memory was all it took to summon the tears back in full force? My stomach twisted over the fact that we'd have to repeat the charade all over again at Morgana's Revelation Day. Eleven months from now, she'd be nineteen and eligible for the Revelation Ceremony like Jules and Meera, our eldest sister, had been. Eleven months were all we had before we relived the horror. By then, I'd have turned eighteen and reached a whole year of my life without Jules.

"Look, Lyr, I'd clean this all up for you if I could, but I don't know where anything goes. Or how to clean. And I—I just can't do this," Morgana said. "Ugh, I miss the maids!"

"You know why they're gone," I snapped.

"Doesn't change the fact that I miss them. And clearly," she gestured around my room, "you do, too. Now, make a Godsdamned decision. Are you seeing Tristan today or not? Because if you are, then I'd get my ass up and march straight into the ocean. That's the size of the bath you're going to need to get this shit off you. You need to do it before he sees you," she sniffed, "and smells you."

"He said she was better off dead," I cried. I couldn't shake the memory of the moment he'd told me so callously to move on.

"Half of Bamaria said the same thing," Morgana said.

My chest tightened. Half of Bamaria had said far worse. Even though we'd all been as still as possible during the arrest, keeping our faces stoic and neutral, Jules's vorkah was Bamaria's biggest scandal in years. For the past month, it had reignited the flames of distrust Bamarians felt over Father becoming Arkasva after Mother died. He'd ruled our country, sitting in the Seat of Power, wearing the Laurel of the Arkasva, for most of my life. But it had taken years for our people to accept him as ruler—many still didn't.

Traditionally, Bamarian rule had always transferred through the direct bloodline of Ka Batavia—a bloodline of women. Power transferred from mother to daughter, sister to sister, aunt to niece or to female cousin. Father was not in the bloodline, and he was a man —and no man had ever ruled Bamaria before.

We'd always had a High Lady, and now for well over a decade, we'd had our first High Lord. A mob of angry Bamarians had formed right after he'd taken the Seat of Power. He'd been making his first public appearance in the streets when the mob had nearly killed him. Arrests had been made, traitors killed, and the rebellion squashed. Years had been spent cultivating the perfect image of Ka Batavia and regaining the trust of our people.

Aunt Arianna had been instrumental in that. She'd been the one the mob wanted in power—and she'd been the one to quell the unrest and stand by Father's side. As my mother's youngest and only surviving sister, tradition said the Laurel would go to her. But it hadn't. Still, she protected our Ka as fiercely as she could even after she'd learned her husband had led the rebellion.

She taught us not only to smile and wave but to control what our people saw, to master the art of public perception. Aunt Arianna had trained us to be public figures even as toddlers. Soturi fight disobedience with swords; nobles fight with appearances, she'd say.

And it was for this reason—to separate our Ka from scandal, from vorakh—that I continued my relationship with Tristan. To keep Ka Batavia from losing everything, from becoming the next Ka Azria.

Arianna assured us that my actions the past month had been instrumental in bringing our Ka back into favor. As an Heir to the Arkasva, I wasn't simply courting a nobleman, I was shaping public opinion. I was keeping Bamaria's most famous vorakh hunter distracted, and thus the people distracted as well.

I received fewer glares every time I ventured out. Nobles who'd shied away from talking to me the first days after Jules's vorakh had been revealed now greeted me warmly and invited me to parties and social gatherings. But it wasn't getting any easier.

Morgana shifted beside me. "Look, Lyr, I get it. Tristan's a piece of gryphon-shit, but he was a piece of gryphon-shit before Jules was—"

"Don't!" I finally sat up. "Don't you say it."

"Before Jules died!" Morgana said. "Myself to Moriel! You're the one courting him, not me!"

I launched forward in bed, ready to scratch and claw at Morgana. "You know exactly why I'm doing it! What I'm giving up to protect us! To keep us from—"

Morgana's hands wrapped around my wrists, and she pushed me back. "You can't fight me, little sister. You're not strong enough. You haven't eaten in days. You're weak," she snarled. "And I don't care if you court him or not. You can shape public opinion without marrying your reputation to his."

"You know that's not true." If it had just been Jules, I could have ended things with Tristan and moved on. But it was also Meera who'd revealed vorakh.

"Fine," Morgana said. "Then do it already. Get up."

"You don't understand."

"I don't understand?" Morgana seethed. "I don't fucking understand?" She released my wrists and sat back, her arms folded across her chest. That was when I looked at her—really looked at her—for the first time in weeks. Her notoriously shiny black hair was dull and frizzy. There were black circles under her eyes, and her pale skin was white, gaunt, and pulled tight against cheekbones that hadn't been as pronounced last month.

"I know," she said slowly. "I know that you...Gods. You and Jules were closest. It's always been the four of us, all together all the time. And I get it. I have a special bond with Meera. You had one with Jules. But she was my cousin, too. My friend, too. Maybe I'd be in bed looking like a fucking akadim victim if it had been Meera who'd been...." She sucked in a breath. "But it doesn't change anything. We're all upset, and we're all doing the best we can. And if we want to keep it from being Meera next time, or me, or you—especially if you keep up this circus act of courting a vorakh hunter—then you need to wake the fuck up, go see him, and convince him again that you're fine."

I knew she was right. I knew we had a duty and a secret to protect.

We four keep this secret. We four die by this secret.

I had given my oath in blood—I had promised to protect Meera. And laying here in bed, crying, grieving, and sobbing, didn't do anything. It didn't help anyone. It didn't change the circumstances.

Jules was dead. Meera, my eldest sister, was alive because we were willing to sacrifice everything to keep her so. I wasn't going to lose one more member of my family or renounce my Ka or our claim to the Seat of Power in Bamaria no matter what happened. I was willing to sacrifice everything.

So, do it. Get up, I thought. *Get the fuck up. Live your life as Lady Lyriana Batavia, Heir to the Arkasva, High Lord of Bamaria.*

Put on a pretty dress and a pretty smile, and let your boyfriend escort you through the city like a proper noble. It was what I'd been sleepwalking through the past month—wearing the mask of a brave face and then falling apart the moment I was alone.

But it was getting harder to put myself back together again, to prevent my emotions from consuming me. And as much as I tried to logic my way through this, I remained frozen to the bedsheets.

Morgana rolled her eyes. "Fine. I'll tell Tristan you're on your cycle bleeding, and your stomach hurts too much for you to get out of bed."

I blinked. When was the last time I'd bled? A month? Two? Not that it mattered. But I couldn't remember, like I couldn't remember the last time I'd eaten, or bathed, or smiled, or felt Jules wrap her arms around me, or listened to the infectious sound of her laugh. Most memories since the Revelation were foggy in my mind. There were clusters of me crying, throwing every piece of clothing on the floor after trying each one on in an attempt to look normal and happy, and then feeling doubly miserable and hating how everything looked and felt on my body. I'd meet up with Tristan, a smile plastered on my face as we pranced around the city and rode in litters, and when I returned home to Cresthaven, I'd lose it the moment I was past the fortress walls. I'd taken to running straight for the ocean, wading in in my clothes and shoes deep enough to scream and cry into the crashing waves without fear of anyone hearing me.

Morgana inched closer to my side of the bed, wrinkling her nose in disgust. "Give me your arm."

"No!"

Morgana grabbed my elbow, trying to expose my wrist.

Immediately, I snatched it back from her fingers, hugging my arm to my chest. "Don't touch it."

The blood oath still felt raw on my wrist, the skin burning where Father had cut me as I'd sworn to keep our secrets—that Meera was like Jules and had one of the three vorakh, visions, and that Father had overstepped in the ceremony to save her. The oath bound me to keep the secret with an ancient magic. I could feel its power hissing under my skin, watching, waiting, ready to strike me down the moment I broke the vow.

We four keep this secret. We four die by this secret.

"I don't want to touch it," Morgana snapped. "But I need to make sure it's healing properly. Stop fighting me." She grabbed my wrist and wrenched it into her lap, her sharp nails digging into my skin. In the temple when Jules's vorakh had been revealed, Morgana had held my hand so tightly, she'd cut tiny crescent moons into my skin. Now the cycles of the moon were tattooed over her wrist and up the length of her arm.

"I am going to throw up," she said dramatically, peeling back the white bandage on my inner arm. The bandage may have smelled, but the tattoo underneath was pristine.

A seven-pointed star, the Valalumir, had been inked across my skin in perfect detail. Inside the Valalumir, the sigil of Ka Batavia— seraphim wings beneath a full moon—stood proud. The tattoo was there to conceal the blood oath, to obscure the slightly mutilated skin. A blood oath left no visible mark or scar, but it could be felt. As a noble lady, an Heir to the Arkasva, my skin had never been harmed. And if Tristan noticed the slightest imperfection, then the tattoo artist was my defense to sweep away his suspicions.

"At least you don't have an infection." Morgana released me.

"Are we done here?" I asked, already rolling back to bury my face against the pillow.

"With this," she said. "I assume you're not going to attend your other obligation. I'll send word you're sick, and you can lie here and waste away. But if you think I'm going to let the stench of your room seep through the walls and into mine, you're wrong."

"Clean it up then. I don't fucking care."

Morgana laughed. "Like I know how to clean. You either get the fuck up, wash your Godsdamned clothes, take a bath, and get your shit together, or I will come back in here tonight and throw every single gown you own out the window before I light them on fire."

"Don't threaten me with a good time. That's just a reason to go shopping," I said dully and squeezed my eyes shut.

"Well, luckily, you have a boyfriend with a purse full of silver."

I grabbed another pillow and placed it on top of my head.

"That is, if you ever get up to see him again," she said.

A black hole was settling over my heart and stomach. I was just so...empty. And hopeless.

And scared.

Silence washed over us, before Meera screamed from her bedroom. A blood-curdling, animalistic scream.

I recognized the sound at once. At last, one month after her Revelation, one month since Father had controlled her body and magic to make it appear as if she were some mediocre mage—not a powerful Heir to the Arkasva equipped with forbidden magic—Meera's vorakh was making its second appearance. This was the power, the secret, the curse that had left me with a scarred wrist, a tattooed arm, and a promise that weighed more than my life. This was the same illegal power that had taken Jules and left me a mere shadow.

Meera's vorakh had come to collect its price. She was having a vision.

Morgana was already moving, no longer trying to work her way around my depression-built mountains of dirty clothes but leaping over them. "Meera!"

There was another scream—louder and weaker all at once, as if she was too terrified of what she'd seen in her mind to even express the fear flooding through her.

I remembered seeing that fear in Jules's eyes when she'd looked out across the temple once her magic was revealed. She had been searching for me, for her family, for support. She had needed us—needed *me*—and I...I'd sat there, pinned to the chair, schooling my face to a neutral, noble expression, and holding the hand of the very man who'd have hunted her down in seconds if the Imperator hadn't gotten to her first.

"Stop!" Morgana yelled. There was a crash. Glass shattered against a wall.

Cold seeped into my room. Freezing air. Meera's aura.

Goosebumps prickled across my arms and legs, and I reached for my blanket, determined to burrow back beneath it into endless darkness and warmth.

"Help!" Morgana cried. "Gods! What do I do?"

I burrowed deeper, willing myself to go deaf, to stop hearing Meera's screams or Morgana's pleas. It felt too much like that night. It was too soon, too close.

"Lyr! Help me! Please!"

Meera screamed again, and again I was pulled back into the temple; the memory of how I hadn't been able to help Jules, to save her, was overwhelming.

But Meera was here. Meera was alive. Meera had a chance.

The scar on my wrist itched wildly. Morgana shouted another desperate call for help. Energy I hadn't experienced in weeks surged through me, and I jumped out of bed and raced around the piles of clothes on my floor, my ankle nearly tangling in a discarded gown. It was the same gown I'd worn that night, on my birthday.

A moment later, I was in Meera's room. Her walls were pristine white except for one splotch of red. Blood. There was a cut on Morgana's forehead and a glass vase on the ground. Water leaked from the shards onto the plush carpet and the wilted silver snap flowers that had spilt from it.

Morgana clutched her forehead, moaning in pain, while Meera circled her. There was a feral look to my eldest sister, a look I'd never seen before. She was thinner than she had been a month earlier, her ash-brown hair was stringy and tangled—in desperate need of being washed and brushed—and her hazel eyes were wide, somehow both full of fear and empty.

Meera's gaze turned to me but she showed no sign of recognition.

She lunged, her hands in front of her and fingers curled into claws. I was shocked at the impact. For a second, my mind conjured up some old scroll I'd read about vorakh. The forbidden magic strengthened the mages who had them, in effect making them as strong as a soturion when they were enthralled.

In the next second, my back slammed against the carpet, and I wheezed, barely able to catch my breath.

A growl erupted from Meera, her teeth gnashing as she readied herself to pounce on me. I rolled to the side just in time.

"What do I do?" I yelled to Morgana. "Morgs! How do I stop this?" I'd never been in a fight before. I didn't know what to do or how to help. I only knew I had to keep Meera from hurting herself.

Morgana shifted, gingerly clutching at the wall. Blood dripped down her chin onto her chest, bleeding into the fabric of her black gown. "I don't know," she moaned, pressing both hands to her head as she made it to her feet. "I don't know what to do with her like this. I don't—I can't—She's too strong right now."

Meera grabbed my arm, the movement fast and vicious. Her nails slid down my arm, cutting into my skin, drawing blood.

"Fuck!" I scurried back, scrambled to my feet, and clutched at my arm to staunch the wound. "Meera. Meera! Are you…?"

She screeched, leaping to her feet and running for me. I flinched, and then something settled deep inside of me.

I made a decision. I wouldn't lose anyone else in my family. Never again. And I would do whatever it took.

In that moment, I had two objectives: protect my body and keep Meera from further hurting Morgana or herself.

I ran at Meera, at the vision forcing its way inside of her. Our bodies collided, and I pushed her onto the bed to cushion her fall. I found her wrists, pinned them above her head, and pressed my forehead to hers.

"Come on, Meera! It's me. Come on, come on!"

Her eyes widened, recognition filling them. "Lyr?"

My breaths came sharp and fast as the tension left her body. "Meera?" My tears began to spill. She was all right. She'd survived her first full vision. We had survived.

The room remained filled with a frigid chill as we cleaned the blood off the wall and threw the broken vase and dying silver snaps into the trash. Then the three of us huddled together under layers of blankets as Meera described a scene that didn't make sense. In her vision, there'd been a forest and a girl wandering through it. There'd been voices in the air, cries for help. But the girl couldn't find the owners of those voices, and then everything had gone dark.

After Meera described her vision, the temperature in the room slowly returned to normal, and I made another decision. Not only was I going to meet Tristan, but this was the last time I would let myself fall apart. If I was going to play my role to perfection, I couldn't come home and scream into the ocean. I couldn't break down and cry anymore. It was getting too hard to pick myself back up. Jules was gone. I couldn't change that. But I could protect Meera, and to do that, I'd need to wear my mask at all times.

I took a bath and washed and detangled my hair. For the first time in days, I put on clean underwear, tying bows on either hip to secure the undergarment in place. I gathered every article of clothing from my floor into a pile on my balcony. I gathered everything else until my room was clean—glasses, dishes, and cups that had accumulated in Morgana's attempts to get me to eat, my bedding, anything dirty, anything that smelled, anything I'd touched in my sorrow or grief, anything that reminded me of the fear that had plagued me for the last month or conjured up feelings of how scared and helpless I'd been. It all went to the balcony.

When I stepped onto my balcony, the salt-kissed wind blew at my hair, and my locks turned red beneath the sun and blew across my face. I tossed everything, every last memento of my depression-piles, over the railing. It landed in a heaping dump on the waterway of the fortress grounds below me. One dress remained in my wardrobe untouched—a black gown that cut a low v down the front, nearly to my belly. Silver threading beneath the material made it sparkle and shimmer in the sunlight, and silver rope crisscrossed over my waist and ribcage. Tristan would love the silver. He'd love the low cut of the dress, too.

You must let her go. She has to die in Lethea.

I pushed away the memory of Tristan holding me back and whispering those hateful words into my ear when Jules had been arrested.

I fixed my hair into long, loose waves, the way my hairdresser used to before we'd sent her away. I watched the locks transform from dark brown to bright red whenever I shifted into the sunlight. I couldn't make it look as good as my stylist could, but it wasn't bad either. I draped my diadem across my forehead for the first time since my seventeenth birthday and applied makeup, watching the gold center catch sunlight between my dark eyebrows. I looked beautiful and calm. The perfect Lady Lyriana Batavia, Heir to the Arkasva, High Lord of Bamaria.

Giving myself a final once over, I realized I only had one flaw: a scratch on my arm from Meera. Shit.

The cut ran across my bicep. I turned in the mirror to look more closely at it, gasping as I realized there was another wound from her vorakh. I had a bruise forming on my back as well. No one could know, no one could suspect. My hair was long and thick and hung in loose waves—it would cover the bruise—but I grabbed a black shawl that matched my dress just in case. I couldn't afford to make a mistake; I couldn't afford one misstep. My status in Bamarian society and the future of my Ka was at stake.

But the cut…I couldn't bandage it to hide it. Tristan would notice. I needed some other way to keep him from seeing it. I wandered into Jules's room, the room she'd occupied since we were girls. She'd moved in after her parents had died. It hadn't been touched since she'd been taken.

My eyes watered, but I blinked back the tears and schooled my face. I couldn't ruin my makeup.

On her dresser lay an assortment of jewelry we'd collected over the years. Birthday jewelry, we'd called it. Our own little tradition. Gold necklaces, jeweled rings, bracelets, bangles, earrings, waistlets, anklets—they were spread out in disarray rather than neatly arranged in her jewelry boxes and on her jewelry stands as if she'd been trying on different pieces to see their effect with her dress before her Revelation. While she'd been looking for the perfect accessory for what was supposed to have been the best night of her life, I'd been outside at the pools, kissing Tristan.

I inhaled and exhaled sharply, focusing on my mission, and examined the pieces, trying not to recall the days we'd purchased them or the occasions on which she'd worn them. In the center, under a larger golden necklace, was what I'd been looking for. It was Jules's favorite piece: a golden arm-cuff styled like seraphim wings.

I picked up the bracelet and watched it shine in the light, feeling how smooth and cold the metal was. I slid it over my arm, past my elbow, and up to my bicep. It fit perfectly, complementing my diadem, and most importantly, hiding the cut.

I nodded at my reflection and retreated through the halls of Cresthaven, using the kitchens to access the waterways behind the fortress that led to the garden underneath my balcony. Everything I owned lay in a giant pile. I flagged down one of my father's sentries. He'd been watching me and eyeing my dirty clothes with a mix of curiosity and disdain. But he hadn't said a word, and he wouldn't, since as far as he could tell, I did not appear to be in any danger.

"Your grace," he said, lowering his chin. He paused on the waterway, his golden armor gleaming in the sun.

I smiled sweetly. "Can you have one of the fortress mages burn this?"

"Burn? Your grace." His tone was condescending. I could read his expression as easily as a scroll. He thought I was being a silly, dramatic little girl. Spoiled. Ridiculous. It was exactly what I'd expected him to think. It was unbelievable sometimes, the way men, even those employed by my father, thought they could judge me when I was the one manipulating them.

I lifted my chin. "Did I ask for your opinion?" I used my haughtiest, most affected voice—the voice of an heir, of a girl who far outranked him and dared him to question her.

"No." He bowed. "My apologies. But it appears to be your entire wardrobe, your grace."

I laughed. "And it's all entirely last season. Some pieces even several seasons old. I can't have that, now can I? Wearing clothes that have fallen out of style? What would people say?"

The sentry looked confused but also like he'd decided it wasn't worth arguing. "I will see it done."

I nodded, turning on my heels. "I'll be checking in to see that it is in fact done."

"Your grace," he called. "Shall I alert Soturion Markan you wish to leave the premises? Venturing into the city, I presume?"

My fingers curled at my sides. "That won't be necessary," I said. "I'll have the escorts of Lord Tristan Grey accompany me."

Moments later, I sat in a seraphim carriage with Tristan's arms around me as I willed my body to relax and not shake under his touch. I had to get over this, this weird feeling I had whenever he touched me. His escorts, mages who kept their staves ready at all times, sat behind the partition to give us privacy. It made Tristan bolder, his hands already on me.

The floor shifted beneath us as the seraphim stood and took flight. A cold breeze hinting of fall's longer nights and darker days blew through the window as I watched Cresthaven move farther and farther away from me. Curls of black smoke rose above the glittering blue mosaic tiles of the fortress walls, dancing and licking at the sky before fading into white wisps.

I sucked in a breath. I'd shed my last tear for Jules. I'd fallen apart for the last time. If I was going to protect Meera, if I was going to fulfill my blood oath and my Ka was going to survive, I couldn't break character again.

I turned to Tristan. His brown eyes were full of affection, the wind lightly brushing through his hair. He had no idea of the turmoil thrashing inside me.

I conjured up the memory of our first kiss. Of the butterflies fluttering in my stomach. Of the way that sensation had moved lower when he'd drawn me closer, of the gasp of pleasure I'd made when his knuckles had grazed across my breasts and my nipples had hardened. I remembered the excited beats of my heart and the way he'd looked so handsome beneath the stars, the soft sprinkling sounds of water flowing into the pools. I remembered how I'd waited weeks for him to kiss me, enduring our flirtations and teasing until it all came together in what had felt like such a pivotal, explosive moment between us.

I pulled that memory forward as if I could wear it like armor. I'd desired him once with my entire being. I willed that desire to cloak me, to seep into my skin.

I traced the line of his jaw with my fingers as the carriage tilted. "Do you know how handsome you are?" I brought my lips against his, softly, slowly, tentatively, and closed my eyes, as his mouth opened to mine. I tensed, a feeling of panic surging through me, and then it passed. The faint scent of smoke wafted into my nose, blending with Tristan's scent, a mix of mint and the salt of the ocean.

His fingers pressed into me as my tongue swept past his lips. Our kiss deepened as my old life, the old me, burned to ash, and a new fire stoked inside of me.

CHAPTER
TWO

(Present Day)

You're the fire. It had been hours since the immortal Afeya Mercurial had uttered those words to me. Hours since he'd vanished right off the track in the Katurium, Bamaria's arena and training grounds for warriors. For the rest of my run and through all my soturion classes, all I could hear was the lilting, musical voice of the immortal replaying itself again and again in my head.

All I could hear was the way he'd taunted me and laughed and said I could be the most powerful soturion of all time. He'd seemed to know something I didn't. Something crucial. Something dangerous. Even after hours of lecture on weapons, soturion history, and combat theory, I could barely touch my lunch as I sat down with my friends, Haleika and Galen, to eat. I couldn't stop the dread building in my stomach.

You're the fire.

It wasn't the first time I'd heard those words. That was what made them so terrifying to hear. I'd heard them in a dream, a dream I'd had right after Rhyan and I had been bound together as novice and apprentice soturi—my blood and his blood joining to form a link between our power. This link meant we could never be more than apprentice and novice. Kashonim.

"You're the fire," he'd said in my dream just before he'd kissed me, before we'd fallen to the floor to make love...only to discover we were underground, buried alive, and the dream had come to a crashing halt, startling me awake.

Every time I thought about those words on Mercurial's lips, a chill ran down my spine. Why had he used that exact phrase? Was it a coincidence? Did it mean something different to him? Or could the Afeya see into dreams? Did he have the ability to see, not only into my mind, but also into my unconscious? My stomach knotted.

I didn't want an answer to my questions. Every single possibility scared me. Mercurial scared me.

Of all the people in Lumeria, he seemed to be the most suspicious of me and Rhyan, the most aware of the fact that, on some level, our relationship transcended that of just novice and apprentice. It was a fact Rhyan had just begun to acknowledge two nights before. A fact we had both decided immediately after could never be. A fact I knew was going to grip my heart like a vise forever, the way our first kiss had lingered with me the last three years.

I'd thought about that kiss, of the feel of his lips on mine and his body pressing me against the tree that night beneath the stars, far more times than I wanted to admit. Even now, with all that had happened and all the danger we faced, I was just as captivated by thoughts of him, of his emerald eyes, of the soothing sound of his voice and the light timbre of his northern accent. I could barely stop thinking about the way he moved his body with such strength and determination and the way he talked, as serious and insightful as he could be bitingly sarcastic and full of wit. The way he—Gods. I had to stop.

We were playing a dangerous game, one forbidden on so many levels. I still had a role to play, a duty to protect my family. I was still to be engaged to Tristan, and I still needed the protection of his Ka and wealth. If Mercurial had any inkling of the truth of what existed between me and Rhyan, neither of us would ever be safe when the Afeya was in Bamaria. The immortal had made it clear he wanted something from me, some power he believed I possessed, one I wasn't even aware of. It was a power he claimed even the nahashim—ancient creatures from the old world capable of finding anything—had been unable to detect. After I'd failed to reveal any magic at my Revelation, the Imperator had ordered me to be examined by nahashim. The procedure had been painfully invasive as the snake-like creatures violated my body seeking answers. They'd found nothing.

I didn't know whether or not to believe the Afeya. Mercurial knew I was desperate, that there was something I needed, something so important, I'd consider bargaining with the immortal for it; he knew I needed to find my power.

My lack of magic had led to my arrest and banishment and torn my life apart in a matter of days. It had kept me from protecting my family and from truly following my heart.

Mercurial had the ability to grant me any wish, any desire. It was what Afeya did. But every wish came with a price. And it was a price even I, a Lady of Ka Batavia, could never afford.

I tightened the laces of my soturion-issued sandals—so different from the sandals I'd worn all my life. These were of a heavy, dark brown leather, with straps running up the sides of my legs connected by laces that tied at my calves, thicker than anything I'd worn before. They were the shoes of a warrior, and I was not a warrior—unless Rhyan really could teach me to be one, as he'd promised.

I took a deep breath, trying to clear my mind before I entered our private training room for our afternoon lessons.

Rhyan closed the door behind him, as I dropped my bag on a stack of mats. I was hit with the musty smell of the room, now tinged with my own scent and Rhyan's familiar musk. I'd gotten used to it in the past month. I'd even begun to find it comforting. Safe.

"He's gone," Rhyan said immediately, green eyes blazing. A single red scar ran through his left eye, starting above his brow and ending at the top of his cheekbone. He looked me up and down, his gaze studious, assessing, as he folded muscular arms across his chest. "Are you all right?"

I pushed the loose strands of my hair behind my ears and tucked stray pieces into my braid before I stretched my arms across my chest, trying to relieve the tension still tight in my shoulders. "That depends. Which 'he' are you referring to?"

Quite a number of unwelcome *he's* were currently in Bamaria, not even including the newly formed legion of soldiers from Ka Kormac—two thousand men, all from a foreign country, all loyal to a foreign Ka led by my worst enemy. The Imperator had been gradually bringing the soldiers into our country for years. And recently, he'd used the excuse of unrest in Bamaria to arm the streets with his soturi until we were basically being occupied—even if no one in Bamaria was willing to say it out loud.

"The Afeyan messenger. Mercurial's gone." Rhyan's jaw tightened. He still stood in front of the door, his shoulders tensed. It was a protective stance, one I'd seen him take a hundred times now, as if he was preparing to defend me from anything or anyone who came through that door.

"How do you know?" I switched my arms, reversing the stretch. "He's never supposed to be here, and yet he seems to have a habit of appearing when and where he's least welcome." Like my apartment. Or the track when I was in the middle of a run.

Rhyan shifted his weight, looking uncomfortable, one hand resting on his waist. He wore a black practice tunic and a leather practice belt with seven hanging straps. The weighted bronze ends of the leather pieces reached mid-thigh. Below his tunic were his old boots laced up to his knees. They were his boots from the North, from his home country of Glemaria. I knew he favored them over Bamarian sandals even if we didn't have the right climate for them, at least not for another few weeks. Bamaria had a snowy season, but it was brief.

"I had a meeting this morning, after his appearance," Rhyan said, finally moving away from the door. "Regarding your...security detail."

My nostrils flared. It was still a tense subject between us—the fact that for over a month, Rhyan had been secretly a part of my security team, one of my escorts, a personal bodyguard watching over me. No one had told me, not even him. It had explained his constant alertness, the way he was always tense and ready to fight.

"Right. Of course. Did it occur to anyone that I ought to have been included in this conversation regarding my own safety and security?"

Rhyan flinched at my harsh tone.

In the last few days, we had grown closer. I'd even slept in his bed—I was injured, and he was on the floor, but still, there was an intimacy that had not existed between us before. Not to mention he was the first person I'd ever let see or treat my wounds. He was the first person I'd trusted enough to tend to them. In some ways, it was the most intimate I'd ever been with another person.

"I'm," he coughed, "a rather low-level member on the team—you know, being forsworn and all. I apologize that I can't speak to your lack of invitation to the meeting. But I am telling you now."

I softened. Rhyan hadn't had a choice in the matter to become my guard. He'd been exiled from his own country a year earlier, accused of murdering his mother, wife to the Arkasva, and Imperator of the North. He was also rumored to have killed another soturion in training. I didn't believe that either rumor was true no matter who else believed it. Rhyan could be dangerous and violent, and I had no doubt in my mind he was physically capable of what everyone said. But capable was all. He was good through and through. I'd never doubted that for a second.

When he'd reached our borders, an akadim—a monster of the old world—had nearly breached Bamaria, something that hadn't happened in years. Rhyan had killed it, a feat impressive even for the most powerful and experienced soturi. For this reason, he'd been permitted to stay in Bamaria despite being forsworn—a criminal in exile from his home country. But killing an akadim hadn't been enough for my father to absolve Rhyan of his past. He'd assigned Rhyan to be my guard and my apprentice. And Rhyan was stuck with me—the weakest soturion in history, the girl who could very well be his downfall if I didn't become stronger—as his novice.

Unless Mercurial was right, and the power he'd hinted I could possess was real.

"I know you are. And I appreciate that," I said. "But considering the Star Court Ambassador's penchant for showing up after he's allegedly left the country and then breaking and entering into my private quarters, can you elaborate?" I asked.

"We have eyewitness reports from the Soturi of Ka Batavia that they watched him cross the Elyrian border. They saw him physically crossing it." The Afeya seemed to have the ability to travel, a power that was forbidden. It was the third vorakh—the one I'd feared I'd have after Jules and Meera had been cursed with the first of the three vorakh two years before. They'd both had visions. Morgana, one year ago, had revealed the second vorakh—mind reading. Then there was me, cursed with nothing.

Anyone found in possession of vorakh was immediately arrested and executed. But the Afeya operated outside of the Emperor's rule. They could not be controlled or contained, only closely monitored with many, many peace treaties and trade agreements between us and their three courts.

I shook my head. "Was he invited for this most recent visit?"

"No."

I exhaled sharply, my stomach twisting. Afeya were capable of doing anything, making the impossible happen with their magic. Breaking into an apartment in a country he was not welcome in would be child's play for Mercurial. But there was a catch when it came to Afeyan magic: Afeya could never perform anything by their own free will. Every bit of magic they used, every spell they cast, every action they took—it had to be by request. Which meant someone had wanted Mercurial to seek me out.

"Rhyan, this isn't comforting. Don't you see? He can come back at any time."

"I know. I'm not taking this lightly. Everyone on your team is very aware, but the new wards around your apartment are up. The mages have given them double reinforcements and alarms, so you should be safe."

I narrowed my eyes. "Right. And if they fail, then at least my security detail will be patrolling outside my window."

"With the threat of the Emartis and the way they've targeted you, it's necessary."

The Emartis, rebels who'd been underground for years, had recently reemerged, determined to remove my father from the Seat of Power. Attacking me by attacking the Katurium had been their latest act of terrorism.

I folded my arms across my chest. "And what shift did you pull? Standing outside my window all night? Or sleeping outside my front door?"

He raised an eyebrow. Just one. I was never sure if he meant to lift one or both when he did that. The scar through his left eye cut through part of his eyebrow. His vision was perfect, and he claimed the injury had no impact on him beyond the way it looked cosmetically, but he couldn't move that part of his face at all. And though he'd never admit it, I knew he was ashamed of the scar to some degree. Whenever his brown hair began to curl—usually when it was damp—he had a nervous habit of pushing it over his forehead or running his fingers through the curls until they unwound into loose waves that covered the scar.

"Maybe it's best you leave your questions with the head of your detail," he said neutrally. "I'm merely an employee."

"And who is the head?" I asked. "Fucking Markan? He doesn't tell me shit."

Rhyan's hands clenched at his sides. For a moment, cold air sputtered around me, then just as quickly, it was gone. Rhyan's aura was one of the most powerful I'd ever encountered. Whenever he was feeling a particularly strong emotion or was using large stores of his power, his aura expanded, producing a chill.

I shivered at the sensation, goosebumps rushing up my arms.

"Sorry," he said. "I didn't mean to—"

I shook my head. "If my aura worked, it would react the same way whenever I mentioned him."

Markan had been my escort since I could walk, guarding me around Cresthaven and following me in the shadows when I left the fortress. His job was to keep me alive. But to me, he'd always be the bastard who'd stopped me from chasing after Jules when she had been taken. He'd be the bastard who'd drugged me that night and taken my unconscious body back to Cresthaven so my father could force the blood oath on me, cut my wrist and make me swear to protect our Ka's secrets.

"Arkturion Aemon is the head of your detail," Rhyan said formally, but there was an underlying tension in his words, an anger threading through them. "Any questions you have, I'd take to him." His aura flared out again, something colder and darker in the air, and Rhyan's body went still in a way I'd only seen once before—when he'd first seen me injured outside the other day before a training event.

I'd had to go to the habibellum—a practice fight amongst all my classmates—immediately after helping Meera through a vision. I hadn't had time to clean myself up or inspect every inch of my skin and hide my wounds with jewelry, clothing, and hairstyles. Doing so would have made me late, and because the Imperator had come to observe me, I couldn't afford to miss even a minute.

Rhyan had seen my injuries. He'd seen me limping with blood splattered on my tunic. He'd seen the cut on my cheek. He'd blamed Tristan, who was the last person Rhyan thought I'd been with, and for one moment, Rhyan had frozen like a predator. He'd looked ready to race through all of Bamaria until he'd hunted Tristan down and recreated every cut and bruise he'd seen on my body.

Rhyan didn't know it was Meera's vorakh doing all the damage.

"Rhyan?" I asked. "What's wrong?"

His nostrils flared as he shook his head. "Just...if you have questions about security, take it up with him."

I stepped closer, tentatively reaching out to touch his forearm. "Did something happen at the meeting? Between you and Aemon?"

The muscle in his jaw worked. "How's your back feeling?" he asked. Anger was laced through his words.

I rolled my shoulders gingerly. "Still sore."

He nodded, his expression tense, like he was holding back quiet fury. "No new pain?"

"No."

"Good," he said roughly. "Can I check your ankle?"

"My ankle's been fine since Mercurial healed it." I'd sprained it trying to get to Meera quickly enough to help her through her vision. Mercurial had healed me with a snap of his fingers the other morning, claiming it was a free gift—except the Afeya never gave anything for free.

I shifted my weight, uncomfortable with Rhyan's line of questioning, though I was skeptical myself that the healing would last. I didn't like thinking about Mercurial's motivations or the fact that Afeyan magic had been used on me. For him to have done so meant someone had ordered him to. Someone must have struck a deal with him and requested he heal me. Had it been the same person who'd ordered him to visit me?

But right then, my main source of discomfort came from the fact that I didn't want Rhyan contemplating how I'd gotten the sprain in the first place. I had to keep him from connecting the dots back to Meera and her vorakh.

"What's with the sudden health check?" I grabbed my left wrist in my hand. My fingers pressed into my skin, into the mutilated flesh where my blood oaths lay at the edge of my Valalumir tattoo.

Rhyan gave a somewhat harsh laugh. "It's been one day, partner," he said. "One day since you sprained your ankle, or whatever happened to you. One day since you were lashed by Aemon." His voice broke saying Aemon's name, his fingers flexing and curling into fists at his sides.

I looked up at him. "Did something happen with Aemon to upset you?" I asked again.

Rhyan's eyes ran back and forth across my face, his expression incredulous. "Lyr," he said. "He lashed you."

My mouth fell open. "No. He—He didn't want to hurt me. It wasn't his choice."

The Imperator had arranged it. He'd planned to be in Bamaria to test me. When it was revealed that I had no magic at my Revelation Ceremony, which was confirmed by the examiner from Ka Maras who'd used nahashim to inspect my body, I'd been given a deal. I had seven months to become a soturion. I had seven months to train and pass a test given by the Emperor himself. I had seven months to prove I wasn't wasting everyone's time by training without magic— a feat that had never been accomplished before. But the Imperator had never meant to allow me the full extent of my time or our bargain. He'd made it his mission to ensure that the smallest mistakes were penalized. My time had been cut in half. My test by the Emperor to determine if I'd be allowed to continue training or if I'd be permanently banished had been moved from spring to the winter solstice, Valyati. And I'd been lashed four times across my back.

Aemon had been the one to do it, but it hadn't been his choice.

"I know Aemon didn't sentence you," Rhyan said. "I know the Imperator was behind it. But that doesn't make me want to kill the arkturion any less when I see him. Or strangle him for touching you like that, for hurting you."

A chill ran through me. "He was trying to help. You said so yourself, he spread the lashes so I wouldn't scar. And I...I'd rather him than Turion Dairen." Dairen was Aemon's Second, the one who usually doled out punishments to soturi, and he was a total asshole. But after my father had become Arkasva and the riots had broken out, Turion Dairen had saved my father's life when he'd absorbed what would have been a killing blow—meaning he was praised as a hero in Cresthaven despite being a piece of gryphon-shit.

The moment Aemon had said, *I'll do it*, and taken Dairen's place to whip me would be burned into my memory forever. It had horrified me. But...it was still a better outcome than if the punishment had been doled out by Dairen, who would have no doubt derived some sick pleasure from it.

Rhyan folded his arms across his chest, his biceps flexing as his shoulders tensed. "Just because Aemon didn't do the worst doesn't change the fact that he hurt you."

"I know, but he didn't want to. He's like an uncle to me."

Rhyan's face softened. "When did you learn it was okay for people close to you to hurt you?"

When Jules had been taken and I'd had to sit still and watch like a good little girl. When I had to endure Meera's vorakh taking over her body and attacking me every time she had a vision. When I'd been forced into a blood oath because revealing that Meera hurt me could get her killed and turn us into the next Ka Azria. When I'd endured it all again to protect Morgana. And every day when I played the good daughter of the Empire, madly in love with Tristan.

I stiffened, staring back at Rhyan.

He was watching me expectantly, hand running through his hair and down the back of his neck. "I'm sorry. It's not your fault. It's just…I was raised by an Imperator. I understand the nuances here. The politics. Doesn't make it any easier. Doesn't make me any less…." He exhaled sharply, looking like he was doing all he could to calm down and contain his emotions. "You didn't deserve that."

"I know." I blinked back tears, the lids of my eyes burning. Every time he did this, every time he came close to the truth, I started to lose control and unlock the cage I'd so desperately tried to conceal my emotions within. "It's fine," I said dully.

Rhyan looked pained, his mouth opening like he was ready to argue with me, then seemed to abruptly change his mind. "Will you have a seat, Lyr? I really do want to check your ankle and change your bandages. If that's all right with you."

My hands shook at my sides, but I pressed them against my waist. Though I trusted Rhyan and had let him tend to my wounds before, old habits died hard.

He turned from me, crouching low over his bag and pulling out his medicinal supplies: clean white bandages and what appeared to be uncured golden sunleaves.

I made my way over to a stack of mats and sat down, reaching gingerly behind me to loosen the ties of my tunic. I winced, gasping in pain from the movement. I was feeling far better than I'd expected considering what had happened, but everything still hurt, most of my body still sore and raw.

Rhyan glanced up at me when I made another noise of pain. "Don't strain yourself," he said. "I'll get your tunic off."

I bit my lip, feeling my skin warm, half from liking the idea of Rhyan removing my clothing—liking that idea too much—and half from embarrassment that I couldn't even do this one simple task myself.

I waited nervously as he crossed the room, wondering if he'd noticed the effect his words had had on me. My nerves jumped as Rhyan threw one leg over the front of the mat and straddled the seat behind me, one leg pressed warmly against mine.

"Is this okay?" he asked, leaning in toward me, his fingers grazing the back of my tunic. "If I untie this?"

"Go ahead." My body tensed, aware of his presence, alert to the coming examination. But the knots that had formed in my stomach and around my heart began to loosen. Rhyan always checked in with me about everything he was doing—even when I'd given him prior permission. And he kept me informed of what was coming next and why. It made me feel safe in a way that I couldn't ever remember feeling.

My body for the last two years had become a tool to be used. Against Meera to stop her visions. In public to distract Bamaria from any wrong steps made by my sisters. And for Tristan's plea-sure as I continued to keep up the pretense that I loved him purely and wanted to be with him. Now it was a tool for the Imperator to humiliate the reputation of Ka Batavia. It was a tool for myself to train and strengthen to pass the Emperor's test in three months. But with Rhyan...I never felt any of that. With Rhyan, I had the distinct sense that my body was mine again.

Cool air washed over my back as he slid the laces out down the entire length of my spine. My tunic sleeves rolled down my shoulders, and I held onto the material to keep the front of my body covered. A warm, calloused hand gathered the loose strands of my hair, along with my braid, and pushed them over my shoulder, smoothing everything to the side. His fingers grazed the nape of my neck. I arched into his touch without realizing it.

"Did I hurt you?" he asked.

Heat flushed across my face, making my cheeks redden. "No. Just stretching."

I closed my eyes, focusing on keeping my breathing even as he removed the bandage and cured the sunleaves into a paste for my wounds. But with the feel of his hands on my back, I needed a distraction. He set the jar down beside me, and I stared at the leaves, taking note of their unique design. "I've never seen sunleaves shaped like that before—with the edges so blunt."

"Hmmm?" Rhyan paused, his hands warm on my back, a welcome, soothing pressure. "Oh. They're from Glemarian sun trees."

I twisted my neck to look at him. The movement pushed me closer to him; our thighs pressed warmly together. "From your home?"

He offered a cocky smile. "They're far superior to the sunleaves you have here."

"You didn't have to use them on me." I wasn't sure how rough Rhyan's life had been in exile, traveling from one end of the Empire to the other. When I'd first seen him, his soturion uniform had been in stained tatters, and he'd been in need of a haircut and shave. I suspected anything he carried, anything he'd managed to take when he'd fled his home, had to be of great value to him. It wasn't clear when, if ever, he'd be allowed to return. "You could have saved them."

"Yes, but, your grace," he said, voice teasing, "you're the Lady Lyriana Batavia, Heir to the Arkasva. And if I have superior sunleaves available to treat you, I have to use them. We can't just use any old inferior leaves on an heir, now can we?"

"Perhaps I am of the opinion that Bamarian leaves are superior," I said, following his lead. I knew Rhyan well enough by now to recognize his jokes and sarcasm for what they really were—his own form of distraction. Sometimes for his benefit, sometimes for mine. "What would the Council say if they knew you'd dared to use lesser leaves on an heir?"

"I'd ask to see which studies were done to corroborate this nonsense." His lips quirked as he finished applying my new bandage. "And I'd offer further evidence to support my claim that Bamarian cuisine is actually quite lacking."

I laughed. "You can't be serious! For one, that doesn't prove your point because I see no correlation. And two, you're just flat-out wrong." The fare they served at the Katurium to keep the soturi strong during training did leave a bit—a lot, actually—to be desired. I could barely stomach the food; granted, most days that was from nerves. But I knew for a fact that Bamaria had some of the top restaurants in the Empire plus plenty of access to fresh fruits, vegetables, and spices.

"To counter your points, one, I am very serious, and two, that is a weak argument to make, especially when I am most definitely right," he said, pulling my sleeves back over my shoulders. His fingers were nimble at the base of my spine, bringing the material together and lacing me back up. "I'd wager there's studies which show that the soil in Glemaria has more nutrients, therefore better-tasting food and more effective medical treatments. So there's your correlation, Professor Batavia. Plus, Glemarian food is just better—heartier. Tastier."

"Or you just have a bland taste palate after years of eating all your hearty snow mountain food."

"I'll have you know, partner, that I have an excellent taste palate," he said, leaning toward me. His eyes darkened, and his scent enveloped me—warm and musky with a hint of pine trees.

I still feel the taste of your lips on mine.

My mouth went dry.

Rhyan straightened, looking away, and patted my back. "It's healing nicely." He spoke in a clinical, detached voice. "Just one more...."

It was always like this between us. Serious and tense one moment, and in the next, we'd slip into that overly comfortable banter—flirting.

He swiped the sunleaf paste across my cheek. I'd been punched there by Meera, hard enough for her to break my skin and leave me with a black eye. He studied my face, his eyes assessing and studious. "That looks good. Now your ankle."

Rhyan kneeled before me, taking my foot into his lap. He sucked in a breath, looking up, then deftly unlaced the sandal down to my ankle. His hands were on my calf, his warm fingers pressing and prodding before he lightly turned my foot side to side.

"He really did heal you." He sounded like he could barely believe it. Rhyan brushed his fingers across my ankle, eliciting a small shiver through me. "I mean, obviously, or you couldn't have done the run, but...when he appeared again, I thought maybe—"

"You thought he came back to undo it."

"Something like that." Rhyan's voice darkened again.

I was grateful to the Afeyan for this. The relief from the pain had been welcome, as well as the renewed mobility. I'd been hurt so badly before the habibellum, during it, and especially after it. It was a Godsdamned miracle that not every single part of my body was screaming in pain. But my gratitude only went so far. Afeya did nothing for free. He had come back for something.

You're the fire.

Rhyan slid my sandal all the way off and pressed his palm to the bottom of my foot, slowly moving it in circles. "Does this hurt?" he asked.

"No."

"This?" He shifted my foot again, fingers pressing in.

"No." But it was making me feel something else. Gods. He was just touching my heel, and we'd agreed nothing could happen. But his skin against mine, even on a body part that didn't particularly excite me, was causing my nerves to jump again—this time with anticipation. Anticipation for something that was never, ever going to happen.

He slid my sandal back over my foot as he gazed up at me, his emerald eyes blazing. My stomach clenched. And then his expression became neutral, studious as he looked down and methodically laced my sandals back up my calves. One hand rested behind my knee when he finished, lingering—too long.

"I just had to check. I don't trust him."

"But he's gone," I confirmed again.

"He's gone." He pulled his hand away at last and stood. "Listen, partner, I know it's strange between us—all these oaths and duties. But I swore an oath to you first. I'm going to make sure you stay safe. I don't want you to worry, not on top of everything else. So whatever he's up to, know I'm watching."

"Thank you." I bit my lip. "Rhyan, I think I need to tell you something." All day I'd been debating whether or not to reveal to Rhyan what Mercurial had said to me. Immediately after the Afeyan had vanished, Rhyan had seen me and the ghostly expression on my face. He'd asked what had happened, and I'd brushed it off, claiming Mercurial had just repeated the same nonsense as before. I didn't know how to explain my concerns, not without revealing my dream to him. And now that we were openly deciding not to be together, to honor our oaths and duty, I worried I'd mess things up between us, make everything more awkward than it clearly already was.

Telling Rhyan I'd had a sex dream about him after our Oath Ceremony was not something I'd wanted to do today.

But he had sworn to protect me. When he'd seen I was weak before the habibellum, he'd made me call on kashonim, which had allowed me to take all his strength and magic and power to protect myself when I fought. And he was nursing me back to health so carefully. He really was my friend. I could trust him with this. Mercurial wasn't just a threat to me. If he'd really pulled his words from my dream of Rhyan, then he was a threat to us. And Rhyan needed to know.

But before I could say any more, the door opened.

Turion Dairen stood in the doorway, his golden seraphim armor shining. The sharpened Valalumir stars hanging on the leather straps of his belt gleamed and glittered in the sunlight streaming through the window.

"Soturion Lyriana," he said.

I held back a sneer. It was completely acceptable to address me as such in a soturion setting, but something told me he wasn't just using the informal address because we were in the Katurium. Dairen had shown his true colors in his eagerness to have me lashed. He'd even tried to have me lashed my first day of training when another noble, Lady Pavi Elys, niece to the Bamarian Senator, had tripped me and stomped on my hand.

I could feel his glee emanating from his aura in his ability to avoid saying "your grace," to lessen my title, to strip me of my status.

"We're in the middle of training," Rhyan said. He sounded bored and disinterested—a cold noble High-Lord-to-be who could not care less about me.

Dairen's eyes jumped between us. "Soturion Lyriana has been summoned as witness to a trial taking place in Arkturion Aemon's townhouse. She's to present herself immediately. I was told you were to accompany her. You're both excused from training for the length of the proceedings."

CHAPTER
THREE

"Trial?" I asked, heart pounding. My mind immediately went to the worst—to Meera having been caught. Or Morgana. My hand closed over my wrist, over my blood oaths, and I squeezed.

No. If they'd been caught with vorakh—if we'd been caught concealing it—the trial would be held in the temple, not the townhouse. And the trial would be presided over by the Imperator. He wouldn't have sent Turion Dairen, a general in Ka Batavia's soturi, to summon me. His own soturi would have arrived fully armed. I'd have been bound and carried away.

"Lyr." Rhyan watched me from the corner of his eyes, his voice too low for Dairen to hear. "Breathe." He stepped forward, angling his body in front of mine, his stance protective, shoulders tensed. "I'll escort her grace right over."

Dairen bowed. "I'll alert the Arkturion."

The moment the door closed, I turned to Rhyan. "What does this mean? What trial?"

Rhyan reached his hand out to me but dropped it suddenly, making a fist at his side. Touching me was dangerous unless necessary—unless for teaching or medical purposes.

A truly horrifying possibility entered my mind as I recalled my fight with Tani the day before. She was a soturion from Elyria, not a noble, but she had been absolutely devoted to Soturion Pavi, a noble of Ka Elys—a Bamarian Ka that had taken over power in Elyria after Ka Azria. Since Pavi had been whipped, Tani had made it her personal mission to get revenge on me. When she'd found me in our apartment building yesterday, she'd revealed another horrid secret— she was a supporter of the Emartis, the rebels who didn't want my father on the Seat of Power in Bamaria, the rebels who almost twenty years earlier had tried to kill my father and left him with his permanent limp. She'd taunted me in our clash, questioning my usage of kashonim and why Rhyan had been so eager to give his power to me. She seemed to know or suspect we were more than novice and apprentice.

What if—Gods. What if the trial had to do with me and Rhyan? A trial at Aemon's…he'd preside over any sort of breaking of oaths amongst the soturi. My stomach knotted.

"Rhyan." His eyes locked with mine. "Do you think—I mean— What if…?"

"No," Rhyan said, shaking his head. "No. I don't. Lyr, relax. He said you're a witness. Not the defendant. You're not on trial." He stepped closer. "We did nothing wrong. Remember, I just saw Aemon for our security meeting, and he didn't mention anything. Let's just go, and we'll find out what this is, and once we know, we'll deal with it."

I gave a small nod, his gaze holding me, sure, steady, and calming. But the icy shiver of his aura flared up, reaching out like a cold caress before he tempered it down.

Fifteen minutes later, we were walking across the threshold to Aemon's townhouse in the center of Urtavia. Soturi of Ka Batavia guarded the black onyx wall outside and lined the interior, all bowing respectfully to me as I walked through the entrance.

We were led into a small chamber at the center of Aemon's home, the Arkturion's war room. Flickering torchlights lit the windowless walls, all painted a soft muted gray like the rest of Aemon's townhouse—a stark contrast to his reputation as the Ready. One wall had been detailed with a map of Lumeria. But the soothing tones ended there, as the walls framed black marble floors shined to such perfection, the fires reflected in it. It was the opposite of a waterway; it gave the illusion of walking on fire.

Which was exactly how I felt.

Soturi of Ka Batavia lined one side of the room, standing still against the wall, their green cloaks neatly pleated around their waists and styled with the excess material to cover their heads like a hood, even indoors.

I'd expected our soturi here, but my heart jumped at the warriors standing at attention on the opposite side of the room adorned in not gold, but silver—the Soturi of Ka Kormac. Their silver armor was designed to look like a wolf's pelt. Their sigil, a snarling silver wolf, clipped the top of their green cloaks over their soldiers. These were the Imperator's men. My enemies. The wolves who belonged to the army occupying the city.

I stepped deeper into the war room with Rhyan beside me, my training sandals almost sliding on the smooth floor. The wolves against the wall growled under their breath as Rhyan strode past them. Trained since birth to be the future High Lord and Arkasva of Glemaria, he had been groomed to intimidate others with just a look. Even if Rhyan didn't have that look down to an art, he'd still intimidate with his height and muscles—and impressive as they were, they didn't compare to his reputation as a warrior. Ka Kormac knew damn well he'd easily beaten several of their soturi on duty, and they hated him for it. But in true Rhyan fashion, he appeared aloof and calm against their predatory stares, like he was bored and could barely be bothered to escort me to these proceedings since he had better things to do. I was the only one who sensed the icy tension emanating from his aura. He was keeping his emotions close.

A set of onyx double doors opened at the front of the chamber. Aemon appeared dressed in full arkturion regalia. Unlike the soturi in green cloaks that magically camouflaged their appearance in the outdoors, the Bamarian warlord wore red. His cloak skirted elegantly around his hips, leading into the long piece of material that rose up behind his neck and spilled down his back, flowing out like a cape from his golden armor—armor that had been molded into the shape of sharpened seraphim wings, as was the tradition for all soturi in Bamaria who served Ka Batavia.

His black hair was shorn close to his head, his expression grim as he folded his arms across his impressively muscled chest. He stepped forward, and the Valalumir stars hanging from the seven straps of his leather belt picked up flashes of light from the flickering torches lining the walls.

Arkturion Aemon Melvik, Bamaria's warlord, was known as the Ready—the deadliest warrior in Lumeria. His reputation had been sealed when he'd swung into action the day the Emartis attacked my father. Aemon had single-handedly quelled the riot and killed its ringleader, my uncle Tarek—Aunt Arianna's late husband and the father of my evil cousin Naria.

Aemon was stern and severe yet always fair and kind beneath the surface. But when he was the Ready, a literal death-God incarnate, his face took on another look—a terrifying one that dared any Lumerian or beast to fight him. He wore that face now.

"Soturion Lyriana, your grace," Aemon said and bowed his head. "Soturion Rhyan." He gestured to a small rectangular table carved of black onyx at the front of the room. "Have a seat."

My eyes darted around to all the armored soturi, waiting, alert, and ready to attack. Their energy seemed to crackle with tension. Rhyan's eyes flicked to mine then back to Aemon, still outwardly cool and calm. A snobbish expression overtook his face, as he casually inspected his fingernails and flicked an imaginary piece of dirt.

A moment later, the double doors opened again. My stomach dropped. I'd suspected he was here if his men were, but I wasn't prepared to be so close to the Imperator after what had just happened. I wasn't prepared to be in a room with the man who'd had me whipped and lashed like an animal—brutalized with a magically enhanced weapon meant for soturi who possessed magic in their bodies. The punishment was not meant for someone like me—someone without magic to protect her flesh or withstand the attack.

The Imperator's black robe swirled against the back of his black leather sandals. The Bastardmaker, brother to the Imperator and warlord of Korteria, stalked behind him.

These were the monsters who had taken Jules, the brutes who had been in charge of her, free to do Gods knew what until her transport to Lethea and her stripping—her death.

Sweat beaded at the nape of my neck, and nausea roiled inside of my stomach as pure hatred pumped through my veins. Still, my body knew what to do, how to keep playing my role. I found myself pushing to my feet without thought, standing next to Rhyan as he bowed. Willing my insides to remain inside, I curtsied, offering the Imperator a forced show of respect. My knuckles cracked with the knowledge that I was submitting to him, and some small ember of defiance rose inside me. I pulled my gaze up to meet the Imperator's dark eyes—feral and predatory—as his aura lashed out at me.

"Your highness," Aemon said and nodded toward the Bastardmaker. "Arkturion."

The Bastardmaker grunted in response, then turned to me, a look of glee spreading across his reddened face.

Rhyan gave me a sidelong glance and coughed, giving a pointed look at my hand on the table as we retook our seats. It was shaking violently. I pushed my hand beneath me, sitting on top of it. I needed to maintain my air of defiance and strength, to remember who I was.

But the fear was winning out.

My eyes met Rhyan's. *What is he doing here?* Rhyan was no mind-reader—not like Morgana—but he seemed to understand me well enough and frowned in response with a slight lift of his shoulder. He straightened his back, draping one arm across the table, his fingers tapping a bored beat against the marble.

Aunt Arianna entered the room next, followed by the reason we'd been called to trial: Tani Elwen.

I sat straighter, watching the novice soturion march in with her head held high, her lips in a smirk. The last I'd seen Tani, the day before, she'd been wearing an Emartis mask in the halls of our apartment building, and we'd fought. She wasn't just a soturion with a vendetta against me because of her loyalty to Ka Elys, but a member of the Emartis.

She was the second known member I'd met. The first had been a jeweler I'd stumbled across on my birthday. He'd been tasked with making pins with the Emartis sigil—a bastardization of the sigil for my family, Ka Batavia. Our sigil showed golden seraphim wings beneath a full moon. On the Emartis sigil, the wings had been painted black. It was some kind of dog whistle that I assumed alerted the other members of their identity. When I'd found the jeweler again in Urtavia and confronted him, he'd seemed genuinely afraid for his life and as if he were part of the traitorous organization only for money. But before I could learn more, Soturion Markan had killed him. Right in front of me. Fucking bastard.

The scene was one I'd tried my best to block out of my memory. Markan had killed him because the vendor had looked like a threat to me. But the vendor had only attacked me because he'd seen Markan, he'd been scared he'd been caught. I shuddered with the memory. Seeing Markan's sword pierce the vendor's belly before his body had fallen to the ground had been horrifying.

Whoever the vendor had been answering to terrified him. The leader of the Emartis was someone with great power and money. The Imperator was my prime suspect. I doubted the Imperator cared who sat in the Seat of Power in Bamaria—he only cared it wasn't him. And with the demeaning way he spoke to me and about women, I would have thought he'd have preferred my father, the first male Arkasva in Bamaria, to anyone else. But that wasn't it. He wanted Bamaria. The Emartis created instability in our country. And that instability had been the excuse for more of his soturi to cross our borders fully armed.

Tani was led to the onyx table across from mine. She sat tall and proud, her dark silky hair braided down her back and her orange soturion tunic neatly pressed, her armor showing the sigil of Ka Elys, an ashvan horse flying across the sun.

Aunt Arianna gave me a sharp look. Her red hair had been

pulled into a crown of braids on top of her head. I knew her command at once. It was the lesson she'd drilled into me again and again until I'd become almost perfect at following it.

Control what they see.

In Lumerian politics, perception was everything. I had to appear calm. Powerful. In command. After all, I was not on trial. Tani was. Tani was a member of a dangerous, rebel organization trying to hurt me, trying to hurt my family.

"Arkturion," Arianna said. "Your highness." She bowed to the Imperator.

"Soturion Tani Elwen," Aemon said, "you stand accused of being a member of the rebel group going by the name of the Emartis. This group has been recently classified by the Bamarian Council as a terrorist organization."

I hadn't heard that that declaration had been made. That was good—the Council was taking their threat seriously. But at the same time, it made my stomach twist because this classification was an admission that the Emartis were far more dangerous than just some rebels.

"Lady Arianna, you are Master of Education on the Bamarian Council as well as an eyewitness to Soturion Tani acting in the interest of the Emartis and showing visible symbols of the organization that mark her as a member," said Aemon. "Tell us what you saw."

Arianna nodded elegantly, giving me a quick reassuring glance and a tender smile, the one she'd given me whenever I'd needed comfort over the years. Her expression straightened as she turned her gaze to Aemon and the Imperator. "I was entering the Soturion Apartments designated for the novices yesterday afternoon when I found Soturion Tani attacking her grace, Lady Lyriana Batavia, Heir to the Arkasva, High Lord of Bamaria." She stated my full name and title, pride in her voice, and I gave a small smile. I'd missed being with Arianna in the last month, kept busy with my training. Though my nerves were still on edge from being in the Imperator's and Bastardmaker's presence, warmth bloomed in my chest as she spoke.

"Lady Lyriana found Soturion Tani with a symbol of the known terrorist organization calling themselves the Emartis. It's High Lumerian, meaning 'truth bearers.' Their motto is shekar arkasva, or false arkasva, laboring under the delusional belief that my late sister, High Lady Marianna, *Ha Ka Mokan*, did not name her husband, Harren Batavia, the current High Lord of Bamaria, as Heir Apparent before her death."

The belief among the Emartis was that the Heir Apparent should have been Arianna—my mother's only remaining sister. Meera was the natural Heir at the time and the current Heir Apparent—next in line to the Seat of Power—but she had been only four when my mother passed, too young to accept the Laurel of the Arkasva. And she was too sick with vorakh to take it now.

Tani grinned at Arianna's words, as if she loved everything my aunt was saying about the traitorous organization and their treason. Gods, she was sitting here on trial, and yet…she was proud. A chill ran down my spine.

"Fascinating history," drawled the Imperator, looking bored. "What does the civil unrest over the current rulership of Bamaria have to do with a non-noble soturion from Elyria?"

I clenched my jaw, my teeth gnashing. Civil unrest in Bamaria was his entire excuse for his foreign occupation of my country.

"The organization has created a bastardized symbol of Ka Batavia's sigil, a seraphim with black wings," Arianna said. "The sigil is a full copy otherwise and cannot be attributed to showing off some other breed of seraphim, as black-winged seraphim do not exist. Soturion Tani was wearing the mask of a black seraphim when I found her engaging in a fight with her grace." Arianna produced her stave and pointed it at the double doors behind Aemon. They opened at once, and a black feathery object flew into the room and landed at the Imperator's feet. "Soturion Tani was in possession of this very mask."

"Wearing a seraphim mask with black wings is enough to

convict her?" asked the Imperator, looking down at the evidence on the floor. One sandaled foot pushed the offending object away from him.

"I believe, your highness," Aemon said through gritted teeth, "this is why we're holding trial." He looked like he was out of patience for the Imperator. Aemon turned to Tani. "Soturion Tani, this is a serious accusation. And the evidence is damning. Her grace, Lady Lyriana, was targeted by this organization only a day before your encounter. The Emartis launched an attack that could have proven deadly. An attack that directly resulted in classifying the Emartis as terrorists. And then you proceeded to strike your own attack on her in the halls of her living quarters—a place considered out of bounds for fights amongst my soturi."

Tani shrugged her shoulders like this was no big deal. She was on trial with the deadliest arkturion in Lumeria, the head of the Soturion Academy she was required to graduate from if she had any hope of a future, and the Imperator, the man who could whisper in the ears of the Emperor, his uncle, regarding whether someone in her family should live or die. And Tani looked calm. Almost gleeful. I couldn't fathom being like this in the Imperator's presence. And I knew I'd shrink under Aemon's gaze if he ever directed his anger, the anger of the Ready, at me.

When the Emartis had attacked the Katurium, they'd released an explosion of shadow, glass, and scrolls with their hateful message—one wrong step, and the glass could have sliced someone's throat. But Viktor Kormac, the Imperator's son, had been one of the Lumerians at the scene looking calm, unafraid, even happy. Like he'd known this was coming. My cousin Naria, the daughter of the Emartis's first leader, my uncle Tarek, had also looked pleased. That was how Tani looked now.

If Tani wasn't afraid of the accusation, she must have believed she wouldn't get into trouble.

I didn't think much of Tani, but I didn't believe she was that stupid. Which meant her confidence was coming from more than one place. First, she had backing from the Emartis leader, someone powerful enough to protect her from this trial. Second...she must have been planning to shift the attention to me and Rhyan by accusing us of being more than just apprentice and novice and of using kashonim in the habibellum.

Tani's dark brown eyes met mine, her gaze triumphant.

"Well, let's continue with the trial," the Imperator said. He waved a hand dismissively at Aemon.

"Tani, were you or were you not in the apartments during school hours yesterday?" Aemon asked.

"I was, Arkturion," she said evenly.

Aemon nodded. "Did you engage in a fight with her grace despite knowing you were out of bounds for a fight?"

"I engaged in a fight with her, yes," Tani said.

I shifted in my seat, not liking the ease with which she answered.

"And when her grace found you, were you wearing the mask of a black seraphim?"

"I was," Tani said proudly.

"Do you understand what we have discussed? The implications of wearing that mask?"

"I heard everything you said," Tani replied, eyeing the mask still lying on the floor. Her eyes roved up from the mask to the Imperator standing right before it.

Aemon's black brows drew together. "Are you aware this mask you wore is connected to a Bamarian terrorist organization?"

"I heard your explanation," Tani said. "So, yes."

Rhyan's eyes flickered to me, and his jaw tensed before he turned back to Tani. Arianna grimaced, a look of disgust spreading across her usually beautiful features. She adjusted the golden cuff around her arm. It was stylized in a very similar manner to mine—with seraphim wings—though hers was massive, covering almost her entire bicep. It was a pure symbol of Ka Batavia's power. Arianna seemed to be petting the bracelet as if to remind herself it was still there—untouched by the Emartis and their treachery.

"Under Bamarian law, clear association and participation with a terrorist organization is enough to have you expelled," Arianna snapped. "Not to mention the fact that you attacked an Heir to the Arkasva, an offense of equal severity."

"Lady Arianna is correct, Soturion Tani," Aemon said, "And so I must bring justice to the situation. As Arkturion of Bamaria and the head of the Soturion Academy, I—"

The Imperator coughed, cutting Aemon off. "It seems you're rather quick to judge this case, Arkturion."

"By Empiric Laws, I am the lawful judge here, your highness. Are you critiquing my methods?"

"Of course, not." He offered a feral grin, rolling his shoulders back. "The questions you asked were fair. I believe every member of the Senate would support your performance. And, of course, the soturion's answers were especially damning to her case."

"Then perhaps you'll allow me to finish the sentencing," Aemon said. Only this wasn't Aemon anymore, this was the Ready, and the room darkened with the force of his aura, crackling with its dark, shadowy power.

Tani finally broke character, looking worried. Even the Bastard-maker frowned, his grimy hand moving to grip the hilt of his sword.

"I'm concerned. As Imperator, I oversee the welfare of every Lumerian in the Southern Empire—including Elyria. Not to mention the deep sacrifice my soturi have made to protect the Academy—an academy that has been under siege twice within the past six weeks, first with the appearance of an akadim on the Bamarian border, and now with a terrorist attack right over the very arena where our students learn, where my future soturi—where my son—is studying and expected to not only become a great soldier, but remain safe!" The wolf inside of the Imperator snarled, biting through Aemon's aura until the tension of the two energies pushed forward in a battle of wills against the other. "I have a vested interest in the Academy, I must admit, on a professional and personal level. I am a father. And I have charitably given my men, a full legion, to the Academy's protection. I beg forgiveness and ask for your patience. I want to be absolutely thorough in our approach."

My heart pounded in my chest. No one, not even my father, the High Lord of Bamaria, would have dared interrupt or doubt Aemon's word.

"Then we are united in our goals, your highness, as I also care deeply for the welfare of each student in the Academy. In the interest of student safety, would you not agree that expulsion of a member of a terrorist organization, one that attacked the university you wish to protect, a terrorist organization whose actions could have harmed your son and Heir, is appropriate?"

"Wholeheartedly," said the Imperator, placing a hand to his heart. "Any Lumerian who risks our students, our future, must be expelled at once. But I am unconvinced that this is what we are dealing with today. I wonder if this is truly what Soturion Tani is guilty of." The Imperator stepped forward, his black cloak threaded with gold sweeping ominously behind his back.

Himself to Moriel. He was going to twist this, to do whatever he could to make sure Tani, his little soldier, was freed.

The Imperator spoke solemnly. "I believe we are taking a very black-and-white approach to this nonsense. We speak of extremely serious, dangerous organizations. But that is not what I see before me now. Soturion Tani is not some high-ranking member of the Emartis. She appears to be no more than a little girl, one from another country who would have absolutely no interest in the Emartis's tactics. And considering she is not Bamarian, and her interests and loyalties likely lie elsewhere, isn't it too soon to believe she is a member of this group? Why would an Elyrian girl join a group desiring to unseat the Arkasva of a foreign country—one that has no bearing on her life at home? Perhaps she is merely of the opinion that the Emartis are right. Is that a crime?"

Aemon's eyes narrowed. "The Emartis have been named a terrorist organization. They are not just some group nor are they simply desiring an outcome—they are taking treasonous action to achieve it."

"I asked," the Imperator said slowly, "is it a crime for her to have an opinion?"

Arianna's eyes narrowed on the Imperator. Her nostrils flared as she neatly folded her arms across her chest, highlighting the golden cuff she wore across her bicep.

"Is it a crime? Do we punish all who have differing opinions?" the Imperator asked. "Have we returned to the tyranny of the kings and queens of Lumeria Matavia whose corruption lead to the Drowning?"

"No," Aemon said. "Soturion Tani will be held responsible and have the law applied to her the same as any other Lumerian. But this isn't about opinions. Freedom of opinion is not up for debate today, your highness. Bamaria remains the epicenter of thought, philosophy, and education in Lumeria. We are, after all, the home of the Great Library and the Museion, not just starfire mines and war camps."

The wolves standing at attention shifted, some of their lips snarling at Aemon's simple description of their home.

Aemon continued, "Why don't we remain focused on what is actually in question—not freedom of opinion, but whether or not she belongs to the Emartis, whose previous actions include attempting to assassinate our Arkasva and harm an heir, who is also an academy student?"

"Right, Aemon. Of course. But where I'm stumbling is how we know beyond a shadow of a doubt whether Soturion Tani is connected to them. Soturion Tani, are you a member of this so-called—"

"Terrorist organization!" Aemon said.

"Yes, that," the Imperator said dismissively with a wave of his hand. "Are you a member?"

"No," Tani said.

"That's a lie!" I yelled, pushing my chair back. I'd been sitting frozen, tight-lipped, and nauseated throughout the exchange, furious with the Imperator's twisted logic and application of the law. He'd used the same logic to claim I was a criminal worthy of not just expulsion from school but exile from the Empire when I'd failed to reveal magic.

Rhyan's eyes widened, and Arianna pursed her lips together, shaking her head sharply.

"Patience, Soturion Lyriana," said the Imperator. "A soturion follows the chain of command and does not speak out of turn. I have some questions for you. Perhaps I am rusty on Bamarian court proceedings, but then why else did we call her grace to be a witness if not to put her through an examination? Should not a witness act as such?"

"Tani admitted guilt," Aemon said. "And you seem more interested in squabbling over the basic Lumerian right to have an opinion. That is not and never has been up for debate in Bamaria. What we are debating is whether or not we see evidence of Soturion Tani being part of a terrorist organization. Even if we were to have reason to doubt her membership in the organization, we still have the matter at hand of a student who fought another student out of bounds, and in doing so, she changed her actions from a soturion fighting another soturion to a common Lumerian attacking an Heir to the Arkasva."

"Squabble?" asked the Imperator. "This is not some squabble but an important discussion about the freedoms being allowed in Bamaria, and whether or not they align with Lumerian freedoms as given by the Emperor and Senate. Opinions and freedom of thought should not be dismissed so easily, especially in the Empire's epicenter of thought and education, the home of the Great Library in your ancient pyramids and your little Museion." He shook his head. "If Bamaria isn't going to fight for such freedoms of thought, I will take up the cause. Because it is crucial to the matter at hand. We have the future of a young girl at stake."

I narrowed my gaze. The day the Imperator cared about the future of a young girl or freedom of thought was the day seraphim sprouted black wings. He only cared if Tani could further his view. She was useful to him, a pawn in his grab for power and nothing more. Why couldn't anyone else see or acknowledge that?

"Now," drawled the Imperator, "we have established that opinions are not a crime. My question is, how do we know she is even a member? She said she's not. Is she lying? Maybe. But in my honest opinion, I find it rather unbelievable that she would be. Why would someone want to interfere in the politics of a foreign country?"

I was seething. None of this courtesy had been afforded to me when I'd been expelled from the university for being powerless. And interfering in the politics of another country? That was what the Imperator lived for—what he and his brutes did every day. It was what his legion of two thousand soturi were doing right now as they occupied Bamaria and threatened the safety of my own citizens. His dangerous brutes were armed and causing fights in the streets.

Aemon's dark eyes flicked to me. He no doubt had the same exact thoughts in his mind. He'd been present for my sham of a trial when I'd become a soturion, and he knew as well as I that the Imperator could not be trusted.

I took a shaky breath, feeling Rhyan closely watching me from the corners of his eyes. I had to stay calm. I had to play my role. I had to remember I was not on trial. I was not in trouble—neither were my sisters. And neither was Rhyan. It was my duty to keep it that way.

Control what they see.

But my intuition was igniting with certainty that the Imperator was laying a trap for me with every word he spoke. Like so many times before, I had to decide how to act, what role to play, how to survive his verbal assaults against my life and the safety of my Ka.

"Waryn," the Imperator said suddenly. He turned to his brother, the Bastardmaker, the warlord of Korteria. "It's getting rather chilled outside, even by southern standards. Fall is here, would you agree?"

The Bastardmaker's beady black eyes focused on me, his gaze dipping to my chest as he grinned and nodded in response. "I can feel the cold in here."

"And with fall," said the Imperator, "comes Days of Shadows.

The holiday is, by my calculation...two months from now?" He turned his gaze to me. "A mere month before Soturion Lyriana's test by the Emperor, I believe. Now, Days of Shadows means costumes. Traditionally, black masks are worn. Yes?"

"Masks of akadim," Arianna said.

"Yes," the Imperator agreed and shrugged. "But I also have seen the new trends emerging with the youth. Newer costumes are being created each year. Now they're dressing up as Afeya, as gryphons." He bent down, picked up the Emartis mask, and tenderly brushed back its black feathers. "They've dressed as seraphim. Some are even inventing their own beasts in their creativity. I just think it's a bit irresponsible to expel a girl who may turn out to be a surprisingly talented soturion when there is reasonable doubt as to why she'd associate with this group in the first place. She may very well have been wearing this mask, not because she's an associate of the group, but because she wanted to put together a costume for the upcoming celebration."

He had to be joking. That had to be the most absurd argument ever made in the history of Lumeria.

I looked to Aemon. He couldn't allow this. He couldn't allow the Imperator to roll over the proceedings like this and make such an outlandish ridiculous claim. I was no lawyer, but I'd read enough of the law scrolls in the Great Library to know what a childish, ridiculous, and immature argument this was. Anyone with a half a brain would know! Plus, at the end of the day, this was still a Gods-damned Bamarian matter. Why was he being allowed to have any say at all?

Because we belonged to the Empire. Because the Imperator was not just the Arkasva and High Lord of his country, but the overseer of all six countries below the southern border. Because his uncle was our Emperor.

From the corner of my eye, I caught the Soturi of Ka Kormac grinning and nodding in agreement. Brutish, slimy bastards.

I knew it was over—we'd lost. Of course, we had. I closed my eyes, taking in a deep breath. This was what the Imperator did; he overreached and abused his position, used shoddy infantile arguments for personal gain, and with each argument, he obtained more power—again and again.

"I will remind you that you're here as a courtesy," Aemon said. "Not to offer the final say."

I swallowed, barely daring to breathe, silently begging Aemon to hold his ground and to be the Ready not just on the battlefield but in trial as well. He had to throw the Imperator out, or at least tell him to be quiet. He had to punish Tani for actions that so clearly required punishment.

"And I am grateful for the courtesy," said the Imperator. "I hope you don't think I'm overstepping my bounds. I respect your judgment greatly. The Great Ready. The defender of the Lumerian Empire. Arkturion, of course, I hold you in the highest regard. But I, like all loyal sons of the Empire, understand that it is imperative to follow the law. The law is what keeps us united, and part of that is the chain of command. Let's not forget who has the highest ranking here. Now it is, of course, your final decision, but I am offering a very important, and what many would consider weighted, opinion on a matter that does personally concern me."

He'd as good as said that Aemon had no choice. Gryphon-shit bastard.

"I'm here with the evidence in my very hand." The Imperator held up the mask, turning it over in his hands, black eyes narrowed to inspect it more closely. "And nowhere on this mask does it mention the Emartis. It looks to me like an elaborate costume mask. A mere holiday token." He stepped forward, returning the mask to Tani, who grinned wickedly.

Aemon cleared his throat, watching the exchange closely. He rolled his shoulders back, releasing a black wave of energy from his aura. "After receiving wise council from his highness, Imperator Kormac, with his unusual logic brought forward, we may drop the charges against Soturion Tani regarding her connections to the terrorist organization known as the Emartis for reasonable doubt as to her association."

I clenched my fists at my side. There was no doubt. The evidence was literally right in front of us. She was holding the Godsdamned black seraphim mask in her hands. Herself to Moriel. And the Imperator—fucking bastard. Tears burned behind my eyes at the injustice of it all.

"While we may have dismissed one charge, we are not done here," Aemon continued. "There is the other matter. We are still obligated to punish Soturion Tani for attacking an heir out of bounds."

The Imperator made a sound of irritation, glancing at Tani, a look of derision sprawling across his face. "Fighting an heir is a very serious offense. I am father to one, so I understand. Once again, I'm sorry to interrupt. But I do wonder...Aemon, remind me of the rules for fighting amongst your students."

Aemon sighed but nodded. "A soturion may challenge another at any time during Academy hours with the exception of the morning run. Any group may also engage in a five—five soturi against another—again during Academy hours on Academy grounds in the Katurium."

"And what time, Lady Arianna, did you see Soturion Tani fighting with her grace?" the Imperator asked.

"Close to three in the afternoon when I arrived," Arianna said tightly.

"I see. Those are Academy hours, are they not?" the Imperator asked.

Aemon's eyes darkened, his power surging out again before he called it back.

Fuck. The tide had definitely shifted, and not in our favor. I attempted to remain still, to keep my heart from pounding through my chest.

"Yes," Arianna said neatly.

"Well then, it seems to me if this was during school hours, we're not dealing with a Lumerian who attacked an heir, but two novice soturi. It seems to me that a fight during Academy hours is a legal fight."

"It was off Academy grounds," Aemon said.

"Yes, and so my question now," drawled the Imperator, "is what in Lumeria Soturion Lyriana was doing off the Academy grounds when it was still Academy hours."

Rhyan stiffened in his seat. Fuck. Fuck. He clenched his fists in his lap, his knuckles turning white even as he continued to keep a neutral expression on his face. I'd left the Katurium because he'd told me to. He'd wanted me to rest, to heal after being injured, after being lashed...to think over his offer of extra training. He had been trying to protect me.

"Soturion Lyriana is here under special guidelines. She has barely three months to prove herself as a warrior without magic. And she is to fulfill her end of the bargain by taking training seriously. No special provisions were to be made for her. Those were the specific terms of the bargain she herself agreed to," the Imperator said, voice growing in volume. "Or else we have no deal. Was she not just found guilty of disregarding the rules? Of disregarding the chain of command? Of disregarding the very kind offer I so generously made to her? She is still making her own rules, preferring to be Lady Lyriana instead of realizing that becoming Soturion Lyriana is what her life depends on. Step forward, your grace."

Cold air blasted against me as I pressed my hands to my sides to keep them from shaking. My heart was pounding furiously in my chest so loudly I thought the whole room could hear. Rhyan made a small noise of anguish—too quiet for anyone to notice but me. His lips tightened as the muscles of his jaw flexed while his shoulders tensed, his body poised for a fight.

I reached the front of the room and stood between Aemon and the Imperator, staring out at the soturi lined up to watch me before glancing at Tani and the traitorous mask lying before her and Aunt Arianna.

"Turn around, Soturion Lyriana," the Imperator commanded. "Face the doors."

Rhyan's eyes widened, as did Arianna's. I caught Tani's gleeful look of joy as I willed myself not to throw up. Slowly, I turned my back on the room—the room full of armed soturi.

"Imperator!" Arianna said, her voice indignant.

"My lady," he said calmly, "despite your impressive titles and familial relations to her grace, you have no jurisdiction here."

Deep breaths, deep breaths.

"Imperator," Aemon said, a warning in his voice.

"Nor do you, Aemon, when it comes to our contract. Waryn." The Imperator jerked his chin at the Bastardmaker. "If you would."

"What?" I asked, my breath hitching as a look of disgust came over Aemon. The Bastardmaker was behind me, his grubby hands on my shoulders, his dirty hateful fingers grabbing at the ties of my tunic—the tunic Rhyan had just so carefully laced up after treating my wounds—and then, without warning, there was a sound of fabric ripping all the way down my back.

"NO!" I shouted.

But it was too late. Cold air, infused from Rhyan's aura, hit my bared skin, and the front of my tunic hung off my shoulders. From behind I was bared except for my short-pants, my sandals, and the fresh bandage Rhyan had just applied over my wounds.

I closed my eyes in humiliation, willing myself to breathe and not panic. But my entire body was shaking with cold and fear and dread of what was coming next.

There was a loud slapping sound, and a riot of pain exploded across my back. I fell to my knees, biting back my scream. The Bastardmaker had hit my back, the rough palm of his hand thwacking right across my tender wounds. A tear escaped my eye. My knees were definitely bruised from hitting the marble floor, and my back pulsed in agony.

"Do not touch her again!" Aemon yelled.

"Arkturion," Arianna snapped. Her voice was shriller than I'd ever heard in my life. "She is still under my care as Master of Education. She has not been sentenced anew to punishment. You are out of line!"

A chair had screeched across the floor, and Aemon gestured for the person moving the chair to take a seat. Though I couldn't see with my back to the room, I knew it was Rhyan.

As I watched the flames flicker in the smooth marble beneath my hands, my entire body shook. Then a large set of hands wrapped around my wrists, and I was gently lifted to my feet and pulled against a man made of nothing but sheer, overwhelming muscle and wearing black robes over silver armor.

The Imperator.

"Tut, tut," he said gently, like he was cooing at a baby. His hands ran up my shoulders, still bared from the destroyed tunic. "Oh, this won't do. Not for an Heir to the Arkasva." He squeezed my shoulders, his fingers pressing in with such force I gasped in pain. His hands moved to push what remained of the material back up my arms. The tunic fell right back down and would have completely exposed me if I hadn't been holding the front of the cloth in place.

The Imperator turned me to face the front of the war room once more, my feet stumbling to comply. I couldn't look up, couldn't face their eyes, their glee, or their pity. It was too humiliating. I was too angry. I was Lady Lyriana, Heir to the Arkasva, High Lord of Bamaria. And the Bastardmaker, the fucking Bastardmaker, had just publicly stripped and assaulted me before some of the most powerful nobles of Bamaria. And Tani, who was a traitor, a part of the Emartis, was going to walk free on a technicality and a gryphon-shit excuse for doubt and then tell everyone what had happened, guaranteeing my humiliation and punishment remained endless.

I glared at the Imperator. And the Bastardmaker. I wanted to kill them. I wanted to kill every last wolf in this room with my bare hands.

"I sincerely apologize for my brother's brutish behavior," said the Imperator, his voice full of mock shock and sincerity. He shook his head, rolling his eyes in exasperation. "Waryn is, at heart, a soldier who's rough around the edges. And, well, the Soturi of Ka Kormac mean to be gentle, but we by nature are made of stronger material. So are our tunics. Brother? Maybe you can rectify this. Pay her grace for a new one?"

The Bastardmaker was watching me carefully, obvious lust in his eyes. He wasn't even bothering to hide it. I swear to the Gods, he mouthed "Asherah" as he kept his eyes on me, focusing on my bared shoulder, right where the cloth had fallen and exposed my collarbone. He reached a hand between his legs, and I swallowed back bile, but then his fingers wrapped around a gray velvet pouch hanging from his belt. He untied it and tossed it at me.

The pouch fell to the ground between my feet, the coins inside clinking and thunking against each other.

Had he really thought I would hold my hands out? That I would attempt to catch money and allow my tunic to fall? And the disrespect—the disrespect of offering money to me—and like this! If I ever found myself alone with him, with a dagger between us...I couldn't be held accountable for my actions.

The Imperator bent before me, snatching the coin pouch off the ground. He walked it over to Rhyan and slapped it on the table before him, the metals crashing together as they hit the smooth marble surface. "As the apprentice trains the novice with knowledge, so the apprentice outfits the novice in the clothes and weapons they will need," he said, mimicking the sacred words spoken at the Oath Ceremony, the words that had been spoken before Rhyan and I had been joined. I'd been nearly naked then, and he'd dressed me for the first time as a soturion.

"Buy her a tunic that's a little sturdier," said the Imperator. "One that can withstand opening and closing for punishment. During the next three months, I believe her grace will need it."

Rhyan eyed the pouch, nostrils flaring. Then he sat back, folded his muscled arms across his chest, and stared back at the Imperator.

"I train her. That's it. She can do her own shopping."

The Imperator laughed and returned to my side. His hands were crossed behind his back. He stood close to me. Too close.

"Again, apologies for my brother. The commotion. But a point had to be made."

I stiffened, icy cold fear washing over me. My body went numb. His hand was on my back. His hand was on my fucking back!

"Soturion Lyriana has no power." He pressed his palm into my spine. "No magic. Her own aunt, the Master of Education, had no choice but to expel her from her own country's Mage Academy. Let's not forget that any breach of the contract we made, any special favors, any skipping of classes, of clinics, any being late," his fingers traced across my bandage; he tapped lightly, moving and poking until he found a lash wound, "is a breach of contract." I sucked in a breath, tensing as he leaned closer, his breath disgustingly hot against my ear. "A real soturion would never cry out." He pressed one finger into my wound.

I stumbled forward. Tears welled behind my eyes. My tunic slipped down. Rhyan shifted so fast in his seat, he seemed to be in two places at once.

I tried to hold his gaze, to will him not to move. His green eyes bore into me, his knuckles whitening on the table, the muscle in his jaw working as his fury blazed. I shook my head at him.

"You were punished, Soturion Lyriana, for doing exactly what you swore to me you wouldn't," the Imperator said. A second finger punctured my skin, his nail piercing through the bandage into the wound.

I gasped for breath, my vision turning white before I realized my legs were shaking with the effort to keep from crying, to continue standing.

"And then," the Imperator added a third finger, and my stomach twisted with nausea as my back screamed with pain, "not even a day later, I get word that you're once again guilty of the very same infraction that led to these."

He pulled his fingers away. My back was on fire, aching and sore, the wounds furious from his touch. There was another rip as the bandage was torn off my back. I gasped, some unintelligible sound slipping past the barrier of my sealed lips. Blood dripped down my spine, and I stumbled forward, dizzy from the pain.

"You fucking—!" Rhyan yelled, anguish in his voice. There was a punch, a slap of flesh against flesh, and then the metallic sound of swords being drawn, one by one down the row of soturi lining the wall.

One wolf stared down Rhyan, grabbing his arm, his blade unsheathed.

"Get off!" Rhyan spoke in his High Lord voice. He punched, sending the soturion back against the wall. "I still have to fucking train her, don't I? Put your Godsdamned knives down."

But the Imperator wasn't listening. He was too focused on me, on my exposed body and my opened wounds. "These truly do look so painful," he said, leaning back. His eyes ran up and down my body, tracking the blood as it dripped. There was a splash of blood on the ground, a splotch of red against the pristine black marble. "My sympathies for what you're experiencing grow so much now that I'm seeing it up close. Don't you feel the same, Waryn?"

"They look like they hurt," said the Bastardmaker, glee in his voice.

"Is that not the point?" snarled the Ready. "She broke some rules, and she was punished multiple times for her infractions. This is over! Tell your men to stand down in my house, or my soturi will be within every legal right to stop the threat."

The Imperator waved a dismissive hand at his soturi, and one by one the wolves re-sheathed their swords. The last wolf who'd come for Rhyan licked blood dripping down his chin.

Aemon stepped forward, black mist curling from his aura, his brows furrowed together. "And your highness, you will not touch her grace again."

The Imperator grinned, a wolfish, toothy smile. "I have no intention. In fact, I never have. You were the one holding the whip, Arkturion Aemon. Now, to come to my point. She went home early. Why? Soturion Rhyan?"

"She needed time to heal her injuries. The injuries you yourself ordered," he said through gritted teeth. His good eyebrow was drawn to a tight point. The scar across his other eyebrow seemed to have become redder and more pronounced. "What's so Godsdamned hard to understand here? This isn't a search for the lost shards of Valalumir. It's basic soturion care. She was lashed, now those lashes need to heal. That takes time, that takes rest. Every soturion knows this."

"Yes, except I've never seen another soturion take time off from training after a lashing to rest," said the Imperator.

"We all know the lashes are infused with magic to cause more pain to Lumerians," said Arianna. "They are designed to hurt. They are meant to create a lengthier healing cycle."

"Right. For Lumerians with magic," the Imperator's voice rose again, "Lumerians whose bodies need a bit more pain to counteract their strength, their power. I say this again—if you are going to continue to flout this gift that has been given to you, maybe this is not the right place for you, your grace. I can't even imagine the pain you're experiencing—it's certainly far worse than it should be."

And whose fault is that? I clutched my tunic tighter to me, blinking back the fresh batch of tears burning behind my eyes and threatening to fall. He'd given me an impossible task and at every turn was changing the rules and punishing me for the problems he'd caused.

"I am a patient man, your grace. And I am forgiving. Any soturion, whether they deserved these lashes or not, would be able to bear them without interruption to their daily lives and would not cry out. So if this is too much for you...." His hand reached forward, and I flinched. He gave me a victoriously wolfish grin, replacing his hand on the hilt of his sword. "If you want to be relieved of your bargain before we further waste the Emperor's time on Valyati, say the words now."

I swallowed back bile and spit but stood tall even as my back burned. Even as my limbs shook and fear weighed like a heavy shadow over my heart. I knew I was seconds away from toppling over, but I looked the Imperator square in the eyes. "Tell the Emperor when he's here for Valyati, I hope he'll save me a dance."

The Imperator grinned, shaking his head. "Try to heal that black eye first. The Emperor will not want to dance with a marred face. Now, sit."

I stood there, blood boiling, refusing to follow his commands like a dog. And yet…Gods. I was dizzy with pain. Stomach sinking, I stumbled back to the table.

Rhyan jumped to his feet, pulling my chair out for me and gently sliding it back in. I sat forward, aware of the blood dripping down my spine, the humiliation of having been exposed to the room, and the fact that my wounds were now fresh and vulnerable to pain and new infections—undoing all the work Rhyan had meticulously done and the care he'd given me. He'd wasted the rare sunleaves from Glemaria. Fury and rage boiled inside of me.

"Your grace," said the Imperator, his hand pushing back on the hilt of his sword, the blade jutting forward, "I must say, your back looked like it was healing impeccably."

"Looked that way," Tani said. Her dark eyes glinted as they flicked between me and Rhyan. I remembered her accusation, clear as the Lumerian Ocean. She'd suspected the use of kashonim at the habibellum. She'd suspected something between me and Rhyan.

"Might we finally return back to the original proceedings?" said the Ready with a snarl.

"Of course," said the Imperator. "I eagerly await your judgment."

"Seeing as how the fight occurred during the Academy hours but off the Academy grounds…."

I already knew what had to be done. I knew what he had to say. It couldn't be any other way. He could not punish her for fighting me outside the Katurium without also punishing me for leaving the Academy early. And I couldn't allow Tani to be punished, not when she could say something about me and Rhyan. We were innocent—technically. No lines had been physically crossed. But when the Imperator was involved, truth was irrelevant—truth was what he made it to be, what suited him, what he fancied, and anyone who disagreed with that truth was damned. One accusation against us, even from someone like Tani, would be twisted and perverted by the Imperator's logic until we were both tried for breaking our Oath.

"Arkturion," I said before Aemon could proceed, before he could attempt to defend me any further. "Perhaps, Soturion Tani should be released without punishment. I'm no longer going to be leaving early or arriving late. I see the error of my ways. And I'm sure Soturion Tani will remember that next time she wants to practice fighting with me," I held her gaze, "she will do so at the Katurium. It's easy to see how the error in judgment occurred—on both our ends. I was in fact out of bounds, but we were well within the timeline for a fight, and many consider the Soturion Apartments an extension of the Academy itself. All should be forgiven—just a misunderstanding."

Arianna's eyes widened, but she nodded, a thoughtful expression on her face.

Control what they see, and you control what they think.

"All charges," Aemon said pointedly, looking from Tani to me, "are dismissed. I expect everyone back in the Katurium immediately, and any time lost from being here today is to be made up for after hours. Am I clear?"

"Wise counsel indeed, Arkturion," said the Imperator. He bowed his chin and turned back to me. "Do replace that tunic, your grace. Before you catch a chill. The temperature is expected to fall tonight. We must go now. I am to report to the capitol to update the Emperor on the latest goings on in Bamaria. He'll be very eager for a review after this week's...excitement. We'll see you come winter." The Imperator spun on his heels without another look at me, the double doors at the front of the room swinging open. "Oh, and, your grace, I'll let him know about that dance."

Several seconds passed before the Bastardmaker, after giving me one final lascivious look, stepped forward, his beady eyes flicking to the marble floor—to the spot where my blood had fallen. "Arkturion," he said, "you'll want to clean that up." The head of the dead wolf attached to the pelt across his back bounced grotesquely as he followed his brother. The Soturi of Ka Kormac abruptly turned and marched behind their leaders.

"Leave us," shouted the Ready at his soturi. "You all know what to do."

The remaining soturi, those loyal to Ka Batavia, began to file out. Arianna gave me a sympathetic nod before escorting Tani, who was grinning stupidly with glee, through the doors. Arianna's blue eyes narrowed, and there was a note of disgust in the way she pursed her lips together. She left the Emartis mask on the table, and its empty eyes stared back at me.

Then it was just Rhyan, me, and the Ready. Every door shut at once. Magic hummed around the walls as the war room wards sealed into place.

"What in fucking Moriel?" Aemon shouted.

I started to sit back, as if Aemon's anger was a hurricane pushing me away, but I stopped before I hit the back of my chair. My wounds were exposed, bleeding.

"Your grace," his voice was filled with a deadly rage, "Soturion Rhyan, not a word. Not a single fucking word. I'm going to have a sentry bring her a new bandage and a spare tunic. You two are to march back into the Katurium and stay in your training room until her grace's clinic tonight. Eat dinner publicly in the dining hall—let everyone see you're training—and I swear to the fucking Gods, not one more misstep."

I swallowed. "Yes, Arkturion."

Rhyan nodded, his jaw clenched tight. "You have my word, Arkturion," he said through gritted teeth.

The wards were called back, and the humming stopped as the doors unlocked. We didn't dare speak a word as the sentry appeared moments later with our supplies, nor when Rhyan methodically cleaned and redressed my wounds. We remained silent, a dangerous tension running in an undercurrent between us, as he dressed me again, not daring to talk, not daring to look at each other in the arkturion's townhome. I sat forward before him, elbows on my knees, hands pressed over my eyes to keep from crying and from feeling shame wash over me again. The unbearable silence continued as Rhyan walked by my side the entire waterway back to the Katurium.

Only when we were behind the walls and closed door of our training room, only when we were alone again, did he lose control. A primal scream of frustration escaped from his lips, followed by a string of curses layered with his northern accent.

Rhyan pulled his arm back, his thumb crossed over his fingers, and without warning, he punched the wall. The room shook as a crack appeared in the panel. Shards of debris fell to his feet. His shoulders heaved as he stretched his neck side to side, his breaths rough and uneven.

"Rhyan?" I asked. "Are you—"

"No, I'm not," he said. "Lyr, just…I need a moment."

I stepped back.

He punched again and again, a hole now in the wall. And then he punched once more as he heaved out a breath, something almost like a sob at the tail end of it, followed by another round of curses before his shoulders finally slumped.

"They're all the same," he said, his voice low. "All the fucking Imperators are the same."

Rhyan's father was the Imperator to the North, and a brute. A brute who'd beaten Rhyan mercilessly as he'd grown up. Beaten, imprisoned, bound, and humiliated him until Rhyan had realized he was strong enough to fight back.

I couldn't imagine the depths of the horrors he'd experienced. I couldn't imagine how he felt. The Imperator terrified me more than akadim, more than anything else in the world, and he'd destroyed my life from afar, torn my family apart. Rhyan's father, Imperator Hart, was rumored to be even worse, even more cruel. I didn't know the full extent—in some ways I didn't want to—but I knew what was in Rhyan's eyes, the hurt, the pain, the way he sometimes looked so distant and haunted. The cruelty of Imperator Hart's aura had even touched me when he and Rhyan had twice visited Cresthaven years earlier. I'd hidden in my room, terrified of the powerful gusts of dark, cold power emanating from him. I'd once even feared he'd blow Cresthaven down.

Rhyan's hand slammed against the wall, this time not in a punch but to support himself as he learned forward, his head dropping. His knuckles were reddened with small scrapes and scratches that were beginning to bleed. Had he not been a soturion with magic running through his body, he'd have broken his hands. The tendons in his forearm stood out, and his shoulders rose and fell as his breath remained uneven.

I moved toward him before I realized what I was doing, my hand reaching for his slumped shoulder, wanting to touch him, to comfort him. But I pushed my hand against my hip at the last second. We were in this situation because of what lay between us. And touching him right now…it wasn't going to help anything. It would only make matters worse, make it harder for us to do what had to be done.

"It's over," I said. "He's gone…for now."

"Some gryphon-shit guard I'm turning out to be," he said. "Gods."

"That's not true. You're—"

"Don't," he said. "Don't comfort me when you're the one who…." He shook his head. "You shouldn't have to. Not when I owe you an apology. Not when everything that happened was because of me. I sent you home. It's my fault you ran into Tani, my fault you were exposed to this, my fault the Imperator—" He practically roared in frustration.

"Rhyan."

"Lyr…." His voice broke on my name. "You shouldn't have to see me like this."

"Like what?" I asked. "You still look like Rhyan to me. It's all right."

"No," he said through gritted teeth. "It's not."

"Hey. You're my friend, right?"

His shoulders tensed as he turned slowly, moving his gaze to mine. The edges of his eyes reddened as he looked me up and down, his chest heaving with the exertion of trying to calm himself down. "Of course, I am."

"You've been there for me whenever I needed you. The friendship you've given…I don't even have words for what it means to me, how your support has been the biggest reason I survived the last month. Rhyan, I want to be there for you, too. If you'll let me."

He squeezed his eyes shut and grimaced. "You're the one who was just…who…." His hands flexed. "I caused this. My fault."

"No, you didn't. You didn't sentence me to this life. You didn't rip my tunic apart. You didn't open my wounds."

He took a shaky breath. "Lyr."

"Rhyan, you're the one who's closing them. Over and over again." I stepped forward. "And it means everything to me." I could see the guilt and shame in his eyes. I knew that look because I'd seen it in myself every day since Jules. "I know how sacred oaths are to you. But you've never forsworn yourself to me. I learned the hard way, oath or no oath, I'll never be safe. I can't be protected. Not while the Imperator lives."

He looked ready to disagree with me, one eyebrow narrowed as he frowned. Instead, he asked, "Do you know the motto for Ka Hart?"

"No. Tell me."

"Me sha, me ka."

"My oath, my soul," I translated.

He closed his eyes, hands flexing into fists at his side. "Our word is our soul. If we can't keep it, we're worth nothing. And I'm forsworn. I've broken that oath before, failed the people I loved most in this world. Being unable to keep my oath, to uphold my promise, these were the worst moments of my life." His eyes opened. "I failed." His gaze grew distant. "I couldn't save them. I can't make that mistake again. Not with you."

I stepped forward again. This time, I took his hand. His grip tightened around mine at once, his skin warm and familiar. "I don't know what happened. But I know you. And I know you're not just a good person, you're one of the best. You're so much more than just someone keeping every oath you've ever made—"

"Stop," he said.

"No. Listen to me. I'm the one who just had my back splayed open, displayed for sport. There was nothing you could have done! So take your own advice here. You told me before, it wasn't up to me to save Jules." I stopped suddenly. "Not that I'm suggesting you care about me like—"

His fingers threaded through mine; our palms pressed together. "Partner." His green eyes blazed, glowing like emeralds. "I care." His fingers tightened around mine, and he stepped forward, closing the distance between us. "It's killing me to have to see you get hurt. To not be able to kill every last one of those Moriel-fucking bastards who touch you."

My stomach tightened at the violence in his words. "When you do get your hands on them, save a punch for me?" I tried to lighten my voice, to make a joke. But the words came out with more violence than I thought myself capable of having. A tear rolled down my cheek.

His shoulders relaxed, the corner of his mouth lifting. He reached forward, brushing the tear away. There was something heartbreakingly kind in the barely-there smile on his lips. "You can have them all if you wish. Just leave some scraps for me to pummel."

"Deal."

A shudder ran through him, but his breathing slowed, becoming more relaxed. His thumb rubbed small circles into my skin.

There was a loud knock on our door followed by the sound of it bursting open. Rhyan released my hand at once, moving to the wall away from me. When I turned to see who'd come in, I found Tristan, his head cocked to the side in anger, his hand already drawing the stave from the silver scabbard at his waist.

CHAPTER
FOUR

Tristan crossed the room in quick, predatory strides, his stave drawn and pointed at Rhyan. He looked just like he did when he was on the hunt, when he'd been informed about a situation. The energy in his aura brought me right back to when he'd moved through the crowd in Urtavia, arresting the Damaran water dancer for visions. He was like a mountain cat prowling—fast, powerful, and deadly. Confident he'd catch and kill his prey. And right then—his prey was Rhyan.

"Tristan!" I yelled. He didn't hear me. He was too focused on his goal. "Tristan, stop!"

He kept his stave pointed at Rhyan, but his left hand shot out, his palm facing me. A blast of warm air emanated from his hand. It didn't hurt me, didn't trap me, but it made moving forward nearly impossible.

Fucking Gods! After he'd bound me, assisting the Imperator in my arrest, I'd pulled his stave on him, making him swear to never use it on me again. He was keeping his promise. But this...this wasn't much better. It wasn't the stave that was the problem—it was only a tool after all, a way for him to focus and strengthen his magic —it was the fact that he used magic against me at all; I didn't care if it was by stave or by hand.

I pushed forward, watching in horror as Rhyan remained in place, holding his ground as Tristan reached him. I couldn't believe the change in his face, in his expression. Just seconds ago, when we'd been alone, his eyes had been so expressive, so full of emotion, anger warring with his worry for me and his guilt over what had just happened.

Now, Rhyan lifted his good eyebrow, an infuriating smirk on his lips—one that might have fooled even me before I'd gotten the chance to get to know him as well as I did. But I could see through the bravado, see now the way he masked himself so frequently to protect me. I knew the indifference he pranced around with was only to throw off anyone who might suspect how much he cared. But even more than all of that, I knew this look intimately, knew it deep in my soul, because I wore this look, too.

His mask was flawless and cruel. Gone was my kind, caring friend. Now, face to face with Tristan, Rhyan was every bit the evil, murderous, forsworn bastard he was reputed to be, the savage, uncaring future High Lord of an equally savage and brutal country. Here stood the vicious future Imperator he'd been groomed to become. Rhyan was able to perfectly wear the face of the very monster he despised.

"Lord Grey," he said jovially, eyes darting between Tristan's sneer and the twisted sun-and-moon wood he held tightly in his grip. "By the looks of that stave in your hand, you must be very happy to see me."

Said stave was now pointed at Rhyan's neck, the point poking his skin, yet Rhyan made no move to defend himself or shift his position. Only a slight flex of his fingers and a cool blast of ice from his aura gave away his irritation.

"That's what you're going with?" Tristan snarled, his own aura pulsing in response. There was some odd mix to his emotions, but anger was underlying all of it, giving his energy a red, hot feeling that left my skin itchy. Tristan twisted the stave against Rhyan's throat. "Last time you were cleverer than that."

"I've been busy. But so happy to know I made an impression. If only I could schedule more time between my pushups and face punching, I'd get back to my daily hour of writing insults to you." He exaggerated the shrug in his shoulders. "But since you obviously came for a show, how about a classic, like the fact that you still don't have enough faith in the reach of your stave's magic to actually hold it at a reasonable distance? Which unfortunately only makes me think you don't have enough faith in the distance—or length, shall we say—of other parts of yourself."

Tristan's lips curled, as he pushed the stave harder against Rhyan's skin—hard enough to leave a bruise.

"Tristan! Stop!" I yelled, still furiously trying to push against his magic.

Rhyan continued to hold his stance strong, his expression defiant. While he didn't appear to be in danger from Tristan's magic, the stave on his neck like that could seriously injure him.

"Tristan, stop it," I said. He was so focused on Rhyan that the air he'd used to hold me back had evaporated, and I stumbled forward with the sudden freedom. "What in Lumeria has gotten into you?"

"What has gotten into me?" Tristan yelled. He held the stave firmly in place, the muscles of his arms flexing through the blue mage tunic he wore. "Lyr, you were lashed!"

My mouth fell open. "I-I know. But—Tristan that's—Stop it! That's not Rhyan's fault." When he'd arrived at my apartment last night, he'd listened calmly as I'd explained what had happened the night before. He'd asked if I was in pain, and I'd said no. Then he'd asked if I wanted to see a healer, and again I'd said no, I'd already been bandaged. He'd accepted my answer, hugged me gently like everything was fine, and let me fall asleep on his chest to avoid putting pressure on my back. He hadn't asked to see the wounds. He'd let it go. And this morning, he'd acted calmly, joking with me, walking me to the Academy. If I was being honest, it wasn't the reaction I'd expected from him at all. But so many things had been warring for attention in my mind, I'd brushed off the interaction.

Some part of me had known he'd been underreacting, but

I'd been so relieved, I hadn't seen it for the warning it was. I hadn't wanted Tristan to see me hurt, to see my injuries. Partly from instinct—because I never let him see my wounds—and partly because, well, it had all been so public, so humiliating. It was nice to be with someone who hadn't witnessed it, who hadn't been able to fully grasp the horror of what had happened. In a way, that had allowed me to pass off the fear and pain of it all as less than it was. To pretend it hadn't happened. And I was already so used to pretending with Tristan.

But all my pretending had come to a crashing halt when the Bastardmaker had ripped open my tunic and the Imperator had reopened my wounds and torn off the bandage. My back ached fiercely, and though I knew Rhyan had done all he could, my back was irritated with every move I made and every bit of pressure from my tunic against the bandage.

"I was against this from day one," Tristan said. "You shouldn't be bound to someone like him. For your sake, I've tried to stay quiet, to remain calm. But, Lyr, he let you get hurt on his first test! He was supposed to prepare you, to keep you protected from things like that." He turned his anger once more toward Rhyan, shoving him back into the wall, nostrils flaring as he released his hold on him. "You failed to protect her."

"Tristan! No, he—"

"I failed to protect her?" Rhyan spoke casually, but an undercurrent of anger was threaded through his voice. His shoulders tensed. Gods. He really did believe he'd failed me—Tristan was trying to hurt him, but he had no idea how cutting his words were or how much Rhyan was beating himself up for just that.

For a second, Rhyan's eyes were on me, and I desperately wanted him to see, to believe that he hadn't failed me. But Tristan followed Rhyan's eyes to where I stood, and instantly, Rhyan turned away, staring Tristan down.

Rhyan licked his lips, slowly readjusting his posture until he stood tall, one hand resting casually on his waist. "I'm going to need some more details, Lord Grey. How is it exactly that I am supposed to be protecting her grace?"

"You're her trainer," Tristan said.

I bit my lip. He didn't know Rhyan was part of my security detail. Nor did he know I was secretly paying his own escort Bellamy not to report my activity back to Ka Grey.

"Good job," Rhyan said. "You got one fact right!" He clapped his hands together.

"Listen to me, forsworn. You're not doing your job. If you were, she wouldn't have been whipped."

Rhyan took a step forward and then another. Tristan lifted his stave, and Rhyan shoved him back so far, he hit a stack of mats. "Don't tell me this is you defending her now."

"Of course, I'm defending her," Tristan sneered, stepping forward. "She's a Lady of Ka Batavia, she's supposed to get the best training, to be kept safe. Not fucking lashed! Does her status mean anything to you?"

Rhyan's eyes widened. "Yourself to fucking Moriel, you noble snob! Is that all she is to you? A status symbol? One that's been diminished by her lack of power and some stripes on her back?"

I gasped, a sinking feeling in my gut as Tristan looked desperately at me and then back to Rhyan. Gods. He was right. Tristan was upset about how this looked. His grandmother, Lady Romula, the Master of Finance for my father's council, had been horrified over the idea of nobles being lashed. When we'd had dinner at Lady Romula's weeks ago along with Aunt Arianna and my cousin Naria, Naria had tried to insinuate I'd been whipped, forcing me to reveal that Lady Pavi had been. The dinner had almost ended when Lady Romula had heard. The old lady had nearly fallen off her chair.

Still, she was cunning, powerful, and fully in control of every aspect of Tristan's life—including whether or not he proposed to me and whether or not he wished to.

We'd gone to the dinner to try and gain her blessing because Tristan didn't feel right proposing without it and because, as callous as it sounded, his proposal to me was worthless without the added political and financial protections I'd gain with her support. I'd wanted to use Ka Grey as a shield against the Imperator. And she'd made it clear she'd refuse our engagement as long as the Emartis continued to cause instability in Bamaria.

"You really think I'm that shallow?" Tristan yelled. "That I'm upset over stripes that will heal? What in Moriel's name are you getting at, forsworn?"

"The fact, Lord Grey, that you have no fucking clue, once again, about the words you're letting slip out of your mouth."

"I know damn well—"

"Your mouth is moving, Lord Grey. That's a problem for me."

"Have you been a criminal so long you've forgotten how our world works? This isn't the wild outside the Empire. I wouldn't give a shit if her grace had permanent stripes on every inch of her body—I'd still love her. But Bamarian perception doesn't work that way. You allow her to be hurt, to be humiliated, you put her in danger. It's your job to make sure that doesn't happen, to make sure she's prepared, and to keep her grace out of the line of fire. That's the reason you're here, isn't it? You get to stay as long as she does? So do your Godsdamned duty!"

Rhyan's mouth tightened into a straight line. "Did it ever occur to you that as the forsworn, low-life bastard you constantly tell me I am, that I do not have any say in this matter? Did it not occur to you that you're right, I do need her to remain in training, and therefore, I'm doing all I fucking can?" he snarled. "I am training her, and all I can do is train her. Oddly, I would be training her right now if you hadn't interrupted me. Something you seem to like doing."

"I interrupted nothing. You two were just standing there."

Rhyan's eyes moved to me, the look swift and subtle yet rattling me to my core. "She was taking a break after being lashed! Auriel's fucking bane. Are you really this dense? And speaking of her lashing, where were you? Where the fuck were you when it happened? Not protecting her. Not talking to your precious Imperator to get him to change his mind, to play fairly, or to go easy on her. And you know where else you weren't?

Cleaning out her wounds or washing away her blood. Nor were you bandaging her back to prevent infection. I was there. I was the one."

At the mention of blood, Tristan looked green, like he was going to be sick. He swallowed roughly, his hand falling to his side. His head swayed, and I realized—he hadn't asked to see my wounds, not because he didn't care, but because he couldn't. His own trauma made him sick over the sight of blood and gore.

Rhyan's eyes flashed as he saw this, immediately using the small shift in Tristan's demeanor to his benefit. "What…the idea of blood scares you? Seriously? You're going to be a boy for the rest of your life."

"Rhyan!" I said, my voice deadly serious. "Stop! Stop right now."

He didn't know that when Tristan was three, a mage with vorakh—with visions—had gone mad and attacked his parents. She hadn't just murdered them, she'd ripped them to pieces, empowered by the strength and madness that came with her power—the same strength Meera had during visions. Tristan's parents had died in the most brutal, horrifying way, and up until the end, they'd been trying to protect him. He'd seen the entire thing. I knew deep down, he'd never fully recovered. It was why he hunted vorakh, why he'd never be able to see Meera—and hadn't been able to see Jules—as anything other than a monster.

Rhyan's one eyebrow lifted, and his green eyes were on me, questioning. I shook my head, my expression dire. He had to drop this topic. He had to drop it now.

He frowned but gave me one curt nod, leaning forward toward Tristan, a dangerous mischief in his eyes. "Let's agree on one thing, Lord Grey. I didn't lash her. I didn't order her to be lashed. That's on your precious Imperator."

"The fuck does that mean? I'm not his fan."

"Could have fooled me. Since I've been in Bamaria, all I see you do is carry out the man's dirty work, stalking after vorakh, handing them over to him. You were so eager to bind her grace. Do you get a special bonus after you arrest ten? What is it? A weekend in the capitol with him and his uncle?"

Tristan leaned forward, his aura exploding until the room darkened. "I am doing my duty to keep the Empire safe. Maybe it's not an akadim kill, but until you've seen what a vorakh can do, how it grows in strength, how it kills and destroys—" A pained look darkened his features. Tristan looked truly haunted as he spoke. He shook his head. "Now that's the second time you've criticized me for doing exactly what needs to be done, for following the law, for ridding the Empire of danger." His brown eyes narrowed in suspicion as he assessed Rhyan, looking him up and down. "Tell me, forsworn, is that why you're so far from home? Why you're in exile for murdering—"

"Yourself to fucking Moriel," Rhyan roared. "I swear to the Gods—the amount of wrong, idiotic things you say in so short a fucking time."

By the Gods. Tristan was accusing Rhyan of having a vorakh. I was going to be sick. I tried to take a breath. I was around Rhyan enough hours in the day to know he showed no symptoms of reading minds or having visions. I was too acutely aware of the symptoms, too tuned in to what they looked like. I would have known. Rhyan was just the rare Lumerian who saw people as people, whether they had vorakh or not. Tristan only saw vorakh— the monster that had killed his parents.

"Then how about this?" Rhyan said. "If you really aren't a fan of the Imperator—if you're actually legitimately concerned with his treatment of her grace—then tell me. Tell me why you assisted him with her arrest. Why you bound her in ropes. Have you ever been bound yourself? Did she ever tell you what they felt like? How much they hurt? How much they burned? How your actions left her all alone, suffering in pain for hours?"

Tristan closed his mouth, his nostrils flaring, eyebrows drawn closely together. I stepped back, not wanting to relive that memory, not wanting to dig up that wound with Tristan.

"You storm in here," Rhyan continued, "making this big

useless show of attacking me because you're concerned for her protection, but it's all staves and crystals because you know damn well this doesn't help her. Just like you knew damn well you wouldn't save her from prison. You, the man who is supposed to love and protect her for the rest of your life, have failed her on your first test. You're working alongside the man hurting her. The man who gave her seven months to survive a brutal training or face exile. The one who just took half those months away on a technicality. The one who lashed her. The one who just reopened her wounds."

Tristan turned to me, eyes wide and full of concern. "What?"

"It's nothing," I said. "He...He was just patting me on the back. And my wounds weren't ready for that."

"Lyr," Rhyan said, a warning in his voice.

"You are to address her as your grace."

"Who? Your fiancée—no, sorry, just girlfriend, right? What's the latest title your grandmother's allowed you to say? Special friend?"

"Fiancée," Tristan snarled.

"Oh, well, then! Lord Grey, I would have offered my congratulations, but—where's the ring?" Rhyan looked pointedly at my finger. My empty, ringless finger.

It was in the Shadow Stronghold, being kept as payment by Ka Shavo for looking the other way just long enough for Tristan to break me out of prison. Only the attempt had failed. It had been thwarted by Rhyan—because I'd asked him to. Because Rhyan had been right—it had just been for show. Tristan had had no plan to execute his break out beyond the prison walls.

Rhyan stalked forward. "As entertaining as your interruption has been, I'm done with our little interlude. Kindly get the fuck out of my training room. Now."

Tristan moved to my side, his hand holding mine a little too tightly. "Lyr, let's go." He took a step, but I held my ground, refusing to move my feet.

"Tristan," I waved my arms helplessly. "I can't leave now."

"Yes, you can. The day's over. And this," he said to Rhyan, "is the last time you keep her late."

"And this is the last time you trespass in my training room. You came here because you were concerned for her safety? Because you want to protect her? Shall I do a recap for your tiny little brain? She was whipped for being unprepared. She was just warned by the Imperator again for taking a few measly hours off to heal from said whipping. She's not being given any breaks. And if you really have an in with him and you're actually on her grace's side, you're going to think of some way to leverage favor for her—to get her a break. But until that day comes, she's been ordered to stay late—to stay tonight until her combat clinic, which she is required to observe. I am not forcing her to do this. I am not the one giving orders. I am the one following them—the neutral, low-level, forsworn bastard soldier at the Arkturion and Imperator's command. So stop coming in here to distract and upset her, stop trying to get in the way of her studies. Get out of my room, and for Gods' sake, stop keeping her up late at night. Her exhaustion is hurting her. Just look at her face."

I stepped back, fully self-conscious. Most of my scars, my wounds, my bruises, and my cuts were hidden. But the large cut on my cheek and my black eye from when Meera had punched me, those I'd been unable to hide. Those I'd hoped to pass off as results of the fight in the habibellum. Only Rhyan knew they were from something else—something Tristan could never know about.

"Care to explain her black eye?" Rhyan asked, something deep and primal in his voice. "That cut on her cheek?"

"Rhyan, stop! Enough!" I yelled.

Tristan's mouth twitched. "I blamed you for that."

"Did you now?" Rhyan asked darkly. "What about her limp?"

Tristan blinked, looking honestly confused. "Limp? Lyr?" He wrapped his arm around my shoulder, staring down at my feet. "When were you limping?"

Rhyan watched carefully as I shook my head fervently.

"I wasn't. And I'm not." I stepped out of Tristan's embrace and balanced myself first on one foot, then the other. "See?"

"Then what is he—?"

"I tripped before the habibellum. I thought I'd twisted my ankle, but I had it looked at—twice—it's fine."

Rhyan frowned. Why wouldn't he fucking let it go? Gods. The limp was nothing compared to the way the lashings had felt. But in some weird way, I preferred the lashings to the pains he was pointing out now. The lashings were simple. The Imperator was evil, and he was doing evil things to me. Every other bruise and wound on my body, every scar, my blood oaths—they'd been given to me by people I loved, by people I would die to protect. And they hurt, and they were complicated. And Rhyan wouldn't let them go.

"I need to finish training tonight," I told Tristan. "I'll send word once I'm finished with the clinic—I'm just observing tonight. I'll take it easy, I swear. I'll be with Haleika and Galen, they'll watch out for me. It's fine."

"I'll watch out for you," Tristan said. "What time is the clinic?"

I blinked. "What?"

"What time?" he asked again.

"Seven," I said.

"Finally taking an interest in kicking and punching?" Rhyan taunted.

Tristan ignored him, pulling me to the side of the room—away from Rhyan's ears. "Lyr," he said, his voice hushed. He took both of my hands in his, drawing me closer, his aura cocooning around us like a protective shield. "Do you want him as your trainer?"

"Tristan," I pleaded. "We're bound together. This isn't a decision you can just pay your way out of. Not when the Imperator's involved. Not now when I'm on borrowed time."

"You didn't answer the question."

"I do. He's good at his job—and you're not making this any easier for me."

"I'm sorry. I just…lose it at the thought of you being hurt. I'll come tonight. I'll meet you at the southernmost entrance to the arena." He pulled me against him, his lips on mine in a lingering, claiming kiss.

I knew what this was—he needed reassurance. Rhyan had dug up old wounds and issues between us, bringing them straight to the surface. I felt weird kissing Tristan in front of Rhyan, but I also didn't want Tristan feeling insecure. So I did what I always did—I deepened the kiss. My fingers were still entwined in his, and I guided them toward my back to pull our bodies closer.

Tristan lost focus as our lips moved together, his shield coming down.

I released his hands feeling his palms slide across my waist and up my back. But the moment he touched me, I cried out in pain, unable to help myself. His hands were exactly where the Imperator had touched me, had broken through my wounds.

Tristan immediately stopped, his hands on my shoulders to turn me around so he could inspect the damage.

Rhyan shoved his way between us before I could turn, his hands around Tristan's neck, slamming him into the wall as a cold blast of wind pushed me backwards.

"You idiot! Don't touch her fucking back. Why is this so hard to understand?"

"I'm all right," I shouted. "It was my fault!"

Rhyan released Tristan, slowly stepping away from him, holding his hands up in surrender.

Tristan's eyes met mine, hurt and anger swirling in them. "Are you all right?"

"I am, I'm sorry. I…That was my fault. I need to be more careful until I heal."

"Lyr?" Tristan asked, starting toward me. But he changed his mind suddenly, stave back in his hands as he stalked toward Rhyan. "This overly protective gryphon-shit attitude you have? It stops now. Remember your place." The threat in his voice was clear. "Or you will lose it."

Rhyan breathed out a long, hard breath, his nostrils flaring as he stared at Tristan with hate in his eyes. "You'll join her at seven. Now get the fuck out of my room."

"I'll be right at the door at seven exactly," Tristan said, barely containing the anger raging inside of him. He slammed the door shut, knocking a mat leaning against the wall to the floor.

I turned on Rhyan, hurt and fury rushing through me. "By the Gods!" I shouted.

"Lyr?" Rhyan was by my side in an instant. "Did he hurt you?"

"Auriel's fucking bane! You really won't let that go!" I yelled. "I told you already. Why won't you fucking believe me?"

Rhyan closed his eyes, his jaw tensing. "I didn't mean…." He shook his head, running his fingers through his already loosened waves. "I meant, just now. I saw where his hands were. I heard you. After what the Imperator did today, that had to have hurt."

"It did." I looked up at him as tears blurred my vision. "And it does. But that was my fault. After that little pissing contest you just had, I had to reassure him. Fuck, Rhyan. What the hell was that?"

"He came at me—not the other way around. I'm sorry I snapped. But you know he needed to hear all of that," he growled.

"No, he didn't. Do you know what you just did? We're going to be fighting all night now."

"I'm sorry. But tell me honestly. Was I wrong? Was I, Lyr? Did he do anything differently than I said?"

"It's not about that. It doesn't matter. He's my—We're—Fuck. It's not that simple, and as my friend, I don't want you stepping in like that. I mean it. Rhyan, don't do that ever again."

"Don't what?" he asked, voice dangerously low. "Defend you? Call your boyfriend out for being a sack of gryphon shit? Lyr, he's hurting you, he's putting you in danger. What am I supposed to do?"

"Nothing!" I shouted. "Nothing! Because he's not doing what you think he's doing!" It was the same fight we kept having, the one he was so convinced he was right about that he wouldn't let go. My heart hammered as I said, "I know you're trying to protect me, but you're overstepping here as my guard!"

"I'm not being your Godsdamned guard. I'm being your friend."

"My friend? Really? Partner?"

"What else would I be?" he asked. His chest rose and fell, his eyes blazing.

I didn't know if he was thinking of our almost-kiss but pushed the thought away. "Then as my friend, you're not protecting or helping me. What you just did back here, you made it worse. Did you ever consider that I've known Tristan my entire life, and I care for him deeply, and he cares for me? Did it ever cross your mind that he actually loves me, and he's doing what he thinks is best?"

"If that was true, then why are you hiding your injuries from him? Why are you pretending you didn't have a limp? You looked like…like…Gods, Lyr, do you think I haven't seen this before?" His voice caught, his eyes reddening. "Do you know how many times I watched my mother pass off a new injury as an accident—pretend her cheeks weren't bruised, that they'd been painted that way for fashion? The amount of times she styled her hair to hide a wound or bruise or just fucking covered it up with jewelry?"

I flinched.

"Every single time she was hurt, it was him. And I knew it. We all knew it, and we couldn't say a Godsdamned thing. And now you're doing all the same things as her," he said. "And I can't—I can't just be a bystander. Not when I can see so clearly. Not when it's you. I can't go through this again."

My chest heaved, my breathing fast and uneven. "Rhyan, I'm sorry. I know how this looks, but I swear to you, it's not what you think. And I can't show my injuries in front of Tristan because…." I trailed off, biting my lip to stop from crying out. My scars were on fire.

"Because why?" He slammed a fist into his hand. "Tell me one good reason."

My mind blanked. I couldn't tell him. I couldn't explain the real reason. Quickly, I had my excuse. "His parents were murdered when he was three," I said. "He watched the whole thing. A mage with visions tore them apart. He can't stand the sight of blood because of that."

Rhyan blinked. "Gods," he said. "That's…That's horrific." He stared at his feet, silent until he looked back up at me. "I understand if he can't stand the sight, but why can't he know you're injured to start with?"

I balked, having no more excuses, no more ideas to throw him off course, to make him drop the subject.

Rhyan watched me carefully, his eyes studious. He stepped forward, something dark and cold in his aura sweeping through the room. "I could make you tell me, you know. You're my novice, and I'm your apprentice. I am within every right to do so. Because when you're in this room, I outrank you. And because you already know the price you'll pay if you don't comply with the chain of command."

"You wouldn't dare."

He closed his eyes, pinching the bridge of his nose as if I'd caused him physical pain. His aura pulled back, and the room instantly warmed several degrees. "Fuck." He practically exhaled the word. "No, I wouldn't," he said, his voice softening. He opened his eyes again, hand dropping helplessly to his side. "I'm sorry. Fuck. I'll drop it. I swear. I just…. From a very practical, logical point of view, taking all emotion out, with what you need to do to prepare for the Emperor's test, you cannot be hurt on top of all the training you're doing—the training you're about to add on."

"I know. And I'm not," I said desperately. "I just need to watch where I'm going and get some more sleep. Simple solution. I'll do that, I'll do my part, I promise. I'll do what I need to do, and then you can just do the training part."

He huffed. "Great. And then you'll let me know when it's okay again for me to do the caring part?"

"Rhyan."

"Because I do. I care. And I can't just turn it off. Much as I wish I could. I don't know what's going on with you, but I know something is. And I know it doesn't feel simple, but sometimes it is when we pull back all the chains and shit that come with our status. You think I didn't see this play out before? That I didn't have a dozen noblewomen at home all vying for my attention, purely for political gain? That I don't see the layers of your union with Lord Grey?"

I stepped back, my belly tightening with a sickening feeling. With jealousy, I realized. Jealousy at these nameless noblewomen who at one point in time had close proximity to Rhyan. I couldn't bear the thought of him in someone else's arms, yet I had no right to feel jealous. He wasn't mine. He could never be mine. I was with Tristan. I had to be with Tristan. Rhyan was my bodyguard, and he and I were part of a kashonim—making a romantic relationship forbidden.

I folded my arms across my chest, willing the feelings to vanish.

"If he's not proposing to you," Rhyan said, sounding pained, "and not offering you political protection, providing you with backing from an additional Ka, if he's not making a case to the Imperator on your behalf, what is he doing? Why else would you, of all people, you, who are kind and brilliant and—" He cursed under his breath. "Why would you be with someone like him?"

"Stop it," I said. "I don't have a choice. He's not as bad as you think he is. And knowing what I'm up against—knowing what I stand to lose—I had to give myself my best chance possible. And that's him. That's always been him."

Rhyan flinched, his good eyebrow narrowing, his mouth tight. "Lyr, that can't be it. Especially now when he's not fulfilling a single need."

"I'm done discussing this with you. You haven't earned the right to question me," I said. "My relationship is not your concern."

"It is if it interferes with your training. And that is my concern." The muscles in Rhyan's arms flexed in irritation. The light from the window was shifting from gold to red, giving his hair a bright bronzed hue. There wasn't much day left. The sun was already setting.

"Are we done here?" I asked, ready to walk out the door with permission from the chain of command or not. I wanted to be out of this room, away from Rhyan, away from everyone so I could forget this day had ever happened.

"Lyr, stop. Please. I'm sorry," he said. His fingers curled help-lessly at his sides. "I know you've been hurt before. I mean, just earlier, when the Imperator had you up there, I knew exactly what he was doing behind your back, and you barely cried out. You barely reacted when it was over. You seem barely shaken now. I know you're strong and resilient, but I also know it's not the first time."

"What happened to dropping this?" I asked, voice low. I closed my eyes, taking a breath before looking at him again.

"I told you before I wouldn't push, like I just did, and I...I mean it," Rhyan said apologetically. "I need to uphold my word. I owe you that much. I said I wouldn't force you to tell me before you were ready. And despite my words, my offer still stands—I'm here for you, here to listen, here for whatever you need—anytime you want. But if it is Tristan doing this—"

"It's not."

"—I will end him." He spoke the words quietly, without force, without aggression. He spoke with the same preternatural stillness he'd possessed when he'd first threatened to hurt Tristan—right after he'd seen my initial injuries from Meera.

But I knew deep down in my core that despite the fact that Rhyan and Tristan could never—should never ever—be left in a room together, this wasn't about Tristan. It was about ending my pain. Rhyan, though I didn't like how he was going about it, was on my side in a way so few people ever had been.

Tears fell down my cheek. I wanted to tell him. I wanted to offload the burden. I wanted him to soothe me and to understand and to stop the pain. It was what I had so desperately wanted for the last two years, but I couldn't have it. Rhyan couldn't help me in this. I'd never be able to tell him, I'd never have his comfort, I'd never be able to break my blood oath.

A long silence stood between us that Rhyan broke.

"You deserve better. And you deserve...you deserved to be asked one more time," he said. He blinked like he was holding back his own tears. "I was there, Lyr. I was hiding my scars and wounds. I was lying to my friends and to my family, trying to protect the people around me who didn't fucking deserve it—I was trying to

preserve the honor of my Ka. And then it was too late. And I wish
—" His voice broke. "I wished that someone—anyone had circled
back, hadn't taken my word, hadn't believed my lies, and had asked
me—asked me just one more time if I was okay. Because I think if
I'd been asked once more," he squeezed his eyes shut, "I would
have told them everything." The words poured out of him in a
hushed whisper.

Instantly, I was walking to him, and before I knew it, my arms
were wrapped around him, my face pressed into his chest. He pulled
me to him, one hand wrapped around the nape of my neck, the other
low on my waist—carefully avoiding my wounds.

He breathed in slowly, his body shaking just a little before he
relaxed. "I didn't mean to push—"

"Rhyan," I whispered, my heart breaking. "I know." He'd been
hurt, too, terribly and too many times. He'd been alone in Glemaria,
hurting without anyone to protect him, lying to his friends and his
family while his father had beaten his mother, beaten him, and left
him to rot alone in a Glemarian prison. I just wanted to hug him, to
hold him until his pain went away. And then I wanted to march to
Glemaria to murder his father, to tear him apart limb by limb for
every hurt he'd caused Rhyan. I held him tighter, rubbing my hands
up and down his back. "I'm here for you, too."

"Lyr?" he asked under his breath. "I know I'm asking too much.
But, by the Gods, I have to know. Swear to me the truth. Is he
hurting you?"

"No."

Rhyan let out a shaky breath, his chin resting on top of my head.
He was silent as I clung to him. "Is it someone else?" he asked.

"I can't tell you that."

"Lyr."

"I swear, I have my reasons. Rhyan, trust me. Don't ask me
again."

"Lyr," he pleaded.

I pulled back, pressing a fist to my heart two times before I flattened my hand against my chest. It was the same gesture he'd made

to me when I was in prison and he'd promised me protection, that he'd always keep me safe. "*Me sha, me ka*," I said. *My oath, my soul*—the motto of Ka Hart, the one Rhyan had spent his life trying to live up to. "I swear."

He shuddered as he pulled me back in and held me closer. "Okay," he whispered against my hair, sounding heartbroken but like he'd finally accepted I wouldn't say more.

I wrapped my arms tighter around him. His head dipped down as he gathered me against him. My face rested in the crook of his neck, and I inhaled his scent: musky and fresh, like the pine trees that filled the lusher, greener parts of northern Bamaria. His breath softened, and our breathing synced together.

"Why did you defend Tani?" he asked, his thumb rubbing across the back of my neck. "Why did you let her go?"

"Because when I confronted her, she said," I pulled back, looking up at him, "she said she suspected something between us. And she knew we'd used kashonim."

Rhyan released me from his arms. My skin tingled, my body suddenly cold without his touch. "Every time I try to help, to protect you, I only make it worse."

"No, that's not—"

He looked away from me. "If I really am going to keep my oath, to keep you safe and protected, I can't keep doing this. I need to step away from you."

"Step away how? By not talking to me again?"

He grunted in frustration. "I tried that. And I can't not talk to you."

"Do you want to…." I heard my voice get smaller. "Do you want to back out of our deal—of the extra training?"

"No. That's on."

"Then what?"

"I don't know." He cleared his throat and rolled his shoulders back, a look of determination on his face. "You need to eat dinner before the clinic. Keep up your strength so you can heal."

"What about you?"

"I'll be down in a few minutes."

"Okay."

"And, partner, I'm eating alone." He turned around, busying himself with the mats.

We hadn't agreed to anything. He hadn't changed anything about our relationship or our plans. But my gut was sinking. He was trying to pull away again, and the idea of Rhyan pulling back, separating from me, even on just an emotional level, left me gutted.

I rubbed my hands up and down my arms, full of goosebumps from a chill in the air I could feel through the windows. Bells rang, the hour being called, and little blue lights from the ashvan horses lit up the sky.

I grabbed my soturion cloak, wrapped it around my tunic and over my shoulders and head, and without a word, I walked out of the room, leaving Rhyan alone.

CHAPTER
FIVE

An hour later, I stood at the entrance Tristan had specified to the arena, my heart still hammering. I'd eaten dinner alone in the dining hall, but I'd barely been able to touch, much less stomach my food. I had been too aware of Rhyan's presence on the other side of the room; I'd felt his distance more strongly than I'd felt the presence of the other soturi dining at the table right beside me.

I hated how we'd left things. Knots formed in my stomach every time I replayed his words in my head—every time I thought about the way he'd looked as he'd said them. But as the hour had passed, more and more dread had begun to plague me over seeing Tristan again.

I shifted my weight from foot to foot, both nervous to see Tristan and still trying to find a way to stand in which my back didn't ache and I couldn't feel the ghosts of the Imperator's fingers piercing through my flesh or the bruising on my knees.

Galen and Haleika found me on their way into the Katurium after what I assumed had been a normal, unremarkable day for them —one where they got to leave the Academy, take a break, and have dinner. One where they hadn't been publicly tortured or caught in a position that left them without any easy answers.

They beamed when they saw Tristan approach, neither one

seeming to notice the tension or awkwardness pulsing between us. His head was cocked a little to the side and his neck still reddened —his tells for when he was angry. He was trying to hide it, to act calmly in public like the cool, collected future lord of Ka Grey. But I knew better. Inside Tristan, there was a fire raging, one hellbent on racing back to my training room and seeking out Rhyan for a fight. His silver scabbard was jutting out to the side, like he'd shifted it when slamming his stave back inside of it and was too angry to fix it. He normally never appeared with even a wrinkle of clothing out of place.

I tried to give Tristan a reassuring smile, one that said I was happy to see him and grateful that he was in my life. But his eyes quickly darted to Haleika, who jumped and wrapped her arms around her cousin. Galen grabbed his fist, and they both slapped each other on the back as Haleika bounced over to me and linked our arms. The four of us walked outside into the shouting and excitement that filled the arena.

A cool gust of wind blew through my hair, and I shivered. But it was nothing compared to the icy feeling I had when I spotted the black pole—the Godsdamned pole I'd been tied to and whipped against. The ropes, the ones that had been tied around my wrists, were hanging loosely, their vile ends blowing lifelessly in the wind. I'd of course seen them the morning after I'd been lashed and this morning as well, but seeing the pole and its ropes now, in the dark, against the circle of torchlights above us lighting the rounded arena and beneath the black and starry sky, I was suddenly tied to it again, trapped, exposed, and screaming in pain. The lashes across my back seemed to pulse in response, as if the sheer memory of what had happened could conjure up fresh torture.

The Imperator's recent assault was more likely to blame.

I squeezed my eyes shut and shook out the memories, hearing Rhyan's voice in my head reminding me only to look ahead.

Haleika had sensed my nerves. She pulled me closer to her and asked if I was all right. She'd witnessed my lashing, seen me screaming and crying in pain.

I gave her a shaky nod, not wanting her to realize how upset I was or how much pain I was still in. I didn't want her alerting Tristan. The sooner he forgot his fight with Rhyan and the sooner he forgot I'd ever been injured, the better.

She gave me a strained smile, tightening her grip on me, and we moved forward.

We wound through the stadium seating up several levels until we found four open seats together. The night air cooled rapidly around me, full of an iciness that was less a promise of fall and more like the coming kiss of winter.

"Cold?" Tristan asked.

I nodded, pressing the side of my body against his, seeking out his warmth. I had my soturion cloak wrapped around my arms and torso, but come the end of the week, if this weather continued, I was going to need to trade in my sandals for boots.

Tristan wrapped one arm around me and pulled his stave free from his silver scabbard.

I winced then schooled my expression.

His arm tightening around me, Tristan's gaze narrowed on my face just for a second before he conjured floating flames. The tiny little fires circled around the four of us, spreading a warm, soothing heat. But he still remained tense, clearly uncomfortable holding me —uncomfortable with how I'd reacted to him pulling out his stave.

"Ah, this is what we need mages for," Galen said appreciatively, rubbing his hands together.

"We have a few good qualities," Tristan said, and I could tell he was making an effort to sound normal.

"I'd rather be down there." Galen looked longingly at the arena's center.

I shuddered. I'd be fine never stepping foot in there again, but I slammed the thought down. Thinking like that could manifest that exact outcome in three months, and that was the last thing I wanted. Come the end of the week, I'd have to double my time in the arena with Rhyan, no matter how strained things were between us.

The stadium continued to fill with the sounds of hundreds of footsteps slapping against the floors of each level. I straightened in my seat, moving away from Tristan's embrace when I realized just how full the arena was becoming. There were hundreds of students here—all the elite of the Empire—but apprentices weren't observing tonight, and even if they were, as large as the Soturion Academy was, we didn't have enough students to actually fill the stadium.

Silver armor gleamed in the flickering flames in the seats on the other side of the arena. The seats were nearly as full as they had been the night of the habibellum.

Fuck. It wasn't students entering to fill the seats, it was the Soturi of Ka Kormac. All at once, I heard wolves howling in unison above the din of the crowd. All male voices called out to each other; Ka Kormac was all men. They were the only country of all men. Men and women had both served equally as soturi since Lumeria Matavia, since before the Drowning. The disparity of Ka Kormac's soturi was shocking when they came together like this.

My throat went dry as I stared at the sea of silver. It looked like the entire legion was here. I pressed myself harder against Tristan. His arm automatically tightened around me again, and this time, he relaxed into the practiced touch of the man who'd been mine for over two years.

"Lyr?" he asked. His voice was gentle, but his body still crackled with tension. "Are you all right? Your back?"

I nodded, not sure I could speak in that moment. And even if I could, what could I say? What could he do? Nothing.

"Watch it," Haleika yelled.

I looked up to see her and Galen glaring at Tani, who was pushing her way through our row of seats. There were aisles and empty rows that would have been easier to cross through, but she'd chosen to disrupt us. She wasn't done with me yet, and she clearly didn't care how small or petty the offense. She was going to keep coming after me, especially now that she knew what she could get away with under the Ready and the Imperator's noses. Her eyes caught mine as she stood over me, crowding my space. One of Tristan's flames flew right before her face, nearly burning her own nose off with its proximity.

"Your grace," she said, her voice mocking. "How's your back feeling?"

Tristan's flames expanded, the orbiting fires forcing Tani to duck and lean away. "Move," he said with all the dripping disdain of Bamarian nobility. "You're blocking my view."

Tani shrank back, just for a second.

I narrowed my eyes at her, grateful for once for Tristan's snobbery. It sometimes came out at just the right moment. However far I had fallen from grace, no respect had been lost by Ka Grey. As long as they had their silver, they had their respect. The snide look on Tristan's face was enough to send most Lumerians scurrying.

Tani's dark eyes narrowed in defiance as she turned her attention back to me. She smirked, her golden-brown skin alight. "Where's Rhyan?" she asked sweetly, flipping her silky black braid over her shoulder. "I thought he was always...just a step behind." She placed a hand over her eyes, squinting like she'd find him somewhere in the distance.

Tristan sucked in a breath beside me, the muscles in his arm going taut around my shoulder. In the same moment, I felt Haleika lean into my side. She was still for once, her brown eyes—just like Tristan's—widening.

"Apprentices aren't at clinic tonight," Haleika said.

"No," Tani shrugged. "But Rhyan is usually around her grace anyway."

Herself to Moriel. She'd gotten away with everything today. And I realized with horror—it wasn't just the Ready and the Imperator who had let her go. It was me, too, in my attempt to protect Rhyan, to protect us. Tani was clearly taking this as permission to say what she wanted about Rhyan and I without fear of repercussion.

A gryphon does not shed tears when it's called a seraphim. It knows what it is. Only a seraphim in the mask of a gryphon would be upset—for their truth has been revealed. Aunt Arianna's words played through my mind; they were the words I used to guide my actions at every turn.

Tani had me cornered, for that was exactly what I was: a seraphim in a mask. I was sitting here with Tristan, trying to act normal and pretend our relationship was fine, when deep down in my heart, in my soul, something that felt ancient and un-nameable was calling out for Rhyan.

Galen stood up from his seat, his dark muscled arms peeking out from beneath his practice tunic, flexing. "Are you lost, Tani?" he asked. "We don't talk to you."

Tani rolled her eyes, looking down at me, an unmistakable challenge in the quirk of her lips. She wanted me to fight her, to pick up where we'd left off the day before. Whether or not I was capable of beating her, we both knew where it would end. She would be the victor, never having to face punishment for her actions.

Tristan had had enough. He stood, his posture a mirror of Galen's, the anger of his aura expanding with a vicious pulse. "Go," he said, voice low and dangerous. It was the voice he used when hunting vorakh. "Now."

Tani left, offering one glance behind her as she continued to push her way through the seats. A swatch of orange and purple tunics down the row hinted she was heading for seating with the rest of Ka Elys.

"I thought she was out sick," Haleika said. "She missed the run and all her classes today."

Because she was on trial for being part of the Emartis, for being a terrorist, and for fighting me. I didn't want to get into it, so I shrugged in response. "Must be feeling better now."

Another round of howls erupted as the soturi fighting in the night's clinic took their places, the three groups of five entering the bindings of the silver rings.

Haleika narrowed her eyes, staring across the stadium at the uproar. I stared down, seeing several novice soturi wearing silver in the rings. Their armor was sculpted to look like wolf's fur. Ka Kormac. Guess the entire army had all come to support their pack.

"Gods," Galen said with disgust. "That's a lot of anointed soturi." He'd finally caught sight of the legion occupying the stands. "Auriel's bane." He leaned forward, squinting. "They're all Ka Kormac."

"Isn't the whole point of them being here to offer protection?" Haleika frowned. "It seems like they're just here to sit in the arena and cheer like they're at a sports game."

They are at a sports game. At least tonight I'm not the entertainment.

Aemon stepped into the center of the field. He spoke calmly, reviewing the rules as he always did and announcing the first five. It was clear from the power of his aura he was mad—still furious from the trial—though me and Tani were probably the only ones in the arena who knew why. Everyone else would assume he was in one of his moods.

I wondered if Rhyan could feel it, too, or if he'd gone back to his apartment.

The soturi in the first ring took their positions, and the clock started. Immediately, the novice in the center, a blonde girl from Ka Daquataine in Damara, went on the offensive, targeting what appeared to be the biggest soturion in the ring, a brute from Ka Kormac. She raced forward, springing onto his back and covering his eyes with her hands. He flailed, trying to reach her, his hands stretching behind his back, but his silvered-wolf armor didn't allow him full freedom of motion, and he couldn't get to her. He turned around and around again, trying to stretch his arms farther or shake her off, but he kept failing—he was too bulky, and while clearly strong, he was not flexible, restricted by both his muscle and the contour of his armor. Spinning around once more, he turned his back to the silver circle binding them in. He backed up so fast I shuddered. He was going to slam her into the binding, into the rings that were so cold, they burned through your skin.

Half the crowd cheered while the other half—Ka Kormac— cursed and howled. The soturion from Damara released her grip at the last second, dropping to the ground. She tucked herself into a ball and rolled aside just as the brute crashed into the ring with such force, he fell to his knees with a bloodcurdling howl of pain. Light flashed across the silver circle, emitting a buzzing sound of magic I could feel up in the stands.

The girl unrolled herself, sprung to her feet, and spun on the heels of her sandals, her eyes tracking her next opponent.

Tristan shifted in his seat uneasily, and I turned to see him watching me carefully. "Was that you? The other day?" he asked. "Having to fight soturi that size and…that many at once?"

"Yes."

He bit his lip, his eyebrows furrowed together. "You were in the center?"

I nodded, craning my neck to look back at him. His eyes were fixed on the arena, his eyebrows furrowing.

The fight ended minutes later, and the discussion and critique of the battle ensued, followed by the next one, and then the last. Through all of it, Tristan remained silent, tight-lipped, and uncomfortable, holding me in his arms so stiffly I felt like I was being hugged by a stone statue.

With each maneuver executed, each hit, punch, and kick, I felt Tristan's discomfort grow, felt his anger cresting like a wave through the pulses of his aura. His fury echoed in the flickering flames of the fires circling around us and keeping us warm from the chilled air. I was beginning to feel suffocated by their heat.

Finally dismissed, with my back aching from sitting still for so long, Tristan and I left Haleika and Galen and headed back to my apartment. I took Tristan's hand in mine as we wound over the waterways of Urtavia. I'd wanted to avoid Ka Kormac at all costs, and every single time I caught the sound of a howl or noticed the torches lighting up the city catching on silver armor, I turned or changed direction.

Back in my apartment, I left Tristan alone in my living room while I changed out of my practice clothes and uniform. I reached back to unbraid my hair, but I couldn't. My arms were too sore. Even my fingers felt stiff. Changing my clothes alone had been a miracle, and though I wished in some part that Tristan had been in here helping me, I was mostly glad he'd waited outside. The less he saw of my injuries, the better. Dressed in a loosened tunic to keep pressure off my back and tight riding pants to balance the look, I reentered the living room, barefoot and exhausted, my hair messily falling out of its braid. I found a still tense Tristan sitting awkwardly on my couch.

I swallowed, my mouth dry as I felt the tension crackling in his aura.

"Can we talk?" he asked.

I sat down beside him and nodded, trying to keep my knees from shaking with nerves.

"I didn't know," he said urgently. "I didn't know it was this bad. Lyr. Why didn't you tell me?"

I shook my head, heart pounding. "Tell you what?"

"How badly you were being hurt. You've been brushing it all off —acting like it's not that big a deal. You never once clued me into anything like I saw tonight."

"What?"

"Lyr, why did you underplay all of this with me?"

"I didn't."

"You barely wanted to show me your back."

I bit my lip, terrified he was about to guess—to see through my lies and realize I'd never shown him a single wound because if he saw one, he'd see all. "Because...I know you don't like to see things like that."

"I'd look at anything for you. Don't you know that?" He frowned. "I know you've been busy, that this past month hasn't been easy. But I also feel like...you've been keeping me at a distance for a while now."

"I'm sorry," I said, my stomach twisting. He was always more perceptive than I gave him credit for, and that perception could prove deadly if he got too close. "I've never wanted you to feel like that."

"No," he said, voice gravelly. "It's not your fault. I think since your birthday, I haven't made the best choices with you. I just...I haven't known the right thing to do. I only know I hate the idea of you out there. The idea of you getting hurt." His chest heaved, and he reached for my cheek. His thumb brushed lightly against my cheekbone just under my cut—the cut that had come from Meera punching me in the face.

I tensed, my entire body going cold as fear gripped me. My wrist flamed with pain.

"Aren't there fucking rules against this?" he asked. He traced my cheekbone again, the skin of his hand so smooth against my face —too smooth. I bit the inside of my cheek, heart hammering. Outside, the wind howled, rocking a window that wasn't closed properly on its hinges. His brown eyes widened as he scanned my cheekbone, his thumb tracing the injury slowly up and down.

He doesn't know. He doesn't know. He doesn't know. He couldn't sense injuries from a vorakh. But still, my vision went in and out of focus as icy cold fear ripped through me.

"There are rules," I said, willing my voice to sound even. "But...accidents happen. Especially when you have the whole novice class in a fight."

"Lyr, tell me honestly. Were you limping?"

"No. If I were, wouldn't I still be now?"

"Then what was all that crap the forsworn bastard was spewing? He...." Tristan stretched his neck from side to side. "He was acting like I'd hurt you."

My eyes widened. "Tristan, you'd never hurt me," I said quickly.

"Then what the fuck was going on back there? Why would he think that?"

"I—" I shook my head, my mind freezing.

"Maybe I missed the mark. Maybe I wasn't seeing what I was supposed to see or paying as much attention as I should have been. But he's with you all day, every day. He was at the habibellum. If he didn't see you get hurt, didn't see you get this," he swept his thumb against my cheek before his fingers cupped my chin and tilted my face up to his, "when did you?"

I wracked my brain for a lie, a story, a cover-up. This was exactly why I hadn't wanted Rhyan saying anything. The habibellum had been the perfect excuse to cover up my newest wounds and bruises. It was a perfect alibi for Meera's vorakh. And Rhyan had destroyed it in a single conversation.

"Tani," I said suddenly.

"Who?"

"That girl, the soturion from Ka Elys who tried to push through our row. I didn't tell you because, well, what happened with my back took precedence. But she—we got into a fight the other day. Not exactly a legal fight. And I came out with cuts and bruises that left Rhyan concerned. Because he hadn't been there to see."

"She did that?" he asked.

I watched his mind churn, knew he was deciding to go after her, to report her and attempt to bring her down. He'd drag her back to court, to another proceeding that would only end in her favor and potentially expose me and Rhyan, at best for using kashonim and at worst for being…more.

The fires we lit in my living room crackled and spit, but my heart beat loudly over the sound. I couldn't think. I needed to stop Tristan. I gripped his arm, pushing his hand down into my lap and interlacing our fingers.

"There was a trial today because of it," I said. "Tani was held accountable. That's why she was trying to annoy me in the arena—to get back at me. The Imperator was there, too, to oversee. I had to go to the trial during training hours, and then I had to make up the time. That's why I was training with Rhyan late. Imperator's orders."

Tristan narrowed his gaze. "Then what was the forsworn's Godsdamned problem? Why was he so convinced I hurt you if he knew what happened?"

"He…." I sucked in a breath, stumped for a lie, for a way to keep weaving a believable story.

"Lyr, he's dangerous. I can see it in his eyes. He's not just a killer. There's something off about him. He may be farther than Lethea, too. The way he talked to me—I only left so he'd calm down."

"He's not crazy," I blurted out.

Tristan leaned back, and I realized my error. I'd defended Rhyan.

"I mean, what he was doing…was projecting."

"What?"

"Don't you see?" I asked, the idea forming clearly in my mind. I'd use a truth to conceal a lie. "Tristan, you were right. He left me unprepared for the first habibellum—left me unprotected. And when you pointed that out, he got upset. He tried to deflect and say it was your fault. He just feels guilty. It makes him look bad. That's all it was. His own insecurity. If I don't stay in the Soturion Academy, neither does he—and that's it. He's back on the streets, outside the Empire, forsworn and in exile forever."

Tristan looked deep in thought as he considered my words, his eyes flicking occasionally back to my face, to my cut, to my black eye. I could sense his unease with my lies, how close he was getting to finding the hole in the story I'd fed him.

I knew what I had to do.

I sucked in a breath, tightening my fingers around his and drawing his hand up my thigh, higher and higher, guiding him to the center between my legs.

Tristan froze, his eyes now wholly focused on our hands, his fingers, and what lay beneath.

"I love how protective you are of me," I said, my breath catching as his fingers brushed against me.

He swallowed. "I love you. You know that."

"I know."

"Just the idea of you being hurt, being in danger…." He pressed his knuckles against my center. I widened my legs, gently pushing his hand lower. His hand moved down, his palm opening to cup me through my pants and rubbing up and down. "It drives me farther than Lethea."

My breath hitched, and I let out a small moan, playing along as my fingers trailed up his forearm, digging in, spurring him on.

"Is there anything else I need to know?" He pressed his palm harder against me, fingers switching to a circular motion.

I closed my eyes, focusing on the feel of his fingers. I was numb. But I knew he needed this. We needed this. I exhaled sharply, focusing my world on his hand, on its movement, on the pressure he was creating, on the flow of blood slowly beginning to heat and bring my body to life. I felt the energy in his aura relax; it was no longer pulsing with anger, hurt, and confusion, but desire. As I turned toward him, I caught the scent of mint and salt from the ocean.

Disappointment washed over me. I'd wanted musk and pine.

"I'm adding on extra practices," I said, moving my hand back down to cover his, urging him to use even more pressure, driving the circles faster.

"All right," he said. There was an uncertainty to his words, and his fingers paused. "What does that mean?"

Everything in my body ached, but not in the way I wanted it to. "I have three months." His hand moved up the seam of my pants, and his fingers pushed up my tunic, exposing my belly and sliding along my waistband to just below my navel. I breathed deep, my belly rising and falling against him. "And you saw what it was like out there."

He brushed his fingers back and forth across my stomach, sliding them lower, but only a little. He was teasing, waiting.

"So, longer days?" Tristan asked, voice rough.

"And weekends," I said. "I'll have to excuse myself from most social events."

His jaw tensed, and I leaned in toward him, drawing my mouth to his.

"It's not forever," I whispered against his lips. "Just until Valyati. Three months." I kissed him, but Tristan kept his mouth closed, his lips hardened together. I pulled back, my gaze questioning. "You saw what it's like. You know how behind I am. So until I pass the Emperor's test," my mouth went dry, "I may need to be...scarce."

"Extra training," he said.

I nodded, writhing my belly against his hand, urging him to keep going, to forget what had happened tonight, to let it go, to make me forget, to make me feel.

"Please," I said. "Tristan."

But his hand was still, refusing to do what I needed, refusing to offer me any relief or signal that he was all right with everything that was happening, that he was all right with me.

"Not with him," he said, his voice dark.

"What?"

"The extra training, studying, whatever you need to do, do it. But not with him. I forbid you." Tristan kissed me, his tongue sweeping against my lips. Our kiss deepened. His fingers finally slipped beneath my waistband, reaching down until they were against my bared skin, where they ran up and down my center before moving in slow, sensuous circles. "Not with the forsworn," he said, increasing the pressure. "He trains you for official Academy hours, and that's it."

"Tristan," I protested.

He slipped a finger inside of me, his palm against my center. I arched my back, gasping from both the sudden pleasure he'd evoked and the pain in my back. I could feel the pressure of Tristan's finger inside of me...and I could feel the agony of the Imperator's finger inside my wounds. I cried out, no longer sure what was making me cry. It seemed like pleasure and pain were the same when it came to my life now. One always caused the other. One couldn't exist without its opposite bearing down on me.

He increased his speed, as I braced myself on the couch, my fingers digging into the cushion, my hips rocking against his hand. I was desperate for relief, for something to finally feel good after having been tortured. His mouth was hot on my neck, his kisses repeating the same demand as anger began to vibrate through the lust in his aura.

Some inner part of me rebelled. He had no right to make such demands or to have any say in my training or how I survived these months. But he wasn't supposed to know about my agreement with Rhyan. He wasn't supposed to know Rhyan was the one training me in secret. Tristan never could know—not if we were both going to stay safe.

Tristan slid a second finger inside me, each thrust repeating his demands. *Not. With. Him.*

I arched.

"Not with him," I said breathlessly. The tension inside me was building, and so was the soreness and ache in my back. "I won't be with anyone in particular. Just whoever is around to spar. Mostly… I'll just be…practicing…." My breath hitched. "Training…studying…. I…I have to…prepare."

"I'll help you," he said.

"No," I said. "I…I can't focus when I'm with you. This is serious." I gasped. The tension was building and building—until that's all it was. Tension. Tension strung too tight to be released.

What had felt good seconds ago now left me numb in the part of me I'd wanted to ache and aching in the part of my body I'd wished desperately was numb. I wanted to go to bed. I wanted to crawl under the covers.

I imagined rough, calloused hands on me. Rhyan calling my name. Rhyan's lips on mine.

I dug my fingers into Tristan's arm, my nails piercing him as I moaned and threw my head back. He watched me carefully, his movements slowing as I brought my breath back to normal, praying he hadn't noticed it had been an act.

He watched me carefully like he didn't fully believe I'd come. But then he offered a slight shake of his head, like he was going to let it go as he slid his hand out of my pants. I reached for his, running my palm against his length. He was only semi-erect. "Do you want me to take care of you?" I asked.

"You look like you're in pain."

"My back," I conceded guiltily, biting my lip. "It's sore. But this," I gestured between us, "it took my mind off it. For a little."

He gave me a small smile. "I'm glad," he said. The smile was tight on his lips—not reaching his eyes. "Can you handle sleeping on your stomach tonight?"

"You're not staying?" I asked.

"I think you'll get more rest without me."

A panicky feeling fluttered in my chest as my body went cold. I was fine spending a night without Tristan, but I didn't like his tone or the fact that he was the one suggesting it. He was still upset about what had happened with Rhyan, and despite everything that just happened between us, nothing felt like it was fixed.

"Are we all right?" I asked.

Tristan nodded. "Of course."

But my stomach dropped, my insides twisting. We both knew it was a lie.

He stood up and gently kissed me on the lips. "Saturday night, Ka Grey is dining at Cresthaven. I'll be there."

I tried not to read too much meaning into his words. But Saturday was three days from now, which meant he didn't plan on seeing me for three days. He'd never gone three days without seeing me—except for during my time in the Shadow Stronghold.

"I'll miss you," I said, not even trying to hide the desperation and fear in my voice.

"Good night, Lyr."

I shoved off my clothes after he left and after double-checking everything was locked. I listened for the unmistakable hum of the magical wards meant to offer additional protection around my apartment.

After managing to slide a nightshift over my head, I went to close my opened bedroom window.

Steel reflecting torchlight caught my eye on the waterway below. A lone soturion stood guard on the glass, the water rushing beneath his feet. Rhyan was keeping watch outside my apartment building, staring up into my window. His black armor was dark in the shadows, and the stars of the Valalumirs on his leather belt glittered in the firelight. He was so far below, I shouldn't have been able to tell it was him in the black of the night, but I knew. Despite being at such a distance, our eyes met, and I could have sworn I saw the sharpest movement of his head turned up to me. And just as quickly as I'd found him, he was gone, vanishing into the shadows, leaving nothing behind but the reflection of fire dancing on the waterways in the dark.

CHAPTER
SIX

The rest of the week passed in a blur. And despite Rhyan having promised he would continue talking to me, that he couldn't not talk to me, he was in fact back to being cold Rhyan. He still motioned me over to set my dagger down beside his in the mornings before our runs. He was still a meticulous teacher during our training sessions. But I could see the change in him, in his demeanor. I could feel it, too. Our entire relationship had changed overnight. Again.

He refused to engage in small talk or to even look at me beyond making sure I was using proper fighting form. He spotted me when I needed his assistance in a certain position. He kept his eyes focused on my fists when we sparred, on my legs when I kicked, and on anything else he could to avoid looking me in the eyes. If he needed to touch me to make an adjustment or to deepen a stretch, it was clinical and cold.

When I tried to talk to him about it, he changed the subject with his jaw tensed or lips pursed together. If I tried to get him to admit he wasn't speaking to me, his eyes darkened, and he went into excruciating detail about whatever stretch or move we were practicing, talking at such length I could no longer focus on what he was saying.

By the end of the week, I was miserable. I'd never felt more distant from him or Tristan. I'd never felt more alone. I hadn't seen my sisters since the night after my lashing—the night after Meera's latest vision.

When Saturday morning rolled around, I woke early to prepare to meet Rhyan for our first private training session. But a note had been slipped under my door.

I unrolled the scroll, still scrubbing the sleep from my eyes with my hair tangled down my back in the braids I'd slept in.

Can't today. Start tomorrow.

-R

I tossed the scroll into the flames of a candle I'd lit in my living room and slumped onto my couch. What in Lumeria did that mean?

He'd sworn he wouldn't go back on his agreement to give me extra training. But with the way he'd treated me the last few days, I was worried. And, if I were being honest, I was disappointed.

I was suddenly faced with an entirely open day and no idea what to do with myself. Through my opened bedroom door, I could see my dummy with my armor on it, the golden seraphim wings on the shoulders glittering from the morning light.

I sat up and stretched, my back aching, my calves sore from the previous day's work-out. I didn't want to be in the city, and I'd be at Cresthaven for dinner tonight with my sisters and with Tristan. I was too stiff to try and train on my own—not that I had any idea what I was even doing. I couldn't sit here all day. Even if I wasn't training with Rhyan, I still had to prepare for the Emperor's test.

Suddenly, I knew exactly where to go.

I got back up and threw open my wardrobe. It was time for a visit to the Great Library. When I'd last been there, I'd been able to read a scroll by Sianna Batavia—an eyewitness to the Drowning. According to the title, she'd promised to write about Asherah, the Goddess who'd been an original guardian of the Valalumir in Heaven and had lost her power after being banished to Earth for her affair with Auriel.

But the scroll, The Fall of Asherah and Her Loss of Power, had cut off just before the events of the Drowning occurred, right when the Lumerians lost the war over the Valalumir—the sacred light that had crystalized when stolen from Heaven. When Moriel, the God who'd sided with the akadim, had overrun the Lumerian forces and their land, the scroll had ended.

There was a part two. But Mercurial had borrowed it in the knowledge that I would want to read it—that I would be desperate to read it and would potentially enter a deal with him in order to do so. Such a deal would be one I'd been taught since birth never to make.

As far as I knew, Mercurial was still outside of the country since he'd approached me earlier in the week. Something told me that despite having crossed the Bamarian borders, he still had the scroll in his possession. He wouldn't have let go of his leverage over me so easily even if it was illegal to take a scroll from the Great Library outside Bamaria. Only copies were allowed to leave, and according to Nabula Kajan, one of the lead librarians, all of those were in restoration beneath the pyramid.

Gingerly, I pulled off my sleep clothes to check my back in the mirror. Rhyan hadn't changed the bandage since our fight. He'd promised to do it today, but it looked like it was still secure in place. No weird smell or stains were coming through—a good sign the wounds were healing and not infected after what the Imperator had done. Thank the Gods.

I pulled out a black gown with a high back, and after lacing up my new soturion-issue boots, I brushed out my hair, pulled half of it back with golden pins, and placed my diadem across the center of my forehead. The gold circlet at the center shined and highlighted the golden jewelry adorning my arms, wrists, fingers, neck, and ears. And thanks to the meticulous application of sunleaves on my face and a little bit of makeup, my black eye and cut cheek were nearly invisible. This was the most I'd looked like Lady Lyriana Batavia in days.

I usually didn't like wearing my diadem outside of formal events, during which it was expected of me to present my station to the public. But I needed to make a trip into the restricted section of the pyramid, so I was pulling out every last stop.

On my bureau lay the largest golden necklace I'd ever seen, made of connecting seven-pointed stars of pure gold: golden Valalumirs. Inside the center of each star was a diamond infused with starfire—a rare metal that we forged our weapons from with the help of the Afeya. In the sun, they burned with flames, the steel turning red. Like my hair.

The necklace had been an artifact found in the Lumerian Ocean in a recent fishing expedition. It had been cleaned up and most likely heading for a display case in the Museion, where it would have been lifeless and ogled at by visitors to the exhibit on Lumeria Matavia.

But now it was mine—thanks to Ramia, the Afeyan librarian. She was half-Afeyan herself, half immortal, and half as dangerous as Mercurial...though I'd never considered her to be before Mercurial had waltzed into my life. Before, she had simply been a fun librarian who'd also created and sold my favorite jewelry.

But Ramia hadn't made this piece. It had technically been stolen, and now it was mine. I felt a sudden pull to the necklace, a sudden urge to put it on, to let the gold mold to my shape and warm against my skin. I wanted to let the stars shine with the flames of starfire beneath the sun, to let the Valalumirs drip down my shoulders like armor and feel its weight across my breasts.

But I stepped away from the necklace. Knowing Ramia wanted me to wear it made me uneasy. It made me unsure if I'd ever put it on again even if I sometimes caught myself absentmindedly staring at it, imagining myself wearing it while walking along an unfamiliar golden shoreline.

I'd gotten it on my birthday to serve as a distraction during my Revelation Ceremony; I'd hoped to dazzle every noble and the Imperator with my excessive jewels so they wouldn't notice if I revealed a vorakh.

Now the necklace was just distracting me.

I shook my hair out and left my room, leaving the necklace behind, but before I left the apartment, I added my soturion cloak to the ensemble. I was grateful to wrap the extra material around my shoulders to protect me from the chill in the air, and also to hide my hair from any onlookers. I was in full Lady Lyriana regalia—I just didn't feel like having anyone notice that fact until I arrived in Scholar's Harbor.

A brisk wind pulled at my makeshift hood, and I pulled it tighter against me, my boots slapping down on the waterway as I attempted to hurry, unseen, through Urtavia. Vendors were filling the streets and drawing crowds. Tents had been set up to sell fresh fruit and spices. More harvest stands had appeared with lines of Lumerians forming to purchase vegetables and baked goods. As I looked more closely, I could see soturi camouflaged in the alleys of the city buildings, behind the shrubbery, and alongside the trees. It was the Soturi of Ka Kormac—the occupying army of the Imperator.

I tugged the hood of my cloak farther down my forehead, shadowing my face, and my feet moved faster across the sparkling waterway until I reached the seraphim port.

"You think you're clever."

I whirled around, coming face to face with my least favorite soturion in Bamaria—Markan. Fucking bastard.

"Is this your way of trying to tell me you don't think I am?" I asked.

"You think you can sneak off, fly wherever you please without an escort?"

"We both know I've done it before. So, if that makes me clever, there's your answer."

"It makes you a fool." He stepped closer, his hulking form now in my personal space. I wanted to hit him, but I knew from experience he was like a wall of bricks. I'd been helpless when he'd carried me away from the temple after Jules and Meera's Revelation.

"That almost sounded like an insult," I said. "And I didn't once hear you address me as your grace."

"Your grace," he said, voice even.

"I suppose this means you want to come along with me to the Great Library? To watch me read words too big for you to understand for the next few hours?"

"Insulting my intelligence isn't going to deter me from my duty," he said, already hailing down one of the seraphim attendants to prepare my carriage.

"Well, insulting my intelligence isn't going to make up for the lack in yours. If I in fact am the fool you claim me to be, then let's remember the many times this fool left you behind in the dust or tricked you into staying back while I flew away unescorted. If a fool can outsmart you—what do you call yourself?"

His nostrils flared, and for a moment, I remembered just how dangerous Markan was. He struck first and asked questions later. He always followed orders, including those to drug me and carry me away from the last place I ever saw Jules alive. He'd killed the vendor who worked for the Emartis.

"Impatient," he said. "You know we have terrorists in the city now, terrorists who have targeted you, terrorists who you decided to chase after on your own. Foolish. Don't act so brave when you're hiding behind Lord Tristan's escorts or the forsworn trailing your every step."

I stiffened, not liking the way he'd mentioned Rhyan. Rhyan was officially part of my escort, a member of my security team along with Markan. He'd been ordered by my father to guard me in exchange for refuge in Bamaria. But the way Markan had spoken of him made it sound like Rhyan had been going above and beyond his duty. Like he'd noticed something between me and Rhyan he shouldn't have, just as Tani had noticed.

"Sit behind the partition," I snapped. I turned, rushing forward and climbing up the stairs into the blue topaz carriage atop our seraphim.

The carriage shifted as Markan climbed aboard behind me, the privacy door slamming shut as he grunted. I huddled into my seat, my green soturion cloak wrapped tightly around my shoulders. The floor shifted again as our seraphim stood, preparing to take off.

The wind blew against the carriage as her golden wings flapped, and within another few seconds we were airborne. I called out our destination to the bird and stared out the window, remembering how the Emartis had appeared over the Katurium on black seraphim that had exploded into glass. There was a single dark cloud ahead, and my heart hammered, but then we passed it, soaring into peaceful skies. I squeezed my eyes shut. There were no Emartis in the sky. Not today.

In Scholar's Harbor, I walked through the golden desert of the island. The land had been dried out completely by the magic used to construct the pyramids that housed all the Lumerian knowledge in existence. Elderly ashvan horses raced back and forth across the sand dunes, their jewel-toned bodies and manes shining too brightly in the morning sun. Ashvan foals just beginning to fly raced until their hooves lifted from the sand, tiny blue sparks erupting behind them.

Before me, the three golden pyramids loomed. I headed straight for the smallest and oldest, the one that housed Sianna Batavia's writings. As usual, the entrance was guarded by Apollon and Eger Scholar, two brothers, both trained as soturi who had dedicated their lives to protecting the knowledge kept inside. They both towered over six feet tall, and their skin was nearly black, a trait shared by most of Ka Scholar, who preferred life in the slower-paced desert-like setting of Scholar's Harbor.

Immediately, they parted their swords for me to step inside. Both Apollon and Eger offered warm smiles as I greeted them, surprised to see them in the day since they often took guard duty overnight. I caught a slight narrowing of their eyes and a frown on Eger's face as they noticed Markan stalking behind me.

Inside the pyramid, Nabula Kajan jumped up as soon as she saw me. Leather cases full of scrolls were strapped across her body. She also tended to work at night, but was in the library most days as well.

"Your grace," she said. "It's been weeks."

"I know. I've been busy. It's good to see you, Nabula."

She eyed me up and down, taking in my formal attire as an Heir to the Arkasva. I watched as her gaze settled on my forehead, on the diadem, the mark of my station.

She nodded slowly. "And you, your grace." She took in the soturion cloak wrapped around me, the only aspect of my appearance that hinted I was still powerless, still forced into that path. "Shall I prepare your light for you?" There was an underlying question in her words. I realized she was unsure if I was still without magic.

"Please," I said, a familiar stab of pain in my heart.

She rushed behind the long table at which she'd been sitting and which was full of scrolls of all shapes and sizes, some neatly rolled and tied shut with a leather strap, others open and laying across each other, weighed down by crystals to save her place. After stretching to grab a long golden lamp from a high shelf behind her, she laid the rod across her worktable and reached up to a second shelf to take down one of the oversized amethyst crystals. The amethyst was hooked to the edge of the rod, which she carefully stood against the ground.

She uttered the incantation, her hands sweeping in circles around the stone until a bright, luminescent light uncoiled from the center of the amethyst. Light glowed from within until the entire crystal shined, its light reflecting on the inner golden pyramid walls, turning Nabula's white dress lavender. Nabula placed the rod in my hands as the amethyst rocked side to side.

Her gaze shifted behind me to where Markan stood, miserable and surly.

Good. I'd forgotten how much it annoyed him to come here— this was new motivation for me to make more visits if he was going to insist on following me every time I left the Academy.

"One for you as well, Soturion Markan?" Nabula asked.

"No," he said. "I'll be waiting for her grace right here."

Nabula's face fell a little, and I almost laughed. She was just as miserable at the idea of him being around as I was. She was clearly in the middle of some serious reading and didn't want a brute like Markan hovering over her.

"I can set you up at your own station—we do have some lovely firsthand accounts of soturion training in Lumeria Matav—"

"I'm fine," he said with a cough. He was already stiff and in his guard position: eyes alert and assessing for danger, muscled arms crossed over his chest.

"Follow me, your grace," Nabula said, waving me to her side.

I gave Markan one last sneer before following Nabula down the library's dark corridors. Tiny amethysts floated above my head.

"What are you looking for today?" she asked once out of earshot from Markan. I appreciated that she allowed me to read and research in private.

"When I last came, I'd wanted to look at the second scroll by Sianna Batavia. *The Fall of Asherah and Her Loss of Power.*"

"Ah, of course. You have been waiting for that." She opened a leather case strapped to her bicep and removed the scrolled parchment inside, unraveling it to read, her eyes quickly jumping back and forth across the page. "The available copies are still beneath the pyramid in restoration."

"And the main copy? The one that had been borrowed by the Afeyan Ambassador from the Star Court?"

"It is not available."

I frowned. "Nabula, he left Bamaria earlier this week—were you aware of the scroll leaving the country?"

She shook her head. "He returned what he borrowed prior to leaving. But it was also due for restoration."

Due? Or had he damaged it in some way, determined to keep it from me?

"When will it come out of restoration?" I asked.

"I'm not sure," she said apologetically. "But I do have some ideas of several other titles to pull for you—firsthand accounts from that time."

"I would appreciate being allowed to visit the restoration section today." I tried to form it as a request, keep my voice gentle. I liked

Nabula, and the last thing I wanted to do was ruin the relationship we'd formed over the years. But at the same time, I didn't have the luxury of waiting any longer. Not with less than three months to train, not with my extra sessions with Rhyan approaching. I needed to see what that scroll could tell me, and I needed to read it today.

I stood taller, my shoulders rolled back—the perfect posture of a noble, of an Heir to the Arkasva. It was exactly why I'd worn my diadem.

Nabula looked down at once, and I instantly felt guilty for such a show of power, but the stakes were too high for me not to have resorted to my nobility.

"Of course, your grace," she said formally. "My duties force me to stay on the main level, but I shall summon another librarian to escort you and prepare the scroll."

"Her grace will come with me," said a seductive voice.

I turned to see Ramia sauntering down the aisle, her hips swaying side to side, a tight black dress hugging her every curve. Golden bangles ran up the length of her arms, and a golden Vala-lumir pin held the black material of her dress together over her right shoulder. The amount of jewelry she wore made mine seem minimalist in comparison, and I was always wearing a lot. But then again, she was my prime jewelry dealer. Her bright red hair had been twisted into a loose braid with tiny golden beads threaded throughout. Her eyes, always sparkling and full of mischief, swept over me.

Ramia stood before Nabula. "I take her grace to restoration. You go run your table, yes?"

"Your grace?" Nabula asked, her eyes darting to me.

I nodded even though my stomach had flip-flopped at her sudden appearance. Ramia was a librarian, but she worked with the Afeya collections, which were housed in a different pyramid. She'd given me the first of Sianna's works the last time I'd been here. Ramia had even prepared a viewing glass and gloves for me in advance, like she'd known I was coming.

"I'll go with Ramia, thank you."

The half-Afeyan gave me a mischievous smile, a dark glint in her eyes as she tossed her red hair behind her shoulder. She swiveled her hips, the bangles on her arms jingling as she stepped closer to me and made a shooing motion with her hand to Nabula. "Go. Go. I know my way."

Nabula pursed her lips together, looking like she was resisting the urge to roll her eyes. "You have been spending a lot of time in my library, Ramia."

"Your library? Not Great Library for all Bamaria?"

"You know what I mean." Nabula turned to me, still looking unsure of this new development. She was right. This was not the library Ramia had been assigned to; she was in the larger pyramid with the Afeyan scrolls. But Ramia was an official librarian and was perfectly in her rights to be here as often as she wished. "Your grace. Please send word up to me if you require any assistance."

"Thank you, Nabula. I will."

"She's fine," Ramia said and sauntered around the corridor.

I tried to offer Nabula a sympathetic look but had to rush after Ramia. Despite her being willing to show me my way to restoration, she was speeding forward, as if daring me to keep up.

I matched her stride, and there was a small look of surprise on her face as I caught up to her.

"Quick. Like soturion," she said.

"That's what I am," I said carefully.

She smiled, the giant amethyst hanging from her golden lamp bobbing back and forth as she turned another corner. I gripped mine tighter in my hands as we left the main floor of the library and passed through two golden doors. Beyond them we were in near total darkness aside from our amethyst lights.

"Still," Ramia said, removing a stave from her belt and pressing the tip into a golden circle on the wall. Blue light lit up the circle and Ramia pulled her stave back with a smirk on her lips.

My stomach leapt into my chest as the floor began to move, dropping us miles below the pyramid's main floor. Our descent paused, and Ramia urged me forward.

I stepped onto flat ground, clutching my chest. I never got used to that. And within a few short steps, the floor began to slope down beneath my feet. I held out my lamp in front of me, watching the golden brick walls lit in a lavender hue round and round as we descended beneath the pyramid.

Each circle we made took us deeper into new levels where dozens of librarians from Ka Scholar worked in silence. Some pushed carts full of scrolls, some sat at tables and carefully read newly restored scrolls, checking and editing for mistakes. We passed a few sections with nothing but scrolls made from ancient parchment that had been locked behind glass and no mages in sight.

At last, Ramia made a clicking noise with her tongue. "This level. This one we want."

She walked off the spiraling corridor onto the floor. Dozens of amethyst lamps created an eerie glow so far below the ground. I'd noticed the levels opening at each section growing smaller and smaller. Hidden beneath each of the pyramids in the Great Library was a pyramid underground, built in reverse. Having their points at the bottom, each section we traveled past felt tighter and tighter. In previous visits, I'd descended even lower than this level, but only by one or two floors. Today was my first time being allowed to step onto the restoration level.

Two mages immediately froze upon our approach. A row of golden rods jutted out from the golden-bricked wall behind them, the wall itself on a slight angle. Hanging from each rod was a glowing amethyst.

The first mage, his white robes glowing beneath the light, narrowed his eyes, a small hiss escaping his lips. "What are you doing here?" The question was directed at Ramia.

I didn't have time for inter-library politics or the opinions Ka Scholar had of Ramia. I stepped forward, my chin lifted to ensure the crystals shined on my diadem, and reminded them of my station. "Forgive our intrusion. I've asked Ramia to escort me."

Immediately, both mages dropped to their knees, muttering, "Your grace" as they rose.

I waved them off. "No need. I'm seeking Sianna Batavia's second scroll. *The Fall of Asherah and Her Loss of Power.* I need Part Two, specifically."

The mages eyed each other warily.

"A popular title recently. We went years without it being touched or borrowed. Now...." The second mage frowned. He looked to the first one, older and perhaps more senior in his title. He gave a small nod.

The second mage grunted at this and motioned me forward, though I wasn't sure how he was able to use his arms at all. His white robes were sleeveless, but every inch of his arms was adorned with the small leather cases that held scrolls. He had to be wearing at least two dozen scrolls on each arm. It gave him an incredibly unbalanced look; in the shadows, he seemed to be a thin man who'd made a deal with the Afeya for overly large muscled arms.

I stepped forward. "You have the scroll?"

"Part of it," he said with a sneer.

"What do you mean? Nabula said the copies have been down here for a month, and the original was recently returned."

An irritated grin spread across the mage's face, but the older one coughed.

"Answer her grace's question, Ishan." The older mage nodded at me with respect. He was pale for a member of Ka Scholar, his skin wizened. I wondered how often he left the under-pyramid and ventured into Scholar's Harbor, or even Bamaria proper.

"Nabula was correct," Ishan said, sweeping his scroll-laden arms out to the side. "However, after a recent lending incident, I'm afraid we are no longer in full possession of the text, your grace."

"Mercurial did not return it?" I asked, my eyes focusing on Ramia's. She remained calm, peaceful, sizing up the two librarians before her. She didn't appear surprised or upset by this news.

"The Afeya Ambassador returned the scroll. However, upon bringing it down to restoration for a routine cleaning after each borrow, especially for a text as old as this, we found...well, let me show you." Ishan beckoned me forward. Behind their worktable, beneath the rods lighting their level, the slanted wall held several glass rectangles, each one with a scroll within it, the glass holding the parchment flat. A tiny shelf jutted out on either side of each glass where the ends of each scroll curled and rested.

"May I?" I asked, getting closer.

Ishan looked to the older librarian, who nodded again at me.

The first scroll was full of words that looked incomplete. Many of them were missing inner letters, and many sentences appeared to have blank spaces at random points within them, indicating entire words were missing. There was so much disruption to the text I could barely make out a single sentence. I turned my attention to the second displayed scroll and found the same issues.

I looked back to the first scroll. At the top of the page were the words, *"Asherah's distraught..."* The remainder of the sentence was unreadable between the missing words and letters. On the second scroll, I read at the top, *"a— she f-ars her p—er wil—."* I walked along the wall to the third glass display. In the top line, most of the words had been obliterated or were missing, and what remained read, *"-nd...-ow— —l never..."*

I read back through the first line of each scroll, piecing them together. "Asherah's distraught, and she fears her power will never," I said.

The older librarian smiled at me. "Very good."

I exhaled. "So...none of the scrolls have all of their words or letters?" I asked.

"No," grunted Ishan. "That Godsdamned Afeyan!" He glared at Ramia.

"No offense, I'm sure," she said sweetly.

"Offense was meant," Ishan snapped.

"Hush," said the older librarian.

"You hush, Omur! These scrolls are going to take months to fix, to corroborate and decode with each missing piece."

"So they're complete?" I asked. "All together, all of Sianna's words are here?"

"And her letters, too," said Ishan. "We think."

"You need respect," said Ramia with a hiss. "Her grace deserve your respect."

Ishan glared. "And you, Afeyan?"

Ramia huffed. "I only half-Afeyan. I also Lumerian. Do not forget." She stroked the hilt of her stave.

"Well, your grace," Omur said softly, "I'm afraid that after the scroll was returned, some magic of the Afeyan Ambassador damaged the scrolls—including the ones he hadn't touched. Unless you'd like to spend the next month down here decoding, you'll have to come back to perform a proper read."

"I've already waited a month." I glared at Ramia, wondering if she had known about this, if she'd had anything to do with it. She'd given me Sianna's first scroll to begin with, and she'd seemed to know the state of the scrolls already. "Have you read the text?" I asked.

"Your grace," said Ishan, his voice impatient. "We are reading now."

"But you had the copies. Tell me what you know about this text."

"Are you asking me to summarize?" Ishan asked.

"Give her grace what she ask for," Ramia hissed.

Omur jerked his chin at Ishan—clearly outranking him.

Somehow, despite all the scrolls on his body, Ishan folded his arms across his chest and said, "Lumerians lose the War of Light against Moriel who defected and sided with the akadim. Lumeria sinks. The Valalumir is shattered into seven shards—all the pieces lost. Sianna and Asherah land ashore after the Drowning. Prince Kormac parts ways from them all, wishing to head to the mountains of what becomes Korteria. Asherah mopes about the beach without any power—it seems to have vanished the moment the waves came. There's maybe three hundred pages where nothing happens. We're reminded of Asherah's history. She was a goddess. She was chosen to become a guardian. She was a guardian of the Valalumir until she and Auriel…well, you know. Meanwhile, post-Drowning Lumerians who survive the ocean befriend the Dobrans. They settle, they begin to carve out life and recover. The Afeya," he paused, his eyes flicking to Ramia, "are cursed by the Valalumir for not taking arms against Moriel in the war and are forced to live as immortals, unable to use their magic for themselves, only at the request of others."

Ramia's eyes narrowed to snake-like slits.

Before the Drowning, the Afeya had just been Lumerians. But they hadn't wanted to fight. I'd also heard stories of the Afeya joining Moriel's forces, fighting alongside the akadim.

"Auriel is reunited with Asherah," Ishan continued, "and her power returns."

"How?" I asked. "How does it return? What words does Sianna use?"

"She doesn't. She says it returns."

"That can't—" I threw up my hands, practically groaning in frustration. I whirled on Ramia. "Did you know?"

"I know how scroll end." Ramia shrugged. "Maybe boys need my help, yes?"

"Ramia," I said, "why did you offer to bring me down here?"

"You ask. You want to come down to restoration. Nabula say wait. Ramia takes you."

"Does anyone in this room know anything else about Asherah regaining her power?"

Omur shook his head. "My apologies, your grace. Asherah is most famous for being a guardian of the Valalumir and for inspiring its theft. There's a lot written about her that is myth, so much that is legend, and some that is true. Perhaps when the scrolls are revived, you can do your own research, see what we may have missed."

"Thank you, Omur," I said. "Ishan." I was already turning around. I wanted to get above ground and away from Ramia immediately. This whole thing had been a wild gryphon hunt and a total waste of my time.

"Your grace," Ramia called after me.

I didn't turn around. I was back on the winding floor, racing quickly up the pyramid's center spiral.

"Your grace! Stop!"

I paused at the lift, knowing I needed Ramia to use her magic to bring us back to the ground level. We moved back to the top of the under-pyramid, in silence. When the ground stilled once, I stepped forward, pausing right before the double doors that led back to the main level. I turned on Ramia. "He destroyed them, didn't he? With his Afeyan magic. You're both taunting me."

"I help you," Ramia said.

"I don't trust you."

"Why? I give no reason for you not trust me. I give you information. Information Nabula did not. You want to go to restoration, I take you to restoration."

"To a destroyed scroll! To a scroll missing all the information I need. Destroyed by Mercurial."

"Only temporary. It being fixed. Yes, he did something. But I am not him. I give you great jewelry and at great price. Especially jewelry you not wearing."

"Why?" I asked. "Why do you care if I wear that necklace? What benefit is it to you?"

"I tell you. It sit in display in Museion with countless others. Do nothing. Useless. Should be worn. Should adorn beautiful Heir to the Arkasva."

"That can't be it," I said. "You didn't design it. If anything, my wearing it is dangerous, especially if it can be linked to the other necklaces like it."

Ramia's eyebrows narrowed. "I think it fit for queen. I support you. It just gift."

"Gift I paid for," I snapped, "with your unnamed favor."

She shrugged. "Small price. Still gift."

"I'm leaving," I said, pushing through the double doors. I rushed past several librarians of Ka Scholar before finding my way to the entrance. Nabula was sitting at her table staring at three different scrolls while Markan was sitting off to the side, his eyes wide and wary, two daggers in his hands. He was sliding the blades back and forth across each other, the sound grating.

Nabula flinched and looked up to find me. "Thank the Gods," she said. "I mean, you're back so soon, your grace."

"The scroll was...not fit for reading," I said. "Will you inform me when it is?"

"Of course."

"Going home?" Markan asked hopefully.

"We have another stop," I said.

Twenty minutes later, our seraphim landed on the opposite end of Scholar's Harbor, at the Museion, the ancient building that housed Bamarian's top philosophers and forward thinkers. I'd come here often when Meera's vorakh had first appeared to sit down with anyone from Ka Scholar or any philosopher I could find.

I headed down the golden brick roads laid into the sand. Since the island was surrounded by the water of the Lumerian Ocean, it didn't need waterways running through it to strengthen Lumerian magic. The Museion had been built out of white and gold marble and stood at the top of a great cliff that had been affectionately named Dry Wave, for it resembled the wave of an ocean, frozen in time by rock. The white marble stairs glittered beneath the sun as I climbed to the top of the cliff, and golden tiles came together to form a great Vala-lumir in the center of the steps. Markan followed close behind me.

There was no door to the Museion and no walls on the first level, only white marble columns that twisted up toward the roof. Waves crested against Dry Wave, spraying me with salt water as I approached the entrance. The soturion on duty immediately bowed.

"Here for another meeting, your grace? Class? Lecture?" he asked. "I'm sorry. I should have checked the schedule and prepared for your arrival."

"This was unplanned. But I've been wanting to revisit the ancient artifacts exhibit," I said.

Markan cursed under his breath.

"Ah, well, you know the way. Would you like a guide?"

"No, I'd just like to do a quick walk-through and see some of the new items on display."

Several floors up, I reached the exhibit and walked under the archway separating the artifacts from the recovered and restored paintings—paintings that had all been created with Lumerian magic so that they moved and told a story, paintings I'd never be able to see come to life unless I found my power.

I passed by the usual assortment of broken staves and daggers, wandering down the aisle of old starfire swords. There was a section of parchment scrolls, too destroyed for the Great Library, all kept under glass. I found cases of broken and useless vadati stones followed by an array of ancient helmets and armor in various shades of silver, bronze, and gold.

I found the jewelry section at last. My eyes were wide as I searched for what I'd come here for. Walking through the exhibit, I passed cases full of old rings with missing stones, bangles, pairs of earrings, waistlets, and anklets. Beyond all of those were several new display cases of necklaces.

I slowed down to allow my eyes to focus on each one. Some were forged in silver, some in bronze, but most had been forged in gold. There were delicate chains followed by thick collars and necklaces bound by pearls and gemstones. One even included a vadati stone. Not one was like my necklace. There were newer pieces I hadn't seen before at the end of the aisle, but even those were barely a third of the size of what I was looking for. Not one came close in size, scope, or design. I perused the necklace display three times and retraced my steps, circling the exhibit and searching for anything that could be seen as remotely related or similar to the necklace Ramia had "gifted" me.

There wasn't a single one.

I stared hard at the display cases like I could will the copies to appear.

"Need something to wear to dinner tonight, your grace?" Markan asked.

"Remember when you didn't talk to me? Or...really talk at all?" Markan raised an eyebrow.

"I preferred you that way."

He sneered but stepped back, his eyes assessing the empty exhibit for threats.

I stared back at the necklaces one last time before drawing my own soturion cloak closer around my shoulders as I turned back for the archway leading out of the exhibit.

Ramia had assured me multiple times that there were plenty of necklaces like the one she'd given me on my birthday. She'd insisted they were all sitting here, all useless…so what was the point of one more? But she'd lied. Had the necklace even come from the Lumerian Ocean? It had been in pristine condition. The styling and feel…it seemed so ancient, so authentic. I was sure Ramia hadn't made it—she would have told me if she had. She would have charged me. Which meant it had to be an artifact of Lumeria Matavia. But it hadn't been in the Drowning. It had survived, had been carried or worn across the ocean. Not fished from it.

After climbing onto the seraphim, Markan and I headed for Cresthaven to prepare for tonight's dinner. It would be my first time seeing Tristan and my sisters in days. I tried to relax, to calm myself before the storm that I expected dinner to turn into, but I couldn't stop thinking about the necklace. Who had made it? Why was it mine? And more importantly—since Ramia was so intent on my wearing it—who did it benefit?

CHAPTER
SEVEN

A loud knock on my apartment door woke me from my slumber the following morning. I rolled over, groaning, bleary-eyed and exhausted. My stomach was unsettled and nauseous. My head was pounding, and my nightshift was twisted around my waist like I'd tossed and turned all night.

The knock came again, and I groaned, shielding my eyes with my hands from the sunlight that had suddenly decided to parade its way into my tiny apartment bedroom.

I'd had way too much to drink the night before back at Cresthaven. Half of the Bamarian Council had been in attendance at dinner, including Tristan and his grandparents, Lady Romula and Lord Trajan. The whole evening had been so stressful that the wine being poured had seemed like the best thing to ever touch my lips.

Things were still tense with me and Tristan. No matter how many times I'd smiled at him or slipped my hand into his lap or how often I'd leaned into his warmth with his arm around my shoulders, everything had felt wrong between us. Even though we'd touched each other in some capacity all night, the strain on our relationship was palpable.

It definitely didn't help that Lady Romula had been watching me carefully, her eyes full of judgment and distaste, while across the table, my cousin Naria, who'd had the audacity to proposition Tristan while I'd been imprisoned, had stared with such undisguised lust that my blood had boiled.

But before I had been able to do anything I'd have regretted to Naria, my sisters had drawn my attention away. Morgana had laughed too loudly for a noble, and Meera had looked ready to faint. Suddenly, I didn't have enough energy to focus on Naria or to really care about Tristan or his grandmother's impression of me; I was on Morgana and Meera duty.

Just like it had been for over two years, it was my job to make sure they appeared normal. Lady-like. Noble. Strong, yet demure. Two perfect Heirs to the Arkasva who were without scandal or anything for the Bamarian people to feel concerned over.

Neither sister was up to the task.

Meera had appeared frailer-looking than ever, even after she recovered from her near-fainting spell. Somehow, she'd seemed to have dropped several pounds since her vision earlier that week even though she'd sworn up and down she was eating. Her hair was thinning, which had made styling it a challenge. I'd had to apply extra blush on her cheeks to make her look even somewhat healthy. She'd looked hollowed, gaunt, and so far from the demurely beautiful Heir Apparent she'd been growing up. When I was younger, I had always looked up to her, admiring her beauty and delicate grace. She'd always been rather on the quiet side for nobility, but many saw this as refined. She truly would have been a picture-perfect image of the High Lady of Bamaria, and I'd always wished I could be as effortlessly poised as her.

But now Meera's polite, quiet nature felt like it was fading. Instead, her wild animalistic side was thrashing, bubbling just beneath the watery nature of her aura. The haunted look in her eyes had caught my attention, and my mind couldn't stop flashing to her attacks on me while in the thralls of her last vision—a vision she still wouldn't share the details of with me. During the vision, her voice had changed, and I still couldn't get the sound out of my head.

It had sounded like multiple voices, both male and female, thrown into one body.

The only comfort I'd truly had during the Cresthaven dinner—aside from the wine—was that Meera had had a recent vision. We were once again in the safe zone between her visions for at least a few weeks. I'd known her vorakh wouldn't rear its ugly head that night. But its side effects had seemed to be in full force.

Morgana had arrived at the dinner already drunk—a necessity with her vorakh acting up. Having so many Lumerians dining in Cresthaven gave her a migraine, and she'd needed to dull her senses as much as possible to avoid hearing every person's thoughts echoing through her mind. She'd been smoking moonleaves half the day, but I knew from past experience that Lady Romula was hypersensitive to the smell and was likely to make some negative comment that would have only drawn more negative attention to Morgana. So, when I'd arrived at the fortress after my failed visit to Scholar's Harbor and the Great Library, I'd taken away Morgana's leaves, doused her in perfume, lit all the incense in her room, and left her alone with a silver flask to further wash away the scent and dull her senses.

During the inane dinner conversations, the banal comments about the weather, the snobbish insults and gossip about nobility disguised as compliments, and the leading questions that attempted to get me to reveal some secret or scandal, I had been completely drained. I had downed at least three glasses of wine. Though I was usually the one wound too tightly, insistent on staying in control, I hadn't been able to help myself.

I'd been feeling a shift since my birthday—a kind of recklessness and an exhaustion when it came to following the rules of embodying the essence of the perfect lady. I didn't know what was wrong with me. It was almost like my mask had been my Binding, and though no magic had been revealed, some powerful will within me had been desperate to get out. I'd been letting my mask slip with Tristan, letting my true feelings shine when I was with Rhyan. Maybe the two years of following every rule, of being the good girl

I was supposed to be, had taken its toll on me. There'd been no reward for my sacrifices. Following the rules hadn't made my life better. It had only brought more suffering.

But I couldn't afford not to continue playing my part. So, I drank.

I was drunk by the end of the dinner when Lady Sila had arrived exceptionally late to the gathering. We had been at dessert—a dessert I was barely touching because no one else seemed to be eating at that point. And with the arrival of my father's Master of Spies, the Lady of Ka Shavo, and the current owner of my would-be engagement ring from Tristan, even the drinking had come to a halt.

Lady Romula's eyes had widened when she saw her, and her bony fingers had flexed in anger as she'd settled her wine glass on the table. She'd looked like she was going to leap across the entire dining hall and rip the ring right out of Lady Sila's hands—if she'd even been wearing it, which I'd doubted. Since Tristan had used his mother's engagement ring as payment to buy time in the Shadow Stronghold, to buy a minute of the shadows looking the other way, Lady Sila had had it in her possession. My guess was she had tossed the ring in a safe somewhere without a second thought.

I'd never once seen my father's spymaster in any form of clothing or jewelry that could be considered remotely distinctive or eye-catching. She always wore a blandly colored robe with a hood that she kept over her head so often I wasn't entirely sure of her hair color or texture—or, actually, if she had any hair at all. I'd seen her in her spymaster robe thousands of times and still could not, for the life of me, identify the color. The robe had been treated with the shadow magic her Ka specialized in, the magic that allowed them to cast their shadows through the walls of the prison and attack. I knew from my research that a similar magic was used on soturion cloaks except I could always spot those if I knew the soturion wearing them. The robes worn by the shadows were far too intense even for my sight. It was an ancient magic they kept inside the Ka, never sharing their secrets with anyone.

Lady Sila had pulled my father away from the table for a discussion, and Eathan, his cousin and Second, had arrived in his place, assuring everyone everything was fine and to enjoy dessert but that Arkasva Batavia would not be rejoining the dinner. No one had touched their plates.

Eathan's eyes had flickered to me, his hair a soft gray in the torchlight. As Second, he was always wherever my father was not. His eyes had crinkled, and he'd given me a concerned but reassuring smile before asking a servant to bring me some bread and water—meant, I'd figured, to sober me up.

But I hadn't been able to eat. My stomach had turned the moment my father had left. I'd assumed it was more news about the Emartis. Lady Romula had assumed so, too, from the dirty look she'd thrown my way. Her red, cracked lips had frowned in disapproval as she'd resumed slowly sipping her red wine. I swore I'd heard her hateful words in my mind, forbidding a marriage between me and Tristan until I had stopped the threat of the terrorists. As if it were all up to me.

The moment it had felt like it wouldn't break decorum, I'd excused myself to leave and stumbled to a seraphim carriage with Tristan, whom I had a hazy memory of straddling and kissing mid-flight. I remembered fighting him once we'd arrived back in my apartment as he'd helped me change into night clothes. Even drunk, even with my own personal bonds breaking, I'd still known I had to uphold my blood oath, control what he saw, and never let him see what was written all over my flesh and body.

He hadn't stayed with me. I had definitely slept alone. And now I was definitely hungover.

And I was seriously going to kill whoever was knocking on my fucking door.

Holding my head, I stumbled from my bed and banged into the doorframe of my bedroom. I pulled my nightshift down my hips and retrieved a strap that had fallen down my arm, practically exposing my entire right breast.

The knocking grew louder. "What?" I yelled as I opened it.

Rhyan was leaning against the wall across the hall, one knee bent, his foot casually resting on the wall behind him as he inspected his fingernails. Seriously, he'd been knocking one second ago.

I glared. "We get it. You're fast."

I stumbled back to my couch, sank down onto the cushions, and rested my head in my hands, groaning in pain.

"Good morning to you, too, partner." He closed my door behind him, and headed for my kitchen, his boots loud against the floor. I heard him pouring water into a glass, and a moment later, he was in front of me, forcing the water into my hand. "I'm going to go out on a limb here and assume you need this."

I stared, dumbfounded, not making any move to take the glass from him.

He frowned, looking down at me, his good eyebrow raised. "I knew you weren't a morning person, but this feels extreme."

"I'm hungover," I snapped. My fingers closed around the glass, and I sat back, taking a slow sip as the room spun around me.

"Forget we're training today?" Rhyan took a seat on the opposite side of the couch.

"You canceled on me yesterday. How could I predict you'd show today?" I breathed through a bout of nausea and took another very slow, very small sip. "Not to mention, you're doing that thing again."

He rolled his shoulders back, exhaling sharply. "I'm sorry about yesterday. Something came up."

"That's it? That's all you have to say?"

"Well, I'm still puzzling out what you meant by 'that thing' I'm allegedly doing." He held up his hands, making air quotes with his fingers.

I slammed my glass on the table and ran for the bathroom. I was going to throw up, and I was going to do it all over the floor if I didn't hurry.

I reached the toilet just in time, feeling Rhyan's presence instantly behind me, his hands sweeping my hair back as I heaved. His fingers were cool and soothing on the back of my neck. After I was pretty sure I'd thrown up an entire bottle of wine and at least my last three meals, Rhyan helped me stand, waiting patiently in the doorway as I spit into the sink basin and brushed my teeth.

"Better?" he asked.

"My head hurts," I said pathetically.

"Hmmm." He frowned, tilting his head to the side. "Do you want to lie down? Or would your head prefer if you sat?"

I closed my eyes to think, but that only made me dizzy. "Sit," I said.

"Come on, partner. I'll get you to the couch." He wrapped an arm around my shoulder, and I leaned against him as we walked back into the living room and sat down together. "Still nauseous?"

"No." Thank the Gods for that—but I did feel raw inside.

"Good," he said. "Because we're still training today. You thought drinking would get you out of it?"

"Drinking got me out of an insufferable Council dinner at Cresthaven," I muttered. "I assumed you canceling again would get me out of training."

"I see. So, because I had to cancel one time, despite the fact I've been training with you every day for a month, you went ahead and decided to establish a pattern?"

"Rhyan," I said, voice scratchy.

"Lyr?"

"Just…don't talk to me. For, like, ten more minutes. Should be easy for you."

He huffed in annoyance, rising from the couch. "You're dehydrated. Drink your water. I'll make tea."

"I want coffee," I said with a groan.

"Oh, I know you do," Rhyan called from the kitchen. Water ran as he rummaged around my cupboards, moving around glass bottles of spices and metal boxes full of assorted teas I never bothered to make. "I've seen you in the mornings."

I groaned again in annoyance.

"If this is going to work, partner, you need to listen to me. Chain of command is in effect—even in your apartment, even hungover.

First, you're going to drink your tea. Settle your stomach and rehydrate your body. And then we're training. And then, if I think you do a good job, you can have coffee."

"First coffee, then soturion training," I whined.

"Let's start with how well you handle your tea."

"Fine," I said, closing my eyes.

When I opened them after possibly falling back asleep, Rhyan was sitting next to me on the couch, one arm around my shoulders helping me sit forward, his free hand holding a steaming hot mug of tea under my nose. I glared at the offending drink.

"It doesn't smell like coffee."

"That's because it's tea," he said slowly, like he was speaking to a child.

I grimaced. "I ordered coffee."

Rhyan laughed.

"You're a terrible server."

He laughed harder. "You're fun when you're hungover."

I responded with a moan of pain.

"Come on, partner," he said, voice gentle now. "Be a good girl and drink up. That's an order. I put ginger in there for you and some moonleaves. I promise, it will settle your stomach and make that headache go away."

"Fuck," I muttered as my head pounded. "Fine." I put my hands around the mug, feeling its soothing warmth rush over me as I took a small sip.

Rhyan smoothed my hair back behind my shoulders, his calloused fingers brushing the loose strands sticking to my neck from my morning sweat or from throwing up or…who knew at this point. I stilled as his fingers brushed against my neck again. He froze, our eyes meeting, like he only then realized what he was doing, and he pulled his hand back to his lap.

"Tea helping?" he asked.

I narrowed my eyes at him but nodded, starting to take bigger sips. "What time is it?"

"Eight."

I wrinkled my nose. "So early."

He huffed again. "I thought you'd say that."

"What do you know?"

"I know plenty. I know you don't get enough sleep. I know you stay up late doing things you probably shouldn't be doing. And I know you hate mornings, but you love coffee. It's the only thing you consistently consume in the dining hall every day."

I let out an angry huff. "We're talking again?"

His jaw tensed. "We were never not talking."

"If you say so. Then what came up yesterday?"

"How's your head?" he asked.

"Rhyan, what in Lumeria happened? I seriously want to know."

He frowned, eyeing me carefully. "You didn't hear anything at your dinner last night?"

I set my mug down on the table, angling my body toward him. "My father was called away early by the spymaster. I thought…I thought it might be about the Emartis." Shit…I shouldn't have been drinking. I'd sat through a hundred of those dinners before. Why had last night been any different? I was sick of playing my role, but I had to do it. I could have pushed through. I should have pushed through sober. Now, I might have missed something important.

Rhyan bit his lip, his good eyebrow narrowed.

"Did something happen? Something new?"

"No," he said. "The Emartis seem to be in the pattern of making themselves known with some sort of show and then going completely quiet. Having been named a terrorist organization this week by the Bamarian Council, they will most likely be exceptionally quiet. For a time. My guess is they went underground. We probably won't hear from them for a few weeks. But when we do, it will be big."

My stomach twisted as I thought of how they were probably together now, plotting, planning. I closed my eyes, hearing the now familiar hum of the magical ward protecting my apartment. The wards had been doubled, so the sound was even louder than before, though within a few days I'd become almost numb to it. Now, I listened, feeling incredibly comforted by the extra level of protection Aunt Arianna had put in place.

"So not the Emartis?" I asked.

He shook his head but offered no more information.

"You're going to have to bring me coffee if you want me to keep guessing."

"It's just not the kind of news that's fun to wake up to, especially hungover."

I tensed. He was probably right, but not knowing was worse. "I can deal. Tell me."

He scrunched up his face like he really didn't want to tell me but sat forward as he said, "Scouts are reporting an unusually high level of akadim activity in the south."

"What's a high amount of activity? What scouts? Where?"

He ran his fingers through his hair. His curls looked like they'd been brushed out earlier, loosened into bronzed waves. The movement of his fingers highlighted the scar running through his left eye, but then his hair fell over his forehead, hiding most of the mark. "They're not typically found below the northern countries except during winter, and even then, you usually only find about a handful of akadim barely making their way past Cretanya."

The southern country was a close neighbor, sitting just above Elyria. I mentally mapped its location and distance from Bamaria in my mind. "So were they spotted in Cretanya?" That was close. Too close. It left only one country between us and those demons.

Rhyan shook his head grimly. "There was a nest discovered in Elyria."

"Auriel's bane! Elyria," I said. Elyria shared our northern border —it was where the akadim attack had happened at the end of summer, right when Rhyan had arrived. "Um, how many akadim are usually in a nest?" I was still catching up on my akadim reading since becoming a soturion, but even in all my years of study, I never recalled nests being mentioned.

Rhyan shrugged. "The nests are kind of a new thing. Most akadim historically are loners, traveling in small packs, only forming brief alliances with each other. This is usually due in-fighting for control of, well, their food supply."

People. Souls. The monsters ate souls. That was their main source of food. Sometimes they ate bodies, and sometimes they did worse. And sometimes it wasn't all in that order.

"Most of the nests I've known about in Glemaria have perhaps a dozen akadim at most, though from what I've seen, the number frequently shifts. They're very territorial—not willing to let many into their packs. Hierarchies form and reform all the time. More often than not, fights break out, and civil wars erupt with different akadim backing different leaders. The groups usually shrink on their own and disperse without any soturion aid. But this nest in Elyria showed evidence of about…we think maybe two dozen akadim in a pack."

My stomach sank to the floor. Two dozen akadim, only one country away from mine. The akadim that had made its way to the Bamarian border, the one Rhyan had slain, had been the closest brush with an akadim I'd ever had. We never got reports of them coming this close, this far south in the Empire. Never so far from winter and never in such numbers. I'd been taught to fear them and take precautions my entire life the way I'd been taught to never make a deal with the Afeya. But the akadim had always been so distant. It was hard to imagine, to really understand, the danger they presented when they'd never gotten close before.

"There's growing concern about the way the akadim are inter-acting with each other. Like they're…organizing. Planning. No one knows why. It's a complete aberration from their normal behavior."

I shivered, understanding why Rhyan had been reluctant to explain this first thing in the morning.

"I was ordered by Aemon to track the nest in Elyria all day yesterday. Even with all the changes, akadim nests don't last long. It was urgent to be on the scene as quickly as possible, so that's why I…. I'm sorry for canceling our first training."

"You went to Elyria yesterday?" That was a full day's trip. He had to be exhausted. "When did you get back?"

"Late last night." He lifted his good eyebrow when I only stared in response. "Or one might say early this morning. Let's just say the sun hadn't risen just yet."

So, he'd gotten absolutely zero sleep and had spent a day traveling to another country and tracking akadim.

"But you look perfect," I muttered. Realizing what I'd said, I stared down at my tea mug. "I mean, you look—"

"Like I didn't drink my weight in wine last night?"

"I didn't drink that much," I scoffed, looking back at him. "What happened?"

He sighed. "We destroyed the nest."

"Did you...were there any akadim?" My stomach twisted, but not from nausea—this time, it was with fear. The idea of Rhyan going near even one akadim left my heart racing and my body cold despite knowing he'd killed one. I didn't doubt his strength or skill, but akadim had the strength of five soturi, were brutally vicious, and were giant. Anything could happen. To anyone. There was nothing more dangerous or sinister than these ancient and immortal demons. Of all the things that had drowned in Lumeria Matavia, they should have been the first.

"No," he said. "We tracked a few for a while. They weren't near any of the cities, staying in the woods to avoid the sun. But it looks like they escaped through the hills of Korteria."

So now they were Ka Kormac's problem. "But why were you sent to Elyria? Why didn't the Soturi of Ka Elys handle this?"

"They were. But since I, um, well—I am the most recent soturion to kill one, at least the most recent south of Numeria, so they asked Aemon if he'd send me."

"I don't like that, the idea of you just being pulled around on someone's whim, just thrown into a dangerous mission for another country."

"It was to stop a threat. It's a good cause. I'd rather lose a night's sleep than learn some innocent person lost their life."

"I still don't like it. Your place is—" I cut myself off before saying here. "I mean, you should have a say in where you go."

"Thank you."

"And you weren't hurt at all?" I asked, still concerned. Knowing Rhyan had killed an akadim when I'd barely known him was one thing, but knowing Rhyan had gotten close to one now—had been inside a nest—even if it was empty of the demons, that was leaving my heart pulsing.

"I'm fine. I wasn't in any danger. I promise." He eyed my discarded mug. "Done?"

I debated saying no and prolonging having to get up and push my body through training on what was previously my day off. But I was committed. I had to be. And, of course, some small, wildly traitorous part of me was looking forward to the day, excited to simply be with Rhyan.

"If I say yes, does this mean I have to train?"

"We'll wait until your headache's gone."

"It's better," I said.

"Good. I'm going to go. I'll be on the track waiting. I think it's better if we arrive separately," he said grimly. "Eat something, too, okay? Promise? As soon as you're ready, meet me there."

He closed the door behind him a moment later. The magical wards buzzed to life. My stomach finally grumbled, and I stood to find he'd left a bowl of fruit on my kitchen counter: apples, pomegranate, and figs.

I picked up an apple, touched. We didn't have a ton of apple trees in Bamaria—they grew better farther up north. I knew Rhyan enjoyed them and wondered if he'd found time to bring them back from Elyria. But remembering he'd been in Elyria made me worried again as I returned to my room to get dressed. Now we had akadim entering the mix of things to worry about in Bamaria. I exhaled a sharp breath, determined to put it all out of my mind. I could only do one thing—train, get stronger, and prepare for the Emperor's test.

CHAPTER
EIGHT

Thirty minutes later, I was stepping out onto the track inside the Katurium dressed in my practice tunic, leggings, and soturion-issued boots. Unsure if Rhyan wanted to spar or not, I'd packed my armor in my bag. He was in the center of the arena moving swiftly and elegantly through the 108 Postures of Valya, his powerful legs holding him in the deep stretches as he rose and fell, twisting and turning through the positions with more grace than I'd ever seen another soturion possess.

The pole caught my eye as I moved toward him. A shiver ran through me, and a foreboding sense of panic and pain ran through my back. The bite of the whip. The feel of the Imperator's fingers. I shook them off. I was here to make sure I never ended up in that position again.

"Partner!" Rhyan yelled jovially. "You're alive."

"Hangover cured," I said. "Thanks to your tea. And fruit. Thank you."

He smiled. "You're welcome," he said, his eyes roaming down my body and back up. "You switched to boots?"

I shrugged. "It's getting colder, and you switched. So…." I looked him over. He was in his old, worn leather boots from Glemaria, laced up to his knees. They were a perfect complement to his black leather armor, which had on its chest the face of a golden seraphim in profile opposite the face of a silver gryphon. The tips of their wings spread as if in flight above their heads, framing the sun. A full moon below them completed the newly forged sigil Rhyan had been granted at our Oath Ceremony. The symbol was half Ka Hart and half Ka Batavia. Inside the design, running through his armor as it ran through his veins, was both my blood and his blood. Our blood. Binding us together, forming our kashonim.

I wondered where he kept his old armor—the armor that represented only Ka Hart and was filled with blood from his previous kashonim. His previous kashonim's line had been broken since he'd become forsworn. He never talked about his old lineage, but I had a feeling being cut off from it had been harder for him than he'd ever admit.

"Good choice," he said. "Boots are far better for running in."

"I'll take your word for it." I grimaced. "Does this mean we're starting with a run?"

"Would you prefer to battle with the longsword?"

I held my hands limply in front of me. I'd never be able to hold a weapon like that. I wasn't strong enough.

He nodded with understanding. "We're going to get you there."

Rhyan threw his dagger onto the track, the blade easily sliding through the dirt to the hilt. I placed mine beside his.

"We're sprinting," he said. "When I say go, we run. Run as hard as you can around the track and reach the dagger."

"That's it?" I asked suspiciously. "Once around the track?"

"How many times you do this will depend on how fast you go. Once around the track is a half mile. Your average speed in these runs," he squinted, his right eyebrow dipping, "is around six minutes. I want to see you run it in four."

"Four minutes." I nodded. "All right."

"Four minutes, three times," he said.

"What?"

"You're more than capable of covering a half mile in that time. You get three half miles in under four minutes each time, and we're done. That's it. But if you come in at more than four minutes, even by a second, you run again. We'll go until you get three. So you decide if we run for not even a quarter of an hour or if we run for several hours."

I sucked in a breath. "And then what?"

Rhyan grinned, a mischievous glint in his eyes. "The sooner you finish this, the sooner you find out."

"You look too excited…like maybe I shouldn't get to the next task."

His gaze dipped again down my body, then quickly shot back to my eyes. "It's worth it. But you need to prove to me and to yourself first that you're taking this seriously. That you can do this. That you will do this."

I sighed. "Let me stretch first."

Ten minutes later, I collapsed on the ground, gripping my dagger in my hands, sweat stinging my eyes while Rhyan stood over me, gloating.

"Three minutes and fifty-eight seconds," he said.

"Impressive after my hangover."

"What you've been capable of doing this entire time."

"I believe you told me to think stamina, not speed."

"Stamina doesn't mean slow, it means not wearing yourself out in the first minute showing off. It means knowing how much energy you have and being able to spread it out over the maximum amount of time. And you had more than you were giving." His emerald eyes blazed, and the morning sun made his hair glow golden bronze. "Don't try to debate me right now over the exact meaning of stamina. Let's get this done."

"I wasn't going to debate you!"

"I see it in your eyes, partner. I know exactly what you're think-ing." He extended his hand, and I reached for him, letting him hoist me back to my feet. "One down. Two to go."

My second sprint was four and a half minutes long. Which meant I still had two to go. My third run was four minutes exactly. Rhyan let me rest and guzzle water before starting on round four. I only needed to finish in four minutes one more time, and it would be over.

But I came in at five minutes. And then six.

"Ready to go again?" Rhyan tossed me a towel from his pack.

Sweat was pouring down my face, and my stomach was twisting from my latest cramp. I wiped down my forehead and the back of my neck before throwing the towel at him. He caught it just before it hit his face. I was frustrated and tired. But I wanted to finish. I wanted to prove to him and to myself I could do this—I could get through our first day of his training.

"Let's go," I said through gritted teeth.

I came in at eight minutes and collapsed to my knees, trying to catch my breath. Another cramp was forming in my stomach, and hot tears burned behind my eyes.

"Eight minutes? That's worse than your average," Rhyan said. "I thought you were taking this seriously."

"I am taking it seriously," I spat. "I'm exhausted. I've run for practically an hour already. The same Godsdamned thing we do every day."

He stood over me. "We're not here to do what we do every day."

"I've done what you asked for twice. Maybe that's all my body can do."

"I didn't tell you to do it twice. I told you to do it three times. And I told you to do it three times because I actually know what your body can do, and it's more than what you just did. Now are you going to run another four-minute lap, or am I wasting my time?"

I swallowed a curse and several nasty things I could have called Rhyan. He extended his hand, and I grabbed it, his fingers immediately tightening over mine as he pulled me to my feet.

"What's the problem, Lyr?"

"I'm fucking tired."

"Then you should have finished this exercise a long time ago. I told you, you could have done it three times, not even fifteen minutes of running, or we could be here all day. It was your choice."

"How was it my choice? I can't help the way my body is built."

"This has nothing to do with how your body is built," he snarled. "This has to do with your mind. You ran two four-minute laps. There's not a single reason why you couldn't do a third one."

"You try running without magic—hungover."

"I have," he said. "And I did it whipped and lashed, with my wounds still healing."

"And?" I asked through gritted teeth. "How did that go for you?"

His eyes narrowed, his gaze on me sparking with intensity. "I ran them in three."

"Ugh."

"Lyr, I'm serious. You think that it's your body's fault, that it's your hangover's fault, that it's because you don't have magic, that you stayed up late. None of that matters now. None of that makes a difference. You're in a different arena, and you are not the girl who walked through those doors a month ago. You can do this."

I sucked in a breath, wanting to believe him, but I was just so tired.

"Remember what I told you?" he said. "The soturi relying on their magic and not themselves for speed will run out of their energy stores faster than they realize. They will never know true strength because they never needed to build it, to cultivate it, or to feel it for themselves. Not like you. Not like me. If you'd wanted to run the lap three times in four minutes, you would have. I've been watching and training you for a month. Even hungover, you could have done it. But you didn't." His eyes darkened. "So tell me, why didn't you want to?"

I shook my head. "I don't know."

"Try harder," he said.

"I don't fucking know! I don't have a reason. What sane person wouldn't have wanted to finish already?" I threw up my hands. The wind was gathering speed, cooling my face down from the heat that had built inside my body.

"Are you tired of running?" he asked.

"Yes."

"You want that coffee I promised you?"

I glared. "Of course, I fucking want it."

"Then why haven't you taken it yet?" he asked.

"Because." I bit my lip.

"Because?"

"Because—" I closed my eyes. "Because what if I do try? What if," my voice shook, "what if I give it my all? What if I throw everything I am, everything I have left at this, and…." I sniffled.

"And what?" he asked, his voice gentle. "Come on, partner. Talk to me."

I squeezed my hands into fists at my sides. "And what if I still fail? What if I let them all down? And after this, all I tried, all I did, all you sacrificed for me—"

"It's not about me. Don't worry about me," Rhyan said firmly. "This is about you."

Too tired to hold it back in, too tired to lie, I let the truth spill out of me. "What if I'm still not enough? What if the Imperator's right, and I'm wasting everyone's time?"

I wondered then if this was why I'd been slipping so much lately, why I'd drunk last night, why I'd been forgetting to control my emotions with Tristan and breaking the rules. Maybe it was my fear that even my best wasn't enough…and it wasn't worth trying.

Gripping my shoulders, Rhyan leaned forward. "Lyr, listen to me. You are enough. And every fucking word out of the Imperator's mouth is a Godsdamned lie. You are enough," he said again, punctuating each word. "And I will tell you that until it sinks in. Every single thing you do is enough. But right now, you're in your head. And I need you to get out of it. Because what you're doing is making excuses." He shook his head, cutting off my protest. "You're not weak. These are thoughts born of fear, and that makes them lies. You can do this."

I sniffled again, nodding.

"You think that the two times you did it were flukes? That they were luck? They weren't. They were you. Your strength, your power, your will. Even tired, even hungover, even without magic, you did it. You! And if you did it before, you can do it again. You can do it another time. And next time, you're going to do it even faster. And you're going to do it more times than ever. Because you decide to and for no other reason. You hear me?"

I exhaled a shaky breath, my stomach turning with nerves and the remnants of a cramp, but his message was starting to sink in. "I hear you."

"Good. Now close your eyes."

I closed my eyes, which burned with tears. I hadn't even realized I was feeling all of that. I had been too focused on recovering from my hangover and assuming I was still powerless.

"Are you mad?" he asked.

"No," I said.

"Liar."

I opened my eyes to glare at him.

"I said eyes shut."

I closed them again.

"Tell me, partner. Why are you mad?"

"I'm not mad." I squirmed a little, but his hands on my shoulders steadied me in place.

"You could say that more convincingly."

"Or you could take me at my word," I seethed; that time even I could hear the anger coating my voice.

"I will," Rhyan said, his voice deepening, "when you give me an honest one."

My nostrils flared, as I refused to give in and play his game.

"That coffee is just going to get colder and colder," he said.

"Well, brew me fresh coffee then."

"I will when you admit why you're mad."

My eyes snapped open. "Fine! You want to know why I'm mad? Because I shouldn't have to do this," I said, surprised at the anger and bitterness in my voice. "Because it's my day off—because I should be engaged and planning my fucking wedding, because Jules should be alive. Because I should be home at Cresthaven. Because I should be powerful. Because it was my destiny. Because I was supposed to be a fucking mage." My shoulders heaved as all my emotions rose to the surface and washed through me.

Both of us were silent, watching each other. When my breathing slowed to a normal pace, Rhyan nodded, uneasiness in his expression.

"I know," he said softly. "But we've got to let that go. All of it. Not because any of it's okay. Because it's holding you back, carrying all of that. Take a deep breath. Inhale...exhale. We can't control every instance of our life or what happens to us. What you can control is how you react. And no matter how much you complain or how much you pretend you can't do this—"

"I'm not pretending."

"I'm going to pretend you didn't just interrupt me. You are pretending. You've already proven to me you can do it. When it comes to you, Lyr, I have zero doubts—about you or your strength. You've got this."

I squeezed my eyes shut again and inhaled and exhaled in sync with Rhyan. I felt his breath against my cheek and his aura wrapping around me, cocooning me.

"I'm tired, too," he said. "I returned from Elyria in the middle of the night. I want to sit down. I want to relax. I want to drink some Godsdamned coffee with you. Let's get this done. No more playing. I want you to see yourself in your mind. See yourself running. Running fast. See your feet. Imagine your boots, see the leather, see their color, visualize their laces. See your boots hitting the ground again and again and again. See the dirt shifting beneath you, the dust rattling behind. See your feet running so fast they become a blur. You're moving through the track. You feel the wind in your hair, against your cheeks. You keep running. You feel strong. You feel ready."

"I see it," I said. I saw every image he planted in my mind. As I visualized, I became aware of my legs and how tired they were, how I'd barely recovered from my last stomach cramp.

"Are you slowing down?" he asked.

"I didn't mean to," I said, unsure how he knew I'd suddenly seen myself do exactly that. I felt his hands, warm on my shoulders. Had my body language changed with my visualization? Or my breathing? Or did he just know me that well?

"You got in your head again. You're trying to find every reason why this can't work. Right?"

I nodded, standing straighter.

"That's the old you," he said. "Not you now. Remember the reasons it can work. You've gotten this far. You're going farther. See yourself picking up speed again. It's just your mind. You don't have to be tired in your imagination, your body isn't real there, it's whatever you want it to be. Remember, your body is being still now, it's getting a break. Resting. So why in Lumeria would you see it getting tired in your head when you can imagine it running faster than ever? Come on," he urged. "Let's get your dagger. Let's finish this."

I visualized the curve of the track in my mind, the arena jutting up around me. I saw the fucking pole being left in the dust as I tore across the ground and the hilt of my dagger gleaming in the sun. I grabbed it, held it above my head as I yelled out in victory, and imagined Rhyan screaming that it was four minutes. I opened my eyes, staring into his.

"I saw it," I said, determination sweeping through me.

"One more run. You've got this. No rope can hold you. No cage can trap you."

My chest was heaving. It was time to end this, to prove I could do it. "I'm ready."

His thumbs rubbed against my shoulders as his expression hardened. "Tear the fucking rope apart," Rhyan yelled, releasing me to get into position.

He called time, and we were off. He quickly sped ahead of me— something that had left me feeling annoyed every single time he'd done it before. But this time, I remembered what he'd told me. His father had made him run bound, made him prove himself without magic. If Rhyan could do it, so could I. In fact, I had just done it—in my mind. I closed my eyes, remembering the image, seeing myself run faster and faster, not tired, not weak. Rhyan was right. If I could imagine anything, why not imagine myself succeeding, improving, faster and stronger than ever? I was ready to do this one more time.

I sped up, rounding the curve of the track. I'd done it before. I could do it again.

"Two minutes!" he screamed when he reached for his dagger. I was still yards away from mine. "Come on, partner! Are you fucking done yet?"

Tears burned behind my eyes. My legs felt like lead, my stomach was on fire. But I couldn't imagine running one more time. It was too painful, too humiliating.

I could do this. I had done this. I was going to do it again. I pumped my arms and closed my eyes, seeing myself at the finish line just like I'd visualized. I only allowed myself to see where I wanted to go. I wasn't slowing down, I wasn't out of energy. It didn't matter how many times I'd done this earlier—all that mattered was right now, this time, this moment.

In my mind, I saw it all perfectly. I was at the end of the finish line, the hilt of the dagger in my hands. Rhyan was bringing me a cup of coffee, and then I was sinking into a steaming hot bath. Gods, a bath was going to feel so fucking good after all of this. And then Rhyan—I pushed that thought away, pumping my arms, giving my body, my run, my muscles, and my mind every last bit of power I had left.

"Three minutes, fifty seconds!" Rhyan roared. "Lyr, you did it!"

I collapsed on the finish line, clutching my dagger to my chest, completely out of breath, sweat everywhere, and the hugest grin in Lumeria on my face.

Rhyan stood above me, an unfamiliar look of pure excitement and pride on his eyes. His smile was wider than I'd ever seen it, matching my own. I'd never seen him look so victorious and joyful. And relieved. Gods, he looked beautiful. Even though for once, he was sweating, too. He was tired, exhaustion written all over his face. There were bags under his eyes, his scar had reddened, and his hair, bronzed gold in the sun, was curling from his sweat. I wanted to jump to my feet to hug him and thank him.

But his expression of pure pride and joy quickly vanished. The lines of his face hardened as he pursed his lips together. I could see the mask of cold Rhyan, distant Rhyan, locking itself into place. The closeness and warmth I'd felt just looking at his eyes disappeared like a wall had been erected between us.

His hands flexed at his sides, almost as if they were itching to reach for me, to help me up.

I stood on my own, watching him carefully, noting the tension now swirling through his body, the almost jagged-edged feel to his aura.

Rhyan nodded at me and jerked his chin toward the doors. "Hit the baths. Meet me in our training room in thirty."

I threw my hands on my hips. "I just ran for over an hour—after being hungover, which I've never done before. Plus, I completed three half-miles, each in under four minutes. I think you mispronounced 'good job.'"

"I know you did," he said darkly. His entire body stiffened, his stance protective yet distant, his eyes moving slowly back and forth behind me. I suddenly wondered if we weren't alone. "Don't correct my pronunciation, *partner*. Take a bath."

Before I could respond, he was walking away from me. Only after he was gone did I see that coming down from the arena's seating onto the opposite side of the track was Haleika and Leander, her apprentice. Shit. Had they seen us?

We hadn't done anything illegal; no lines had been crossed between kashonim, between apprentice and novice. But Rhyan wasn't supposed to go off training protocol or offer anything beyond the official Academy training. And I wasn't supposed to receive any extra or special favors per the Imperator's agreement. No wonder he'd acted so distant.

"Lyr?" Haleika shouted. Her voice was laced with shock.

"Hal," I said, heart hammering. She sounded so genuinely surprised I was thrown. Had she not realized it was me? "What are you doing here?" I asked, carefully schooling my voice to sound neutral and innocent despite the sweat running down the nape of my neck.

"Extra practice. You?" She nodded tersely. Her brown curly hair had been braided, but there were curls falling out, loosened into waves that went in every direction, almost like…like someone had been running their fingers through her hair.

My mouth went dry.

"Same," I said. "Since…my test is coming up."

Haleika frowned. "Lyr, just so you know, if you ever want to run with us, you can. Just," she fidgeted with her hands, "so you're not alone when running." She was speaking oddly, like the words were foreign to her or like she was choosing them extremely carefully.

Leander nodded vigorously, his blonde hair also looking slightly disheveled. He was paler skinned than most Bamarians, having come from Damara. And in this moment, his skin was red, his cheeks flushed. "If you ever want any extra help, your grace," he said formally, "I know you're Hal's friend, and I'd be happy to do so. I don't agree with the Imperator's decisions at all."

"Thank you," I said stiffly, barely believing what I heard. "That means a lot." It was a good way to make sure Tristan didn't realize I was training with Rhyan. Maybe I could take them up on the offer and hope Haleika said something the next time she was with her cousin.

But by the Gods. Neither Haleika nor Leander had mentioned Rhyan. They were inviting me to run with them so I wouldn't run alone, which meant they thought I was by myself.

They hadn't seen him.

I glanced nervously at the stadium seating surrounding the arena. They'd been up there while we'd been running, and they hadn't seen us. I took in their appearances again, how flushed and awkward they were both acting.

They'd been together, using the stadium seats as their cover. Haleika had had a very obvious crush on Leander during the process of kashonim being assigned. But once she'd been bound to him, she hadn't said anything. Plus, she had a constant flirtation with Galen, who seemed to be…with her.

Auriel's bane.

"I'm going to hit the baths," I said. "I'm all," I gestured at myself to indicate the sweaty mess I'd become.

"Let me know next time you're coming for extra training," she said.

"Of course," I said. "Have a good run."

CHAPTER
NINE

I entered our training room wearing my hair in a wet braid down my back and a fresh tunic over new short-pants. After the bath, I'd switched to my sandals, my body still heated from the run. I closed the door behind me, locking it before I took a few steps in and set my bag down.

Rhyan stood in the center of the room, tensed, his arms folded across his chest so tightly his biceps were bulging from beneath his tunic. The veins in his forearm looked ready to pop.

"You saw them?" I asked. "Was that what caused the change in you?"

His jaw worked, but he nodded.

"They, um," I paused. I'd been replaying what had happened over and over in my mind as I'd bathed, trying to work out what it meant and what I was supposed to do with the information I now had.

Haleika was having an affair with Leander—something that could get them expelled from the Academy at best. At worst, they'd be stripped of their power. And the procedure for being stripped... that almost always led to death. It had killed Jules.

My mind was still reeling. Haleika and Leander were kashonim. According to Lumerian Law, they could never be together. And they'd been...Gods...I was sure they'd been together, hiding in the seats of the arena while Rhyan and I had been on the field.

I didn't want to share Haleika's secret with Rhyan, partially out of respect for her, and partially because I didn't want to burden Rhyan with this knowledge. Maybe I hadn't sworn a blood oath this time, but I knew the weight this secret carried, and knew how much weaker the secrecy became with every person who knew. But I also needed to ease Rhyan's mind that he hadn't been seen. That we were okay.

"They didn't see you," I said at last, hoping he wouldn't ask me how that was possible. "I guess because you move so fast."

Rhyan breathed an audible sigh of relief, his arms loosening from his hold. "You're sure."

"They invited me to run with them, so I wouldn't have to do it alone."

"What?"

I shrugged. "I don't know, but they weren't paying attention, and they didn't see you."

He shook his head, squinting in concentration like he couldn't believe it. "Either way, we can't do this again." He pinched the bridge of his nose. "Not here."

"I know," I said sadly.

"That doesn't mean we're not going to continue," he said, stepping forward. "I'll just have to scout out a new location for runs. Or watch from the sidelines if I have to."

"You're sure you want to go through all of this trouble?" I asked.

"I'm sure I want to keep you in Bamaria," he said, his gaze intensifying. Then he winked. "It's the only way I get to stay."

"That still means a lot." I bit my lip, grateful for the lengths he was willing to go to for me.

He jerked his chin toward the center of the room. "Ready for the next part of training?" he asked.

"Only if it involves coffee," I said. I perked up at the thought. I had smelled coffee the moment I'd entered the room but had been distracted with thoughts of Haleika and Leander until now.

He'd rearranged a stack of mats we usually kept off to the side into the center of the room, and as I looked beyond them, I realized he'd done more than just brewed me coffee. He'd laid out an entire feast, and it smelled amazing. The aroma of freshly brewed coffee, baked goods, and spices filled the air, drowning out its usually musty, chalky scent.

"Here's your, how do you say, good job?" he said, tapping his finger against his chin.

I walked forward to the pale blue blanket laid out across the floor. A silver carafe full of steaming coffee stood in its center, the scent emanating from it now overwhelming. Surrounding the coffee lay fruit platters full of pomegranate seeds, strawberries, figs, dates, and grapes. Beyond those were silver plates heaping with hummus, olives, tomato salad, and toasted pita bread.

I spotted a jug of water, tiny bowls full of roasted nuts, and a larger bowl filled with hardboiled eggs. And to top it all off were three plates stacked with desserts. One held tiny sculpted chocolates, the second was filled with honey-glazed pastries with dripping icing, and the third plate had been layered almost ridiculously high with lemon cakes.

"You just put all of this together?" I asked, stunned by the display. My mouth watered, my stomach panging for once with genuine hunger and excitement over what I was about to eat.

"You shouldn't just have coffee. You need something to go with it."

"This is a lot more than something," I said. My stomach growled, as my heart felt like it was swelling up to three times its size.

Rhyan gestured for me to sit down on the blanket, and I did as he reached for the silver carafe, filling a mug for me. Smoky tendrils of steam rose from the cup, and I noted additional spices tangled with the scent of the coffee beans.

"Rhyan, this is…." I didn't know what to say. It was so sweet, and kind, and…exactly what I'd needed today. "You didn't have to do all of this." I paused. "Wait, this isn't, like, some sort of bribe or attempt to get me to trust you, and then the next thing we're about to do is some sort of torturous training routine. Is it?"

A mischievous smile played across his lips. "I thought you knew better than to trust me by now."

My eyes widened. "What?"

He chuckled, his gaze pausing on me before he returned his focus to pouring coffee into a second mug. "Believe or not, partner, the next part of your training is this. Eating."

I didn't fully believe him but definitely wasn't about to argue. "We could have gone to the dining hall for that." I frowned. "Separately."

Disappointment flashed in his eyes, but just for a second. "Well, this is maybe a little more than that. Eating, yes. And I promised coffee. But," his jaw tensed for a moment, "I took a well-educated guess that this past week was probably not the best of your life. And as your friend," he said carefully, "I thought you could use some-thing nice at the end of it."

He handed me a mug, and I cupped it between my palms, bringing it up to my nose to smell its divinely delicious scent but also to conceal all the emotion no doubt spilling across my features.

"I just wanted to do something nice for you, and maybe…say sorry for missing yesterday."

"I really appreciate that." Emotions swirled inside of me. "This past week probably made it into the top three worst weeks of my life."

He frowned, offering a small nod in solidarity.

"Do you want to know what the other two weeks were?" I asked.

Rhyan sat beside me on the blanket, his own mug between his hands. He offered me a small smile and another nod.

"The others were, well, the week we," I sighed, "the week we found out that Jules was—she was—"

"Gone?" Rhyan offered, his voice soft.

I nodded. "And then there was my week in the Shadow Stronghold. That's second place."

I'd left off my list the week of Jules's Revelation Ceremony, when everything had turned sour in my relationship with Tristan, Jules's vorakh had been exposed, Meera's vorakh had been revealed to us, and my first blood oath had been sworn. But every week that month had felt the same. One long endless miserable week.

"I'm glad this wasn't the worst week then," he said.

"There's really one big reason why it wasn't," I said, watching him carefully.

He stared down at his coffee, the steam rising up around his chin as he inhaled, then looked back to me. "Why is that?"

"You were in it."

"Lyr," he said, his voice barely above a whisper. He leaned toward me. His expression was so open, so vulnerable and sweet, a shy smile spreading across his lips. But he seemed to catch himself, cleared his throat, and sat back, lifting his mug to cover his mouth. "Try your coffee."

I gestured at his mug. "I thought both mugs would be for me," I said, trying to lighten the mood. I knew I shouldn't have said what I had. And yet, nothing could have stopped me from telling him that. Despite his non-reaction, I knew he understood. That feeling of safety I felt with Rhyan when he treated my wounds and when I trained with him, it was growing in strength, overwhelming me with its power.

He smiled over his cup. "I actually make a pretty strong brew. Go on," he said. "Drink up, partner."

I brought it up to my nose again, letting the heat and scent rise before I took a slow, hot sip. I moaned. I'd been expecting a strong cup of coffee, and I'd been wanting one all day long, so I'd known this was going to be good. But I'd never dreamed it would be this good. Rhyan had sweetened it, and there seemed to be some sort of spice topping it off. I inhaled again, realizing how complicated and sweet the combination really was before taking another sip. It was the most delicious coffee I'd ever had.

"You like it?" he asked, offering me a furtive glance from behind his mug before taking a sip.

"Um." I took another sip. "I am going to need my coffee to taste just like this every single day for the rest of my life. What's in here?"

"Ah," he said, grinning. "That I can never reveal." His accent had intensified into a parody of itself. "Secrets of the north," he said with a wink.

I laughed. "Guess you'll just have to make it for me every day."

"Hmm. I think this means I win."

I narrowed my eyebrows. "Win what?"

"Win our argument. Glemarian cuisine is far superior to Bamarian."

"Unless you had this coffee imported from Glemaria, I believe this is Bamarian coffee," I bluffed. He had Glemarian sunleaves, so who knew what else he'd carried with him across the Empire?

"It's my personal recipe," he gloated. "Which is Glemarian."

"You didn't specify recipes. You said food, from the land. You were arguing about minerals and soil. So you still don't win this one."

He watched me from the corners of his eyes, a smile spreading across his face that he hid behind his mug. "Yet," he said and took another long sip.

I followed suit, practically devouring the coffee. I didn't need the second mug for its caffeine, but I was tempted to have a refill simply for the taste.

"If you can wake early," he said, "before dawn, I'll make you 'Secrets of the North.' Every morning until Valyati."

"First coffee, then soturion training?" I teased.

"First coffee, then soturion training." He downed the rest of his mug and set it down, reaching for a plate and piling it high with everything he'd collected for the feast. Pita bread was heaped with mountains of hummus, olives, nuts, and salad. He added a hard-boiled egg, then he topped it off with a chocolate, a pastry, and three lemon cakes.

"I had a feeling you'd be excited by the coffee, but you haven't mentioned the food." He placed the plate in my hands. It was heavier than I'd expected.

"Oh," I said, staring dumbly down at it. The plate was intimidating. "This isn't for you?"

"I made this plate for you."

"I don't think I can eat all of this."

"It's food you like, though, isn't it? I know you like lemon cakes. Other than coffee, it's the only thing I've seen you gravitate to in the hall."

I could only nod in response, a bubbly feeling in my stomach as I looked over at him. Sunlight streamed through the windows, creating a golden halo around his curls.

"I want you to eat more of them," he said, voice serious again.

"What, right this second?" I asked. "What about you?"

One eyebrow narrowed, his green eyes carefully assessing me. "I'm going to make my plate now and eat with you, but you have to promise to finish whatever I give you." He set himself to work, piling his own plate with food. I noticed he tripled the amount of hardboiled eggs on his.

"Why the sudden focus on how much I'm eating?"

"Take a bite." Rhyan tore into his first lemon cake, licking the icing off his fingers. "You want the lemon cake first? Eat that."

I gripped the plate on my lap, eyeing him suspiciously. I'd never started with dessert before, nor had I ever allowed myself two— forget three—pieces of lemon cake. I'd never even thought of it. Ladies who were Heir to the Arkasva only ate one piece and usually just a bite of it. And only at the end of a meal. Somedays I was so stressed or injured, I could barely stomach food at all, much less get to dessert.

Rhyan took another bite. When he swallowed, I finally bit into my lemon cake, chewing slowly, allowing myself to really taste the sweetness on my tongue.

"Eat the other," he said, as soon as I finished the cake. My stomach growled in response, but before I could feel embarrassed,

Rhyan smiled. "Mine used to do that, too, in my early days of training."

I took another bite, aware of how carefully Rhyan was watching me.

"I did say that eating was part of training, so here's the lesson. I've been watching you in the dining hall, and I think you've been eating like an heir—a very stressed one. From what I've observed of Bamarian culture, including during my previous visits, there's an expectation of small portions, of eating only what is considered polite, or eating only when guests are. I was trained to do the same," he continued. "But from now on, I want you eating like a soturion. You need more nutrition and sustenance to keep up with the warrior you truly are."

"I'm n—"

"You are a warrior, Lyr. You stood up to Ka Kormac on my behalf, not to mention the way you faced them this week after all they did to you. You spent a week in the Shadow Stronghold. You've been training with soturi for over a month, and you survived your first habibellum and whipping. Now you're already back to running mere days later, and you just beat your average run time. You are a warrior. Now eat like one."

Tears burned behind my eyes as his words sank in. He was right. I had barely eaten in the past month, barely eaten when I'd used more energy than ever. I'd been through so much—Gods, even last night, I'd eaten according to what I'd seen Lady Romula consume and stopped eating dessert when everyone else had, and that had allowed me to get too drunk from the wine.

"This is the next part of our training. Whatever was keeping you from combat clinic was also keeping you from sleeping enough and eating enough. From now on, you're getting more of both."

I blinked the tears back. I hadn't been undereating and under-sleeping for a month—I'd been doing it for years. "How did you know?"

He scooped another serving of hummus onto my plate, motioning for me to try the bread. "You were wasting away, getting thinner, looking weaker," he said, nostrils flaring. "You were practically sleeping on the field before the Emartis showed up. But I knew for sure the other day. When I treated your back, I could see just how thin you were becoming." He grunted. "Go ahead. Try the bread."

When I took a bite, he continued, "After my Revelation, I was eating the same amount of food as my friends when I started training. The amount I'd been taught to eat. But they weren't being bound like me. They hadn't grown up with the experiences I had. Their stress levels weren't the same. Only when I realized magic was making up for a portion of their energy did I make the connection. I had to increase my food intake to compete—to match the physical energy levels expected of me and that I wanted to achieve.

"You can do the same. Eat bigger portions and until you're actually satisfied, don't just eat the amount expected. And no skipping meals. From now on, we're always going to have snacks in this room. Always. No more depriving yourself. You want to eat the lemon cake first, do it, fuck what anyone else thinks. And when you're with me, you don't have to be an heir, you don't need to put on a show or perform as Lady Lyrianna. You're hungry, you eat. Especially these next three months. If you have needs, you see to them. If there's something you want, something you enjoy, something that will help you get through this, I want you to have it. What you're doing is hard enough without you depriving yourself over silly societal norms. Understand?"

I took another bite, and then another. Rhyan did the same until both of our plates were cleaned. When I hesitated to grab seconds, he pushed every bowl toward me with a grin.

When I was completely full and satisfied and Rhyan was convinced that I had in fact eaten my fill, we started to pack away the food.

"I wanted to take a walk around the track after this," he said. "To digest. But um...." He ran his fingers through his hair, clearly irritated.

"We can't risk being seen."

"How are you feeling?"

"Full," I said. "Satisfied. And tired. But good tired. For once."

"Why don't you take a walk through the city?" he suggested.

"Doesn't that open up even more possibilities for people to see us together?"

"I won't be walking with you. I'll be," he grimaced, "I'll be watching."

"So I'm going to take a walk by myself while you play bodyguard?"

"I'm not *playing* bodyguard. I take that role very seriously."

"Fine," I said. "When's our next training?"

"Tomorrow morning before dawn. I'll bring you coffee."

I tried to hide the smile forming on my lips. The idea of Rhyan's coffee first thing in the morning—of Rhyan first thing in the morning—was the best thing I'd heard all day. But I was still annoyed at him for suggesting he revert back to being my bodyguard, even if I knew it was for the best and something my father and Aemon had ordered him to do.

"Isn't that going to be suspicious? You showing up to my apartment first thing in the morning?"

He sighed. "With the new information we have about the akadim and the likelihood of the Emartis making another appearance in the next few weeks, I've been assigned to your detail every morning before dawn until you step foot in the Katurium. So I'll be there no matter what. This way, there's coffee."

"Okay. Sounds good," I said.

"When you walk," he added, "just be careful of your surroundings. I'll be with you the whole time even if you can't see me. But the Emartis, they're hiding in plain sight."

Hours later, I was back in my apartment, snacking on leftovers Rhyan had packed me from the picnic and trying to catch up on some scrolls. The sun was setting, and I was ready to call it early and crawl into bed.

But there was another persistent knock on my door. I assumed it was Tristan coming to check on me. I was only just realizing now how odd it was that he hadn't been over earlier in the day—unless I'd missed him. I had told him I'd be scarce, and he seemed to be respecting that, but I still had a pit in the bottom of my stomach whenever I thought about him.

When I opened the door, I was greeted by the brown hair and eyes of Ka Grey. Haleika stood impatiently in my doorway. For once, her expression was serious, her mouth thin and without joy.

"Can I talk to you, your grace?" she asked formally.

"Of course, Hal." I gestured her inside and closed the door. "Do you want to sit?"

She shook her head, her curls bouncing. "I'm not staying. I only came to tell you something."

I stopped breathing, waiting for her to speak.

"What I said earlier today, I was covering for you. Leander didn't see Rhyan on the track with you—he didn't see how close you two were. But I did."

"Hal, I—"

"Did you tell him? Did you tell him we were there together?"

"No," I said. "I didn't."

"I'm not blind," she said, twirling a brown curl nervously around her finger, her cheeks red. "I know what you're doing. And I know what it means. And what consequences there might be. To your place here. To his. To your place in my family, in my Ka."

"Hal, no. It's not like that at—"

"Don't insult me, Lyr. We've known each other too long. I am trusting you to keep this secret because it's the only way I'm keeping yours."

"Hal, there's no secret. I swear, I love—"

"The rumors have already started. They'll reach Tristan soon. Or worse. Keep my secret, Lyr, or yours gets out."

"I have no secrets," I said, my voice shaking. I felt like I was standing in front of a stranger, an enemy, not one of my oldest friends. I'd never seen Haleika anything less than bubbly and sweet, flirting with Galen or any other noble she fancied. But threatening me—blackmailing me? I'd never imagined this.

She scoffed. "Spoken like a true heir. If word gets out, if I find out anyone has been told about me, about us, I will expose you. Tristan will be the first. And I think you know what he'll do."

My heart hammered. I was going to be sick. "Nothing has ever —" My mouth was so dry it was hard to speak. "Nothing has ever happened between us. Nor will it."

"Yes. And I can say the same," she said, storming out the door.

THE SECOND SCROLL: BLOOD DEBT

CHAPTER
TEN

No one was more surprised than me when I woke the following morning at dawn and didn't feel completely awful. It certainly said something of Rhyan's methods. But as far as my mood went, that was an entirely different story. I was never happy to be awake before the sun, especially knowing I was going to be running again in a few short hours. But Haleika's threat kept replaying in my mind over and over again. I debated telling Rhyan—he was the only person I could tell. But I couldn't explain to him what had actually happened without breaking my promise to Haleika.

I decided as soon as he knocked on my door that I wouldn't say a word. He was already aware of the threat against us, how seriously we were expected to take our kashonim. He knew the whispers that had been lying under the surface of everything we did, knew what Tani had said, and I had no doubts he suspected how jealous Tristan was.

But when I opened my door, I couldn't help the relief I felt in just knowing he was near, nor the way I immediately felt safer in his presence. Nor could I help the smile spreading across my face as I caught the light in his green eyes.

"Sleep well, partner?" Rhyan asked, setting the carafe down, the warm, spicy scent already beginning to waft its way to me.

"Better than last night," I said, inhaling the coffee. I glanced anxiously around, hearing the bells calling out the hour. Through my kitchen window, tiny blue lights lit up the morning sky as the ashvan took flight over the city.

"What's wrong?" he asked.

"Are you...?" I sucked in a breath, my stomach knotting.

The rumors have already started. They'll reach Tristan soon. Or worse. Haleika's words wouldn't stop racing through my mind.

I tried again as Rhyan raised his good eyebrow questioningly. "Are you sure that you being here is, you know, safe?" I leaned back, my hands grasping the sink basin.

"Would you feel better if I brought you the official schedule?" he asked lightly. "I can tell you exactly who is outside, where they stand on the perimeter, and what time the guard changes."

"You know what I mean."

"I do." He opened a cupboard, pulling out two mugs and setting them onto my counter. "And, yes. If I thought for one second this would put you in danger or raise suspicions," he gestured at himself in my kitchen, "I'd never step foot in here again."

My heart sank so fast at that idea I nearly lost my hold and slipped back.

"Why don't you sit on the couch? Relax for a moment while I pour your coffee, then we'll train," he said.

"In my apartment?" I asked, skeptical of what he had planned. The place was tiny. Not really set up for any sort of fighting or exercise sequence. Plus, I was pretty sure any noise we made would carry to the apartments below.

"You'll see," he said as I took a seat.

Hot steam swirled from the mugs as he grabbed them, heading to the coffee table.

I sat and brought my mug to my nose, the warmth of the cup in my hands welcome in the chilled morning. It smelled exactly like it had the day before, and when I took a sip, I closed my eyes in bliss. At least I had this to look forward to each day.

"I think I found a new location for us to train in," he said.

"Though I wouldn't use it consistently. Mornings we'll be here, evenings in the Katurium. But on our days off, can you meet me on Gryphon Island?"

"On the beach?" I asked.

"The caves behind the Guardian of Bamaria. I've ventured out there a few times, and it's always been abandoned. The interior has a pretty flat surface, which would be good for practicing combat."

I took another sip of my coffee. "I can fly there," I said. "But Markan has been following me more closely lately. I don't see how I'd meet you there without him or another escort realizing what I'm up to."

Rhyan frowned. "I thought about that. There's a few days on the schedule where I'll be on duty all day."

"There's one escort who will remain quiet," I said carefully. Since I'd realized that one of Tristan's escorts, Bellamy, was also following me, protecting me on behalf of Ka Grey, I'd been paying him to be silent—to not tell Tristan about anything he saw me do or report on anything he had to protect me from. Bellamy had kept his word so far, and I'd been sure to keep the coin flowing. If I could get word to him on the days I needed to reach Gryphon Island or anywhere else Rhyan and I might meet, this could work.

"What escort?" Rhyan asked, one eyebrow narrowed in suspicion.

"He's not officially a member of the security detail," I said carefully.

Rhyan's face tightened. "I don't trust the mage from Ka Grey."

"I bought him," I said carefully.

Rhyan's eyes darkened. "Then he's loyal to money and not you."

"What other choice do we have?"

"We'll figure it out. If we need to, we can meet separately in our training room. You can also run on your own. As important as the extra training is for you, it won't help things if you get into more trouble."

I exhaled in frustration and took another sip of coffee.

"Sorry," he said. "We'll figure it out, we have a pretty solid plan so far. For now, though, let's focus on our morning training."

Morning training turned out to be guided visualizations and meditation, similar to what we had done on the track the day before. Rhyan guided me to map out each part of my day, asking me how it was going each step of the way. Every time I imagined it going poorly, I revised the scene in my mind. If he thought I was imagining something weakly, he had me redo it to an outcome where I showed more strength. I saw myself successfully completing the morning run, sitting energetically through classes, nailing every combat move in our training session, and victoriously fighting my way through combat clinic—even though, thank the Gods, I wasn't back on the schedule. Yet.

When he was satisfied that I'd mapped out a successful day of soturion training, he ended our session with some deep breathing before he took off, still having refused to tell me what was in the coffee.

I arrived at the Katurium to meet Galen and Haleika for breakfast, surprised to find she was back to her normal, happy, bouncy self. I froze as she greeted me with a hug, starting to wonder if the day before had been a fever dream brought on by exhaustion or my hangover.

She was flirting with Galen, sipping the dining hall's coffee—which now paled unbelievably in comparison to what I'd had earlier—and talking excitedly about attending the fall festival in the city that weekend. I politely excused myself from making any plans, saying I'd need the time to study and train.

A group of apprentices walked by, their trays full of food. Leander was among them. Haleika didn't look at him, nor did he look at her. But I could feel the tension cutting through them. Only in this moment did her eyes narrow on me, a glimmer of the Hal I saw yesterday poking through. Her eyes flicked to Rhyan sitting across the room, holding court at a table by himself, his gaze on me as he peeled a hardboiled egg.

Haleika cleared her throat, and then her pointed expression was gone, and she returned to discussing the fall festival.

My stomach twisted with nerves, and right in that moment, Viktor and his wolves decided to stalk past our table, their eyes leering, predatory. Tani sat across the room with Naria, Pavi, and all their little Ka Elys followers. I took several more bites of my breakfast platter, knowing I needed the energy.

"You feeling all right, Lyr?" Galen asked, eyeing my plate. It was the biggest plate I'd ever made for myself.

For a second, I was embarrassed. I'd never eaten this much in front of him. It wasn't proper. Then I remembered Rhyan's words. Fuck it. I needed the energy and strength. I took another bite. "Hungry," I said.

Haleika gave me the side eye. "It's good your appetite's increasing."

My stomach turned at her words, unsure what her point was. There was no way she could know who'd influenced me. But she had such a knowing look in her eyes that my mouth went dry. I held her gaze, determined not to cower, and took another bite.

"Go for it, Lyr," Galen said. "Eat whatever you want. I think I'm going to get some more, too."

Outside, I wordlessly set my dagger down beside Rhyan's before falling easily into our warm-up routine. The stretches felt the best they ever had. I'd been practicing, but an unusual look of approval from Rhyan made me wonder if the visualizing was working already.

"You look good," he said.

"Thanks," I said, as my heart did a little flip. "Quite a far cry from Lord 'You'll-be-the-worst-one-out-there.'"

"Oh, you'll still be the worst one out there," he said.

I practically growled at him.

"What?" He held up a hand in surrender. "I'm already forsworn, I can't lose another title, especially one as important as Lord 'You'll-be-the-worst—'"

"Fucking Moriel," I muttered.

"All right, partner," he said. "In all seriousness, you're a hundred times better than when you started. That girl who walked onto this track a month ago, she and you are not the same. I still say stamina over speed. But today, I want to see you pass someone. Wait for the right opportunity to come, and go for it."

I deepened my stretch, accepting my little assignment even as I wanted to growl in frustration. I knew Rhyan was right—I was still the slowest one out there, and it irked me every time I had to be reminded of it.

But I kept remembering what he'd said about gryphons. When they were babies, they were too weak to break the ropes holding them down. And when they got older, when they were strong enough to break free, they wouldn't, because they didn't realize they were stronger. No one had told them—they'd never had the opportunity to see their own growth, to understand the true power they possessed. Their reality was constantly reflected back to them —gryphons of all shapes and sizes and strengths were held down, so they never learned they could break free.

Yes, I was still woefully behind. I was still in great danger of failing whatever test the Emperor threw my way. But I remembered how I'd felt the first time I'd stepped onto the track. How my body had felt, how slow I'd been, how excruciatingly painful and embarrassing it had been, and the way I'd retched afterward. If I could travel through time and race myself from the first day, I could see clearly in my mind how much faster I'd be now, how much surer I was of my footing and pacing. I was stronger. The ropes that had bound me were starting to unravel, if not tear apart completely. I was no longer the girl I was a month earlier.

After my third loop around the arena, I did outrun another soturion. Twice.

Rhyan ran past me, winked, and sped forward.

. . .

S oon the weeks began to blur, each one passing more swiftly than the last. The days were shorter, the air crisper, the nights longer and colder, until another full month had passed.

Only two months remained before my test with the Emperor. Unsure what I might be asked to do in the test, Rhyan introduced wooden swords for us to spar with so I could become comfortable wielding weapons. These were only practice swords, not able to do any real damage other than the blunt kind. But they were heavy. It didn't take long for my smooth, soft noble hands to feel nearly as calloused as his.

Every night after our formal training ended, I stayed late through dinner, and we picked up the wooden blades. I'd needed tons of breaks at first when my hands and arms had grown tired from holding the swords after only a minute. Rhyan patiently gave me those breaks, though he always pushed me to make up for them. But soon my strength began to increase, my fingers stopped cramping, and I held the practice sword higher and steadier as the weeks went by. What I'd barely been able to grip on day one was now beginning to feel like an extension of my arm—I could swing with force and hit my target as precisely as I would with my finger.

Over the course of that month, I established a routine with Rhyan. Coffee and meditation every morning. Running, classes, training. Then we both stayed in the Katurium through clinic or late-night training before I was escorted back to my apartment— often by Markan while Rhyan watched in the distance. We kept exploring options for training on the weekends, but with the shifting schedule of my escorts and the whispers growing again of Emartis activity, we stuck to our training room after I did solo runs on the track with Rhyan guarding from afar.

A few nights—the nights I had no clinic—I made it out to dinner with Tristan in the city. But since I'd drunkenly straddled him in the carriage after the Cresthaven dinner, we'd almost completely stopped being intimate. At least, not in the way we had been before. We kissed when we were together, sometimes a lot. But his kisses had changed. They used to be flirtatious, hot, possessive. Now, they felt almost like a question. Like he was unsure if this was what he wanted. He still told me he loved me, and he still held me fiercely, but he was no longer spending nights in my bed, and we were no longer exploring each other's bodies in every way possible without getting fully naked. He always said it was fine, he didn't want to take away from my time training.

But I was worried. I knew without a doubt that if Meera hadn't also revealed vorakh all those years ago, I would have ended things with Tristan immediately. I could have taken the heat for being sympathetic to vorakh if it had just been about Jules. She was gone —we'd let her go, performed our role flawlessly—and if not for Meera, we would have had nothing more to hide.

Being with Tristan had always been about protecting Meera.

Over the last two years, I'd wished so many times that Meera hadn't had her vorakh, but for selfish reasons. So I could have grieved. So repairing our reputation wouldn't have been all on me and wouldn't have been so urgent. So I wouldn't have these damn scars.

Keeping the eye of the vorakh hunter on me and off my sisters was my duty. The only problem was I wasn't sure I was doing my job well anymore. Even if Tristan had never outright said anything, I knew it in my gut Rhyan was coming between us.

The rumors have already started. They'll reach Tristan soon. Or worse.

My feelings for Rhyan had been a shadow over my heart for years. Some part of me had been claimed from that first kiss between us three years ago. If Tristan suspected Rhyan had any role in our relationship falling apart, the consequences would be just as deadly as if he'd discovered Meera and Morgana's vorakh. So I kept plastering on my smile, kept initiating touches, and kisses, but there was a split between us—one that would not easily heal. One I wasn't sure I wanted to fix.

. . .

T he days and nights were all seamlessly spilling into each other. I'd been meditating, running, and sparring with the wooden blades every day. When just over one month remained before my test with the Emperor, Rhyan deemed me ready, and we switched to swords with dulled blades during our sessions.

He had me memorize choreography until I moved across the room like I was dancing with the sword, changing positions with each step. Every day, we added onto the choreography so I could hold the sword without thinking, so I could use it relying entirely on muscle memory, and feel as if it were an extension of my arm.

While I gritted my teeth and cursed him under my breath, the training was working. My arms had been sore as fuck when we'd begun, but soon there was only a dull ache in my muscles after each session. I noticed a change in my arms. In fact, a change was happening over my entire body.

This change had been subtle, both to me and to everyone else at the Academy, especially since the colder days and nights meant I covered up more of my body. Even in the baths, it had become an unspoken agreement that no one talked to or looked at me, not out of respect, but as if I'd been shunned. Even Haleika, who I was still on shaky grounds with, barely acknowledged me beyond what was polite. But on a rare night back at Cresthaven, preparing for another mindlessly boring and highly stressful formal dinner, Morgana walked in on me changing.

I stood in nothing but my undergarments, staring at my wardrobe and trying to decide on a dress. None fit right. They were too loose where they used to be too tight or too tight where they used to fit comfortably.

"Holy fucking Auriel's balls," Morgana said.

"Get out." I glared.

"Meera!" she yelled. "Look at Lyr."

"Why?" I asked. *Morgs, stop gawking at me!*

"I can't hear you!" she sang.

Morgana marched into my room—without an invitation—
followed a moment later by Meera, who also stared at me wide-
eyed. "All right there, Arkturion," Morgana said.

"Stop it!"

Neither of my sisters listened. They each grabbed one of my
arms and dragged me before my full-length mirror.

"Lyr, those are muscles! You have fucking muscles," Morgana
said like she could hardly believe it.

I looked at my body, finally taking it in. It was still mine, curved
where it always had been around my hips and breasts, and my
stomach was still slightly rounded, but there were lines in it now—
muscular ones. When I flexed…Gods. I could see it now, the newly
defined ridges and the reason why my arm cuff on my bicep felt too
tight at times. Three months of soturion training had had an impact.
Especially with Rhyan's private training on top of it.

For a moment, I was elated with my body, with the training it
had completed and the strength it had accrued. Then a dark thought
clouded my mind.

I watched Meera carefully in the mirror's reflection, all my
nerves on edge. Tristan would be at dinner, along with the full
Bamarian Council. We were well into Meera's danger zone. A
vision could come at any moment, and if it did in front of anyone,
we'd have to create a distraction as we rushed her to safety as
quickly as possible. For the last several weeks, the knowledge of her
impeding vision had kept me on edge, made me want to fly back to
Cresthaven to check on her every night after combat clinic.

Morgana had talked me out of it, promising the situation was
under control, and if I was needed, she'd find a way to get to me as
soon as possible. Considering her methods of alerting me to Meera's
last vision—binding her to the bed and flying out to find me—I had
my doubts. Still, there was nothing more I could do about it; I had
to keep up my training. My time was quickly running out.

The dinner itself was fine in the end. Meera didn't have a vision,
and with the dropping temperatures, the guests seemed inclined to
leave Cresthaven early.

My father excused himself, off again for another conversation with Lady Sila. Morgana had told me there'd been a sudden increase in her meetings with Father. They were still tracking the akadim situation, and concern was growing over the Emartis, who seemed to have switched tactics in an attempt to be more subtle. In their new strategy, a single black feather would be found outside a business, some spell used to keep it sticking to the doors and walls of the city buildings.

Turion Brenna, my father's Master of the Peace, reported an increase in painted graffiti. *Shekar arkasva* had been found painted all over Bamaria, and her soturi had enlisted the help of mages to erase the messages.

"Your grace," Eathan said, pulling me aside after the dinner. "How is training?"

"It's going." I eyed the door my father had walked through with Lady Sila. "What can you tell me about the Emartis movements?"

Arianna had joined my side and wrapped her arm around my shoulder. "My lord," she said, bowing her head to Eathan. "My dear," she said, giving me a squeeze.

"The Emartis are preparing to make a move," he said solemnly. "I don't know when. But the influx of their signature across the city seems to be hinting at some coming event."

I swallowed, noting Lady Romula glaring at me from across the room. She turned, her silver gown swishing at her heels. She loved to pretend she was old and frail when it suited her—moving slowly, stealing people's time and patience—but she was quick on her feet when push came to shove. She called Tristan to her side, linking her arm with his and falling against his shoulder as if she were too weak to hold herself up. She directed Tristan to a corner where Naria stood and engaged her in conversation, looking back to check I was watching. I turned my face fully to Eathan's before I could sneer or reveal some other emotion.

"I don't want you to worry, Lyr," Arianna said. "We're watching this all very closely. I've had an extra eye on the Academy since that girl thought she could attack you."

"Thank you," I said.

Eathan bowed. "I must speak to Brenna. But I'll find you before you leave."

"Sure," I said.

Arianna moved in front of me, reaching for both of my shoulders. "How are you holding up?" she asked. "I know these months haven't been easy for you."

"They haven't." I stared into my aunt's eyes, her face so like mine. She was my mother's youngest sister, third in line to the Seat of Power like I was. Growing up, everyone always said how much I looked like my mother, especially when I went into the sun and my hair turned fiery red. Arianna's hair had faded; it was still red but without the flames that made it true Batavia red.

Though I loved hearing I looked like my mother, I knew I looked more like Arianna. Her paintings from her youth were almost exact replicas of my face.

"I wish your mother were here," she said. "I think things would have been easier for you."

If she had been alive, she'd still be ruling Bamaria as High Lady. My father wouldn't have a limp from being attacked by the Emartis. The Emartis wouldn't even exist. And even if I was found to be powerless in this alternate version of reality, I wouldn't be dealing with the threat of a rebellion while I tried to survive the Emperor's decree.

A tear rolled down my cheek, and Arianna pulled me in for a hug. "Oh, my dear," she said. My wrist itched, my blood oaths acting up the way they did whenever I wanted to tell anyone our secret.

She drew back, her blue eyes scanning me up and down. "Be safe." She turned her head toward the dining room doors. They'd both opened suddenly.

Rhyan stepped through them, dressed in his full soturion uniform. His black leather armor shined with the design of our merged sigils, the gryphon and the seraphim. The sun and moon. Gold and silver together.

My breath caught. He just looked so beautiful.

"Looks like your ride is here," Arianna said.

"What?" I asked.

"To escort you back to Cresthaven," she said, eyebrows scrunched together in confusion. "You seem so surprised."

"Oh, no...no," I stuttered. "I didn't know that you knew he was on my detail."

As far as I'd known, only Aemon, my father, and the select soturi assigned to guard me had this information. It had been kept secret so Rhyan could offer me extra protection in the Katurium, a place where traditionally even heirs were expected to be on equal ground with everyone else. In the Academy where fighting was encouraged, there was no place for a bodyguard to step in. I was the exception.

"You think I don't know everything that concerns your safety?"

I coughed, feeling like an idiot. Of course, she knew. I was so used to hiding everything to do with Rhyan that I'd overcorrected. "I just didn't realize I was getting picked up," I said, trying to cover myself.

"You can leave whenever you want. I'm making sure you're watched over. At all times." She wrapped her arms around me, squeezing me tightly to her. Her giant golden arm cuff cut into my arm, and I flinched. Arianna immediately pulled back. "Gods! I'm sorry, Lyr. Us Batavia women and our big jewelry. Did I hurt you?"

"I'm fine," I said, noting her eyes darting to my own arm cuff. Immediately, my wrist itched again. My cuff held Meera's vision log, on which I recorded every vision she had, its duration, her symptoms, and the date, always leaving space to record the next one. "I probably should retire for the evening."

"Be safe, my dear," she said.

Rhyan's eyes blazed as he strode across the room. He reached my side at the exact moment a second set of arms wrapped around me. I caught the familiar scent of mint and salt.

"Lord Grey," Rhyan said jovially.

"What are you doing here, forsworn?"

"Taking in the scenery."

"Forsworn don't attend formal functions at Cresthaven."

Rhyan squinted, looking around the room. "The formality appears to have left this function in particular. In any case, don't bother reaching for your stave." He held up both hands. "I know how stick-happy you get when you see me. I'm just here after being summoned by Arkturion Aemon."

Even in Rhyan's snarkiest voice, the one he seemed to have tucked away specifically for his interactions with Tristan, I could still detect the undercurrent of anger he felt toward Aemon.

Lyr, he lashed you.

"Ah, speak of the Ready," he said, turning to Aemon, who had appeared across the room.

"Let's get you home," Tristan said. He was frowning in disgust, looking at Cresthaven's formal dining room with its high ceilings and golden columns inscribed with text from the Valya as if we'd gone to eat at some dump in the city.

"Fine," I said, making my way through the room to formally excuse myself from all the remaining guests. Gods forbid I left in a timely manner. After Tristan and I had seen every last Lumerian present—including his grandmother, who pulled me aside and whispered into my ear as she smiled sweetly at Tristan, *He has other options*—we reached the carriage outside the front doors.

"Your grace," Aemon called, marching across the room with Rhyan beside him. "Soturion Rhyan is going to fly back to the Academy in your carriage. I want extra security with you."

Tristan cocked his head to the side, his nostrils flaring. "She has a full team and my mages, does she not?"

"One might argue that her grace can never have enough. Wouldn't you want her to have the most protection possible?"

"As long as it's someone sane and balanced. I don't put my trust into the hands of criminals."

"Luckily, neither do I," said Aemon darkly, and he turned and marched back to the dining room.

Rhyan raised his hand. "If I say that I don't trust criminals either, does that mean we have something in common and can be friends?"

"You're sitting behind the partition this time," Tristan said.

"Hmmm," Rhyan said. "You cut me deep, Lord Grey. By the way, did you ever decide to reach out to the Imperator? You know, see if her grace could have an extra month to train?"

Tristan stiffened. "You know that's not possible."

Rhyan leaned forward, his voice low, "If given the choice between you and the criminals, I'd choose them." Rhyan climbed inside the carriage and sat behind the partition.

Tristan gripped my hand, holding it too tightly throughout the ride as if Rhyan could see through the partition walls.

I stared out the window, watching as the landscape shifted from the fields beyond Cresthaven to the city. Beside the Temple of Dawn, the building shaped like the Valalumir, bonfires erupted in the field. Viewed from above, the bonfires spelled out a very simple message:

Shekar arkasva.

CHAPTER
ELEVEN

I woke early the following Thursday. The day before, we'd all celebrated the final fall holiday of the season, Days of Shadows. I was looking forward to my morning routine with Rhyan. The schedule, the consistency of it, was one of the few things I felt I had control over in my life, especially as Tristan continued to pull away and the whispers of *Shekar arkasva* returned. But instead of finding Rhyan outside my door at the usual time with coffee, there was a note written hastily onto a scroll:

Away until this afternoon. Back for training. Sorry.
-R

My stomach knotted. The last time he'd canceled our training session, he'd been called away to hunt akadim. If he had been called away again, it could be because the threat was growing. Maybe the packs were larger, or they'd moved closer to Bamaria.

I poured myself a glass of water, trying to process whether I was jumping to conclusions. Aemon had been consulting with Rhyan more often, almost interrogating him about the akadim kill he'd made. That was why he'd been summoned to Cresthaven. Aemon had heard more reports, and he'd wanted to make sure our soturi were equipped with every detail needed. But Rhyan hadn't been called away until now.

Where had he gone this time? Elyria again? If he was in Elyria, he must have left last night after dinner, or even in the middle of the night. Which meant he probably would be returning this afternoon without any sleep. Unless the akadim were closer.

I sipped my water and tried to relax. I'd been meditating every morning with Rhyan for two months, and it had done wonders to calm my nerves and relieve my anxiety—I hadn't had a panic attack since we'd started. Now, I was having trouble focusing by myself. I was too used to listening to Rhyan's soft breathing and guidance as I visualized. I slowed my breathing like I'd been trained, but I couldn't stop thinking about his note and worrying about him.

So, I went to the Katurium early, sensing Markan and Bellamy following me. The stores hadn't opened yet, leaving the city's waterways nearly empty. The air was chilled, and fog clouded the sky, leaving me shivering down to my bones. We were at the end of fall, when the weather reached that in-between phase of cold that left my teeth chattering.

As I walked, I caught flashes of silvered armor, of wolfish pelts. Ka Kormac was on guard duty this morning. Their presence in the streets had been a growing shadow in my mind the last two months. During my morning walks, I usually spotted soturi from Ka Batavia, their golden armor flashing from their camouflaged cloaks. On sunny mornings, I saw their starfire blades light up in the sun. But everything today was cold, gray, and silver. I wrapped my soturion cloak tighter around me as I passed through the sleeping city.

I was one of the first to arrive at the Katurium. I ate a full breakfast in a nearly empty dining hall before heading out to a silent track to digest and stretch in peace and quiet. I fell forward, my fingers easily reaching my toes. I exhaled, deepening the stretch until the palms of my hands were flat on the ground. Slowly, like I'd practiced countless times with Rhyan, I rolled my body up, my arms reaching for the sky as I completed the stretch.

After I moved through the 108 Postures of the Valya, I took another walk to clear my head before everyone else arrived. I lost

track of time, the walking becoming its own form of meditation as
soturi spilled from the doors into the arena. The usual groupings
began to form on their designated parts of the track. Loud laughs
and chatter sounded as they each began throwing themselves into
their stretches and warm-up routine.

Though I knew he said he'd be back this afternoon, I still
watched every time a door opened, hoping I'd see Rhyan's tall
frame, his brown hair curling, and golden in the sun, and his black
leather armor and belt shining with Valalumirs.

I was in my usual starting spot, my dagger hilt jutting from the
ground, when Viktor and his beady-eyed apprentice Brockton tossed
their daggers on either side of mine.

"Where's your bodyguard, Lady Asherah?" Viktor asked. "Get
called away again?"

Viktor and the wolves of Ka Kormac constantly casted their
lewd stares my way, always trying to intimidate or throw me off
balance. But since I'd increased my training with Rhyan, I'd noticed
them keeping their distance. I hadn't been called Lady Asherah in
weeks. Even Naria, Pavi, Tani, and every other soturion from Ka
Elys who hated me had been quiet.

"Brave now that he isn't here?" I snarled.

Brockton, his face resembling the Bastardmaker's more and
more each day, leaned toward me. "You scared now he isn't?"

"A real soturion wouldn't need her little protector to keep her
safe," Viktor said.

Glaring at Viktor, I pointed at Brockton. "Then what do you call
that?" I asked, my pulse spiking.

"You—" Brockton started, but Viktor cut him off.

"Don't say something you'd regret, Brockton. She's still Heir to
the Arkasva. For now." His nostrils flared, his eyes focusing in on
me, so predatory and wolflike I wondered if Ka Kormac had a
connection to the animals closer than merely as a symbol for their
sigil.

I stood taller even as my mind reeled. Had that been a taunt, or was there a threat laced in there? Viktor's father was the Imperator, the one funding the Emartis, who didn't want my father on the Seat of Power. If my father was deposed, depending on who took his place, I might no longer be an heir. My stomach twisted. The Emartis had been ramping up their messaging recently, and perhaps the quietness of Viktor and his supporters these past weeks should have also been a warning sign.

Sweat beaded at the nape of my neck despite the chill in the air. My mouth opened to form a retort, to show him I was still Lady Lyriana, Heir to the Arkasva, High Lord of Bamaria, no matter what the Emartis thought or how well Ka Kormac paid them, but in that moment, everyone stood at attention, including Viktor and Brockton.

Aemon had entered the field, followed by Dairen. I locked eyes with the Ready, wanting to run over to him and ask about Rhyan. But he was clearly already in a mood, his dark aura swirling through the cold morning mist. Whatever was bothering him was now bothering everyone in the arena as his aura pulsed and darkened the already foggy stadium. Clouds moved across the sun, shadowing the sky further and filling the air with moisture.

"Something's up," Viktor sing-songed. "If the all-mighty Ready is in such a sour mood, that spells trouble for Bamaria," his voice became low and deep, "and trouble for you."

"Shut up," I sneered. I didn't have the energy for anything else. "Just shut up. You have no idea what's going on."

"Do you?" he asked pointedly.

I stared straight ahead. Viktor had been a gryphon-shit asshole his entire life. He was a nasty, spiteful, cocky know-it-all. But he was Heir to the Arkasva, son of the Imperator, and grand-nephew of the Emperor. My heart pounded in my chest, nearly beating out of my tunic. The Imperator was far more calculating than his son— anyone who'd observed them longer than five minutes could see that. I found it unlikely the Imperator would involve Viktor in his plans or arm him with dangerous knowledge that he could leak.

And yet, Viktor had seemed aware of the Emartis's last attack over the Katurium. He'd delighted in it beside Naria, not showing an ounce of fear even as sharpened blades of glass had fallen from the sky.

"Not one to chat in the morning?" he crooned. "Or do you only like talking to the forsworn?"

My hands pressed into my hips. I had to stay calm, present. *Be a gryphon, not a seraphim disguised as one.* Haleika was stretching a few feet ahead of me, close enough to overhear the conversation. She turned her head, her eyes widening on me standing between Viktor and Brockton. Leander sank into a deep stretch beside her.

Haleika took a step, like she was starting toward me to help. She'd done it countless times before—told off Tani or other soturi who thought I was free game now that I was a soturion.

But I shook my head carefully at her. Viktor outranked her. She could not safely come to my aid. Not this time. I had to handle them myself.

Her brown eyes—so like Tristan's—widened with sorrow when she realized what I was doing, and I offered a small smile, hoping to convey my full meaning. It was the most genuine interaction we'd had since the day she'd come to my apartment.

She turned back to Leander, catching her foot in her hand as she did a standing stretch. On either side of me, Viktor and Brockton moved closer to me, the smell of bad coffee foul on their breath.

"Be careful, Asherah," Viktor said. "You made it this far, but your time is running out. You have one month left, to be exact."

"Feeling brave because your big uncle's coming?"

Viktor cursed. "Enjoy your run." He lifted his foot, his black eyes boring into mine, and without warning stomped the heel of his boot down onto my dagger. The hilt vanished as his heel drove the blade deep into the ground.

Fuck. I was going to have to get on my hands and knees and literally dig to get it free before I could finish the run.

"Yourself to Moriel," I snarled, glancing over my shoulder to the center of the track. Had Aemon seen this? Or Dairen? Would anything be done? Had it been the other way around, and Viktor had accused me of some slight, Dairen would have been dragging me to the pole at once. But despite Dairen's glee in punishing fairly, even punishing heirs, I had never once seen Viktor called out for his behavior.

"Oh, no, how will you get your dagger back without a shovel? Brockton," Viktor chided, "so clumsy of you."

My hands curled into fists at my sides—they were replicas of their fathers, of the Imperator and the Bastardmaker.

Aemon called out for everyone to prepare just as the clocktower bells began to ring out and the ashvan shot into the sky.

I took off, my arms tight at my sides, my pace picking up. Fuck stamina. Today was about speed, about running faster than Viktor and staying the hell away from him until the hour was over. It was too bad Rhyan wasn't here. Between my anger at Viktor Kormac burning through me and my anxiety at Rhyan's absence, I ran the fastest I ever had, passing three soturi at one point.

When the hour ended, I crouched on the ground and dug up my dagger, the cold dirt caking beneath my fingernails. Thankfully, Haleika and Galen came to my rescue, using their blades to dig. I was grateful to have Haleika back on my side, or, at least, acting like she was. Especially when Naria, Pavi, and Tani began to circle closer to me in the dining hall, clearly because of Rhyan's absence.

There was a shout of "*Shekar arkasva*" as I ate lunch. I froze, glancing around, but there was no way to figure out where the shout had come from. Everyone in the dining hall seemed to delight in hearing the phrase—the phrase used as the call of terrorists—pronounced so boldly to me. Classmates I hadn't expected to turn on me were now leering in my direction or laughing. Across the dining hall, Viktor, Brockton, and every other brute from Ka Kormac was sitting at the table Rhyan usually occupied, howling.

I leapt from my seat. I couldn't take it anymore, and I retreated to the training room, hoping to find Rhyan. It was empty. I set down my bags and sat on a stack of mats, drawing my knees up to my chest and taking deep breaths to stay calm.

The door burst open, and Rhyan stumbled in. He looked at me, his eyes glassy and unfocused, as he closed the door behind him.

"You're back," I said, relief spreading through me.

Rhyan opened his mouth as if to say hello, then collapsed to the ground. Face first.

CHAPTER
TWELVE

"Gods! Rhyan!" I shot across the room, crouching beside him.

He didn't make a sound or move.

"Rhyan?" I shook his shoulders. "Rhyan!"

Fuck! What the fuck had happened? Was he breathing? I wrapped my arms around him and rolled him onto his back, using my hand to support his head, as I pressed my ear to his mouth. He was breathing, but it was shallow, his chest barely rising with each inhale. His face had paled more than usual so it was nearly white, and his scar stood out, red as if it had just been bleeding, but there was no sign of blood. In fact, I couldn't find evidence of any injury anywhere on his body. I ran my hands up and down his arms and over his chest, checking for cuts, bruises, or rips in his clothing. There was nothing.

Icy cold fear began to settle inside me. What if he had been akadim hunting? Getting mauled, cut, or bitten by an akadim wasn't the worst thing it could do to you. Being beaten to within an inch of death by an akadim was the best outcome one could wish for in most cases.

Akadim were known to rape their victims—sometimes alive, sometimes not. And even that wasn't their worst offense. The most horrific outcome of losing a fight to an akadim was becoming one—

becoming forsaken. They did this through soul-eating—sucking out the soul of their victim and devouring it. It had given me nightmares as a child. Even then I'd known this was a fate worse than death.

The evil act of soul-eating left only a single scar—a black circle over the victim's heart—marking the place the soul left the body.

My hands shook with fear. I had to know, had to see for myself. Rhyan showed no other sign of injury. If he'd been attacked, his skill in fighting might have left him unscathed, but his soul.... When akadim planned to create a forsaken, they left the body whole. My fingers were unsteady as I reached for the top of Rhyan's tunic. I pulled the neckline down to expose his collarbone, revealing the edges of his black gryphon tattoo, followed by his chest, his heart.

There was no mark. I slid my hand down his skin. So warm. And strong. And whole.

"Checking for a heartbeat, partner?"

I yelled, releasing Rhyan and falling on my ass beside him.

He'd lifted his head, only one eye open as he watched me, a bemused look on his face.

"You can check the wrist for a pulse in the future," he said wryly. "Unless you were just trying to steal a feel?"

"I—You're okay?" I cried out.

He lifted his good eyebrow. He looked so tired, like a ghost of his former self. His jaw and chin were lined with dark stubble, and his hair was wild with its curling waves.

I shook my head, feeling half-hysterical. "I-I was checking for a black mark. From akadim. I thought...." My heart was still hammering, and a vision of him falling flashed in my mind. "I thought that's where you were. Hunting them."

Rhyan instantly sobered, lifting himself up onto his elbows, gingerly coming into a seat. "Oh, Gods. I'm sorry. No black mark. I promise, I'm fine."

"You weren't! You fainted. And you didn't have a single cut or bruise on you. So I—Gods—"

"Lyr, I'm not hurt. I promise. Everything's fine."

I was shaking. I'd been worried all day for him, and then seeing him faint like that—Rhyan, the strongest man I knew, the most energetic, the most powerful soturion, the man I—I swallowed the thought. I couldn't think that, I couldn't feel that.

"You scared me."

"I'm sorry," he said softly. "I didn't mean to. I'm not hurt. It's okay. It's okay," he said again, his voice urgent for me to believe him. "I promise."

"Then what the hell happened?"

Rhyan rolled his head from side to side, one hand reaching to rub the nape of his neck, his bicep flexing. He groaned as he straightened, a worried look in his eyes. "It's hard to say," he said, his gaze distant. He bit his bottom lip, his eyebrow narrowed in frustration. "I don't know. It felt like someone had called on kashonim."

"I didn't."

"I know. I know what it feels like when you do." He looked up at me, the green in his eyes deepening.

"Do you think it was from your old lineage? I thought being forsworn, the line was broken."

"It was." Rhyan leaned forward, resting his elbows on his knees. His breathing was heavy, uneven. It was obvious he wasn't feeling well even though he tried to convince me otherwise.

"Were you bound to another novice?" I asked, a sharp pang in my chest as I said the words.

"No. Just you." He stared at his hands, looking uncomfortable. "The cutting…happened with my father." His jaw tensed, a haunted look in his eyes he got whenever he talked about him.

I knew then I needed to drop the subject. The idea that his previous kashonim hadn't fully broken made sense—spells were never a guarantee, and there could be endless consequences if they were not being performed correctly. A mage may have misspoken the words or been unpracticed in the spell or simply had a weak will. This could have explained how I'd drawn as much power as I had during the habibellum. Rhyan had been pale then like he was now—my calling on kashonim had depleted him of energy and power, but he'd still been able to stand upright, to carry me home afterward, and to care for me all night.

"Fuck," he said, his voice shaking.

"Maybe we can go to Scholar's Harbor," I suggested. "Check in at the Great Library, see if there's some sort of explanation. Or talk to Kolaya? Arkmages create the kashonim, maybe she'll have insight. And you can decide what you want to do from there—keep the line open or cut it off for good."

He nodded sadly. "I'll think about it."

"It could also be important for us to understand, especially if I ever—not that I'm planning to—" I was rambling, trying to find a solution to whatever this was but also sensing Rhyan's growing discomfort with the topic.

"If you ever need to call on our kashonim again," his gaze intensified, and his hand rested on my arm, "if you ever need my strength, Lyr, promise me you'll call on it."

"As long as you're safe—"

"No. I swore to keep you safe. If you need it," he said, voice low, "promise me you'll use it."

"What if I want to keep you safe?" I asked.

"I'll be fine," he said, his jaw set.

"Says the man who just fainted."

"For ten seconds," he groaned. "Just promise me."

I refused to promise what he was asking for. I would not exchange my life for his. But, since the likelihood of that situation seemed impossibly small and far away, I nodded. "Fine. Were you hunting akadim?"

Rhyan rose to his feet and gestured for me to come with him into the center of the room. I watched him carefully. He pinched the bridge of his nose, and I could see the bags under his eyes. I'd only ever seen them once before—after his all-night hunting trip to Elyria.

"I was," he said, shifting his weight from foot to foot. He seemed to be covering up a slight wobble.

"Where?" I moved toward him.

He swallowed, his lips tight. "They were back in Elyria. The same nest from before. It had been rebuilt. And…the pack has grown."

"Auriel's bane," I muttered.

"Yes," he said, that one simple word holding an infinite amount of gravity within it. "It was the same as last time. The nest was abandoned, and we destroyed it, but something's changed. Almost like they're planning or organizing. Akadim, as far as we know, have never organized themselves."

My stomach twisted. "What's causing it?"

"Either they're evolving as a species or something has learned to control them." He pushed his fingers through his hair. "I'm going to be making more trips as we head into winter. They're taking volunteers—anointed soturi and any apprentices who want to go. We're going to have to start hunting."

"Are you volunteering?" I asked, my pulse racing.

His mouth tightened again. "I have to go."

"Aemon?" I asked. "Is he forcing you?"

Rhyan shook his head.

"But you have to go on these hunting trips?"

"Lyr, there were victims in the nest. I…you don't want to know the things I've seen, the things they did to these people." He looked a little green as he spoke, squeezing his eyes shut and shaking his head as if he could shake out the images. "I have to stop the threat. It's what it means to be a soturion." Rhyan shrugged his shoulders back and shook his arms out, like he was still trying to wake up, get his energy back.

"I know what it means," I said. Rhyan had driven the lesson home on my first day: soturi stopped the threat at any cost—even if it meant not saving the life of a loved one. Everything in the warrior's life was sacrificed to kill the akadim, to keep it from killing again, to keep it from making more. "But it's not your job to kill every akadim out there. You said they're taking volunteers. But you didn't have that option? That doesn't sound like volunteering to me."

"I swore an oath. End of story. We need to start training. This whole thing has already cost you time you can't afford to waste."

If Rhyan had the ability to stop a threat, he would take it—he always acted to keep others safe. But he was also focused on my success. He knew he needed to train me, that his ability to remain in Bamaria was dependent on my ability to pass the Emperor's test. Killing an akadim before hadn't been enough to absolve him of his crimes. He'd been forced to become my bodyguard as well. Going on all these extra trips didn't make sense, they wouldn't get him back to Glemaria, they wouldn't—

"Fuck," I said, realization dawning on me. "You promised your sword to my father. Didn't you?"

A small nod was all he gave in confirmation.

"And that extends beyond being bound to me, being forced to protect me. Now you're hunting akadim for Bamaria?"

"Let's just practice, partner."

"It's not right," I said.

"Lyr, stop. I can take care of myself. I'm more than capable of handling this task. I mean, I literally came here and offered my sword after killing an akadim. Are you really surprised that I'm now being asked to stop a threat that's moving closer to Bamaria—closer to you? You had to know," he said. "I'm a killer. It's in the fine print."

"You're not a killer."

"You don't know everything about me."

"I know you're not a killer."

"Then you don't really know me."

"I'm starting to. And I know a killer wouldn't give all their power away to someone else to protect them. I know a killer wouldn't give up their mornings and nights to train and coach someone who didn't have a chance of succeeding."

"You are succeeding. We can debate semantics later. I'm tired.

I'm still your apprentice in this room, and it's time for you to listen to me," he said, voice hardening. "Begin your stretch."

We spent hours in tense silence as we moved through each position, posture, and combat move. Rhyan was adamant that his being forced to hunt akadim wasn't up for discussion, but it was clearly bothering him. Since I'd known him, I'd seen how moody he could be, how cold and withdrawn he could become when he was trying to distance himself from me. I'd seen him act this way at the start of our training and then again for those few days after my first habibellum when he'd thought he was making things worse for me. And now he was doing it again. I didn't know how to get through to him.

For dinner, we left the training room separately, eating on opposite ends of the dining hall. I watched Rhyan out of the corner of my eye. When it was time for combat clinic to begin, he still looked drained and ready to pass out. His color and energy levels hadn't improved.

I narrowed my gaze as he walked out of the dining hall and continued out to the arena. Then I remembered, it was the apprentice's turn to fight while the novices observed. Which meant…it was another habibellum.

Rhyan was going to be fighting every other apprentice—and he wasn't feeling well.

Fuck! Why didn't kashonim work both ways?

Either something had drained him of his energy, something magical, or he was working too much. He still had to complete his own training while teaching me and guarding me, and now he was hunting akadim as well, flying back and forth to Elyria to do so. Maybe even Rhyan Hart had his limits. I was going to have a word with my father about this the next time I saw him. Rhyan was forsworn, but that didn't mean he needed to be punished for it over and over again. Wasn't he doing enough for me? For Bamaria?

Galen approached the arena doors as I was about to walk through them.

"Ready for the show?" he asked.

"If you can call it that," I said, my gaze still lingering on Rhyan, who tightened the leather cuffs around his wrists and stretched his neck from side to side as he crossed the field, his stride quick and confident.

"Don't tell me you're worried about Hart," he said with a snicker.

"I—No. I'm not. I'm just tired," I lied.

Galen's eyes darkened as he looked at me carefully. "You had this look in your eyes just now. And Hal's been going on and on about Leander all day." He leaned in, his voice lowering. "Lyr, we never really established any rules—Hal and I—but," Galen frowned, "do you think that she and—"

"NO!" I yelled. Way too loudly. I softened my voice. "Of course, not. Haleika would never do something like that. Plus, Haleika likes you," I said. "She's farther than Lethea for you."

His eyes searched mine. "I thought she was. But lately—"

"No, Galen. I don't think so," I lied. "Don't worry about it. She's always been a flirt—but it's you. I'm sure of it. Tristan and I talk about it all the time."

He seemed to relax a little at that, his dark eyes moving back and forth across the arena before he turned to me, a solemn expression on his face. "Is everything all right between the two of you?"

The rumors have already started. They'll reach Tristan soon. Or worse.

Tani knew the rumors about me and Rhyan, and so did Haleika, which meant Galen knew, too. And Galen talked to Tristan. What had Tristan told him about our relationship?

I plastered on a smile. "I miss Tristan," I said wistfully. "So much. It's been hard between us with all my extra training. And, well, his grandmother, she's quite stubborn. But soon, this will all be...." My voice caught in my throat. "I just hope things calm down, so I can spend more time with him."

Galen shook his head, his expression sympathetic. "I'm so sorry, Lyr. Whatever happens with the Emperor, I know you'll be okay. Ka Grey adores you. We all do."

I blinked back a tear. He was being earnest, trying to reassure me. But he was so wrong. At least we'd moved past discussing me or Haleika breaking our oaths with our apprentices.

Apprentices who were both standing in a battlefield at this moment.

"We better get seats," I said, tugging his arm. The stadium was filling quickly, and nearly every row was occupied. Galen and I walked higher and higher through the stadium, searching for Haleika and any set of open seats. As we sat at the top row of the arena, with the crackling flames of the torches just over our heads, I realized why empty seats were so sparse.

Ka Kormac had come for entertainment. Their bodies took over the stadium, their howls erupting across the field as they cheered on their apprentice soturi. Brockton Kormac, son of the Bastardmaker and Viktor's cousin and apprentice, preened in the field's center.

The fucking bastards. They were here because we allegedly needed them for protection, because we were supposedly so un-fucking-stable that a legion of soldiers was required to keep the peace, and yet all they did was attend clinics in the arena, start fights in the streets, and sow seeds of distrust amongst the Bamarian citizens who didn't understand why they were here. I knew the story was that their presence had driven the Emartis underground, but they hadn't been underground when they'd been lighting the fields on fire last week. Nor were they capable of catching a single member leaving their feathers around or creating graffiti.

And now that a real threat had emerged—the akadim gathering, migrating, and forming larger packs—where were the Soturi of Ka Kormac? Why weren't they traveling back and forth overnight to Elyria? Why weren't they hunting the akadim in their own country when the demons had escaped to Korteria? A spare legion should have been completely devoted to stopping the threat—the real threat roaming through the Empire. But no, they were sitting here, howling and cheering like they didn't have a care in the world. Rhyan was the one being forced to risk his life.

I wanted to scream as Aemon walked onto the field, his red

arkturion cloak glowing from the silver lights of the binding circles across the arena. Aemon called the habibellum to order, and I watched in horror as Rhyan walked through to the center of the third silver ring on the field. He was now bound in the center of a five. Brockton and two other wolves from Ka Kormac joined him.

The silver rings glowed, their magic buzzing through the Katurium, the sound mixing with the howls of Ka Kormac and traveling up to where I sat.

The fight began, and immediately, every single soturion in Rhyan's circle turned on him. I leaned forward in my seat, my stomach twisting. A moment passed where no one seemed to move. There was just a huddle of soturi surrounding Rhyan. Then one soturion from Ka Elys flew backward. Their back slammed into the circle, which buzzed excitedly as the soturion screamed and slid to the ground, unconscious.

That left four soturi for Rhyan to defeat. I sucked in a breath. Any other night, I wouldn't have been worried, but he'd looked so weak, so tired, so unlike himself.

Another soturion fell, this one from Ka Daquataine. Now it was Rhyan against the three Kormac wolves. They spread out in the circle, forming a triangle around Rhyan in the center. His body was tensed and poised to fight. A moment passed, the soturi all sizing each other up.

Was it a coincidence that the full force of Ka Kormac was here rather than on duty? Or that Viktor had decided to harass me again this morning?

My heart hammered, and I noticed Galen watching me closely. I tensed my jaw, sealing my mask across my face—the neutral, beautiful, poised face of the Heir to the Arkasva. I forced a look of calm, of mere interest in the habibellum.

"Lyr, are you all right?" Galen asked.

Only then did I become aware of Tani sitting a row away, openly watching me. Another dozen soturi from Ka Elys sat around her, and each one turned my way until goosebumps ran across my arms.

You must control what they see.

"Of course," I said, clearing my throat. "I was just trying to figure out where Haleika was sitting."

Galen leaned closer. "I spotted her." He pointed halfway down our row.

Haleika's face was contorted into deep concentration and focus. I followed her gaze to Leander, who was battling a soturion from Ka Maras in Lethea. Leander charged, knocking the Lethean soturion onto their back.

"I can't believe she sat down without us," I said, trying to keep my voice lighthearted. Haleika was transfixed, and even from this distance, it was obvious who had her attention. "I'm going to get her after this. I thought friends saved seats for each other."

Galen chuckled, but his eyes remained fixed on Haleika, and he frowned as he watched her watch Leander.

"Galen, what's that maneuver called?" I pointed to a random brawl in the arena's center. Two soturi from Ka Daquataine with blonde braids were taking turns kicking and ducking.

Galen turned back to the field, humoring me with an explanation and instructions for executing the move as I pretended to listen intently. If he suspected Haleika and Leander…if anything happened to them…Rhyan and I were next, guilty or not.

Slowly, the fight took Galen's focus again. I found his apprentice on the edge of the arena and noted how Galen observed him. He seemed engrossed in the fight, but it was obvious he was looking at it from a technical perspective. When his apprentice was hit, he showed no emotional reaction, unlike me and Haleika.

I drew my gaze back to Rhyan. He stumbled. It was a slight movement, but I caught it. The biggest of the three soturi remaining advanced on him. Rhyan ducked, rolling aside, his boot thrusting into a powerful kick that knocked the soturion against the buzzing ring. He went down, immediately unconscious.

Rhyan sprang to life with a sudden burst of energy. He was moving impossibly fast, his movements precise, deadly, each strike meant to knock the opponent unconscious. And within seconds, he'd achieved that—save for one. Brockton.

By this point, every wolf from Korteria had noticed the contest between their darling Brockton and Rhyan, the forsworn from the north. The wolves yelled and clashed their swords and daggers, mimicking the drums of war.

Galen tensed beside me, and I felt Tani's eyes on me again as I strained to hear their jeers through their metallic cacophony.

"Fuck forsworn! Fuck forsworn! Fuck forsworn!" they screamed. A war cry.

Some of the apprentices across the field paused mid-battle, staring up at the chanting legion of Ka Kormac.

Even at a distance, I knew Rhyan could hear them and was being affected. I couldn't make out the features of his face, but I could see the lift of his shoulders, the tension in his body as he turned, the muscles flexing beneath his armor, his hands balled into fists.

Rhyan fired himself across the ring at Brockton. The Kormac soturion absorbed the hit, and their arms locked around each other. Rhyan pressed forward, pushing Brockton back against the ring.

"Fuck forsworn! Fuck forsworn!"

Rhyan had the upper hand. Time was almost up for the silver rings to dissolve, for each five to be freed. He could take Brockton down and then hopefully vanish into the fight, evade everyone else with his speed.

The mood of the arena shifted. Something dark tainted the habibellum, as if the aura of every soturion in Ka Kormac had joined together and was spreading like a fog across the Katurium, dark, heavy, and full of spite.

"Mother-killer! Mother-killer!"

"Northern bastard!"

"Northern fuck!"

I felt the change in Rhyan's aura the moment the chants shifted, I was so attuned to him. His aura exploded, an icy chill tampering down the darkness of Ka Kormac's presence. I shivered in my seat, my heart twisting.

"Mother-killer!"

Brockton pushed. Rhyan stumbled. He blocked a hit, then another, ducked, kicked his foot out, and missed. Then Brockton was on top of him, pressing him down, his forehead bashing into Rhyan's head.

The rings dissolved, the buzzing hum from each binding gone.

"Shit," Galen muttered. "I've never seen anyone take down Hart."

"He's having an off day."

Any other time, he would have had all five of those bastards unconscious in a minute. He would have been standing in the center of the habibellum for the four extra minutes, flicking dirt from his fingernails, looking exceptionally bored.

He was obviously still one of the best fighters in the arena, but I hated seeing this. I hated seeing him hurt. I hated seeing Brockton Kormac, of all people, get the upper hand. I hated those bastards of Ka Kormac for using his mother's death against him.

"Looks like you don't have the strongest apprentice anymore," Tani yelled.

I stared straight ahead.

"Where's your boyfriend?" she called. "No one here to defend you?"

Rhyan rolled out from under Brockton as the screams grew louder. They were cursing Rhyan, yelling obscenities, and calling him a mother-killer, a murderer, weak, a traitor, a criminal, and…a whore.

"What?" I said under my breath. *Where did that come from?*

Rhyan threw his arms above his head. His hands gripped the ground as his legs kicked out, and he flew back to his feet. There was something reckless in his movements now as he charged at Brockton. This time, the bastard was ready for him and kicked out so hard Rhyan flew backwards, breaking a fight between two Bamarian soturi. All three collapsed to the ground before they saw

Brockton and rolled away, leaping to their feet and leaving Rhyan behind.

Brockton was on top of him again as the chants of "Whore!" and "Mother-killer!" intensified. Brockton slammed his fist into Rhyan's face. Rhyan turned. Brockton reared back, his mouth opened wide, teeth bared, before he threw his head down on Rhyan. He clamped down on his forehead. Gods! He was biting Rhyan's scar.

Rhyan's scream pierced through me, and without realizing it, I was screaming, too.

"Out of bounds! He's out-of-fucking-bounds!"

Galen grabbed my arm, holding me back from flying out of my seat, but I couldn't stop screaming as Rhyan fought back, trying to pry Brockton's mouth from his face.

All fighting was supposed to be below the neck, and this was Brockton's third attack on Rhyan's face.

Galen kept his hold on me, his deep voice now carrying across the stadium, yelling for Dairen's and Aemon's attention, but we were drowned out by the jeers and howls of Ka Kormac.

I screamed louder, and then I heard Haleika. As soon as she yelled, Leander froze, turning toward her in a move I prayed no one else had noticed. How he'd heard her through the racket...Gods. But then he saw Rhyan on the ground and took off, throwing Brockton backwards, crouching over Rhyan until he got him to his feet. They locked arms, Leander supporting Rhyan's weight as he steadied him. Blood dripped down the left side of his face.

I covered my mouth with my hands as Leander punched Brockton, and some other Kormac soturion who was attempting to join the fight.

Rhyan stumbled from Leander's grip, his arm reared back. His fist flew forward, smashing Brockton in the face. Brockton's head snapped a second before his body flew backward, knocking over another soturion. Neither got back up. Leander rejoined Rhyan's side. The two shared a nod, and then positioned themselves to fight back-to-back.

I turned to Haleika. Her focus was intent on our apprentices, but somehow she must have felt my gaze, as she turned.

"Thank you," I mouthed.

Her expression was sorrowful as she offered a single nod.

But as Galen continued watching her, staring straight past me, his expression full of curiosity and jealousy, I wasn't sure how long our secrets could remain hidden.

CHAPTER
THIRTEEN

The moment the habibellum ended and I could leave without being reported to the Imperator, I was gone. I needed to get to Rhyan, to make sure he was all right. Leander had stayed by his side for the rest of the fight, but Rhyan had taken some brutal hits, his feet dragging as he'd left the field.

Haleika began flirting with Galen as soon as we were inside the halls. She grabbed his arm, hung on his every word, and laughed and smiled so genuinely even I started to believe she was completely in love with Galen.

The halls were overcrowded with novices and apprentices, plus the bastards of Ka Kormac, moving slowly, their voices loud. I kept my hood up, blending into the crowd of soturi surrounding me. Most were discussing plans to meet in the city for drinks.

I weaved through the rounded halls unseen, breaking apart from the crowd, keeping my hood up until I reached our training room. Rhyan sat slumped on the floor, his head tilted against the wall, a blood-soaked cloth over his face.

"Hey," I said, closing the door behind me. He didn't move or respond. I was by his side instantly, sinking to my knees. "Let me look at that for you."

His jaw worked, his throat moving, as he turned his head away from me. It broke my heart.

"It's okay," I said gently, keeping my hands to myself. I knew how important it was for him to feel in control. "I'm going to help you."

He sucked in a shaky breath, turning his head ever so slightly toward me and opening his right eye, which was swollen and blood-shot. "I meant to come meet you," he said roughly. "I need to get you home."

"Forget about that. We need to take care of you first."

He scoffed, but the sound was weak, like he barely had any energy. "I'm your guard tonight," he said, his voice low and scratchy and hardly more than a whisper.

"I thought you had the morning shift."

"Had to switch...." He trailed off, too tired to finish. One hand lifted as if to explain and then fell back against his knee. "Other plans this morning."

"Rhyan," I sighed. "Forget it. You're off duty. Taking care of you right now is more important. How about you give me five minutes to be your bodyguard?"

He made a noise low in his throat. "You haven't applied for the position."

"I doubt that's necessary," I said, trying to keep the banter going, knowing he needed it to distract himself from the pain. But seeing him like this, seeing what Brockton had done to him, was slicing through my heart.

"And your qualifications to be a bodyguard?" He lifted his good eyebrow.

I gave him my most patronizing look. "I know how to hold a protective stance, and in less than thirty seconds, I can contort my face to look very serious and grumpy." I spoke in an exaggerated northern lilt.

A small smile barely crossed his lips before it faded, and he closed his eyes. "Partner, do whatever you want to me. But a formal evaluation of the grumpiness of your face is coming."

He still sounded exhausted, but at least he was engaging with me.

"I'd expect nothing less," I said. "Let me see. Please. I promise I'll be gentle."

"Okay."

I pulled the cloth from his hand to reveal the left side of his face.

His eyes were on mine instantly, his mouth tight and his body still. I let out a shuddering breath, trying to stay calm, trying not to make him feel any worse. But there were bite marks all around his eye. Fucking bite marks. His scar was irritated, raised, and shining in a sickly pink. Blotchy red skin, bruised and bleeding, spread from his forehead to his cheekbone. I wanted to kill Brockton.

"That bad?" he joked. "Doesn't matter. That side was already mangled from my father. He said after he gave it to me, 'Now the outside matches what's within.'" Rhyan deepened his voice to match his father's, then laughed. "What's a few more scars?"

"Your father's the one that gave this to you?" I asked, horrified. No wonder he hated the scar so much.

"Mmmhmm. The night my mother…." he trailed off again, his eyes squeezing shut, his nose scrunching like he was trying to hold back some emotion. I squeezed his arm, my hand sliding down to his. Our fingers entwined, our palms pressing together.

I knew what he couldn't say. His father had scarred him the night his mother died.

"I'm going to kill him," I said.

"Which him?" Rhyan asked.

"Both," I snarled. "Brockton and your father." I wanted to kill anyone who had ever laid a finger on Rhyan. I wanted to rip those fingers from their hands one by one, to crush all the bones in their hands and arms.

"I'd like to be there for that," he said, but there was none of the usual snark in his voice, just bone-weary exhaustion. Even his aura felt stagnant, its usual coolness barely leaving his body. "You get first punch. I'll take second."

I released his hand and reached into his opened bag to grab a fresh towel. Using his water bottle to splash clean water onto it, I sopped up what remained of the blood on his face. When I was satisfied he was cleaned, I peered down at the bites, knowing I needed to clean out any bacteria that might have gotten in there, especially from Brockton's disgusting mouth.

Rhyan had been still while I'd cleaned his wounds, but sensing what came next, he opened his eyes, and his hand reached past me into his bag. Our fingers brushed as he found the bottle he needed and pushed it into my hand.

"Don't warn me," he said. "I know it hurts."

"I'm sorry," I said, unscrewing the lid. I poured its contents onto a fresh cloth and lightly dabbed at the toothmarks around his eye. His nostrils flared, and there was a twitch in his right hand, but other than that, he was stoically still as I worked.

"For the record, your father was wrong," I said, moving the cloth as gently yet thoroughly as I could.

"About what?" he asked, wincing as I attacked a particularly deep toothmark.

"I'd wager everything he's ever said to you, but let's start with the scar and it matching you on the inside." I paused in my ministrations, catching his eye. "You're beautiful, Rhyan. You were before you were scarred. You are after. And you're so, so beautiful inside." I kept cleaning his wound, wanting to finish the job quickly. "His opinion of you, of everything, is total and utter gryphon-shit."

His hand found mine again and squeezed just once before lowering.

Satisfied I'd kept him from infection, I grabbed a bottle of cured sunleaves and smoothed the golden paste over his forehead and cheekbone. I bandaged both areas and applied sunleaves to the scratch across his nose. He kept his gaze fixed ahead, his eyes barely blinking.

"All done," I said at last.

"Thanks partner," he said quietly. He pushed himself off the wall, starting to stand, but wobbled as he did so.

"Hey," I said, jumping up. I wrapped my arms around his waist, and he leaned his weight against me.

He coughed and straightened, running a hand up the side of his face, the shadows of his stubble darker than before. "I'm fine," he said. "Let's get you back to your apartment."

"How are you feeling?" I asked.

"I'm patched up. No more scarring," he said dryly.

"That's not what I meant," I said. "What they were shouting out there—Ka Kormac—that was a lot. A lot you didn't need to hear, you didn't deserve to hear. And, I don't know, I just wanted to see if you needed to talk."

He grunted in response. And I noticed him scratching at his right palm.

"Is your hand okay?" I asked, reaching for it.

Rhyan fisted his hand. "Just an itch." His gaze met mine and I felt there was something he wasn't telling me.

"I'm here if you do want to talk. You know that, right?"

"I'm just ready for the day to be over," he said.

"I get that."

We moved slowly through the city, huddling into ourselves as the wind picked up. There seemed to be shouts of victory from Ka Kormac coming from everywhere, leaving chills running down my spine. There had been no victory. Despite Brockton sinking his teeth into Rhyan, Rhyan had still bested their soturi in the end. But I could hear their howling through every open bar and restaurant window we passed.

We reached my apartment door together, but before I could unlock it, Rhyan put a hand on my shoulder, his fingers firm as he gently tugged me back. The door had been left ajar.

"Did you lock it this morning?" he asked, eyes jumping back and forth, assessing our surroundings.

"Of course," I said, my stomach twisting.

"Wait here." He stepped in front of me, angling his body to brace himself against any threat that came from inside. He held his hand up to stop me from following him, his body shifting protectively in front of me. "Lyr, just wait until I know it's safe."

"I'm coming with you," I said. "You're two seconds from falling over."

"I'm not going to fall over," he hissed.

"And I'm not waiting."

"Can I do my Godsdamned job and protect you?" He inched forward, one hand on the hilt of his sword, the other reaching out to block me. "Fuck, Lyr! Stop! If you won't obey my orders as your bodyguard, then remember I outrank you as apprentice. Obey that!"

"Rhyan—"

His hand closed around mine, and our fingers interlocked. His grip tightened, and I stepped forward. It was an unspoken acknowledgment that neither of us would win this argument, so we were going in together, and we'd watch each other's backs.

I slowed my breathing, wanting to be as silent as Rhyan as we stepped into my apartment. We moved soundlessly through each room, lighting candles as we went until the entire space was glowing in flickering candlelight.

Every corner was inspected, every door checked. There was no one here. And by the looks of it, nothing had been taken—no coins, none of the gold jewelry I'd left out. But when we brought the candle into my bedroom, we discovered that whoever had been in here hadn't come to take something from me. They'd come to leave something behind. A message.

There was a bulge beneath the covers of my bed. Rhyan squeezed my hand before releasing it and stepping in front of me, his body shielding mine. I sucked in a breath as he pulled the blanket back.

"Fuck," he cursed, his hand shooting out again to protect me as he stepped back.

I side-stepped him, peering over his arm, and covered my mouth with my hands. A baby seraphim's severed head had been stuffed under the covers, its feathers painted black. Red blood, tinged with the darkened paint, was still running from its neck onto my sheets.

I ran to the bathroom, bile rising up my throat.

"Lyr!" Rhyan chased after me.

I heaved as I reached the toilet, but nothing came out. I gripped the edge of the seat, dizzy, feeling like the walls were closing in on me, the ceiling sinking.

No, no, no.

"Lyr?" Rhyan asked, stepping in the bathroom behind me. "Lyr, you're all right. I'm right here. I've got you."

I spit and wiped my mouth, standing slowly, my pulse racing, heart pounding, a sick feeling still washing through me as I washed my hands and face.

"It's okay. Come here," he said, pulling me to him. "Come here to me. Breathe."

I buried my face in his neck. His arms wrapped tightly around me. The broad expanse of his chest, his warmth, his scent—it all began to wrap around me, to absorb my senses, to slow my breathing, to bring me back from the brink of panic.

"You can't stay here tonight," he said, rubbing my back. He stopped and cupped the nape of my neck. "I'm going to get you somewhere safe."

I nodded against him, swallowing back the rising bile. I was tired of falling apart, tired of being affected like this. "I thought with all the new protections in place, this wasn't supposed to happen anymore. Arianna was looking into it, every protection was doubled. How are they getting in here? And...Gods...how could they do something like that? To a baby?" Tears burned my eyes as the image flashed before them again. My entire body was shaking.

Rhyan held me tighter, making soft shushing sounds against my ear. "Hey, partner. Hey, I've got you," he said. "I've got you."

He led me out of the bathroom, away from my bedroom, and into the living room, where he sat me down on the couch. He sat beside me and wrapped one arm around me as his free hand moved to the vadati stone in his belt pocket.

"Aemon," he said, holding the stone before his lips. His voice was clipped with the anger that hadn't faded for the arkturion's role in my whipping. The stone glowed milky white before swirling into a shimmering blue that shined against his skin.

"Hart," Aemon's voice called through the stone. "What happened?"

"Apartment breach. Place is empty. No sign of forced entry or the intruder. Her grace is secure. Nothing stolen. Emartis left another message."

"What was it?" Aemon asked, the stone brightening with his voice.

Rhyan frowned, his eyes on me before he said, "Seraphim head. Baby's. Painted black."

"Fuck," he said. "She with you?"

"I have her," Rhyan said.

"Fuck," Aemon said again. This time I could hear the shift in his voice, the subtle change that marked him as the Ready. "Give me a minute."

The stone stopped glowing, the blue fading until the light inside vanished.

"You all right there, partner?" Rhyan asked, his arm tightening around me.

"I just want to get out of here." I felt dirty, gross, and violated. And like I'd never be able to sleep in my own bed again.

"I'm working on it," he said. "You want something to drink?" He was already standing, facing my kitchen.

I shook my head, noting the bags under his eyes and the way his skin was still pale, aware of how fresh the wounds under his bandages were.

"What about you?" I asked. "Rhyan, you need to sit down. Do you need anything?"

He shook his head quickly. "Not until you're sorted out and safe."

I was about to offer him something to eat anyway—he needed it no matter how much he denied it—but the stone began to shine with light again, returning to a bright, glowing moonstone blue in Rhyan's hand.

"Hart," Aemon's voice came through clearly.

"Arkturion," he replied coolly, returning to his seat beside me, his body stiff. "How do I proceed?"

"Her grace is not cleared for seraphim travel given the Emartis's penchant for sky tactics. Let her know Cresthaven's secure. No threats discovered. Fortress security has doubled and will remain so overnight."

Rhyan looked at me carefully as Aemon's message sank in. I'd spent so many years protecting my sisters, being the shield between them and danger, it was so weird to think that I was the target, that I was the one who needed protecting.

"We don't have many options for her right now." The stone glowed blue again as Aemon's voice came through. "And I'm not risking her out in the streets."

Rhyan frowned. "She can't stay here."

"Hart, I want you to take her to your apartment," Aemon ordered. "It's the nearest safe spot. We'll have her place cleaned up tonight, locks changed, new wards cast. I already have an escort team surrounding her building. Half are going to give you back up. They'll follow and stay outside your building all night. Let me know when you're inside—her grace secured, the door locked."

"Will do," Rhyan said. The stone went white, and he replaced it in his belt. "I'm going to pack an overnight bag for you, so you don't have to...go in there."

I nodded, still shaken, watching as Rhyan got off the couch. I focused on taking deep breaths, inhaling and exhaling. I stared at the flickering flame of the candle on my coffee table, watching the smoke tendrils swirl sinuously into nothing.

"You're all set," Rhyan said, closing my bedroom door behind him. He had a large overnight bag slung over his shoulder. "Change of clothes, hairbrush, and...basically every item I found in your bathroom. If you need anything else, I'll provide it."

I stood at once, moving toward him, my arm outstretched. "I'll carry the bag," I said.

"I've got it."

"You're exhausted," I said. "Let me."

"And you've just been through...." He shook his head. "Absolutely not. I've got it. Let's go."

Back in Rhyan's apartment, I paced the living room as he boiled water for tea. I hadn't been here since I'd been lashed and spent the night two months ago. I peeked at his bedroom door—slightly ajar. In the corner was Rhyan's single bed, the bed I'd slept in that night, my open wounds bleeding all over it.

We sat down for tea, silent as we'd been since we'd left my place. I watched Rhyan as he sipped. His color was starting to return, and after attacking a bowl of nuts, an apple, hummus with pita, and three hardboiled eggs, it looked like some of his energy was refueling. But he was still nowhere near the Rhyan I interacted with on a daily basis. He looked far weaker than he had after he'd given me his kashonim.

"You take the bed," he said when we were finished.

"No," I said. "You were hurt today, you're exhausted. You need your bed. I'll stay on the couch."

"Lyr, I am too fucking tired to argue with you."

"Exactly! You fainted earlier! So don't fight me."

"You don't fight me. You're taking the bed. And if you don't, I will simply wait until you're asleep, and when you are, I will move you there myself. So you decide. Bed now or later."

"What if I don't go to sleep?" I asked. "What if I wait for you to pass out?"

"You won't. Because we had a deal. You get enough sleep to train. Tonight is no exception."

"And how am I supposed to train with you if you're not getting any sleep?"

"I'll recover. Far faster than you will."

"No!"

He ran his hands through his stubble, up his scalp until his fingers were in his hair. "Myself to Moriel—you are so fucking stubborn."

"And you're not? Rhyan, look at you. You were in Elyria

overnight, a whole other country, hunting akadim. You were beaten up in the habibellum, and now you're forced to have me here. The least I can do is let you sleep in your own bed."

"I've told you." His neck was turning red. "I'll worry about me. You worry about you."

"So only you get to do the caring part?" I snapped.

"When you let me!" His jaw tightened, nostrils flaring with a sigh of exasperation. "I'm not changing my mind. You can decide. Either we both get some sleep tonight, or neither of us do. But I am not sleeping in my bed."

"Fine!" I grabbed my bag and marched into his room, slamming the door behind me. I changed out of my practice clothes and into the nightshift he'd packed for me. I let the door fly open as I went to the bathroom to wash my face and brush my teeth.

I sat on top of his blankets, noting his bed was made, unslept in from the night before, and tried to think of something else to say to him, some way to relieve the tension between us. I felt guilty taking his bed, and yet, the day had left me exhausted, too. And I knew how stubborn he was—how seriously he took his word once he'd given it. His word was his promise, his promise was his oath, and his oath was his soul.

I stood and grabbed the edge of the covers, about to pull them back, when suddenly, I was back in my room again, seeing the baby seraphim's head, the blood and the black feathers—

I jumped back, letting go of the covers like they'd bitten me.

"What's wrong?" Rhyan's frame appeared in the doorway.

"Um, nothing," I said, embarrassed. Fuck. It was just a blanket. There wasn't even a bulge in it—the cover had been smoothed perfectly against his mattress and sheets, the edges tucked with perfect precision into the corners. There was nothing here. No message from the Emartis, no threats. Just Rhyan's soft, warm bed.

His gaze narrowed on me. "Partner, if this is some attempt to get me to—"

I backed away from the bedframe, and his expression softened.

"Oh. It's all right. I'll pull the blankets back."

I squeezed my eyes shut, pressing my palms against my temples. "I'm sorry, this is so stupid."

He stood before me. His hands wrapped gently around my fists, pulling my hands down to my sides. My heart pounded, and my stomach clenched as he continued to touch me, his palms turning to press against my palms until our fingers twined together.

"No, it's not. Not stupid at all," he said. "What just happened, that was all kinds of fucked up. I don't know what kind of monster could...." He sighed. "That would have shaken anybody. Don't be embarrassed. You didn't deserve to have that happen to you. You deserve to feel safe in your home, in your bed. I'm sorry they took that from you."

"You deserve that, too," I said.

Rhyan's eyes darkened, hooded with desire. And suddenly I could feel it. I was alone with him, in his room. His scent was everywhere, all musk and pine. In his bedsheets, on him...and I wanted him. He bit his lip, his breathing slowing as his gaze dipped down my body, taking in the nightshift that barely covered my chest and fell to mid-thigh. His fingers tightened around mine, his thumbs rubbing circles against my skin.

He coughed, releasing my hands. "I've got it," he said, pulling the covers back for me. "All clear. You're safe. Get some rest."

Then he stormed out of the room, closing the door behind him.

My breath hitched. Fuck. My desire for him...it was always there, lurking under the surface. But we'd become so practiced during training at ignoring it, keeping our flirtation down to a minimum. For two long months, we'd done everything we could to maintain the unspoken boundary between us. Almost like we were actors playing roles in a performance. The teacher and student, the apprentice and novice, the bodyguard and his charge. Rhyan and Lyr ceased to exist as we put on the masks of two people who had a job to complete and nothing else. But the closeness, the bond between us—it was always just under the surface, ready to bubble up at a moment's notice, only for us to take turns squashing it back down.

I climbed into his bed, inhaling his scent, letting it cocoon me alongside his blankets as I snuggled deeper into the pillows. I turned on my side, blowing out the candle he'd lit on his nightstand, and pulled the covers over my shoulders as I stared at the door, hoping he was all right out there. I hoped he'd get the rest and peace he so desperately needed and deserved. I wished I could give it to him. And...I wished that his arms were wrapped tightly around me, holding me, pulling me closer, instead of just his blanket.

I listened to his footsteps on the other side of the door and watched the tiny lights and dancing flames from the candles flickering beneath the edge of the doorframe. I followed their sinuous movements until all the lights were vanquished, and there was only silence, save for the bells ringing out the midnight hour. I fell asleep.

Cold. I was so cold. I was wandering in the woods, lost, calling out for help. My limbs ached; my entire body was freezing. I had to get out of here, find help, find shelter, find warmth before I froze to death. Snow fell upon my head.

I opened my eyes. I'd been dreaming, but the freezing cold of my dream had been real. My teeth chattered, and I drew the blankets up higher around me, looking to see if the window had been left open. I huddled down, deeper into the blankets. Winter was weeks away, but it never got this cold in Bamaria—even in the dead of the wintry season. There was a gust of wind blowing, howling ferociously. But not against the window—the sound was beating against the bedroom door. I threw the blanket off and hugged my arms across my chest. My entire body shook as I got out of bed. Something icy and wet pushed through the door against my bare feet.

Snow. It was snowing inside Rhyan's apartment.

I opened the door and rushed into the living room. Snow fell from the ceiling, and wind pulled the snowflakes into a cyclone. The force of the gusts increased, rushing toward me. A glass of water that had been left on the coffee table had frozen into a glass of ice. And lying deep in the center of the storm was Rhyan.

He sat on the couch, his head fallen back onto the cushion like he'd been stubbornly trying not to sleep but had passed out anyway. His eyes were squeezed shut as if he were in pain, and he thrashed, his body jerking.

"No!" he yelled, his face contorted with anguish. "No! Don't! Don't!"

"Rhyan!" I yelled.

"Don't touch her," he snarled.

Rhyan was having a nightmare. A nightmare terrible enough for his aura to summon a blizzard.

CHAPTER
FOURTEEN

"Rhyan!" My teeth chattered as I fought my way across the living room. Snow battered against my nightshift and my bared legs and arms, as the cold bit at my face. "RHYAN!" I reached the couch, crawled onto it beside him, and shook his arms. His skin was like ice, shaking and thrashing. He'd taken off his shirt before he'd fallen asleep, and his chest was turning blue, the black wing tips of his gryphon tattoo standing out in stark contrast.

"No! No!" he screamed. "Don't!"

I was starting to lose the feeling in my hands, my fingers growing painfully numb as the temperature continued to plummet. I shook him again, but I wasn't getting through to him, and his skin was even colder than mine. It was painful to touch, almost burning like the silver bindings in the arena.

"Rhyan!" I yelled again. I straddled his lap and pushed my body as close to his as I could. I wrapped my arms around his neck and pressed my face against his chest, desperate to create warmth between us, hoping to give him some of mine before I lost it all and hoping my weight would startle him awake. I squeezed him tighter, rocking against him, and yelled into his ear, "Rhyan! Wake up!"

One second, I was sitting on his lap, the next, he'd pinned me beneath him, his body pressed over mine across the couch, my legs wrapped around his waist. His hand reached for my neck as his hips pressed deep against mine. I gasped, pushing against him.

His eyes sprang open, and for a few seconds, he looked confused, like he was caught somewhere between wakefulness and the images of his nightmare.

"Rhyan," I said. "Rhyan, it's me." I coughed; his grip on my neck had tightened.

"Fuck," he said, eyes widening, finally awake. The wind vanished, and the snow stopped falling, leaving behind only whatever had already accumulated on top of us. "What?" His green eyes raced back and forth across my face as a look of horror filled his expression. "Lyr!" He pulled his hand from my neck like he'd been burned and sat back, looking horrified.

"What—What just—Are you all right? Gods! Did I hurt you?"

"No." I sat forward, pushing down my shift, which had risen nearly to my waist.

Rhyan was breathing heavily, staring at me in a mix of horror, shame, confusion, and…desire. I wrapped my arms around myself, the cold now deep in my bones.

"You were having a nightmare," I said. "I was trying to wake you."

He planted his feet back on the ground, elbows on his knees as he leaned forward and buried his face in his hands. "Fuck. Lyr, I'm sorry."

I inched closer to him, making an effort to keep my teeth from chattering. "It's not your fault. You can't control that."

He shook his head, still in his hands. "I wasn't supposed to fall asleep."

"What?" I pressed a hand to his shoulder.

His shoulders rose and fell, but he kept his face hidden.

"Rhyan, hey, come on. Talk to me."

He looked up, face full of anguish. "I didn't want you to experience that." He took a deep breath, his chest heaving. "I get these nightmares—usually it's not a big deal when I'm by myself. The storm stays…with me. Gods." He leaned forward, brushing his hand through my hair, his fingers light against my neck.

Snowflakes fell onto my shoulders. I shivered.

"I'm sorry," he said. "I should have stayed awake."

"Rhyan, you need to sleep, too. It's okay," I said, but he only shook his head again. "What about the other nights we were together? When I stayed here? And the night you guarded me in the Shadow Stronghold?"

His jaw clenched as he shifted his body to face mine. "I didn't sleep," he admitted. "I stayed up for both of those nights."

"Rhyan."

"Lyr, I was on duty both times. Guarding you, protecting you. I couldn't sleep even if I wanted to."

"You needed to sleep tonight, though." I slid my hand down his arm to his hand, taking it in mine.

"Usually, I'm not so drained. But between the Elyria trip and the habibellum," he groaned in frustration, "I didn't recover fast enough for my energy to return."

"Because you haven't slept in two nights. You might be the strongest soturion I've ever met, but even you need to rest."

He closed his eyes, giving a mirthless laugh.

"Do you—do you want to talk about it? Your nightmare?"

He frowned. "My father. My last night in Glemaria. It was," he exhaled through his mouth, his fingers twitching in my hand, "it was not so much a nightmare as it was a memory." He looked away.

"You remembered your mother?"

"It was my fault," he said, almost too quietly for me to hear. "I watched. I couldn't save her. I couldn't…it happened so quickly. There were witnesses—a dozen sentries, his personal guard. They watched him cut her down and swore one by one that my blade had done it."

I squeezed his hand.

"I wasn't fast enough for her, for me—to stop this." His eyes flicked up to his scar. "I fucked up. That night. This night."

I leaned toward him. "You didn't fuck anything up tonight. Or that night."

"Yes, I did."

"No," I said firmly. "You didn't. You couldn't have saved her. Your father's the Imperator, he stacked the deck against you. He knew how strong you were, how strong you were becoming. He knew you were growing stronger than him every single day. And he needed a dozen bought-and-paid-for sentries to stand between you and him." I was almost yelling now, so fueled with anger and hatred for his father and so desperate for Rhyan to see how faultless he was. "What happened wasn't your fault. It was his."

"I tell myself that. And yet, I still feel like shit. Still have these dreams."

"You won't always. I don't know when it'll stop, but I know you won't always feel this way." The pain I felt for Jules hadn't changed, but somewhere in the last few months, some of the guilt, some of the shame, had begun to lessen. To eat at me less in the moments I was alone. "But even so, Rhyan, this doesn't make you weak," I said gently. "You don't always have to be the strongest one."

He bit down on his lip. "I didn't know it was you when I woke up." His eyes were on my neck, his hand twitching again in mine. "Are you sure I didn't hurt you?"

"I'm sure, I promise."

"Let me, um," he cleared his throat, pulling his hand away. "Let me find you an extra blanket."

He stood from the couch, but I reached out, taking his hand back and squeezing it. "Rhyan, come to bed with me."

His eyes widened. "What?"

"Just to sleep," I said. "As friends."

He shook his head, almost violently. "No. We can't."

"Rhyan, you need sleep. So do I. You can't stay out here, you'll freeze. And I will, too, if you have another nightmare. Just come with me. I'll watch over you, wake you up if I need to."

"Lyr," he pleaded, his voice almost desperate. "It's a bad idea."

"Why? It sounds like the perfect solution."

"Lyr, stop." He jerked his hand away from mine. "Just go back to bed. I can't be in there with you. I don't trust myself right now. I'm not in a good place."

"I trust you."

"Well, you shouldn't."

"You don't get to tell me that. I do trust you, and I'll trust you enough for the both of us if I have to. You deserve that trust, you've more than earned it. As well as my friendship and my caring about you."

"Lyr, no. If you'd seen my dreams, if you knew the horrors in my memories—I'm not good."

"Yes, you are. This isn't you. This isn't the Rhyan I know. You were dreaming about your past—about a Rhyan who isn't here anymore. About a Rhyan who was living under a tyrant and did whatever he had to do to survive. You're not there anymore. You tore that rope apart, remember? You're good."

"No! Don't you get it? I've killed before, killed with my bare hands."

"Akadim."

"People! My own people when I fled. And you know the rumors. They're all true. I killed one of my friends with my bare hands. *My friend.*"

"I don't believe you."

"Then how about this?" he said, stepping in front of me. His arms wrapped around my waist, pulling my body flush against his as he walked me back into the wall, pushing against me, his hips pressed to mine. I could feel him then. And he was hard, so fucking hard.

Heat pooled between my legs, my core clenching at the feel of him, his length thick and pressing up against my belly. My nipples peaked, feeling the growing warmth of his bare chest through the fabric of my shift. I stared up into his eyes, my breath hitching at the sight of his hooded gaze full of heat and desire. It was enough to melt the remaining chills from my skin. If Rhyan had been frozen a moment ago, he was burning with fire now, flames threatening to consume me.

"Do you know how much I want you?" he growled. "How much I want to throw you on the bed, tear this off of you," he lifted the hem of my shift, pulling it up my thigh, "and fuck you until the sun rises and sets again?"

I sucked in a breath, my heart threatening to hammer through my chest into his.

"Every second I spend with you, I grow closer and closer to breaking my oath." He leaned in, his lips just a breath away from mine, his hand clenching my shift, pulling it higher and higher.

I lifted on my toes, pressing my body closer against his, not caring that this was reckless, not caring that we were both farther than Lethea and there were a hundred reasons why I needed to stop this—oaths, politics, the Emartis, Tristan....

But I wanted Rhyan. I'd wanted him for years. I was losing patience, losing focus, losing control, crawling out of my skin with need and heat and a soul-deep desire that felt like it would swallow me whole one day. Every part of me was lit by a living flame that breathed through my blood, beat through my heart.

Oath be damned. All I could feel was his heated desire, his breath, and the delicious way he was pressing against me, exactly where I needed him to. His hips rolled forward to make his point until I gasped. He lifted my leg around his waist and pushed me up against the wall until both my legs wrapped around him. His hands were on my ass as he ground into me. His lips pressed against my collarbone as he inhaled, a shaky sigh escaping his mouth like he was dizzy from my scent. His lips whispered against my neck, trailing up to my ear until my entire body shivered.

"Tell me," he commanded, "is this what you want? For me to throw everything we've worked for out to sea? For me to take you like this?"

I exhaled my own shaky breath, my chest heaving from exertion like I'd just finished a run. My heart squeezed at his question.

There he was, rising to the surface under all his anger and

desire. There was my Rhyan. My Rhyan who would never do anything without my permission. My Rhyan who was losing control because of his grief and stress and anger and desire but still managed to check in with me.

"You have so much to lose if you give into me, partner. But I don't. I'm already forsworn. Why not break every last oath I have?" he said, his breath hot against my ear.

"No." I pushed my hand against his chest.

Rhyan set me down, strode across the room, and slammed his fist into the wall.

I didn't doubt his desire for me in that moment, only his intention. After the day and night he'd had, he'd gone to a dark place. A place I could only guess he'd inhabited under his father's cruelty and possibly also when he'd spent a year exiled from the Empire. He was bluffing—trying to prove he was bad—to convince me of the darkest thoughts racing through his mind, thoughts that had been planted by his father, thoughts that were completely, utterly false.

"You did that on purpose," I yelled. "You're on such a path of self-destruction that you're even trying to convince me you're not good because some stupid voice got into your head. You really want me to let you wallow out here, not sleeping and sinking deeper? You think after all these months, I don't know you? That I don't care so fucking deeply for you that it hurts? Do you still truly believe you're not worthy of being part of my life? That even as complicated as it all is, you're the best part?"

"The best part of your life can't be some criminal, killer forsworn," he said, sinking to his knees.

I crossed the room and crouched behind him, wrapping my arms around his waist, resting my hands on his stomach, pressing my head against his back. "Rhyan, you are so much more than your oath. I'm not letting you do this to yourself. Or to me. Please, come to bed. If you really want to prove how awful and forsworn you are, then this is it. Stay awake, be exhausted, don't train me tomorrow. Don't give me every chance I have before the Emperor's test. But I don't think that's what you really want. To prove your father right?

The Imperator? To let him win? You're stronger than him. I know you are. You need to remember yourself." I traced the tattoo across his back. "Remember you tore the rope."

He sat back on his heels and turned to face me. I reached out a hand to his forehead, my finger gingerly tracing the path of his scar beneath his bandage. My hand stopped at his cheek, and I let him rest the weight of his head against my palm.

"This doesn't define you," I said. "It doesn't take away from who you are. It never has. And for me, it never will."

His face fell. "Gods," he said, shoulders slumping. "I'm sorry."

"I know," I said. "It's okay."

"Not after what I just did to you."

I stood, reaching my hand out to his in response. He watched my hand, wary, his expression full of guilt before at last, his fingers wrapped around mine as he stood. We silently walked back to his bedroom, and I closed the door behind us. I crawled into bed first, pressing my back against the wall and holding the covers up for him. The mattress dipped beside me as he slid onto the sheets. He lay on his side with his back to me as he adjusted the blankets to cover the two of us evenly.

His shoulders shook as he released a shuddering breath.

I pulled him closer, my arm curved around his waist, my hand on his stomach. "I've got you." I hugged him against me, and slowly his shaking subsided, and his breathing became even.

He squeezed my hand. A small acknowledgement, a thank you that I knew he was too tired and too emotional to voice. I squeezed back.

"You can rest now. Let go for the night," I said. "I'm right here, watching over you. I'll keep the cold away."

Moments passed in silence as his breaths slowed and the tension in his shoulders released.

I closed my eyes, ready to sleep at last.

I woke with a start, the room black. A chill ran through me as Rhyan shifted beneath the covers. I tightened my grip on him, reaching under his body until he was wrapped in both my arms.

"Shhhh, Rhyan. It's just a dream." I stroked his forehead, smoothing his hair back, my fingers tracing the delicate shape of his ear until his breathing slowed again. I pulled my arm out from under him, pressed myself tighter against him, and closed my eyes.

"You're…fire," he whispered.

"What?" I froze.

But Rhyan didn't respond or stir again. He was sleeping deeply in my arms.

CHAPTER
FIFTEEN

The sun streamed in through the window, casting a golden-reddish glow behind my eyelids. I didn't want to be awake yet. It was too early. I was too tired. And I was so wonderfully warm and cozy. I hugged the pillow in my arms tighter, trying to burrow my face into it, to hide from the day, to sleep just a little longer. Except it was definitely not a pillow I was holding, nor a pillow under my head. It was something far larger, sturdier, and warmer.

My eyes flew open. I was laying across Rhyan's chest. His arms were wrapped around me, and his hands were on my back, holding me close.

The events of last night flashed through my mind. I'd been holding Rhyan as we'd drifted off, and somehow, in the middle of the night, we'd shifted until I was the one in his arms, and it was my head resting on his chest.

I shuddered, closing my eyes, not wanting to wake up, not wanting the spell to be broken.

But Rhyan's chest rose beneath my head, and a small moan escaped him as he stretched his legs, his arms tightening around me. "Morning, partner."

I opened my eyes, embarrassed to be on top of him. Quickly, I rolled out of his arms and onto my side as far away from him as the bed would allow. Which wasn't much. He turned toward me, one hand beneath his pillow, the other resting on the sheets between us. Our eyes met.

"Morning." I tried not to stare at his naked chest, at the gryphon wings tattooed across his chest. I tried not to think about how my head had just been there.

He smiled. "So are you like this every morning before coffee?"

I wrinkled my nose. "Like what?"

"Pretending to sleep even though you're awake?"

"I thought you were still asleep," I said. "I didn't want to disturb you."

His eyes bore into mine. "Did you sleep okay? Were you comfortable?"

My cheeks flushed. That had been the most comfortable I'd felt sleeping in months. Years. "I slept perfect."

"Good," he said, sounding relieved.

"How did you sleep?" I asked.

"No more nightmares." He swallowed. "Lyr. I'm so sorry for everything last night. I was," he stared up at the ceiling, "I was a gryphon-shit asshole. And I—"

"It's okay," I said. "I meant what I said. I forgive you. It's no different than me trying to push you away all those months ago when you were trying to help. And you forgave me. We're all right, me and you."

He let out a mirthless laugh. "You called me a forsworn and said you didn't need my fucking help with a bandage after clinic. Not quite the same as me backing you into a wall and—I was out of line. I shouldn't have touched you."

"What if I wanted you to touch me?" I held his gaze as the emerald green of his eyes darkened beneath his lashes. "Because I did. And I think you knew that."

He stilled. "But that wasn't why I did it. And you knew that."

"I know."

"I'm sorry."

"Rhyan, please. It's okay. I promise. If it weren't, I'd have left you out there on the snowy couch."

His lips quirked into a hint of a smile. "Thank you. For forgiving me. And stopping me."

"You wouldn't have done anything truly inappropriate."

"How can you be so sure? I was…not myself."

"Because I've seen you when you're 'not yourself.' And you still put me and my safety first. Every single time."

He shifted, rising on his elbow. "Sometimes, I don't know. I think about what I've done, what I was dreaming about, and then… what he's like—my father—and I—"

"Rhyan, you are not your father." I reached out for his arm. "You couldn't be if you tried. I was never afraid of you. Never worried about what you might do or what would happen between us, not even for a second. I trust you, even at your worst."

He closed his eyes, squeezing them tight. I shifted closer to him, my fingertips brushing against his abdomen.

"I wish I could take it back," he said, voice barely above a whisper. "I wouldn't—I wouldn't have acted that way. If I had the chance, I wouldn't have used the opportunity for anything other than to show you how much I wanted you, and how much it would mean to me. I would be gentle. I would take my time with you, the way I imagined. I would push your hair off your face." He did just that as he spoke, the movement slow. His eyes were transfixed on me, like his words were creating some spell we'd both fallen under. "Smoothed it behind your ear." His fingers brushed against my earlobe. His hand slid down the nape of my neck as my unruly waves fell down my back.

"Then what?" I barely breathed.

"I would have stared into your eyes and told you how fucking beautiful you are to me."

I cringed. "Not first thing in the morning."

"I've never woken to a more beautiful sight." His thumb ran across my lips as a throbbing heat pooled in my stomach, coiling lower and lower. My core pulsed, and my inner walls clenched painfully around nothing. "I would take you in my arms. And I would have told you I want to kiss you."

"Like you said the first time."

"Like the first time." He smiled. "I want to kiss you. Can I?"

I froze, my heart pounding, my thighs clenching. "Are you asking me now?"

His eyes searched mine. "Are you saying yes?" He leaned toward me, so close to me, so very close. The mattress was small enough that our foreheads were nearly pressed together, and I could feel his breath on my lips. I didn't even care that it was first thing in the morning. This was Rhyan, and I would have him any way I could, I would take whatever he had to offer.

My lips hummed, coming to life as they felt the nearness of his. His chest was rising and falling, pushing against my nightshift, which barely concealed my peaked nipples. Pleasure rushed down between my legs.

I didn't know if I moved toward him or he inched toward me, but our bodies were suddenly flush against each other as we lay on our sides. His palm moved between us, sliding over my hip, drawing me even closer against him.

Our eyes met, a barely formed question in his—a question clouded by hungry need and a storm of desire.

I tilted my chin up in response. One nod.

His lips brushed against mine. Once. Twice. His movements were so soft. So controlled. He kissed the corner of my mouth, his lips lingering there as my heart pounded furiously, and then he slanted his lips over mine.

It was like a dam burst open. Our mouths joined together in a frenzied kiss that felt like it had been happening for centuries. A thread existed between this kiss and our last—like there had been no end, no beginning, and these past three years apart had been a mere dream because the true reality had always been this, us, our lips joined, our bodies straining to be together, to be closer until they were one.

Rhyan groaned as his tongue swept across the seam of my lips, my mouth already opening for his. He deepened the kiss, connecting us not just to that first kiss, but to something that felt far more ancient and eternal. I wasn't in my body, and yet I'd never felt more alive, every nerve ending on fire. His stubble was rough against my fingers as I slid them up his face and tangled them in the wild, bronzed waves of his hair. One of his hands cupped my chin while the other moved to the nape of my neck as he rolled me onto my back without breaking the kiss. His weight settled over me, his knee pushing open my already spreading legs.

I ran my hands down his spine, reveling in the warmth of his bare skin. I pushed them just under the waistband of his pants, gripping his hips, unable to stop touching him, unable to get enough of his surprisingly soft skin over his hardened muscles.

Rhyan growled into my mouth as I pulled him down harder against me, needing him closer, rougher. His arousal was straining through his pants, and I could feel him growing even thicker against the light material of my underwear. I was slick between my thighs, already so wet for him, and I rolled my hips up. Rhyan arched, rearing back before he rolled forward, thrusting against me. I gasped into his mouth. He circled his hips, his cock stroking me exactly where I wanted him, needed him. A moan escaped my lips as his tongue captured mine, massaging until I couldn't catch my breath.

His fingers tangled in my hair, tilting my head up, as his other hand snaked down my side. The feel of his calluses stroking my skin lit every inch of me he touched on fire until his fingers closed around the hem of my nightshift. He hiked up what little fabric remained between us to my waist as he grinded faster against me. He squeezed my naked hip, his fingers tangling in the ties of my underwear, attacking the bow at my side.

His deft fingers easily undid it, the bow strings unraveling as the undergarment came undone, baring me. I could feel him through his pants, the only barrier remaining between us. My hips rolled and bucked, frenzied with the need to feel more of him, to get closer. I was losing control, losing my mind, farther than Lethea with the desperation to feel more of him, to touch him. My hands slid back into the waistband of his pants, lower until I grabbed at his ass.

We kept kissing and kissing, unable to stop, unable to catch our breath. Like if we pulled apart from each other we'd drown.

His fingers dug into my hip like he was grasping for control before they slid towards my core. His forehead pressed to mine. His eyes opened, and he stopped kissing me just for a breath, a question in his eyes.

There was a loud knock on the front door.

Rhyan froze. "Fuck."

I clamped a hand over my mouth, my eyes squeezing shut in horror.

The knock came again. Sharper. Louder. The fog that had descended, pulling us into this dreamy, hazy world where nothing mattered—nothing but kissing and touching and licking and feeling —lifted in an instant. My body quickly turned cold as I felt the world of responsibility and politics and promises and oaths and duties come crashing down on me.

"Probably Aemon," Rhyan said, already sliding off of me and out of the bed. He pulled his pants back up over his hips as I pushed my shift down to cover myself. "Don't move," he ordered, not looking back at me.

He closed the door behind him.

I scrambled from between the sheets, my legs tangling in his blankets. I practically fell off the bed, taking half the covers and a pillow with me. I searched for my bag on the floor, desperately opening it to find my clothes. I shimmied on pants, tugged my shift over my head, pulled a tunic down over me, and twisted around trying to tighten the laces. I ran my fingers through my hair, spitting into my hands to attempt to smooth it down as best I could.

In the mirror over Rhyan's dresser, I stared at my reflection, assessing what Aemon would see when he looked at me. Would he see the desire thrumming silently through my body? Would he notice how swollen my lips were, or the deep flush across my skin?

How often does Aemon stare at your lips? Probably never!

Panicking, I scrambled for my leather arm cuffs and belt.

I had to be logical about this. Aemon had no reason to suspect anything. He was the one who'd ordered me to stay here, after all. I looked like I'd just woken up, I decided. I looked like my apartment had been broken into by the Emartis, and I'd had to shelter here because they'd left a deadly message in my bed. If I looked odd, that would be the explanation for it—not kissing Rhyan, not sleeping in his arms, not knowing what it felt like to have his arousal pressed against mine first thing in the morning, not having been slicker with my own need than I ever had been in my life.

Aemon's commanding voice echoed through the apartment as I opened the door and stepped out, my mask in place. I could do this. I could play my role. I could be Lady Lyriana Batavia, Heir to the Arkasva, High Lord of Bamaria, demanding a report from her country's warlord.

Too late, I realized I was Lady Lyriana Batavia, the girl without underwear beneath her pants. Fuck. Rhyan had only untied one side, but they must have slipped down my other leg when I was tangled in the sheets and trying to get up. The undergarment was basically two pieces of triangular cloth with strings on the side. I tried not to flush with the memory of his untying the bow and not to think about having to search his bed for my missing underclothes later.

It wouldn't have been such a big deal if I wasn't soaking wet with desire, so much so I was worried it would seep through my pants.

"Aemon," I said curtly, the affect of an heir settling over me.

He bowed. "Your grace."

"What's going on with my apartment?" I demanded.

"Didn't sleep well, your grace?" he asked.

I exhaled sharply. "I prefer sleeping in my bed in my apartment that has not been broken into. Especially when I have a security team constantly on my trail." I tried to speak neutrally, to make up for overcorrecting, but even I was internally wincing at how spoiled I sounded. Better than sounding guilty.

"I'll make coffee," Rhyan said loudly, heading into the kitchen as Aemon stood stoically across from me in Rhyan's living room. Dressed in his full arkturion regalia, he looked out of place but commanding as ever as he gestured for me to take a seat on the couch.

"Her grace looks like she could use a cup," Aemon said darkly.

I was toeing the line. Even as Lady Lyriana Batavia, I was still expected to show respect to Bamaria's warlord.

"Arkturion, would you like some?" Rhyan asked. Impressively, he looked completely put together. His facial expression was devoid of emotion. He wore the sort of bland, alert look I'd seen thousands of times on Markan or anyone else on my escort team. His hair, which I'd just run my fingers through, was pushed back, wavy, but somehow neat-looking. If I hadn't been the one lying beneath him, kissing him, touching him, I would have never guessed he'd done anything but woken up and maybe knocked out a hundred push-ups before starting breakfast.

Aemon shook his head at Rhyan. "Thanks, Hart, but I can't stay." He turned his attention back to me and perched on the armchair of the couch. "I assume you didn't want your sheets or blankets anymore?" he frowned.

I shuddered. "I'd prefer the entire bed to be burned."

"Yes," he said wryly. "I'm aware of your penchant for lighting old items on fire."

I stiffened. Aemon hadn't been there when I'd tossed everything from my room after Jules had died, but of course, he'd know. He knew everything.

But not about Meera and Morgana. Not what had just happened in Rhyan's bedroom.

"We didn't burn the bed. But it has been removed. I think you'll sleep easier tonight. Brand new frame, mattress, all the fixings you'd expect for an Heir to the Arkasva."

"This doesn't go against my deal with the Imperator?" I asked. "No missing training? No comfortable bed sheets without severed heads in them?" My voice shook.

Rhyan's eyes locked with mine behind Aemon's in the kitchen, and then he quickly turned around, gathering spices.

"You're being threatened outside of the Academy and threatened for being an heir. That is outside of his jurisdiction."

"Are you sure?" I asked bitterly. He'd managed to step in every other time, twisting whatever happened to me into a national emergency that required both his hand and further occupation by Ka Kormac. "Seemed like his entire legion was there last night, exercising his jurisdiction."

"I know," Aemon said.

"And while we're on that topic," I said, my eyes flicking briefly between Rhyan and Aemon, "would you enlighten me as to why we're receiving reports of growing akadim activity in the south, and yet with a spare legion of soturi—of southern soturi—not one of them is being dispatched to deal with the issue?"

Aemon growled at this, his hands flexing and fisting on his lap, the tendons in his forearms straining against the golden cuffs at his wrists. "I am negotiating as best I can," he said. "Unfortunately, the chain of command in Bamaria comes second to the command of Lumeria. And I think you know exactly where the Imperator sits, and who his legion is answering to." His expression hardened. "Which is why we are going to keep what happened in your apartment last night quiet. We're lucky that this time they decided to send a private message to you."

"Finding a severed seraphim head under your blankets is not exactly what I would call lucky," I seethed.

"Would you prefer those heads falling from the sky for everyone to see? To give the Imperator a reason to return?"

I swallowed. "No."

"That's what I thought." He stood. "We are looking into the breach. You're to have two escorts with you at all times moving forward until this threat is stopped. No more running off to Scholar's Harbor unless you're bringing a team with you. You will only be unescorted during Academy hours. And then you'll have Hart. Be on your guard, both of you."

I shivered. "I know what they want, but...why me? Why am I being targeted? Why aren't they attacking Cresthaven? I'm not Arkasva, I'm not even Heir Apparent."

"I think, your grace, it's because they can. You're the most exposed."

I bit my lip, hating that answer. They thought me weak, powerless, expendable. So they planned to take me out first.

"Don't let this distract you," Aemon said. "You have one month to go, and you're making great progress. Do not lose that—do not lose sight of your goal. The Emperor is already making preparations to arrive." He sketched a quick bow and turned for the door. "Hart, good work. I need you on tonight. Days of fucking Shadows."

And then he was gone. I slumped onto Rhyan's couch, my mind reeling.

The scent of Rhyan's spiced coffee wafted to me. I looked up to find a steaming mug on the table in front of me.

Rhyan's eyes were wide as he watched me, his mouth tight. I looked up, not sure what to say or do. Minutes ago, he had been removing my underwear, kissing me like I was his air and he'd have died without it. And now...I felt like an ocean stood between us.

"What are you thinking?" he asked.

"What are *you* thinking?" I replied.

He ran his fingers through his hair. "I know," he groaned, "I know what lines I just crossed."

"We crossed," I said.

"We crossed." He sighed. "I'm your bodyguard, your kashonim."

"I don't need a list."

"And you're with Tristan."

I closed my eyes. It was hard to breathe with the weight of everything settling over me.

"Lyr, I never should have—"

"Don't," I said, holding up my hand. "Don't."

"Don't what?" he asked.

"Just don't do this," I said. "Don't try to take all the blame or dig into the reasons why it shouldn't have happened."

"I don't know what to do!" he shouted. "I know it was both of us," his voice softened, "but as your apprentice, I should have stopped it. I should have been responsible. I lost control. And I just, I need to know if you're okay."

"I'm not," I said.

"Because of what I did?" His hands flexed.

"Because of what we did," I said. "Look, I think we both know what happens next." My gut twisted. "Let's just…forget it. We have to. We're supposed to be on the track in less than an hour. You should get ready. I need to drink this coffee."

He closed his eyes, a look of finality in the tightness of his mouth when he looked at me again. "I'll be in the shower."

CHAPTER
SIXTEEN

The moment the clocktower announced the final hour of the day, I bolted from the training room. It had been my longest day of training yet. Rhyan and I hadn't said a word to each other, not since he'd showered. We'd gotten ready for our morning run separately and silently, hadn't spoken on the track, and had barely spoken in the training room.

The training room had been its own kind of torture. Rhyan had to occasionally touch me to help me go deeper into a stretch or to make an adjustment so I was in proper form. Every time he did so, it was awkward. He hesitated. I tensed up.

There'd always been moments when I'd be hit with a sudden wave of need or desire as Rhyan touched me during our training sessions. Sometimes it made sense that the touches sent me into a spiral, like anytime he put his hands on my ribcage, his fingers dancing so dangerously close to the underside of my breasts. But other times, the touch could be something so innocent, like his fingers on my ankle, and I'd fantasize about him running his hand up my calves and thighs, pushing between my legs.

I'd always been fully capable of ignoring those desires before, of taking a breath and letting the simmering heat cool down inside me. Today, I was useless. Just the fact that the sun was shining reminded me of laying underneath him. Every breath he took, I heard his breathing against me as his hips drove into mine.

I'd never been so relieved to hop onto a seraphim at the end of the day, to let the night air cool my heated face as I took off for Cresthaven.

I found Morgana in Meera's room, both only half-dressed in their black dresses for Days of Shadows when I arrived.

"Lyr," Morgana said happily as I walked in. "You have to try this wine." She stood up from the bed, her words slurred.

"Myself to Moriel," I muttered. "Already?"

"Already," Morgana mimicked. She batted her eyelashes at me and rolled her shoulders back in what I assumed was an impression of me. A really bad one.

"You're right," she said. "I just forgot," she grabbed her ass, "to put a stick up there."

I groaned. *Can you give me five minutes before acting like a bitch?*

"Five minutes was five drinks ago," she snapped.

"Don't listen to her. She's not that drunk," Meera said. She was standing before her mirror trying to curl her hair. "She's just excited for her date tonight."

"Terra. She's an apprentice mage…." Morgana closed her eyes and moaned. "Beautiful. Also, Lyr, if you're going to call me a bitch, say it out loud. It's rude thinking mean thoughts about your mind-reading sister."

"I didn't call you a bitch. I said you were acting like one."

"I'd like to point out that it's rude to think thoughts in front of your oldest sister when you know I can't hear them," Meera said. She was trying to join in the banter, but she already seemed completely drained and exhausted. The bags under her eyes were purple, and she was bracing herself against her dresser, like she was too weak to stand up on her own even just to do her hair.

Maybe it was too much of a risk to go tonight.

Morgana caught my eye in the mirror. Her jaw clenched, black eyebrows narrowed, as she made a cutting motion with her hand across her neck.

I exhaled sharply. We'd had this fight before, about lessening Meera's public appearances even further. But she had to make public appearances at least weekly—in class, at parties thrown by nobles. Hiding her away from Lumeria would be just as suspicious as letting her be seen in this state. It was why I'd made myself so prominent, and even more so after Morgana's Revelation. We tried to keep Bamaria satisfied with at least one Batavia Heir.

What if it's just tonight?

Morgana's nostrils flared, clearly disagreeing with me.

Meera paused, her pale hazel eyes watching, alert. She knew we were discussing her—when she'd literally just asked us not to.

"Ugh. Give me the wine." I was too tired to argue. Too emotionally exhausted to deal with one more thing.

Morgana smiled gleefully as she danced to Meera's night table and poured me a glass.

"I just want you to have fun," she said coyly. "You've been so serious lately and working so hard."

"I have fun," I said, pouting.

I moved behind Meera and took over curling duties, wrapping her long ash-brown hair around the next curler and pinning it to her scalp.

Morgana placed the glass beside me on the dresser. "Drink up. It's Days of Shadows, ladies!"

I picked up my glass, as did Meera, though I'd never seen her take more than two sips of anything in her life.

"We need to toast," Morgana said, holding out her newly filled glass to us.

Meera gave me an exasperated look from the side, and we clinked our glasses together.

"Rapatayim!" Morgana cheered, the glass already halfway to her lips, one hand waving in the air.

"Rapatayim," Meera repeated calmly.

"To your feet," I said, deadpan.

Morgana groaned. "Why do you always do that?"

I took a sip of the wine. Sweet, which was good. "Because that's literally what you're cheering every time you toast!" Rapatayim was the traditional toast in Lumeria, a shortened version of an old Lumerian blessing: *La ra patayim vrata al mar.* Basically, it meant "may your feet always walk above the water." Most likely, the saying had originated after the Drowning. But toasts had shortened it to rapatayim—your feet. I'd found this hilarious ever since I'd learned it.

"Drink your feet wine, then," Morgana said, taking another sip. I followed suit and then set my glass down to add another curler to Meera's hair. Pretending to focus on organizing the remaining curlers and pins for her, I thought, *Morgs, pull your hair into a ponytail if you call truce.*

She rolled her eyes at me in the mirror but swept her raven locks up, gathering it on top of her head in one hand before letting it fall back down her back. She held her hand open, her fingers tensed, before she leaned forward, staring up at me, an expression that clearly meant, What do you want?

How is she doing? Any changes?

She shook her head. I smoothed out a new section of Meera's hair to roll. Meera watched me in the reflection, a hurt, accusatory look in her eyes.

I glanced away, feeling guilty for talking about her in secret—right under her nose. My gaze caught the painting she'd created of the vision she'd had on my birthday three months earlier.

The painting on her wall, one of many that had turned the once plain white room into a clash of colorful murals, was a depiction of me. Meera had perfectly painted my nose, my chin. My hair was red as if I were in the sun. The more disturbing part of the painting showed my arms sprouting into black seraphim wings—my entire body transforming into a seraphim. A black seraphim. The symbol of the Emartis.

"Wait!" Morgana sat forward, her wine sloshing in her glass. "Fuck!"

I whirled around to face her. "What? What did you hear?"

"How your fucking night went? Shit—Lyr. I didn't know. I never would have...Gods! In your bed!"

Meera turned around, too, her eyes wide. "What happened in Lyr's bed?"

Morgana pulled the whole story of the Emartis break-in out of my head to share with Meera, down to every last grotesque detail. All three of us ended up cuddled on top of Meera's bedcovers. Apparently, the escort team at Cresthaven—while doubled—hadn't bothered to inform their heirs of the threat faced by the youngest one—me. As Aemon had said, I was the target, not Cresthaven, not Meera nor Morgana.

Because I was easier to get to.

I marched back to Meera's dresser and downed my wine, holding the glass out for Morgana to refill. She raised one eyebrow, then both, her eyes widening as she filled my goblet to the brim.

"Drink up," she demanded. "That's an order from your older sister."

I did, after finishing Meera's hair to perfection. But before I could start on Morgana's hair, she wrapped her arms around my waist and hauled me from the bedroom, down the hall, and into my room where she practically threw me onto the bed and slammed the door. She pressed her back to it like she was trying to keep someone from getting in.

"What in Lumeria?" I demanded, trying to roll off my back into a seat. I ended up splayed across my bed. Maybe I was a little drunk already.

"You and Rhyan," she hissed.

"Morgs!"

"I know," she said. "I know I can't tell anyone. Myself to Moriel. But...fuck," she whispered. Her dark eyes ran up and down my body before she laughed. "Did you ever find your underwear?"

Fuck you.

She cackled. "Perfect Lady Lyriana Batavia, losing her under-garments in the bed of her forsworn bodyguard. Scandal."

"Morgs, stop." I couldn't talk about it, couldn't deal with it. I felt awful. Awful it had happened, awful it had stopped, awful for wanting to throw my life away so it could happen again. But above all, I was scared and confused…and still so Godsdamned turned on. I buried my face in my hands. "I don't know what to do."

She sat on the bed beside me, giving me one of her rare hugs. "Don't worry about it," she said.

"Great advice," I said.

"No," she said. "I mean it. Everything's fucked right now. Don't feel guilty. Don't feel guilty for even a moment for allowing your heart and body some amount of pleasure when you spend so much of your life denying it."

I sniffled.

"Myself to fucking Moriel," she groaned. "Don't cry. It's Days of Shadows. Of all nights, tonight is the one to let loose, have some fun. Get a little drunk. You need it."

"What do I do about Tristan?"

"What do you want to do?"

I hadn't thought about what I'd wanted to do in years. My thoughts were always consumed by what I had to do, what I should do, what I needed to do. How to sway public perception, how to hide our secrets. Nothing I did came from a place of what I wanted. Acting on desire…I didn't know what that was like. Except for this morning…

"I don't know," I said at last. My mind felt foggy. "I've never been with Tristan for the right reasons except maybe the first day. And it's not like ending it will make it any better or allow me what I want. But with everything that's happened, and how everything is and how he's been, I don't know what my reasons are anymore."

She took my arm in her lap, her fingers tracing the outline of my tattoo, of the Valalumir stars running up and down my inner forearm. Then she pressed her fingers above my wrist, easily finding the invisible marks of the blood oath—the unseen, mutilated skin, the mark of my promise to protect not just Meera but her.

"You have one reason," she said. "To protect Meera. It's always been to protect Meera."

And you.

Morgana gave me a sad smile. "But it doesn't have to be that way. You've had to do too much. I see that now."

"And it's still not enough," I said, wiping my eyes. "I can't end things. Even if…if my relationship isn't protecting our family, ending things could put the spotlight on Rhyan now. Tristan's jealous. I don't know what he suspects, but I'm afraid. What if I put him in danger?"

"There may be other things we can do," she said. "To keep her safe. To keep everyone safe."

"Like what?"

Morgana shrugged. "Who knows. I'm just saying, the first answer isn't always the best one."

"You'll let me know when you find one?" I asked.

I was met with a smirk and a mischievous look in her dark eyes before her nostrils flared. "I need another drink."

Let's go.

Morgana plastered a smile on her face and slammed my door open.

"Gods! Do you ever do anything quietly?" I yelled.

"NO!"

When the hour rang out, we were ready, our hair curled and pinned back. We traded our golden diadems for black masks—masks of akadim.

I thought of the black seraphim mask Tani had worn the day she'd attacked me, the stupid mask the Imperator had been able to twist into a silly costume instead of the symbol for a terrorist group. My hands clenched involuntarily at my sides and sharp pain shot up my back.

As promised by Rhyan, my back had not scarred, and no mark had been left behind by the lashes or the Imperator's cruel attempt to reopen and infect my wounds. But sometimes, when I thought about the trial in Aemon's war room, my body remembered. It remembered the Imperator's fingers, and I felt the pain course through me anew like I was being touched again.

"You need another drink," Morgana said. "Thoughts are too dark."

We were walking through the fortress's double doors and waving bye to Euston and Rhodes as cold night air swept into a gale-force wind against us.

"When we get to the festival," I said, pulling my soturion cloak closer to my body, "I'll have another drink."

"Or sooner," she winked, lifting up her black gown. Underneath she wore black boots laced above her knee; I had on a matching pair. Above her boot, a black silk garter circled her thigh, a silver flask tucked within it.

I shook my head. My gown's skirt had two slits than ran from hip to floor. I slid the material over to the side to reveal the expanse of my leg. A black leather holster was around my thigh just above my boot, but mine held my dagger.

Morgana burst out laughing as we righted our gowns and stepped onto the waterway, heading for our carriage. Walking in the shadows were nine personal escorts, three for each of us, including fucking Markan. Before I could give him the finger, Morgana grabbed my hand.

"You're not being productive with that." She squeezed my hand in hers.

"I'm expressing myself."

Before she could retort, Meera tripped in front of us. Her escorts appeared by her side impossibly fast, each one catching her arm and helping her to stand upright.

My pulse spiked, eyes widening as I turned to Morgana.

She shook her head. The message in her eyes was clear: *Not a vision. Calm down.*

"Thank you," Meera said softly to the soturion who'd flown across the waterway to catch her arm. "Started the party too early."

It was a perfect answer to offer from an Heir Apparent, only she delivered it like a woman who'd never tasted alcohol or partied in her life.

Her escorts didn't seem overly concerned and separated, returning to the edge of the waterway, their boots slapping against the glass. But they remained closer than protocol demanded for being inside the fortress walls, I assumed because of the Emartis. Still, it made me uneasy. I didn't like anyone getting too close to her when a vision was imminent.

Inside our seraphim carriage, Morgana closed the partition between us and the escorts as we soared into the night. She reached into her skirts, pulled out a small silver flask, and shoved it in my hands. "Drink this," she said.

"What? No. I'll wait. This one's for you," I said. She was already wincing in pain from being around so many soturi. Once she found Terra, her date for the night, she'd feel better. Sex was one of the things that took away the pain of her vorakh. Between her flasks and the sex—most likely in the woods outside the festival —I hoped she was in for a pain-free night.

Morgana smirked. "Not just pain-free, but fucking fantastic. Are you sure you don't want more?"

"Morgs, don't encourage her to drink," Meera said. She still sounded tired, as if even to speak was too much effort for her.

"That, there!" Morgana pointed at my face. "Serious face. Come on, Lyr. I want you to have a good time."

"I need to be on guard," I said. "Saying the wrong thing tonight...." I shook my head. "I can't. I've had enough."

I was meeting Tristan. It would be my first time seeing him since I'd spent the night in Rhyan's bed, in his arms, underneath him.... The thought of facing Tristan and kissing Tristan and continuing to pretend everything was fine and nothing had happened made my stomach twist.

"Give me that," I said, swiping Morgana's flask and letting its contents slide down my throat. There was just enough of a burn for me to cough, but instantly my stomach warmed, and a light buzzing ran through my limbs.

Meera rolled her eyes, but Morgana opened the window and yelled out in celebration.

"You can enjoy yourself tonight, too." Morgana winked at Meera before turning to me. "Now show me that smile! No, Lyr, the real one." She laughed. "Okay, your drunk smile's good, too."

"I am not drunk," I said.

"You were always a lightweight, little sister."

We landed in the field beside the Temple of Dawn, amidst bonfires and water dancers sensually stomping and twisting their bodies through black ribbons. Drums played, their beats vibrating at volumes enhanced by magic. Nodding to our escorts, we donned our akadim masks, black and grotesque. Days of Shadows had once been a solemn holiday, a day of remembrance for the victims of akadim—those who'd lost their lives, or worse, their souls. Because there were so few attacks in the south, at some point a certain bravado had emerged in the ritual, a mocking of what we feared. Admittedly, now Days of Shadows was more of an excuse for a drunken costume party, though akadim costumes—despite what the Imperator claimed at Tani's trial—were still the most common.

We stepped forward, and I could sense the escorts spreading, their soturion cloaks easily allowing them to vanish into the cover of night. Bodies clothed in black were undulating and gyrating to the music, moving themselves in a sensuous rhythm. On their faces were the monstrous masks, full of fangs, snarls, and vicious faces.

It was perhaps the coldest night yet this year, but the field was so full I could already feel the heat and desire to lose my cloak. Most of the Lumerians dancing had done so already, and their bare arms, and in some cases legs, had a reddish tint from the crackling bonfires.

Bellamy, Tristan's escort, emerged from the crowd walking toward me along with a second Ka Grey mage I didn't recognize. Tristan strolled between them before rushing ahead to my side, squeezing my hand and pulling it to his lips, the only part of his face that remained uncovered by his akadim mask.

Our party moved deeper into the crowd, which easily parted for us and our escorts.

I only stumbled a little before I adjusted to the darkness of the night, the uneven terrain of the field, and the wine coursing through my veins. Tristan grabbed my arm to steady me as we made our way into the party's center, clearly on display, all eyes on us. The moment we could be sure we'd been seen and noted, we dispersed. A mage named Brandon I'd seen at a few noble functions over the years walked boldly toward us. Morgana pushed her mask back and grinned before grabbing his arm.

Aren't you meeting Terra?

She smiled wider and nodded, then pulled Brandon off to a cluster of trees bordering the party. I caught a flash of silver—one of her escorts following.

I grimaced, but Morgana had never particularly seemed to care about privacy. Although, from the looks of it, it wasn't her escort I needed to worry about. A group of mages, obviously eyeing Morgana's retreating form, was talking loudly in disgust.

"She's always been an Asherah," one said.

"Disgusting."

My pulse spiked, my mind immediately racing to figure out how to spin the situation, how to draw attention back to me.

I tossed my hair over my shoulder, pulling my mask up and shifting my stance so the slits of my dress revealed the full expanse of my legs. The slits were so high I'd had to tie the bows of my underwear up around my waist. But it was a cheap trick, and no one cared about my legs. I could start kissing Tristan, but our courtship had been so publicized for so long our kisses were no longer newsworthy. My only choices were to publicly slap him or fuck him, and I definitely didn't have plans to do either.

I took a deep breath. I needed to get a grip. Better they were scandalized over Morgana's sex life than they came to any other conclusion. That had been our stance since she'd started to sleep around after revealing her vorakh.

Meera frowned in concern. She still looked so tired and weak as she was absorbed by her own group of friends, mostly quiet yet high-ranking nobles related to members of the Bamarian Council. The observers turned their attention on Meera. I tensed, watching them watch her, and grabbed my wrist, my hand twitching over my blood oaths.

Fuck. I had to relax. Meera always got tons of attention in public as the Heir Apparent. I forgot this sometimes due to how little she'd left Cresthaven over the last two years.

I entwined my fingers with Tristan's. "Dance with me."

We weren't far from the dance floor. Mages had spelled it to float nearly fifteen feet in the air. Dark clouds surrounded the edges of the floor, creating the illusion of dancers twirling across the sky. Thin staircases cascaded down from each corner of the floor. I grabbed Tristan, dragging him to the steps, and we climbed up, his hand steady on the small of my back.

The drums beat, the music earthy and sensual. I pulled Tristan close, centering us in the middle of the crowd—making sure I could easily see over the entire field, see Meera.

Our hands linked, then our bodies, undulating to the music. Torches crackled and smoke snaked into the blinking lights of the cold night's twinkling stars. I threw my hands up, as the drums grew louder and the tempo increased. My dance training kicked in, and I closed my eyes, quieting my mind, releasing my body in a way I hadn't let myself in years, allowing myself to just feel the music, to let it move me. My body felt so different than it had the last time I'd danced like this with Tristan. I was stronger, surer of my footing and every move. Every roll, step, and shake felt so good. Each step was backed by muscle and strength that hadn't been there before. My hips rolled as Tristan tightened his grip on me.

I closed my eyes, feeling Rhyan's hand digging into my flesh, Rhyan's hips bucking against mine, rolling in circles, grinding against me, his lips against mine, his fingers untying....

Fuck. I needed to clear my head. Rhyan was all I could think about. Without realizing it, I'd spent the past few minutes looking for him. Aemon had ordered Rhyan to guard me tonight, but he hadn't shown up at Cresthaven, which meant his security detail tonight would keep him bound to Urtavia.

Unless...unless he'd been sent at the last moment on another hunting expedition to Elyria or wherever the akadim packs were currently roaming.

I glanced beyond the stage, desperate to catch sight of him. I peered at the different bodies of soturi all camouflaged to be unseen, looking for the outline of simple black armor.

But Rhyan was nowhere in sight.

Tristan eyed me carefully through his akadim mask, pulling me back to him. "Who caught your attention, your grace?"

"Galen and Haleika," I blurted out. They danced on the other side of the floor, their bodies tangled together. Haleika tossed her head back in laughter. Her bouncy brown curls were unmistakable despite the grotesque mask she'd chosen to wear.

Galen brushed a loose curl from her cheek, hand gripping her waist to pull her close. She arched back, and his lips grazed against the curve of her neck.

Just beyond the dance floor watching Haleika openly was Leander.

I began searching again for a sign of Rhyan, for a glimpse of his golden-brown hair, for the silver of the scar across his eye, for the slope of his northern-issued boots. But noticing Tristan's eyes on me, I focused back on our friends.

"Seems they're ready to take it up a notch." He raised his eyebrows. "Didn't we have a bet going? I can't remember now if I lost or you did, but I'm pretty sure one of us owes the other something."

"Like this?" I asked and drew Tristan's mouth to mine. My blood pulsed. His hand slid down my back, squeezing my thigh, lifting my leg around his hip as the drums grew louder.

I closed my eyes, and Rhyan was there with me, his hand on my hip, his calloused fingers brushing against my skin, untying the bow, my undergarments opening, the feel of his....

My heart hammered. Kissing Tristan, being with him like this, felt wrong in a way it never had before. Like I was betraying Rhyan.

I gripped Tristan closer and broke the kiss, feigning the need to catch my breath, a response bred from years of practice. I pressed my face against his chest, allowing myself one moment to squeeze my eyes shut before I set my gaze over his shoulder and watched the crowd of soturi and mages—all having fun, all letting loose, all dancing with the person they wanted to be with.

After another useless sweep of the festival, my eyes landed on Meera holding court deep in the crowd. She was surrounded, everyone seemingly vying for her attention, wanting to ask a question of Bamaria's Heir Apparent.

She waved at someone and turned to answer another question, her hands clasped neatly in front of her body, stiff with tension. She looked so uncomfortable. Only years of training seemed to keep her standing tall and her head turning with regal precision.

The music slowed, and I lowered my leg to the ground as a more formal slow dance began to play. Tristan twirled me in a circle, spinning me away from him before pulling me close. I took the lead, turning our bodies so I could better see Meera.

A cold wind swept over me, brushing through my hair. I shivered, and Tristan pulled me against him. There was another gust of wind.

No. Not wind. An aura. The cold I felt, I knew far too well. Meera stiffened, her entire body tense.

Alarm bells screamed in my head. *Oh, my Gods. MORGANA!*

I jumped back from Tristan, but he grabbed hold of my hand.

"Lyr, you all right?"

My vision blurred. My pulse pounded, and the world spun and tilted on its side. The wine. Fuck. I shouldn't have let Morgana get to me.

"Lyr?" Tristan squeezed my hand.

"Morgana plied me with wine—really need to pee! Dance with Galen and Hal!"

I launched myself at the stairs, nearly falling off the stage.

Racing down the steps, I covered two at a time before leaping off. My boots crashed to the ground, sinking through the grass. I covered my head with my cloak, hoping I'd blend into my surroundings like a true soturion before I tore through the crowds of Lumerians dancing, kissing, and passing drinks.

I pushed into people, not giving a gryphon-shit who I hurt or offended. I had one goal—reach Meera. I was already losing precious time. Every second that passed and I wasn't by her side, we were in greater danger.

Morgana! Help!

I broke into the circle of nobles all watching Meera and talking in that loud, obnoxiously showy way nobles did when they wanted to command more attention. It had always grated on me, but in that moment, it worked in my favor as a cousin of Lady Pavi's preened while fake laughing.

Meera, I mouthed her name, not wanting to draw any more attention to her.

Her eyes went out of focus, and there was a slight snarl to her lip. It was starting. I had maybe a minute at best before the thrashing came, just as long as no one looked at her too closely. If they did, there would be no mistaking what was happening, or who she looked like.

Jules. She looked exactly like Jules had as her first vision came. And she looked like the dancer that Tristan himself had arrested on my birthday. She looked like the countless other mages who'd had vorakh through no fault of their own and had lost their lives because of it.

"Meera, I need to pull you away," I said, throwing every bit of noble affect I could into my voice. I wrapped my arm around her, my hands closing around her arms and locking into place.

She immediately jolted at my touch, but my grip was vicelike. She wasn't going anywhere. Not yet. Her full force of strength hadn't activated yet, or she'd have thrown me off.

Sweat beaded at the nape of my neck despite the chill rising from her aura. The feel and sound of shattering glass was all around me.

MORGANA! Where the fuck are you? It's Meera! Fuck! Fuck! I knew she should have stayed home tonight.

But Morgana didn't come. I had no idea where she was. Off with Brandon or Terra or whoever. It was up to me. Only me. Meera had to be moved immediately.

In the distance, hiding behind the dark of the forest, was one of Meera's escorts, invisible to all but me. I shook my head, waving him off—she was fine. I signaled again, warning him not to come any closer. He frowned with concern and reluctantly sank back into the shadows on my orders. I spotted her second escort a few feet away, the tip of his sword catching firelight.

Meera snarled at me, and I tightened my grip.

I started to pull her back. She struggled against my hold as the attention of the nobles surrounding us began to draw our way.

I laughed. "Sorry, I need to borrow my sister. You can have her back in a few minutes."

Her guard watched carefully, his posture tensed and alert. We couldn't disappear into the trees, and I couldn't take her to the escort. He'd turn us in. Betray us. A burning sensation cut across my left wrist, tingling and scratching. My blood oath.

Remember. Remember. We four keep this secret. We four die by this secret.

We had to disappear. Now.

There were crowds surrounding us in every direction, drunk, dancing, completely giving in to debauchery. I took stock of our assets. Meera's mask hung around her neck. Mine was over my hair. I also had my soturion cloak.

Meera pulled away from me, her strength growing. In a few seconds, trying to control her would be like battling a fully powered soturion.

Another escort moved behind the trees, and then coming from the opposite end was Bellamy, Tristan's escort, and mine, and since I'd begun paying him.

I waved him over, my plan forming.

"Your grace," he said. "How can I help?"

"Follow me out of here. I'm taking my sister home," I said, my voice low. "Can you make a shield to shadow us?"

His eyes narrowed, flicking to Meera and back to me.

"Please. I will pay you ten times over."

He gave a simple nod and took a step back, his hand on the hilt of his stave in his silver scabbard. "When you're ready."

My heart was hammering in my chest as I took in my surroundings, assessed our location, and mapped out our escape route. I had a window of opportunity here, but there was no room for mistakes. I sucked in a breath, preparing to act, to run.

Silently I counted down. *Three...two...one....*

Bellamy withdrew his stave.

I pulled Meera's mask up to cover her face and pulled mine down, my hand leaving her arm just long enough for her to thrash and flail away from me. Grabbing hold of the edge of my soturion cloak, I wrapped my arm around her again, her body now half-hidden by my camouflage. My grip tightened around her, and we were off.

I started running straight into the crowd of onlookers, praying that between my cloak, our masks, and Bellamy's shadow, we'd go unnoticed. Everyone else at the party was in the dark, drinking and high off moonleaves. But I couldn't take any chances. Even if the crowd did not notice us, our escorts wouldn't be far behind.

Meera fought against me, starting to yell and snarl, but I kept going, half-lifting her off her feet, her boots dragging in the ground as I raced, dodging around the unaware partiers.

I dragged her into the middle of another group, off to the side where the torchlights were low, faking a smile, pulling her close, pressing her face against my shoulder. Meera stumbled, falling into me, then abruptly pushed back, trying to escape my hold. I grabbed her around the waist and pushed through the crowd, stumbling into another group of nobles.

Meera shook in my arms as icy cold air from her aura swirled around us. The vision was getting stronger. Already, her nostrils were flaring beneath her akadim mask. A single drop of blood dripped from her nose, marking a red trail on her otherwise pale pink lips.

It was happening. Faster than I'd be able to get her to safety. In the shadows, golden armor stalked alongside us. Markan had joined our watch.

Come on, Bellamy! More shadows!

How was I going to get her away from the party? Away from our escorts? She was already half-gone.

I had to keep running. I had to get her out of here. I was going to get her out of this.

MORGANA!

I crouched down, grabbing under Meera's knees and scooped her into my arms, holding her close to my chest. She yelled as I wrapped my cloak over her and stood back up, the backs of my legs burning. And then I ran. Faster than I'd ever run before.

We weren't far from the seraphim port. If I could keep running, I could get us on the next carriage, be airborne before our escorts discovered us.

I had to keep running.

I dodged more guests, raced around bonfires.

Meera, as if sensing her escape route was about to be taken from her, thrashed wildly and screeched. I tightened my hold, screaming internally for my legs to move faster, for my arms to be stronger, for my hands to hold onto her just a little longer, but Meera freed her arm from my hold, and her nails slashed at my neck, drawing blood. A thick droplet rolled down my collarbone.

I tightened my grip on her, ignoring every bit of discomfort and pain pushing through me, but I wasn't going to be able to hold on much longer. She was becoming too strong, too violent. The seraphim port was in sight. We were close. So fucking close. I just had to get her onto a carriage.

Come on. You can do this. You HAVE to do this! You're strong!

I ran faster, weaving my way in and out of the partygoers,

careful to stay where it was most crowded, where we could blend in, where I could hide Meera from our escorts. I couldn't even look to see if they were following or check on Bellamy. If I looked, I'd slow down. If I slowed down, I'd lose her.

Meera thrashed, and I tightened my grip as I entered the port. I could barely hold onto her as I raced forward, my boots slamming into the ground until my feet tangled in the folds of my dress, and I lost my footing. I was going to fall. I was going to drop Meera. My grip was failing, my wrists hurting from carrying her. I couldn't make it, I couldn't get there, I couldn't stop it, I couldn't save myself, I couldn't save her.

We were falling.

And then we weren't. A tall soturion appeared before me, grabbing Meera, the strength of his body unmistakable as Meera's weight was lifted from my arms. I hit the solid muscle of Rhyan instead of the ground. I grabbed his leg, pushing myself up to see Rhyan holding Meera, who was thrashing against him, scratching at his face as she shrieked in terror.

"What's wrong?" Rhyan asked, shifting his weight and Meera in his arms. "What happened to her?"

"She's drunk!" I said frantically. "High—I don't know. I just need to get her home."

Meera clawed at Rhyan's armor, shaking and screaming. Her strength was increasing so much with the vorakh that even Rhyan stumbled holding her.

His eyes narrowed, as he caught her fist in his hand before she could punch him. "Tell me what's wrong."

"She smoked something, I don't know, it's stupid! Just help me into a carriage. Now!"

Rhyan turned and ran as I bounded behind him, sprinting for the nearest open door. The seraphim's wings spread in anticipation of us.

He stepped back as I climbed inside and held out my hands to receive Meera, but then Rhyan climbed aboard, too, still clutching her in his arms.

"Give her to me," I snapped.

"It's all right. I've got her." He closed the door behind him, still managing to hold a thrashing Meera in his arms.

"What—no!" I screamed. "We have to go!"

"I know. Lyr, I'll come with you. I'll help. Where to?" he asked. "Cresthaven?"

"I'm going alone! I've got it."

Outside the carriage, Markan shouted my name, asking if I was all right and demanding to board. Meera's three escorts were calling out from behind him, demanding we open the door at once. They'd finally caught up. *Shit! Shit! Shit!*

I pushed past Rhyan and locked the door, telling the seraphim to go. The floor shifted beneath my feet as the bird began to stand, and I raced around the carriage, shutting the windows and closing the curtains in a blind panic.

Markan snarled from outside. "Meet you at Cresthaven. Foolish girl!"

I wanted to scream. Meera cried out in pain, blood spurting from her nose as she thrashed and kicked in Rhyan's arms. I couldn't do it anymore.

We four keep this secret. We four die by this secret.

I squeezed my eyes shut, my stomach sinking as I knew I was about to do the one thing I'd sworn I wouldn't. My wrist was on fire. I wanted to scream. But it was down to this—her life, or mine.

I made my choice. My wrist was enflamed, engulfed in heat and pain.

The carriage floor shook, and we were airborne.

I needed a place to go. A place where Meera would have privacy. Not home…not…. I stared at Rhyan's armor in terror, at the sigil of the gryphon and seraphim. The gryphon.

"GRYPHON ISLAND!" I shouted, and immediately the bird began to turn, wind slapping against the carriage windows. I looked out through the curtain to see another seraphim taking off, heading in the opposite direction—toward Cresthaven. I clutched at my chest.

"Set her on her feet," I said, ripping off my mask from where it'd fallen around my neck. Meera's had vanished in the struggle to get her inside. "But don't let go of her."

Rhyan did as I asked, keeping a firm grip on her waist. Meera slammed her head against a wall, blood spilling from her nose.

"Meera!" I yelled, reaching out for her. She kicked, and I flew backwards, my back smacking into the wooden paneling. Lights flashed before my eyes as I closed them.

"Lyr!" Rhyan called.

Blearily, I opened my eyes, seeing his grip loosen so he could come to me.

"No, don't let go of her—I'm all right."

Rhyan nodded, backing Meera away from me, trying to angle her body away from mine, to avoid my getting hurt again. But I was already crawling back to her on my knees before I stood and stepped forward on shaky legs. "Please, Meera. Please."

Her aura exploded, the feeling of ice and glass cutting through me. Even Rhyan flinched from the impact, but I pushed through. I grabbed her arm, but she swatted at me until I stumbled back. She was too strong already. Too far gone.

"Lyr," Rhyan said, eyes widening. "Tell me what to do—how to help you."

I swung open every cabinet door, throwing every blanket and pillow in the carriage onto the ground.

"Lay her down," I ordered. Wind screeched out the windows as we soared higher, our seraphim moving faster. A tear escaped my eyes, and my throat went dry.

When Meera screamed again, and I sprang into action. "Hold her legs down. I'll take her arms. She needs to see my face and hear my voice. Now. Before we lose her." I sucked in a breath. "She's having a vision."

CHAPTER
SEVENTEEN

"Meera. Meera, listen to me. It's Lyr. You're safe. You're—Stop fighting me."

She writhed, thrashing to escape my grip. Her nails raked up my arm, cutting through the skin until it burned.

"Meera! You have to come back to me."

"No!" Her voice was dark, menacing, with a foreign undertone full of hatred. Just as it had the last time I'd helped her, it sounded like multiple voices were coming through her mouth, male and female, all echoing and twining together. "You won't have her blood! You no longer have a claim on her life. She's ours. She belongs to us. You'll know before the end." She coughed, bleeding freely from her nose, the blood staining her lips. Her arm broke free again, and this time she ripped her fingernails down my back until I cried out.

Tears ran down my face. She was so much stronger than she'd been last time, so much more violent. Her voice was terrifying, sending chills down my spine. "Meera. I don't know what to do," I sobbed. "I can't do this."

The seraphim turned, and the entire carriage shook.

"Give up," the voice from Meera said. "You don't know what we are. You don't even know who you are. You're going to fail."

"Don't listen to that. You know what to do," Rhyan said, his voice full of confidence and reassurance. "Do it."

I'd almost forgotten he was there, right behind me, helping.

"You're stronger than you think," he said. "You've done this before, Lyr. Do it again. Now."

I leaned forward, no longer trying to restrain her, and rubbed her temples. "Meera. Meera, it's me. It's Lyr. It's your sister. I know you're in there. Fight back. Whatever's with you, whatever's scaring you. Fight. Come back to me. Come back."

She thrashed again, and I rubbed her temples, my fingers sliding over her skin. She reached for me, and then her arms fell like dead-weights at her side.

The carriage lurched in its descent. Meera's eyes widened with recognition. "Lyr?" Her eyes shifted back and forth, falling on Rhyan, who still restrained her. She jolted.

"Let her go!" I shouted.

Rhyan released her at once, moving aside. Meera sobbed in pain and curled her knees into her chest, shivering.

I pushed her hair out of her face and used my dress to wipe up her blood. It was already staining her cheeks and lips.

"It's all right," I said.

The carriage rocked gently as the seraphim settled on the ground. We remained in silence until the floor stilled.

"Where are we?" Meera asked. Her eyes sought mine in confusion. They sharpened as she again looked at Rhyan, and she buried her face in her hands. She shook, a tiny animal suddenly discovering it was prey.

"Gryphon Island," I told her.

Rhyan walked to the door. "I'll give you some privacy."

On instinct, I reached for his hand. His fingers closed over mine, and our eyes met. His grip tightened in response.

"I'll be right outside, standing guard." Rhyan released my hand and left.

I rummaged through the overhead cabinets for extra blankets. The night was already so cold, and Meera's skin was turning to ice.

I draped them over her, rubbing her arms, asking her if she felt warm enough. But she only stared back at me with a blank expression.

"What have you done?" she asked, voice cold. "Lyr, what have you done?" Her hand snaked toward my wrist, turning my palm up, exposing my star tattoo and the oaths branded beneath them.

Rhyan knew. Rhyan knew the secret I'd spent years spilling my blood and sweat to protect. I felt like my heart was going to explode. My oath was broken. It was my own fault. It was my own weakness. I'd allowed myself to be cornered, I'd waited too long to act.

"I had no choice," I said. "I had to get you out of there without anyone seeing, without the escorts catching us. I almost had you safe, but I wasn't fast enough. If he hadn't...." I shook my head, feeling the panic start to come over me. "We would have been exposed completely. We had four escorts trailing us after I carried you away from the party." Plus Bellamy.

She squeezed her eyes shut. "I know. I know you did everything you could. But Lyr," she said, her pale eyes flicking to my wrist.

The oath was embedded with consequences. I'd broken my oath. And I was going to pay the price.

"What does it mean?" I asked frantically. "What's going to happen to me?"

"I don't know. I've never known anyone who broke a blood oath before." Her teeth chattered. "Just that...the magic finds a way."

I wracked my brain for any sort of information I'd gleaned over my years of research. But I'd been so busy trying to protect the oath, I'd never read about what would happen if I broke it. I never could have imagined I would.

Meera's thin shoulders shook as she let out a cold gasp, her breath frosting in the air. She ran her hands over her face, fingers catching in her hair, pale and disheveled. "He knows."

My stomach twisted as I nodded.

"Lyr, what are we going to do about him?" Her eyes dipped down my leg, to the soturion dagger strapped to my thigh.

My breath came faster. I was going to be sick. I couldn't hurt Rhyan. Unless...Fuck. Gods.

Meera drew the blankets tighter around her shoulders. "It's too crowded in here, I need some air. I can't. I just...can't right now." Her whole body shivered. Her gait was uneven as she stumbled to the door of the carriage. Holding her hand, I helped her step out. She moved silently through the sand to the shoreline, her moonlit hair blowing in the breeze, the blanket dragging behind her back, erasing her footprints in the sand.

Rhyan stood at the edge of the shoreline, gazing into the ocean. The rolling waves lapped against his boots before retreating. His dark green cloak lifted in the wind. Beneath the moon and stars, the golden sands of Gryphon Island were muted to a soft bronze. The great statue of a black onyx gryphon, the Guardian of Bamaria, loomed in the distance, a silent protector of the shores.

Heart pounding, I made my way through the sand, my boots sinking with each step. I joined Rhyan's side, hugging my arms to my chest, painfully aware of the dagger sheathed to my thigh, of what I might have to do to protect my family. The wind blew at me, frigid with the salt of the ocean water, spraying against my arms and face. And all at once, the pain I was in from Meera's attack, the stress of getting her to safety, and the fear of how and when the magic would strike for breaking my oath and whether or not I could trust Rhyan with what he now knew hit me. The secret I'd carried, the pain...every choice, every sacrifice including Jules... I couldn't breathe. Couldn't believe this had happened.

Rhyan turned toward me, his right eyebrow furrowed in concern. The breeze lifted the edges of his cloak up behind him.

My chest heaved, heart pounding. My hands and feet felt numb and my chest hollow, as tears burned behind my eyes.

Rhyan took a step closer. "Is she all right?" His voice was full of concern.

Not the question I was expecting.

I was imagining Tristan. I was imagining Meera already being tied up, bound in black ropes and dragged away as his aura raged with fury and betrayal.

But this was Rhyan. Rhyan, who swore he'd never hurt me. Rhyan, whose touch could light my body on fire. Rhyan, who even in his darkest moments of the night, even barely conscious from his nightmares, still managed to protect me.

But he was also Rhyan, forsworn. Rhyan, who couldn't afford to lose his place in Bamaria over a secret that didn't affect him.

I shook, my body growing colder, my stomach plummeting.

"Lyr?" he asked again.

I reached for my chest, clutching it through my dress as my breathing grew more erratic. Everything tightened inside me.

Rhyan knew. He knew about Meera. He knew our secret. I didn't know what he was going to do about it. I didn't know how the magic was going to punish me. I didn't know if Meera was going to be all right or how long we had before our escorts found us and questioned us. Or if someone at the party had seen something they shouldn't. Or if Bellamy would talk. Tristan was probably looking for me by now and freaking out.

Fuck. Fuck. Fuck.

I gasped, unable to breathe. My vision blacked out and blinked back, but everything was too bright. The stars, the moon. There were spots on the ocean, exploding and glittering with starlight, and the light of the Valalumir buried in its depths was too bright, too much....

Rhyan's arms were instantly around me. "Shhh. Hey. Hey," he spoke softly. "I've got you. I've got you. Deep breaths. It's all right." He pulled me closer, and my face buried against his chest while my hands remained protectively wrapped around my body. "Breathe with me. Come on, Lyr. You can do this. It's all right, I've got you. Take a breath. In...and out. Lyr. Lyr, calm down. You're safe. You're safe with me. Nothing's going to hurt you. I swear."

My breath hitched instead of improving.

"You're all right. It's all right." Rhyan slid his arm behind my knees, scooped me into his arms, and cradled me against his chest.

He walked forward toward the lapping waves, their surface reflecting flashes of starlight. "I've got you."

"W-What are you doing?" I asked.

"You see the waves?" His hand was on my cheek, brushing loose hairs away from my face. He angled his body, offering me an easy view of the ocean. "The waves," he said again, his voice a whisper. His arms shifted and tightened against me. "Just watch the waves, rolling back and forth. Back and forth. Nice and easy. Just keep watching. I've got you. You're all right."

The full moon reflected on the water, and the wind picked up, icy cold but oddly soothing. Rhyan's chest rose and fell against me, deeper and slower than before, as he breathed in and out in time with the rolling waves. We stayed like that for several moments until I found my own breathing matching his as it had so many times before. Together, our breaths slowed to the pulse of the ocean.

I closed my eyes, letting myself fall into the darkness, peaceful and soothing. I blinked my eyes open, meeting Rhyan's. Immediate relief spread across his face.

"There you are, there's my partner," he said. "Nice and slow." He stepped forward, the water rushing around his boots. "Hang onto me," he said, hand pushing mine up around his neck.

I clasped my fingers together, the movement pushing my face closer against him. We dipped down, and I strained my head to see Rhyan cupping his hand into a fresh wave that rolled against his boots.

"It's just the ocean," he said, rising. "Close your eyes." He let the water drip down my face. The sensation—cold, wet, but refreshing—pulled me back to myself. Small details. Being present. He smoothed his palm against my cheek. "Feeling better?" he asked.

I swallowed, mouth still dry. "I can breathe."

"Good. Good. Breathing's always a good start," he said. He frowned. "You're hurt."

"No, I'm…." My body seized. *Don't let him see. Don't let him know.*

But he'd already seen. He already knew.

We four keep this secret. We four die by this secret.

Not any longer. Now I was forsworn.

"I know," he said. "I know. I'm going to help you."

Rhyan walked us back from the shoreline, just beyond the reach of the waves, before gently setting me down on dry sand and sitting beside me. He reached into the pouch of his belt, pulling out sunleaves and looking at me with his expression full of concern.

"HART!" Markan's voice roared from Rhyan's pouch as a blue light emanated from inside it. The vadati stone.

He scooped it into his palm, his eyes on me. "Markan, I'm here."

"The fuck you're not. We just landed in Cresthaven, and there's no sign of you or their graces. You better be on your way with both of them intact."

My heart caught in my throat, but Rhyan, still watching me, offered a single nod, one hand sliding to my thigh and resting just above my knee. He gave me a light squeeze, keeping his hand a steady, reassuring weight on me as he replied, "Their graces are having," he wriggled his nose, "a bit of holiday fun. They decided last minute to direct the seraphim to Gryphon Island."

"We're on our way."

I gripped Rhyan's arm, shaking my head.

"No need. We're getting ready to come back. It'll take you longer to get here than for us to meet you at Cresthaven."

"This is against protocol," Markan sneered. "Lady Lyriana was ordered to have two guards, and Lady Meera three. I know you think fives beneath you, but you are one man."

"Which is why I am bringing them back."

"You better hope you're back with their graces within the hour —not one hair on either head harmed. Or your ass is gone— forsworn forever."

"Understood," Rhyan said calmly. The stone's blue light faded until it was nothing but a clear crystal that he deposited back in his belt pocket.

Rhyan turned to me, his jaw tightening. "Where's Lady Meera?"

"I think walking along the shore...cooling off."

"We'll get her. The island's abandoned. I flew out here a few times when I was scouting training spots. She should be fine. Let's clean up these cuts and scratches."

Rhyan leaned forward, taking my arm in his hand and turning it, then the other. He released them and leaned back, examining my back, pushing my hair aside, and then both his hands were on my face, turning me toward him. He nodded then counted the sunleaves in his hand before he popped them into his mouth and chewed, alchemizing them into gold paste.

He studied my face again, pushing more of my hair behind my ears, and smeared sunleaves over a scratch on my neck. I sucked in a breath, but the burning sensation vanished almost instantly, replaced with a cool relief.

"Did I hurt you?" His hand lingered on my face, caressing my cheek.

"No."

"This was who was...." He coughed. "This is what's been hurting you? What gave you the limp? The black eye?" He ran his hands over my shoulders, chasing away the cold. "The whole time?"

Tears fell down my cheeks.

His hands ran up and down my back, soothing even as he made a low growl in the back of his throat.

I turned to him. "She doesn't mean to—She can't help—"

"I know," he started, but I cried out in fresh pain. A burning stab ran through my wrist.

"What happened?" He moved closer. "Where does it hurt?"

I gripped my wrist before I could stop myself. Gods, it felt like my arm had been set on fire. Rhyan shifted me to face him, taking my hand in his, turning my palm up.

"Did you strain it earlier?" he asked.

A finger ran up and down the length of my inner arm, across my tattoo. I shivered as he paused at my wrist over the scars that marked my oath as a soturion, that marked where I'd been cut when I joined his kashonim. Gently, his finger ran over the raised, mutilated skin, invisible to the naked eye.

"Blood oaths?" His jaw tightened. "Gods. That's why you got the tattoo. To hide the feel of the scars."

I nodded.

"When?" He held my hand, his thumb rubbing small circles over my scarred skin.

"The night they took Jules," I said, my tears freely falling. "They discovered her vorakh at the Revelation, and you already know—I had to sit there and watch. Watch the Imperator take her away, right in front of me." I sniffled. "I wasn't allowed to move or cry. I wasn't allowed to make a single sound. I had to control what they saw, pretend I didn't care. Tristan held me down while it happened, telling me it was for the best."

The muscles in his jaw clenched. "Was he the one who—"

"No."

He squeezed my hand, continuing to rub circles, and then pulled me closer to him, wrapping his free arm around my shoulder.

"And then after she was outside of the temple, my father ordered the ceremony to go on like nothing was wrong. It was Meera's turn, and she was the same. My father covered it up. Kept her vorakh secret. After the ceremony was over…Gods." My voice broke. "I told you what happened next. Markan drugged me, dragged me home. But what you don't know is when I woke, I was in the Arkasva's Seating Room with my sisters. My father had a dagger." I clutched my chest, trying to contain the sobs. I'd never spoken of this night before. Not even with Meera or Morgana. "I had no choice. I would have never betrayed my family, my Ka, but…."

"You swore the oath anyway," he said.

"He made me. *They* made me. And a year later, I got my second."

Rhyan blinked, his jaw tensing as he realized what I'd just admitted. "And this is why—fuck. This is why you're with him?

With Tristan? Because otherwise, he might have guessed the reason you broke up? And this is why he didn't know about your injuries? Gods. Lyr. This whole time, you were just protecting them."

"I was," I sobbed, squeezing my eyes shut and burying my face against his chest.

He held me, letting me cry. I cried for all the hurt, for Meera, for Jules, and for Morgana. I cried for myself and how what I'd done for my family had never once been acknowledged. How I'd been a casualty in this mess, one no one could see because I was hiding the secrets, holding the family together. How for two years, I'd been punishing myself over Jules, denying myself to keep Meera and Morgana safe, and staying with Tristan so I could keep up the charade and protect our Ka.

"You're not the first to get a tattoo for that sort of thing," he said, when my sobs slowed. He lifted my chin, drawing my gaze up. His thumb brushed away the tears on my cheeks, and he lifted my wrist to his lips. He paused, watching me carefully, then pressed a soft kiss to the scar. "Don't be ashamed of it."

I sucked in a breath. The sensation of his lips against my skin was suddenly the only thing in the world. Like it had been that morning.

He released my hand from his. My wrist tingled.

He began methodically unhooking his armor.

My eyes widened. "What are you...?"

He pulled the black leather off and pushed aside his green cloak, turning away from me to reveal the full gryphon tattoo on his back. The beast, beautifully rendered in detail, was taking flight over snowy mountains, its wings spanning beyond his shoulders to his chest. A torn rope was tied to the gryphon's eagle-like leg.

No ropes can hold you. No cage can trap you.

The source of Rhyan's strength, his inner power, and the love he had for gryphons and his country, all so beautifully rendered across his back and shoulders.

Tentatively, I ran my fingers over the beast, tracing its wings. Rhyan shuddered beneath me, and I paused. I'd touched him there this morning, but this was different. This was somehow far more personal, more intimate. Because now I understood.

"Put your hand against the rope," he said.

I let my fingers trail down his spine to the torn rope beneath the gryphon and landed on a line of raised skin.

"A blood oath," I gasped.

He straightened, pulled his cloak over his back, and reached for his discarded armor. Once he'd returned his uniform to the proper position of an apprentice soturion, he looked up at me. The full moon cast enough light to highlight his scar, silver through his forehead and eye. The bandages I'd put on him the night before had come off when he was holding Meera. Brockton's bite marks around his eye had faded a little, though he was still sporting several nasty looking bruises.

"Why a blood oath on your back?" I asked.

He stared down.

"You don't have to tell me," I said. "But...you also deserve to be asked one more time."

He turned his gaze up and inched closer to me. "My back was getting covered in scars. I was whipped and lashed by my father so many times. So many times, he bound me. And one day...." His gaze grew distant. "It's a long story."

"I want to hear it," I said.

"I want to tell you. Not tonight. First, we need to get Meera. Get you back to Cresthaven before anyone becomes any more suspicious."

I sucked in a breath, bracing myself for what came next. "We should go."

"Lyr, I hope you know, you don't even have to ask. You have my word in this. My oath. Always." His hair blew wildly in the wind, curling over his forehead and eyes, eyes that were now fixed on me with an intensity that left me shivering. "I know you've been given many reasons to believe no one could be trusted with this." He picked up my hand again, his finger running lightly over my scars. "Maybe most can't be trusted, maybe we live in a world full of people who fear others, but I'm not most people."

My heart pounded louder. I believed him.

A large wave crested, and we were forced to scoot farther back. An icy, watery breeze came with it, and I shivered again.

"Cold?" he asked.

"I'm all right," I said.

He laughed. "I felt your hands, remember."

Before I could deny it, he held up the extra material of his cloak, and I inched closer to him, close enough for him to wrap it around my shoulders. Fresh pine and musk surrounded my senses. The scent that always clung to him, clung to his bedsheets. "Better?" he asked.

"Thank you."

"Lyr," he said. His lips were so close. "Can we talk about this morning? I can't stop thinking about it."

I could feel his breath on my skin. We froze, our lips close, our eyes boring into each other's, my heart thumping.

"We need to find Meera," I said. "And get back."

"I know," he said. "But soon—can we talk? Please?"

"We'll talk."

He exhaled, his shoulders relaxing as he rose to his feet, a hand extended to help me up.

"She went that way." I pointed. In the distance was the Guardian of Bamaria. It was why the place had been named Gryphon Island. The structure seemed to predate even Ka Batavia—there were no records of who'd built the statue or when; I knew because I'd checked the Great Library.

We started walking, the uneven piles of sand causing me to wobble and slide as I walked.

Without a word, Rhyan took my hand in his, his grip firm and stabilizing as we continued on.

His eyes, dark green in the night, flicked to me and then straight ahead again.

Warmth bloomed inside my chest as my world came down to

my hand in his, the calluses on his fingers, the stroke of his thumb against my knuckle. I felt completely safe with him—safer than I'd ever felt before.

"Did you know we have a seraphim statue at home on Gryphon's Mount? She's made of pure moonstone."

My eyes widened. "No!"

"She's less famous than your Guardian. Smaller, and most of the time buried under snow. I think she tends to be forgotten for that reason. But her origin and purpose are equally unknown."

"Did you research her origins in the library?" I asked.

"Probably as much as you've researched the origins of the Guardian."

"I love that—" I started, then cut myself off, feeling self-conscious. But I loved how interested he was in history, how he got lost in research like I did.

"Me, too," he said.

We approached the statue constructed of three stories' worth of black onyx. The gryphon's head was lifted high, its eagle-eyes staring into the ocean. Its front haunches stretched before him, vanishing into the golden sand.

"Reminds me of home. Our sigil is everywhere. And every place it's not, there's a live gryphon. We even had a life-sized stone gryphon watching over the toilets in our Katurium. One of the mages thought it would honor Ka Hart to infuse it with life, so it always shifted slightly, its wings and eyes moving, watching. Took me years to manage pissing without jumping every time I saw it staring down at me."

"Seriously?" I laughed.

"As if I'd lie about an embarrassing story." He squeezed my hand. "But one time," he said slyly, "my friend Dario and I moved the beast, just after a morning run. This poor novice came in, didn't realize what we'd done until it was too late. Completely pissed himself."

I burst out laughing.

"Needed a brand-new cloak and everything." His right eyebrow lifted. "Pissed that one a week later when we returned the statue." He joined in my laughter.

"Is Dario the one you used to dress in the morning?" I asked. He'd mentioned him once before.

Rhyan smiled fondly, then seemed to catch himself. "Maybe we should call out to Meera?"

I bit my lip. "We've lingered too long. Are you going to be in trouble?"

"Nothing I can't handle."

"What about us?"

"I've got you and Meera covered."

We started to pass the Guardian's massive body, yelling out for Meera.

The wind howled, and a giant wave rolled through the water, crashing too far over the shoreline, almost reaching the Guardian's paws. We jumped just in time to avoid getting drenched. Another wave, even higher, rose from the waters, rolling toward us.

Then a low drawl came from behind us, "Fancy seeing you two here."

Mercurial, the Afeya messenger from the Star Court, approached us. He wore a loincloth of pure white silk and a silver velvet cloak draped over his shoulder, held in place seemingly by his hand. He frequently appeared with his skin blue, but tonight it was the color of frost, shimmering beneath the gold and silver swirls tattooed across his body.

My heart plunged like ice to my belly.

CHAPTER
EIGHTEEN

Rhyan shifted his body, angling himself between us, his stance protective.

"Holding hands. My my my," said the Afeya.

"Hello, Mercurial," I said, chest tight.

"Mercurial, First Messenger of Her Royal Highness, Queen Ishtara of the Star Court," he corrected. "And how are you, Lady Lyriana Batavia, Heir to the Arkasva, High Lord of Bamaria?"

"Well," I said, voice shaking. "Thank you."

Mercurial bowed to Rhyan. "And how are you, my—?"

"Still not Lord Hart," Rhyan said.

"Of course, *your grace.*" Mercurial chuckled, looking me up and down.

Rhyan released my hand and stepped in front of me. One hand rested on the hilt of his sword, and the other reached for his dagger. "State your business," he snarled.

"Very clever way of not asking me a question yet demanding an answer. Hands off your knives, my not-lord. I'm not here to fight," he purred.

"The fact that you've entered Bamaria without invitation says otherwise," he seethed.

"As ambassador, I am always welcome."

"The way you welcomed yourself into her grace's apartment?"

Mercurial laughed. "This does not look like her grace's apartment. It looks like public land to me. Land I have every right to step on. Land I stepped upon centuries before your soul entered this body."

I stepped forward. "Let me know if you require my assistance."

Mercurial tossed his head back in laughter, the sound rippling against my skin. "Let you know if I am in need of assistance from you? I am Afeya. Immortal. Blessed by the stars. No, I simply came to see the Guardian's great muscular self up-close. It's been, well, centuries since we've had some...alone time."

I stared down the length of the beach. Two sets of footprints led to the statue. Mine and Rhyan's. There was no third set to mark Mercurial's path. My gut twisted. Had he seen Meera?

Mercurial pursed his lips together, pulling his long black hair over his shoulder, suddenly taking a deep interest in his braids. They were unraveling and restyling themselves as he looked down. "And how are you both faring under your oaths? Quite a cold night. Perfect for sitting close together on the shore, cuddling beneath a cloak while the waves lick delicately at your feet. Hands maybe touching, or maybe lips touching hands...." He stared up at us, his eyes like starlight, twinkling and almost too bright to look at. "Or do you prefer early mornings in bed?"

My stomach dropped.

"Good night, Mercurial," Rhyan snapped. Ice puffed from his aura, sharp and burning with cold.

"Such anger from the son of the High Lord and Imperator." Mercurial's voice was dancing with flirtation. "You're more like him every time I see you."

Rhyan lunged. "I am nothing like my father."

"My fierce not-lord. Once again, did I say anything about your father? Just him. And there are many *hims* I've come across in time." He swirled his head back, stretching his neck, which undulated from side to side like a snake.

Once more, I felt myself transfixed, drawn to him, his perfect blend of masculine and feminine features, his otherworldly beauty. His eyes darkening as they focused on me. He pushed his hair off his shoulder and stepped forward, his movements precise like a hunter. Everything about him shouted predator. "Your grace, you should wear your gift more often," he said at last. "You know which one I mean."

"My necklace?"

Mercurial laughed. "The item you, we'll say, *acquired* at the festival."

"Wh—" I cut myself off before I could demand he tell me why he wanted me to wear Ramia's necklace. That would have been a question—a question that would have forced me into a deal with the Afeyan.

"I should think a messenger like yourself has more important matters to concern himself with than the daily jewelry selections of an heir."

"One would think. And you are right. Jewelry does not concern me. But the piece is very becoming on you," he said, "as it was on its former owner." A wind swirled through his hair before caressing my cheek.

I squeezed my hands at my sides. He knew who owned the necklace, but I would not ask. I would not enter a bargain with him.

"You wore it once," he said. "A lovely distraction. Another night will come—when you should wear it again."

I stood taller. "I'll have to see. Depends on my mood. And outfit."

"You do many things based on your mood. I would have thought you more logical. After all, you still never told him your dream."

Rhyan's eyes flicked from me to Mercurial.

"We're leaving," he announced.

"May I offer her grace a kiss on the hand goodbye?" Mercurial asked.

I looked to Rhyan. It seemed like an innocent enough request, though nothing was what it seemed with the Afeya. Still, I had the distinct sense that I could not deny him. Had any other noble or foreign ambassador requested the same, protocol would have demanded I say yes.

Rhyan's hand snaked around the hilt of his sword. "Approach her grace if you must. One kiss to the palm. Anything else, I strike."

Mercurial rolled his eyes like he was dealing with a child throwing a tantrum as he sauntered in front of me.

I extended my right hand forward, palm down.

The Afeyan grinned up at me, his lips puckering.

Then, without warning, his hand shot up. A gust of air blew Rhyan back as Mercurial gripped my arm between his hands, bringing my wrist—my blood oaths—to his mouth. He kissed me there, right where Rhyan had moments ago.

"You bastard," Rhyan growled, pushing against Mercurial's magic.

Mercurial stepped back, released my wrist, and withdrew his magic from Rhyan. "Someone was very naughty tonight. A broken oath. A blood debt to be paid," the Afeyan drawled.

I froze. He knew about Meera.

Mercurial grinned. "Of course, I know. Luckily for you, I don't like to mix my magic with blood oaths. Distasteful. Instead, I will leave you with some advice, and in return, do me one favor."

"I don't do favors for Afeya," I said.

"Then perhaps I will break my own rules and get in the middle of this blood debt." His lips sneered. "I know you lie. I know you owe a favor elsewhere. To one of my kind—to a certain librarian."

Rhyan had reached my side again. "Lyr," he said under his breath. "No."

"Tell me the favor," I said.

"Wear it. Start wearing it on formal occasions, in battle. It was meant to be worn. By you."

I bit my lip, desperate to ask why, to understand the importance of the necklace and what it meant and who it had belonged to and why Ramia had lied about it and why Mercurial was so invested in it and why he'd destroyed scrolls in the Great Library just to hold my attention, to force my curiosity and lure me into a deal.

"Your advice," I said.

"The blood debt is hungry. You are not safe. And you never will be, unless one of two things happens."

Rhyan's arm wrapped around me.

"Either the debt is paid, which I think all three of us can agree we do not want to happen, or the debt is changed."

I looked at Rhyan, who had lifted his good eyebrow.

"Changed," I said, barely keeping the question out of my voice.

"Changed," Mercurial said. "And, unfortunately, that is all I can say without requiring you to give more than you're willing to provide as yet." He narrowed his eyes, stars dancing in them. "But you will give more eventually. You have so much more to give." Mercurial bowed, and another wave rolled, approaching fast, rising higher than the Guardian.

I braced myself to be soaked, but before the water hit, Mercurial lifted a finger. The water froze to ice above our heads. With a flick, the ice melted, and the water formed thousands of tiny droplets, all shimmering in suspension. Mercurial pointed, and the particles united into a gleaming, glittering Valalumir. The star disintegrated back into the wave, which seemed to reverse course, moving itself back into the ocean.

He was using so much magic—magic he shouldn't have been able to use without being asked.

Rhyan moved in front of me again, reaching behind his back to grab my hand. His fingers wrapped around my mine and squeezed. "It's time for you to leave. Now."

"Uh-uh-uh," the Afeya said, grasping Rhyan's chin in his hand. "Naughty boy. You do not make demands of the Afeya. Not until you reclaim your true title."

Mercurial's skin glowed white, then shimmered with the blue he'd worn before. The color went in and out of focus, his skin running through every color of the rainbow before landing on a bright blood red. His aura swirled, separated from his body. The light of the moon vanished, replaced by a black hole, and every star in the sky winked out, blanketing us in total darkness. Dark clouds formed in the sky, and thunder clapped until rain poured straight down, a thick curtained waterfall completely surrounding us.

"I'll never ask you for anything," Rhyan said.

Mercurial's eyes danced, his head snaking side to side again, moving closer and closer to Rhyan's face until their mouths were only an inch apart. He snapped his teeth against Rhyan's mouth, and then he was gone.

"Gods," I cried. "My wrist is on fire."

Rhyan turned to me, taking my hand between his, inspecting my wrist.

"Do you think he was right?" I asked through gritted teeth. "That I can change the debt?"

"I don't trust him," Rhyan snarled. "But he did heal your ankle. He wants something from you. Which means you have value to the Afeya. I don't like it. But I think, in his twisted way, yes. He's probably right."

"We need to get to Cresthaven. Now. Before the guards come. I need to tell my father what happened. See if he can do anything about it."

"If he ordered the oath, his magic will have the most sway."

I hissed as another sharp pain ran down the scar. "It's burning. I think it's going to do this until the debt is paid." I could feel flames licking up and down the scar.

Rhyan rubbed his thumb over my wrist, softly, his touch soothing as he infused it with a blast of cool air from his aura.

"Wait here," he said. "I'll get Meera."

I sat down, bringing my knees to my chest and wrapping my arms around them, clutching at my scar, trying not to jump at every sound. I tried to focus my attention on the waves rather than on the pain in my wrist. I took deep breaths, my shoulders heaving.

Thunder crashed in the distance. I inhaled through my nose. Exhaled through my mouth. I groaned in pain with each breath. I wasn't prepared when a giant wave approached, hovering above me, about to crash down.

Rhyan pulled me into his arms and held me against his chest as he raced backward, just beyond the water's reach. My eyes widened as the water retreated.

"Can you walk?" Rhyan asked, his voice low in my ear.

"Lyr. Gods!" Meera said. She was standing behind him, still wrapped in her blanket.

"I can walk," I said. Sensing the tide returning, the wave growing until it towered above the waters, I amended, "I can run."

"Lady Meera?" Rhyan asked.

"Come on," I said and grabbed her hand. The three of us took off across the sand while the wave crashed and water chased and lapped at our feet. We parted at the Guardian of Bamaria, Meera and me running in front of its paws while Rhyan ran behind, calling out to us.

Our seraphim rested ahead, her head lifted, eyes wide with fear as her wings fluttered nervously at her side. She started to stand, sensing the coming storm and preparing to leave.

"Not yet!" Rhyan yelled. "Hurry!"

I tightened my hold on Meera, running ahead as I dragged her along, but we were both slipping and sliding across the sand, our boots sinking with each step.

"We need to stop the seraphim before she leaves without us!" I yelled over the waves crashing beside us. The tide was moving closer and closer, and our seraphim squawked in annoyance.

Meera pulled out her stave, her other hand tightening in mine.

"Glemata!" Meera yelled. A burst of blue light shot forth, rushing over the seraphim, transforming its wings and body to moonstone blue. The bird froze in a half-crouched position, but Meera's spell wasn't strong enough to hold it. The seraphim's wings were shaking. With another shake, she broke free of the spell.

Rhyan reached her first, the bird now fully standing with no way for us to climb onto the carriage. With a yell, Rhyan launched himself into the air, landing on the bird's upper leg.

She froze in indignation as Rhyan grabbed her feathers, climbing his way up. But instead of going into the carriage, he crawled over to her face and managed to lay his belly across her beak. He stroked her feathers, speaking gently.

Her wings stopped fluttering as she was soothed by his voice or his strokes or both. He was looking right into her eyes. Her body stilled, and her legs began to bend until she laid back down.

I could relate. Rhyan had never lain across my nose, but the rest of his technique was familiar.

At last, we reached the carriage. Meera sheathed her stave in her belt and climbed aboard while I waited for Rhyan to climb down.

"You're a seraphim whisperer?"

He tilted his head to the side, one hand grazing the nape of his neck, an almost sheepish expression on his face. "Gryphon whisperer. Luckily my tricks work on Bamarian birds, too."

Rhyan had wanted a pet gryphon when he was younger. But the creatures grew to such massive sizes he could have never kept one inside, so he'd helped train them with the Glemarian Master of the Horse. A skill I was beyond grateful he had now.

A bolt of lightning lit up the sky, followed by an earth-shaking clap of thunder. Our bird stood as another tide roared to shore, rising and rising as it raced.

"Blood debt," I gasped.

"Fuck!" Rhyan grabbed my waist and jumped, landing on the carriage steps just before they were out of reach.

"LYR!" Meera screamed. The bird was preparing to take flight while we were barely hanging onto her, before Meera had even locked the carriage doors.

"Come on," Rhyan urged, grimacing as he held onto the stairs. The seraphim's wings flapped, picking up speed.

"By the Gods!" The ground was getting farther and farther away from my feet.

"Lyr, climb!" Rhyan commanded. He pushed me against the stairs, somehow lifting my entire body with just one hand.

I grabbed the stairs with both hands as Meera shrieked, leaning out the carriage door, her hand reaching for me.

"Climb!" Rhyan yelled.

I pressed my face against the bird's side, frozen with terror to be outside as she soared.

"Lyr, climb! I'm right behind you," Rhyan yelled, his voice sounding distant as the wind cut between us.

My hand shook—the burning was back in my wrist—but I managed to let go of the step I clung to with one hand and reach for the next, one foot gaining purchase on the step above it. The wind was bitingly cold at this height, and my entire body was shivering both from the temperature and the fear pulsing through me.

Warmth suddenly covered my back as strong arms appeared on either side of me. Rhyan had climbed up behind me. His body shielded mine against the wind and endless sky around us.

"You won't fall. I'm right here." His breath was warm against my ear. I could feel his aura, soothing and trying to warm and calm me.

"Come on, Lyr!" Meera yelled.

I reached for the next step and the next, Rhyan climbing just behind me, until I found my way into the carriage and collapsed into Meera's arms. She hauled me back, as far from the carriage door as possible, until we landed on the ground on top of all the blankets I'd pulled out.

Rhyan slammed the door shut, locking it in place, and exhaled sharply. "Partner," he said. "Let's never do that again." He sank into a seat, looking uncharacteristically shaken.

I tried to say something in response, but words weren't quite forming in my mouth, so I simply stuck up my thumb.

"You're all right," Meera said.

I nodded, and she helped me to make my way to the bench.

"Everyone's inside," Rhyan said. "All limbs and fingers accounted for. Heartrates beating…semi-normal."

"I think," I gasped.

Meera nodded, stiff with tension again.

"Right, then next order of business," Rhyan said. He moved before Meera on the bench, dropping to his knees. "I swore to your sister I would protect her. That she would always be safe with me.

And that means protecting you as well. Protecting your secret." He pressed his fist to his heart, tapped twice, and flattened his hand across his chest. "*Me sha, me ka.* My oath, my soul. Lady Meera Batavia, you have my word."

Meera eyed him nervously, her face skeptical, and I thought of how she'd insinuated I might have to kill Rhyan for what he knew. I understood her reluctance to trust him. We'd been forced to bear the burden of the blood oath—mere promises or sworn oaths weren't enough for Ka Batavia.

Rhyan seemed to understand that as well.

"I offer you a token to prove my trust," he said. "A secret for a secret." He reached into the pouch attached to his soturion belt where he usually stored spare sunleaves and lately bags of nuts and chocolates that he offered me during training breaks. He pulled his fisted hand free, taking a deep breath. Whatever he was about to show, it made him nervous, too.

When he opened his palm, he revealed three clear stones swirling with mist.

Vadati stones. And not the Bamarian-issued stone he used for communication with my escort team when on guard duty. These were smaller, their shapes uneven.

Meera gasped in disbelief as Rhyan rose, placing one in her hand and one in mine.

"This is so you can reach each other for help when you're apart. They were my mother's," he said, "hidden from the Empire for centuries. Her ancestors carried them across the ocean." He glanced away, his gaze distant as his lips quirked into a small smile. "I took them before I left. I was already forsworn—I just wanted something of hers."

These were illegal to own. Priceless artifacts from Lumeria Matavia, heavily controlled by the Empire…like my necklace.

Meera tried to return hers. "I can't. It's too precious."

Rhyan pushed her hand back, closing her fingers over the stone. "I could be arrested for having these. Thrown out of Bamaria if you told anyone. They'd be confiscated, and I'd be forsworn again, in exile with no chance of refuge."

Meera's eyes widened as she understood. A secret for a secret. But it was too much. Rhyan had already given us his oath. To give these, when they'd been his mother's....

He closed my fingers over my own stone. My skin warmed, and our eyes met.

"These will be better served in your hands than hiding in the dragon pile I've hoarded the past year."

Meera's eyes shone. "I accept."

"You have my oath." Rhyan took Meera's hand and kissed it, but his eyes remained on me.

He sat down beside me, the length of his thigh pressed along mine. I pushed my leg back against his, reveling in the feel of his closeness, his warmth, his scent, his…everything.

Meera carefully placed her vadati stone in the pouch attached to her belt beside her stave, a look of awe in her eyes. Even as Heir Apparent, she'd never actually been allowed to touch or use one of the ancient stones.

Rhyan returned his single remaining stone to his belt. My only secure place was in the holster circling my thigh. I pushed my skirt aside, the entire length of my thigh up to my hip bone exposed. I was suddenly aware of Rhyan's eyes on my exposed skin, and my stomach tightened, my core clenching as heat pooled between my legs.

As I looked up, his eyes darkened, hooded with desire. I took hold of the top of my skirt where the slit ended and pulled it back, just enough for Rhyan to see the strings of my underwear. A sound came from Meera, and I pulled the material back down, hastily leaning forward to secure my vadati stone inside the holster—in a pocket just beside my dagger.

When I looked up again, Rhyan's green eyes were full of unbridled hunger. His hand on his leg slid to mine. His fingers brushed past the material of my dress, through the opened slit, and just barely touched my thigh.

Outside, the bells announced a new hour.

Or, I thought they did. The wind was loud outside the window, but the distinct sound of bells rang through the noise.

Then it hit me. These weren't the bells for time. They were warning bells.

Our carriage shook, the movement so violent we were turned on an angle. I slid down the bench and grabbed hold of my seat before I could fall off. Meera slammed into me. There was a crack, and all the cabinets opened and slammed shut above our heads.

"Are you two all right?" Rhyan asked. He opened his window, pulling back the curtains to peer out.

"We're fine," I said. "Anything out there?"

Rhyan shook his head and frowned, eyebrows narrowed, continuing to scan the night's sky.

There was silence save for the wind as we soared. And then it happened again. The whole carriage rocked.

"Fuck!" I yelled. My wrist. The blood oath didn't seem to affect me constantly. The pain came and went at irregular intervals.

Our seraphim shrieked, a horrid, terrifying, high-pitched sound.

Rhyan was by my side in an instant, pulling back the curtain of my window.

A burst of magic rumbled beneath us, black and glittering, moving quickly against the wind until it took shape, sprouting a beak, and wide, black, glittering wings.

A black seraphim was flying right at us.

Our seraphim, already upset from the storm, shrieked in panic, her wings flapping ferociously to change direction. She jerked her body, and the carriage tipped sideways. The cabinets spilled open, and the blankets we'd covered the floor with flew at me until I was tangled underneath them. I scrambled to my feet just as the seraphim turned again. Meera was teetering too close to a window. I launched myself across the carriage and pushed her out of the way.

"Lyr!" Rhyan yelled, reaching for me, his hand outstretched as I fell, my back smacking against the wall. We turned sideways again. "LYR!"

There was a shriek, a sudden turn, and the sickening feeling of the carriage turning too quickly to the other side. My heart leapt into my throat then plunged directly into my belly.

A window burst open, and a gust of wind exploded inside the carriage.

One second, I was holding onto the wall, and the next, I'd been flung across the carriage right out the opened window.

CHAPTER
NINETEEN

There was nothing beneath my feet, just air and sky and wind. I reached blindly as I flew out the window, grasping desperately for anything to hold onto. My fingers landed against the bottom of the seraphim's harness, but I didn't have the strength to pull myself up, and my hold was already faltering, my arms sore, my fingers sweaty. The carriage jerked with another shriek of our seraphim, and my grip loosened.

Rhyan hung half out of the carriage window. He seemed to have soared out chasing me. He screamed for me to take his hand, tried to get hold of me. But I couldn't move. If I lifted one finger, that was it. I'd fall.

Meera screamed, crying, begging Rhyan to save me.

The wind whipped against my face, blowing my hair in every direction. I couldn't see, couldn't focus. I could barely breathe from the pressure of it. Was this it? Was this the price of the magic? Of breaking my oath?

Another jerk. My hand flew off the harness. The wind swallowed my scream.

My hand flew right into Rhyan's. He was leaning too far out the window, as Meera stood behind him, holding onto his cloak. He wrapped both of his hands around me and hauled me up and up to the window's ledge, and with a final grunt, he hoisted me inside.

We flew across the carriage, landing with Rhyan on his back with me in his arms.

He tightened his grip around me, pressed his head to mine. "I've got you. I've got you. You're safe." His voice shook, like he was trying to convince himself. "You're safe."

My whole body was cold, my limbs shaking. I wanted to hug him back, to wrap my arms around him and hold on, to reassure myself that this was real, that I was alive and in his arms, inside the carriage, not falling, not dead. But my arms were useless, shaking and shivering at my sides.

Meera pulled me off him and cradled me against her, squishing my face before bursting into fresh tears. "You're all right, Lyr. By the Gods, you're all right." She hugged me tighter, but I couldn't hug her back. My arms were still shaking and useless. "We need to go straight to Father. I never," she shook her head, "I never should have let you swear that oath."

Rhyan got to his feet, jaw muscles flexing as he closed and locked every window.

There was another shake of the carriage, and our seraphim turned so abruptly beneath us that we slid into the wall. Every window opened again, and a gust of wind swirled around me.

"It's the oath!" I screamed.

"NO!" Rhyan dove forward, wrapping his arms around me and laying me on the ground beneath him. His body tensed, hovering over mine. He kept one arm around me, cradling me, the other lifted to the window. "The magic will have to get through me first."

Meera crouched beside us. "And me."

"Land!" he screamed to our bird. "Land now! Lady Meera!" He grabbed her arm, pulling her to the floor beside me, so we both lay beneath him.

She took my hand as the glass of the windows all smashed and the carriage jerked violently. Then the bird began her descent. My belly jumped through my chest with the drop.

A moment later, we were on the ground.

"Where are we?" I asked as Rhyan moved off us. His hand was on his dagger, his stance ready for battle, as he eyed our surroundings.

"Urtavia," he said, glaring out the window. "We just passed the gates of the city. I see the Katurium." Shouts came from outside.

Meera helped me sit up, using the blanket to brush aside the broken glass littering the floor. I leaned against the carriage wall, my knees drawn up to my chest, still shaky. I took deep breaths as she wrapped both arms around me.

"Are you both all right?" Rhyan asked.

"What's happening?"

"*Shekar arkasva! Shekar arkasva! Shekar arkasva!*" The chant was coming from outside, growing louder and more passionate with each cheer.

The Emartis. They'd conjured the black seraphim in the sky, and now they were out.

When Rhyan opened the carriage door, it was mayhem. Ashvan were taking off with soturion riders on their backs. Mages were running in all directions while the Soturi of Ka Kormac shouted orders for everyone to go inside. In the distance were the chanting Emartis wearing black robes with hoods pulled over their faces. Puffs of black glitter exploded in the sky like fireworks, all in the shape of black seraphim. Every time a new explosion erupted, people screamed and ran as tiny fires broke out amongst the ashes.

"We've got to get to Cresthaven," Meera said. "Now."

Rhyan closed the doors, and the floor immediately shifted beneath us as our seraphim stood, preparing for take-off.

"Sit in my lap," Rhyan said.

"What?" I glanced between him and Meera.

"Now, so I can hold onto you. I'm not having you flying out the windows again. Until we solve the blood debt, we can't risk it."

"He's right," Meera said. "Do as he says." It was a command from my future Arkasva.

I sat down, and Rhyan immediately wrapped his arms around

my waist, locking me in place. I straightened, trying not to sink too deeply into his warmth, into the utter sense of safety I felt around him, especially with Meera watching.

But this time, the flight was smooth. None of the Emartis's black seraphim seemed to be on our route.

His chest rose and fell rapidly behind me, a mirror of my own rapid breaths.

"I thought," I said quietly, "that you were the calm one."

"I wasn't calm last night," he said, voice low.

"Were you calm this morning?" I asked.

"Don't ask questions you know the answer to." His arms tightened around me, his hand splayed across my belly.

I sucked in a breath, noting Meera glancing anxiously out the broken window. She huddled into a blanket and wrapped her arms around herself.

"You know," Rhyan continued, his chest still rising and falling in quick succession, "when I told you to be freer than a seraphim, this is not what I meant." His breath brushed against my ear and neck, and my stomach coiled. "It was a metaphor."

"You didn't specify literal or metaphor," I said, breathless. Too breathless. The unmistakable feel of his erection pressed against my ass, and my body instantly responded. This was not the place nor the time for so many reasons. I knew it stemmed from the fear and energy of what had just happened. Knew it was a natural bodily response. But I couldn't stop myself from grinding back against him, sinking deeper into his warmth.

His nose nudged against my hair, arms pulling me against his chest. "If you keep that up, I won't have any brain cells left to spar with you." He swallowed a moan as the carriage bounced, causing me to shift against him.

I ran my fingers across his arm. "You still have brain cells left?"

"Questionable." He shivered against me, readjusting his seat. I leaned my head back against his shoulder, focusing on his breathing, trying to calm my racing heart, to ignore the throbbing between my legs. One finger began to move idly against my belly, like

Rhyan couldn't feel enough of me, like he needed more—even if it was just an inch of stomach.

"I can see the fortress lights in the distance," Meera announced, still staring out the window. "We're close."

I squeezed my eyes shut, remembering I'd abandoned Tristan at the festival. All the reasons I couldn't be with Rhyan raced through my mind, the same list he'd tried to cite to me this morning. The list I should have remembered before I'd mentioned our morning together or wiggled against him. I stared down at my wrist—calm for the moment—but the sinking feeling in my stomach grew.

"We're at the walls," Meera announced a short time later. Sticking her head out the window, Meera signaled to the sentries on duty that our carriage carried two Bamarian Heirs, and we were immediately allowed to land inside the fortress. My stomach crumbled with dread. I could see even from our vantagepoint that the fortress was crawling with sentries on duty.

"It's probably safe for me to...." I pushed against Rhyan's hold on me, sliding to sit next to him.

He coughed and straightened in his seat, his knuckles white as he gripped the bench for our landing.

Once we landed, I stepped outside, immediately coming face to face with an entire row of escorts waiting to march us inside Cresthaven.

Markan glared at me from under his hood. "A more foolish heir I've never met," he growled. "And you, Hart!"

"I'm going to take their graces inside," Rhyan snarled. "I still need to see them to safety. Then we can talk. Oh, and you should alert someone—this seraphim and carriage will be out of commission for a while."

My body full of tension, we all walked down the waterway to the double doors, an army of guards surrounding us.

The Great Hall was flooded with people—sentries, house staff, members of the Bamarian Council and their immediate families—rushing around; it was protocol for everyone to be called to the fortress during a terrorist attack.

A terrorist attack. I'd been in such shock over the chaos of our carriage ride, it only then dawned on me. We were under attack. And if everyone from the Bamarian Council was here with their immediate family members, then—

"Lyr!" Tristan shouted my name from across the hall. He was taking long strides to get to me, his eyes narrowing when he saw Rhyan was with me. He reached my side in a second and pulled me into a hug. Too tight of a hug. He pulled back, eyes darkening. "What the hell happened to you? You vanished, and then the Emartis—it doesn't matter. You're safe." He pulled me against him again, his hand around the nape of my neck, as I wrapped my arms around his back.

Pain sliced through my wrist, and I let go.

"Is my father here?" I asked. "Morgana?"

"Of course," he said.

"I need to speak to him," I said, unable to hide the urgency or pain in my voice.

"Did something happen to you?" Tristan asked. "You look...." He ran his hand through my hair, smoothing it behind my ear.

I caught sight of Morgana at the other end of the hall. Her expression was pained, and her akadim mask was pushed to the top of her head, pulling her raven hair back. Her eyes widened as she heard me and turned in my direction. I watched as her mouth in opened in horror. She started toward me but stilled when she saw Tristan.

Where were you? I thought, unable to suppress the anger surging through my body.

"Lyr?" Tristan asked again. "What happened?"

I exhaled sharply, knowing Morgana was sifting through my thoughts, putting together the events of the night she'd missed—and in part caused.

"The Emartis," I told Tristan. "One of their birds attacked our carriage."

"Are you hurt?" he asked, eyes widening.

"No, just shaken," I said, automatically underplaying what had happened. I didn't want him digging deeper. I didn't want him to request to see my injuries—not when the blood oath was so close to giving itself away.

A sentry stepped into the Great Hall, ordering everyone to the Seating Room.

No, no, no. I needed to get away from everyone, to avoid people until I could stop the pain. But Tristan took my hand in his and moved quickly through the crowd.

The Seating Room was in chaos. Around a hundred people were moving about, speaking in a mixture of anxious shouts and nervous whispers. Nobles pulled their hair or rearranged their clothing, sliding cuffs up and down their wrists. Council members, their significant others, and children crowded the space so completely there was hardly any room for the servers to slide by with golden trays of wine and plates of figs and dates. It was almost impossible to distinguish one body from the next. Everyone was wearing black for Days of Shadows, and some still had their masks resting on top of their heads or around their necks, partially covering their mouths.

My father stood with a commanding presence at the front of the room, next to the golden Seat. Beside it was the small table from which he'd pulled out the blade with which he'd spelled my blood debt.

He called the room to attention, and everyone began to file into the rows of chairs until there was at last only silence echoing off the tall ceiling. I sat with Tristan beside Lady Romula and Lord Trajan, both looking grim. Lady Romula turned to me, her dried lips painted blood red. She shook her head in disapproval, as if I were behind this attack, as if my inability to single-handedly bring down a secret organization that had been plotting treason my entire life was the reason we were all here. I turned away before my face revealed my anger and disgust and pain. I was finished playing the demure lady she preferred me to be since she'd so boldly reminded me that Tristan had other options at our last meeting.

Across the room, Meera sat with Morgana, surrounded by Meera's escorts. My mouth fell open. With the torchlights filling the room, I had a better view of Meera than I'd had all night, and she looked awful. Her skin was nearly white. Her cheeks seemed to have been swallowed, completely devoid of color, and her lips were white as her skin. She looked more an apparition than a person, more spirit than human. She glanced toward me, her hazel eyes the only aspect of warmth in her appearance, her ash-brown hair messy and unkempt. She looked farther than Lethea.

She looked like she'd just had a vision.

No. No one would think that. They'd think she looked like an Heir Apparent, one who was scared to learn we were under attack. That had to be what everyone was thinking. But even then, she was showing too much fear, too much emotion. Heirs were taught to appear neutral in such situations. She had been groomed to be our future Arkasva, to be a leader, fearless and courageous. I prayed my father would keep his talk short and release us. Meera and Morgana had to be out of sight, away from prying eyes for as long as possible until I could do something about their appearances. Morgana at least seemed able to manage to sit straight, but I could see the concern in her eyes from here—concern for my safety, for what breaking my oath would do to me.

I had to tell my father my oath was broken and what Mercurial had told me—that the debt could be changed.

I took Tristan's hand in mine, entwining our fingers. At another bite of pain in my wrist, I squeezed. Too hard.

Tristan made a sound under his breath. "Lyr? You okay?" he whispered.

"Sorry," I whispered back. "Nervous."

"It's going to be okay," he assured.

I wasn't so sure. Meera wasn't going to have a vision now, but she needed to leave before too many people took in her appearance. Morgana also had to exit the room as quickly as possible. This many people together…it was going drive her farther than Lethea. Too many people were here. It was too much noise for Morgana. There were too many opportunities for people to suspect either of my sisters.

My arm itched, and the blood oath reddened, visible to my eyes for the first time since I'd bled from it. My skin felt hot, and the itch traveled up my arm, until it burst into flames beneath my skin. I bit my lip hard enough to draw tears as I sucked in a painful breath. The room spun, I sucked on my lip, tasting blood, and pinched my waist, taking a deep breath. I had to stay in control. I had to control what they saw…just a little longer.

"Right now, the terrorists previously led by Tarek Kasmar, the traitor, have come out of hiding, calling themselves the Emartis. They are currently engaged in a terrorist attack in Urtavia," my father said. "The group has been engaging in a sort of explosive magic—dangerous fireworks in the form of black seraphim—which are threatening our own seraphim and ashvan from their duties. This comes right as we begin the bridge to winter, which we all know brings longer nights and the possibility of drawing akadim south."

A scared hush came over the room.

"Bamaria has nothing to fear. Our soturi are protecting the border at full strength. But akadim have been spotted recently south of the capitol. We are closely monitoring the situation and do not believe Bamaria has any reason to be concerned about akadim at this time. But these displays from the Emartis, these acts of terror, interrupt our safety efforts, interrupt our students' abilities to finish training, and are a direct threat to our culture, our art, and our lives in the city of Urtavia. Their increased use of fire to send a message is also of great concern. Turion Brenna's soturi are working to make safe the city as we speak while Arkturion Aemon and the Soturi of Ka Batavia are hunting down these spineless criminals, and I have no doubt they will stop the threat very soon." His lips tightened. "An attack like this forces our safety protocol for the Bamarian Council into action. We are currently opening every room in the fortress and our guest homes for overnight stay—until Arkturion Aemon returns victorious, the terrorists bound."

Fuck. The entire nobility was here. And Tristan…Tristan was going to be required to spend the night. I had to keep him from my sisters. Keep him from me. I needed to speak to my father. My heart was hammering wildly in my chest, and another spike of pain in my wrist had sweat beading at the nape of my neck.

My father dismissed the assembly, giving everyone permission to reign free through Cresthaven's walls and the first floor of the fortress until the guest houses on the grounds were ready.

Morgana. Get Meera and yourself upstairs now. You look horrible.

Morgana immediately took Meera's hand and dragged her away from the other Council members before they could swarm her and ask questions. As the rest of the room began to empty, I noticed Rhyan hanging back, watching me and Tristan.

Warning bells rang. The second time tonight.

Sentries from my father's personal guard burst through the doors into the Great Hall.

"Everyone is to take shelter in their rooms now," yelled the commander. "Another display has been spotted a mile away. You're all safe. There's no need to panic, but we're taking maximum precautions."

Immediately, the nobles behind us burst into nervous chatter, saying goodnight and wishing each other well as they dispersed to find their families and their rooms.

Members of my father's staff emerged, helping to direct and escort everyone.

"Tristan," I said, "you should help your grandparents. Make sure they get settled."

He nodded, leaning over to kiss my cheek. "How are you feeling? Not too shaken?"

"I'll be fine."

"Should I try to sneak up to your room after?" he asked. "Check on you?"

Gods, no! I schooled my face, trying to look like I was disappointed in what I was about to say. "I think we better not try the patience of my guards any further tonight, not with the fortress so full. No one will be allowed access upstairs."

He gave me a pouty smile. "I had to try. Be safe. And while I know you're well protected, I'm here, too. I'll find you first thing in the morning." He kissed me again and stood, hand on his silver scabbard, and exited the Seating Room.

Rhyan, who had been watching from the shadows in a back corner, emerged, making his way to me in quick, urgent strides.

"How are you doing?"

Sweat was beading across my forehead, running down the nape of my neck. I wasn't going to last much longer. Either the blood debt would find a way to finally strike me down, or the pain in my wrist would soon be enough to end me.

"It hurts," I said, grateful to see the room had emptied save for two sentries. Now that I was inside Cresthaven, Markan didn't consider me as high a priority though I knew extra eyes would be on me until I retreated to the upper levels.

"Sit here," Rhyan said. "Don't move. I'm going to find your father. We're going to fix this."

I sat back, closed my eyes, and tried to breathe and not focus too much on the pain. Several moments later, far faster than I'd thought possible, the doors reopened, and Rhyan returned with my father, his black arkasva robes sweeping behind him as he rushed to me. Two sentries entered behind him. He gestured for all to stand back, giving the three of us privacy.

"Me bat." He took my hand in his, examining the scar, still red and visible.

I flinched. "I'm sorry," I said. "I tried everything, but...."

He shook his head. "This is my weight to bear," he said quietly. "I know what to do. I've been preparing for this day a long time."

"What happens next?"

"I want you to go up to your room. Get your sisters. You three will need to be together," he said.

"What about you?" I asked.

"I was the author of the oath. I have something else I need to do. Just...be with your sisters. Rhyan, escort her grace to her room."

"At once, Arkasva." Rhyan helped me to stand as my father

raced for the doors, a vadati stone in his hand as he summoned Eathan. His two personal sentries marched behind him.

"He's leaving," I said. "Eathan only comes when he's not here."

"Maybe there's some item he needs for the spell," Rhyan said, but even he looked concerned. "Let's go now."

"You can't be seen going upstairs," I said, "even if under orders. You know how it will look." Sweat beaded my forehead, and I had to exhale from my mouth to breathe through the burning in my arm.

"You go ahead of me. Don't stop until you're safe in your room. I want you to walk in that way that only you know how. The walk of Lady Lyriana Batavia, Heir to the Arkasva, High Lord of Bamaria. Remember who you are. Head up. Don't let anyone stop you. You owe no one here your time. I'll be right behind you."

And I did just that despite the growing pain in my wrist and the dizziness I was starting to feel as the blood price continued to slice and gnaw at my skin from the inside. I moved through the crowd still gathered in the Great Hall, a mix of those who wanted to stay and gossip and those who were waiting for word their rooms were ready. I kept an eye out for Tristan, but Ka Grey seemed to have received their rooms early—not one member of the Ka was in sight.

I reached the stairs, the weight of the scar starting to become physical; my hand was beginning to feel heavy. I made it to the first landing, and then I stumbled, crashing into the wall.

Strong hands gripped my arms and pulled me up.

"It's getting worse?" Rhyan asked, as I leaned against him.

"It just…it's not only burning, it's heavy now, too. I just want it to go away."

His arms swept beneath my knees, and he hoisted me up and carried me the rest of the way.

Morgana, I'm on my way upstairs with Rhyan. He knows every-thing. Meet me in my room with Meera.

Both sisters were sitting on my bed when Rhyan kicked open the door and carried me inside.

"Set her down between us," Meera ordered.

"Father…." Morgana squinted her eyes at me, reading my mind. "Father is going to change the debt of the blood oath?"

Rhyan put me down and immediately retreated to the corner, where he took up his usual posture of bodyguard—quiet, tensed, and alert.

"That's what he said, and we all needed to be together."

"We should never have been forced to swear in the first place," Meera said. "I am sorry for the role I played that night. I was scared. We'd just lost…you know."

"I do," I said, placing my hand on hers.

"Why don't we need to be with him?" Morgana asked. She stood, hands on her hips, and began pacing the room. "That doesn't make any sense."

"I don't know," I said. "Something about him being the author of the oath. I think if he could create it, he could change it."

Morgana still looked unconvinced. "And what, we just wait here and do nothing? And somehow a spell he needed our bodies present for to cast and our mouths to swear will be undone without us being there? Without us saying anything?"

"I—" I sucked in a breath, my entire arm shaking from the pain.

"I know you're the scholar, Lyr, but after my first slash, I wasn't as ready to accept my fate as you. And I did some research on how to undo this fucking thing." She pointed at her wrist, her face twisted in disgust.

I leaned against Meera, the pain becoming unbearable. Rhyan started to move but kept himself back as if he'd remembered his place.

I stared down at my wrist. The scar had doubled in size and was an angry red.

"What did you find out?" I asked.

"That there was no way to undo it," she said. "You either keep your oath, or you don't. And the price is extracted."

"Maybe," I gritted, "maybe you didn't read everything there was to read about it." Sweat was falling into my eyes. "Fuck!" I shrieked.

Meera cried out, too, and Morgana.

The pain had flared up to the point where I thought I'd pass out. My entire body spasmed, and then...it was gone.

I'd been pushed back on the bed from whatever force had stopped my pain, and I lifted my arm up as I stared at my wrist in disbelief. No red mark. No scar. I ran my finger across the skin. Meera and Morgana were feeling their own wrists in astonishment, their eyes wide.

The skin was smooth. No mark, no mutilation...just untouched skin. All that remained were my marks for my soturion oaths.

"He did it," I said, feeling the smooth skin again and again. I felt like I could breathe in a way I hadn't in years, like a weight had been lifted from my shoulders. "It's gone." I sat back up, scooting forward on the bed.

Meera sniffled happily. She looked the most alive I'd seen her in years.

"The fuck?" Morgana cursed. "Well, I assume we're done. I'm going to bed. I don't even want to think about what this means."

"Morgs," I said. "You know we still have your back. Right? And so does Rhyan."

She snorted. "My sisters protecting me? And my sister's protector protecting me? Oh, yes, so very hard to believe." She rolled her eyes. "I'm glad you're all right, Lyr. But I'm telling you right now, whatever just happened, this was not mage magic. I researched this thoroughly. And, surprise, I went to the Museion as well. I didn't tell you because I didn't want anyone to get suspicious of my motives. I just didn't think I needed to be forced into a blood oath with my sisters. We share the same Godsdamned bloodline."

"But they're really gone," I said. "The blood oath scars are gone."

"I can't argue facts," Morgana huffed. "But I know this isn't right. Goodnight."

Do you need anything? For your head?

"If I did, I would have asked," she snarled and strode from the room.

Meera got up. "I'm going to go talk to her." She looked back to Rhyan. "Thank you again for all you're doing for Lyr and what you did for me. I won't forget."

Rhyan bowed formally.

I was left alone with him. He crossed the room and sat on the edge of my bed. "It's gone," he said, "truly?" He cupped my chin, holding my head in his hand. "Gods. I was so worried. One day, I'll tell you the story of the blood oath on my back. It's now no longer needed. The author, he...he died. But since I kept the oath, I suppose I'm to wear the mark forever. This one, however," he pointed to his forehead, to the scar cutting through his eyebrow and the top of his cheek, "this was broken instantly."

"That was a blood oath?" I asked, realizing now how much my own scar had begun to look like Rhyan's after it began to show itself.

"He wanted to humiliate me. Make sure I never forgot. I broke it within a minute of the mage forcing the words from my mouth."

"It didn't kill you?" I asked, reaching forward to run my fingers lightly over the scar. He shivered under my touch, his eyes closing, thick dark lashes brushing against the tops of his cheeks. I cupped his face.

"No. Worse. It killed my mother."

"Rhyan," I gasped. "I'm sorry." I sat forward, still holding him, and pressed my lips down the length of his scar, to his closed eyelid and his cheek. His arms wrapped around me, our foreheads pushing against each other, lips brushing.

Rhyan pulled back, groaning as if it were physically painful for him to do so. "I want you," he said, his hands sliding down my arms, fingers pressing into my flesh. "I want you so fucking much. But we can't do this. Not here, not now. It's complicating everything."

"Everything was already complicated."

"I know. But I think until Valyati, we have to be extra careful. I know the rumors. I know the way Tristan looks at me. Every time I touch you, I'm putting your life in danger. And the way I feel about you—clouds my judgment. My ability to protect you, to train you, to fulfill my oath as a soturion, stop the threat, it's all compromised. Because sometimes when I look at you...." He shook his head. "It's almost too much. I forget. I forget what I must do. The oaths I swore. Maybe our kashonim isn't tied to a blood oath, where a kiss will threaten everything. But the magic still carries weight. And I can't—I won't risk you."

He leaned in, inhaling the scent of my hair, as I took in his, pine and musk. His lips brushed against my forehead. One kiss, and then he was gone.

I lay in my bed for hours, staring at the moon through my window, listening to the waves of the ocean crashing against the shore and the sounds of the people filling the halls of Cresthaven. It had been years since I'd heard so much noise and activity in my home. Not since the scars on my wrist had been forced upon me.

Getting up at some point to pee, I heard a door open down the hall. I moved to mine, cracked it open, and found Morgana creeping past my door. She stopped at the landing, poking her head around the corner to the stairs, cursed to herself, and turned around.

"Fuck," she said when she saw me.

"Is everything all right? Do you want me to get something for you from downstairs?"

"No," she said, wincing in pain. "Nothing's going to help me right now."

"Then what were you—?"

"I was listening," she said, her eyes dark. "The threat has been, I guess we'll call it paused."

"So nothing's changed. We're just not actively under attack."

"Sure. Nothing's changed." She slapped her palm against her wrist. "Except this. And the fact that I was right."

"What?"

"That's what I was listening for—Father's mental chatter in the fuss of all the nobles downstairs. He lied to you. To us. There was no spell. No mage magic can undo a blood oath."

I shook my head, starting to piece it together, my stomach knotting. *But the scars are gone. The blood oaths are gone.*

Morgana's nostrils flared, her eyes darkening with anger as she read my thoughts.

"How?" I asked.

"He went to Mercurial. He made a fucking deal with the Afeya."

My stomach twisted. "What was the price? What did he promise in return?"

Morgana shrugged. "I don't know. He's very carefully not thinking about it—that or he's in denial." Her eyebrows narrowed. "I guess that's one of those things we'll just have to wait and see."

THE THIRD SCROLL: VALYATI

CHAPTER
TWENTY

"Again," Rhyan said. "Lift. Higher. Steady…steady. Good. Loosen your grip. The sword's an extension of your arm. You're not holding onto it for dear life. It is your life."

My arm burned as I followed Rhyan's instructions. We'd been at this for hours. For weeks. Holding the sword, switching between hands, toning my wrists, and building my strength before engaging in battle.

"Now lower. Slow. Nice and slow. Other hand. Back up."

He walked in circles around me, making small adjustments, relaxing my shoulder, pressing a finger into my belly until I tightened my core, lifting my chin. His eyes remained focused, studious, assessing.

"The Dance of Asherah," he commanded, clapping his hands in rhythm.

I twirled, circling my hips, my arms raised above my head, the sword in hand. Rhyan slowed his claps as my hips snaked down following their beat, my knees bending until I was practically sitting on the ground. Rhyan increased his pace, his claps coming harder and faster as I undulated my belly, my arm still lifted, my body rising back up as I balanced on my toes.

His rhythm changed again, as I easily flowed through one of

Lumeria's most famous water dances—a choreography I'd mastered at thirteen. We'd begun adding choreography to my fighting routines months ago to allow my mind to relax, for my muscle memory to strengthen. Rhyan wanted me to feel like the sword was part of me, so we focused our training on movements which I felt most natural engaging in, like water dancing.

I began to shimmy my hips, walking forward, the sword now in front of me before I undulated again, lifting the sword and using my left hand to hold the blade, offering my right hand a break.

Rhyan began to drum on his knees, the final choreography of the dance at the fastest tempo. The dance told the story of Asherah beginning with the Goddess in Heaven being chosen as a Guardian of the Valalumir after the akadim tried to steal it. Then, as the tempo slowed, the dance became more sensual, representing her affair with Auriel. And finally, the fastest part of the dance portrayed Asherah's fall to Lumeria, her becoming mortal. Asherah became arkturion and led her soturi against Moriel's forces, against the God who'd been banished, and took control of the akadim.

I moved the sword in front of me, pointing it at Rhyan, my hips swiveling side to side before they began to shake. I twirled, handing the sword off to my left hand as I spun and completed the performance, my right hand undulating in a final flourish.

Rhyan's eyes darkened, a heated look in his expression as he watched me. He stopped drumming, stood up, and widened his stance to prepare for battle. "Attack," he commanded.

I tossed the sword back into my right hand, my fingers wrapping around the hilt with a quiet practice that almost felt natural. Almost.

"Keep that angle," he said, backing away from me. He raised his own sword, pointing it at me. "Guard your front."

Our steel clashed just as some clouds moved through the sky. The sun's rays burst past the glass window of our training room. Red flames ran up and down the silver blades. From the corner of my eye, I caught sight of my hair, braided and flying over my shoulder, transform from dark brown to bright fiery red.

We pulled our swords back, Rhyan's eyes flashing emerald,

before the clouds descended, obscuring the sun. My hair returned to its original color. Our swords were silver once again as the sky darkened, taking on a grayish hue. The first snow of the season had been predicted for that night.

Our feet danced across the room, lithe and fast, back and forth, back and forth, as we took turns attacking and retreating. Our swords clanged and swung and reset. We began again.

All the while, Rhyan quizzed me for the Academy's first end-of-term written exams. As if I didn't have enough to worry about with the Emperor and his entourage arriving tonight for Valyati's winter festivities.

"First rule of being a soturion." Rhyan charged.

"Stop the threat." I blocked, pushing his sword back. I spun out and attacked, engaging in an old choreography I only used when trying to surprise Rhyan called the Descent of Auriel.

He pivoted at the last second, one eyebrow lifted. "Good. Second rule?" With a swift lift of his arm, our blades slid against each other, ringing until I pulled back.

"Akadim are living weapons." I raised my sword over my head, breathing deeply, fingers tightening and loosening. I let my grip be easy, my movements swift, willing the sword to become part of my arm, my muscles strong enough to withstand its weight.

"Three ways to kill an akadim?"

I lunged, crashing my sword down Rhyan's shoulder. He blocked, the impact so forceful I turned toward the wall. Kicking it, I used the impact to spin back and raced for him.

"Fire," I said as he dodged my attack. I swung, using both hands, turning the sword so quickly he was forced to retreat.

"And?" He feinted left, then lunged right.

I threw out my foot, tripping him. He rolled to the ground, spinning away from me. I was on him in a second, my sword poised beside his neck. "Beheading."

He stared up at me, his eyes meeting mine in an emerald blaze before he rolled again, out of reach of my attack. Jumping back to his feet, he ran behind me. I spun, trying to catch him. But he was too fast, dodging and retreating, spinning back and forth as he feinted until I was nearly dizzy from it.

I stilled, inhaling his scent. It was mixed this morning with the sweet sugary icing left from the plate of lemon cakes.

Since today was the last day of training before the winter break, there was no run this morning, no lectures, only final training preparations between novices and apprentices. Rhyan and I had been holed up in here for hours, practicing and eating and practicing again. The lingering aroma of our morning coffee, sweet and spicy, still roamed heavy in the air despite our emptied mugs. I exhaled, clearing my nose, and started again, observing the training room until I got the clear fresh scent of pine trees, and the deep, sensual, musky scent that always clung to Rhyan. I could sense him, feel the way his scent carried itself, stronger after hours of exertion. The scent was most overwhelming just behind my left shoulder. I turned on my heel and charged, pointing the tip of my blade right at Rhyan's chest, backing him into the wall.

"Heart," I said, out of breath, "is the third way to kill an akadim."

Before I could claim victory, he knocked the sword from my hand. Rhyan gripped my waist and pushed me against the wall. The point of his sword pressed between my breasts, the blade of his dagger flush with my neck. I rose up onto my toes, my heart hammering.

We'd been here before—many times over the past weeks. And still, every time, I felt desire burning through me, that tension that had begun the first time he'd pressed me into the wall and the way we'd barely satiated our hunger the next morning.

Every second I spend with you, I grow closer and closer to breaking my oath.

Rhyan's nostrils flared, his chest heaving with exertion. "And to defeat them?" he asked. His knee lifted, centered between my legs, trapping me between him and the wall.

Desire swelled low inside me. In the same breath, I pinched his armpit, right in the spot he'd shown me was the most sensitive.

He loosened his hold on me, cursing under his breath, his blade pulling back just enough for me to reach down, retrieve my own dagger, and slide my blade against his neck, forcing him back until I had *him* pinned against the wall. At my mercy.

"Use any means necessary," I said.

Deep silver shined against his throat, my name glowing on the blade in golden letters.

"Well done," he said, his jaw tensing as we both stood there, dagger to neck, eyes boring into each other.

I exhaled, my lips tingling, before I relaxed my blade and drew my dagger back.

Rhyan cocked his head to the side, a smile barely forming on his lips before my world turned upside down.

I was flat on my back, Rhyan kneeling on top of me.

"You forgot," he said. "Never ever assume your opponent defeated. Ensure it's been done."

I stared up at him, breathing heavily. His arms caged me in, and his legs, so thick with muscle, were flattening mine into the mat. I twisted and grunted, trying to shake him off, but he was too strong. I stilled, offering a look of surrender. Rhyan's eyes dipped down, assessing my next move, but his gaze seemed to linger on my breasts before returning to my face.

I struck quickly, kicking out my legs and wrapping them around his waist. I locked my ankles together, forcing him down until his body was flush against mine, pressing into me. Intimately. Too intimately. Exactly where I needed him as I wrapped my arms around his neck, pulling his face into my shoulder, choking him.

I flipped him onto his back, pinned his arms down, and held a second of victory before he flipped me again. The movement was fast and violent, but his hand rested behind my head, softening the blow, cushioning me.

"That was your best yet," he said, pulling his hand away from my head. I could feel his fingers catching in my braid, pausing. He stilled, hovering above me, watching. The bells were sure to ring any second. Lunch break. And then the written exams.

But he didn't move. He stayed like that, poised above me. One second too long. Then he slid back, jumping to his feet and extending his hand to help me up. I grabbed hold, pulling him down onto the mat. He landed beside me.

"All right." He released a groan. "I deserved that." He turned on his side to face me, rubbing the back of his neck. "How do you feel?"

I turned toward him. "Like if time travel was a vorakh, I'd wish for it, consequences be damned. I just want to get to the end of two days from now. For my test to be over. And to know I either passed, or I—" My eyes burned, my stomach roiling. "At least I won't have this feeling in my gut much longer."

Rhyan's good eyebrow was drawn in, sympathy in his eyes.

After Days of Shadows, the shock of having broken my blood oath had caused one of my worst panic attacks. It had been made only worse when I'd learned my father had paid a price to protect me from the blood debt.

Meera, Morgana and I had confronted him the morning after, when the threat of the Emartis riots had been quelled. He had refused to speak to us about it except to try and reassure us again and again that he'd paid a fair price to remove our debts, and we were not to worry.

But as we'd gathered back in the Seating Room for Aemon's full report on the Emartis, a gnawing feeling had begun to grow in my stomach, and a month later it hadn't subsided.

No price paid to the Afeya was fair, especially not one to Mercurial. And combined with the countdown to my test, Rhyan's more frequent trips to hunt akadim, and whispers of the Emartis's next move, I'd basically accepted the ball of nerves that lived and breathed in my stomach. Even our morning meditations couldn't release the tension.

At least in two days' time, the ball would burst, either because it was all over or because…. I sucked in a breath. Well, one way or another, it was about to be over.

Rhyan stepped forward. His hand reached for me then closed into a fist as he replaced it at his side. We'd been extra careful with our touches since we'd kissed. If we weren't practicing combat or training, anything like hugs or pats on the back had become off-limits. It was an unspoken agreement we seemed to have come to after Rhyan had left my bedroom that night.

"You're going to your security meeting after this?" I asked.

Rhyan nodded. "We expect the Emartis to make a move with the Emperor in town. It's going to be chaotic and crowded and confusing."

"Their favorite combination," I said dryly.

"Plus," he bit his lip, his gaze giving him away as he looked out the window and then back to me, "there's the possibility of support from the Imperator. And with his uncle in the country—I don't want you to worry, though," he added fiercely.

"It's fine. I'll just add it to the worry list. It's only a mile long. I doubt I'll notice."

"Lyr," he said.

"It's nothing new. Nothing we haven't suspected all along."

The morning after the Emartis riots, Aemon had announced that a dozen Lumerians had been arrested. They'd spent the past month in the Shadow Stronghold awaiting trial. But what was really happening was my father and Lady Sila were waiting for one of the prisoners to break. So far, none had said a word. And it wasn't customary for Bamaria to use torture though I suspected the time was getting close.

For the attack that had occurred that night, and the fights that had ensued across Bamaria, Aemon estimated at least five hundred members of the terrorist organization had been present, yet we'd only arrested a dozen. Tani was not one of them. Every single arrest had been made by one of Brenna's soturi, the Soturi of Ka Batavia. Not one arrest had been made by a soturion of Ka Kormac despite the fact that they'd outnumbered Ka Batavia soturi that night two to one. If it had seemed farther than Lethea to believe Ka Kormac was behind the Emartis before, it seemed perfectly reasonable now.

A new set of bells rang. Not the timekeeper's bells. Not the warning bells.

The bells of the Emperor.

"Oh, Gods. He's here. He's in Bamaria."

"I know," Rhyan said, his voice full of reassurance. But even his face had paled.

This man—the man who'd killed every member of Ka Azria, the man's whose orders had allowed the Imperator to take Jules and have her killed—was now in my country, stepping on my land, and being escorted to my home. To Cresthaven, where his Godsforsaken, Moriel-fucking lungs would breathe the same air as mine, where he would sit in the places Jules had once sat.

"Lyr, you're not due to meet him for hours." Rhyan stepped forward, both hands reaching for my shoulders, the gesture a break from our no-touching-outside-of-training rule. "Deep breath," he said. "He's not in the Katurium. You are. And you have one task right now. Put everything else out of your mind. You need to go eat lunch, take a break, and then go beat everyone at the written exams."

"Meera and Morgana—" I started.

"Have been preparing for weeks," he countered. "They are going to be all right. Morgana knows what to do. And not enough time has passed for us to be in Meera's danger zone, right?" He nodded at my golden arm cuff. I'd had to have it readjusted for my bicep thanks to all my training. Ramia had made quick work of it— and again requested I wear the necklace.

I gave a shaky nod to Rhyan, my eyes following his to my cuff. It was still so strange to have someone know my secret. Know it and not betray me. Know it and still accept me. And at the same time, having Rhyan know felt completely natural.

But his words didn't lessen my anxiety. Even if Meera didn't have a vision, the vorakh was taking a greater toll on her each day. She continued to fade, and even Arianna had commented that it was

odd she had retired to her bedroom so quickly the night of the
Emartis's riots.

"She's not Arkasva," I'd said. "What could she have done?"

Arianna had given me one of her piercing looks with her blue
eyes. "I know, my dear. But they don't see it that way." She gestured
at the nobility milling around the Great Hall, muttering to themselves about the Emartis and their overnight accommodations, all
while searching for more news and gossip.

"Meera is Heir Apparent. And she is of age to become Arkasva.
They expect her to be present at state affairs, to take a role in leadership. To show she is present, concerned, and preparing. If she does
not, many are going to lose faith in Ka Batavia, and we cannot have
that."

I had agreed with Aunt Arianna, but her words stayed with me.
The promise of Meera coming into power was what had set many
Bamarians' minds at ease after the scandal of my father ruling. And
now, it was becoming clear to them that that might not happen. The
longer my father ruled, the more likely our supporters who
remained for Meera's sake might defect.

"Get out of your head, partner," Rhyan said, calling me back.
"One thing at a time."

"Will you be there?" I asked, my voice small. "Tonight?" I
reached for his hand on my shoulder.

"I'll be wherever you want me to be. I swear." His voice was
barely a whisper as he squeezed my fingers in return. His other hand
pressed in a fist against his heart twice before flattening—the oath
of Glemaria. *Me sha, me ka.* He leaned in toward me until our foreheads pressed together. "I won't be able to talk to you. But I will be
on guard with your father's sentries. You're going to be okay. I
promise."

I closed my eyes, the agony of my next two days rivaled by the
knowledge that Rhyan's soft, kissable lips, were so Godsdamned
near.

He pulled away, his fingers releasing my hand.

"I'll see you tonight." I grabbed my bag and walked into the hall just as Haleika turned the corner, Leander walking a few steps behind her.

She froze when she saw me, her cheeks red. Her eyes flicked behind me to Rhyan, still in our training room pushing mats against the wall.

My nostrils flared, but she gave me a single, curt nod. We still had our agreement. Neither of us said a word and walked together to the dining hall to eat lunch while Galen spent the whole time quizzing our table with last-minute questions.

When I entered the examination room and sat down, snow began to fall.

Hours later, I paced across the carpet of my bedroom in Cresthaven, watching the snowflakes burst from the darkening sky and fall outside my window. I wore a long red gown cinched at the waist by a gold belt. The deep v-cut of the dress design vanished behind the belt, essentially putting my cleavage on full display.

Morgana had picked the dress, and I felt sick wearing it, knowing I'd be on display in minutes before the Emperor, the Imperator, and the Bastardmaker. Viktor was also likely to be there since his father and great uncle were present. And Naria would be in the line-up since by blood she was a Lady of Ka Batavia. It would be a whole evening with all my favorite people in Lumeria. Just add Tani, and the entire membership of the Emartis, and we were certain to have a grand old time.

I stared in the mirror again. I'd worn dresses that showed this much skin before, but never one that had...put everything so clearly on display.

As lascivious as the Imperator was, Morgana had gleaned from overhearing conversations during the day that the Emperor was worse. And highlighting my cleavage like it was some work of art could motivate the Emperor to adjust the test or his final decision in my favor. It was no secret that the world worked that way, and I'd played it to my advantage before. But to do it for the Emperor...it made me sick. He was a monster.

The color of the dress was the only thing I liked. It was not just red, but Batavia red. A reminder of who we were—our strength, our ancient role in leading the Empire for a thousand years.

The last light of day finally faded, and the snow could only be seen from the light of the torches the fortress mages had lit at dusk. Any minute now, the bells would ring and the ashvan would soar, leaving blue lights all over the sky from their hooves. And I'd be kneeling before my worst enemies, praying they had mercy on me.

I checked my hair and makeup in the mirror one last time, ensuring my golden diadem was perfectly centered across my forehead. I needed to go downstairs. But I couldn't...not yet. I still felt so naked, so exposed. I didn't have time to change, nor did I have options. The changes in my body from training had altered the way my old wardrobe fit. Perhaps it was time to buy a new one—if I survived the next two days.

Gold caught my eye on the dressing table. Ramia's necklace. I stared at the oversized piece, at the connecting Valalumir stars that would cover me from collarbone to shoulders and drip down my breasts. Starfire glowed red in the center of each star.

It solved all my problems. It matched the dress, it covered me, and it felt like an extra layer of protection against the leering gazes of the men of Ka Kormac. I didn't care if showing my cleavage would better the Emperor's opinion of me.

I picked it up then hesitated. Wearing it because Mercurial wanted me to wear it felt like the wrong reason. But not wearing it because he wanted me to still afforded him some level of control over me.

I swept my hair over my shoulder and fitted the necklace across my collarbone, clasping it at the nape of my neck.

I stared at my reflection, dizzy for a moment. My hair looked redder despite not being in the sun. There was a warm yet damp breeze in the room even though snow still fell onto my balcony. I felt like I was outside, walking the shore in mid-summer, my feet sinking into golden sand. I stared at myself, transfixed. For the first time in weeks, I thought I looked beautiful and strong. Powerful, like a warrior. Like a soturion.

The necklace was doing exactly what I'd sought it out for. It was not just a decoration but a distraction to protect me in a fight I was unlikely to come out on top of. As the bells rang the hour, I left my room.

With Meera and Morgana walking before me, we reached the Great Hall, already filled to the brim with Bamarian nobility dressed in their finest.

Tristan found me first, striding forward to take my hand and kiss my palm. It was a formal kiss, one he'd offered many times at the start of our relationship but rarely since.

My stomach twisted. Was this kiss due to the formality of the night, or was this his way of signaling how far apart we'd grown? He'd been lukewarm for the past month, barely coming to see me anymore and barely touching me when he did. We were more like friends now than lovers. And even that friendship felt delicate and strained.

Lady Romula and Lord Trajan bowed their heads as we approached—a small show of respect for my station. But as Lady Romula straightened, she pursed her dry, wine-stained lips together in disapproval at my necklace. Too garish for her taste. Not enough silver. As if anything I did would satisfy her at this point. Her disapproval of me had only become more intense since the Emartis had forced her to stay overnight in Cresthaven. It had been "devoid of luxury," and the state of Bamaria had her wondering if she might not bring some of her investments out to Elyria. Nothing I did mattered anymore. Unless I was making Tristan the next arkasva of Bamaria, the finish line would always be a few steps ahead of me where she was concerned.

I stood tall, shoulders back, face poised as I'd been trained, the mask of Lady Lyriana Batavia perfectly in place.

Arianna joined the line, looking perfect as usual, her hair swept over one shoulder. She'd traded in her usual blue for a stunning black gown that appeared to be made of endless layers of fish fins all sewn tightly together. Each fin had been threaded in a deep, burnt silver. Every swish of the dress turned the silver from a bright light to a glittering black. Naria was beside her, still as a statue and offering me a death glare.

Eathan shifted around the room, pointing and directing everyone into their place. The lights highlighted his graying hair; he had far more than my father, a marked difference in their appearance. His dark gray cloak flung out behind him as he moved, his lightning-quick eyes checking everyone's position. He gave me a short nod to head into place. Within minutes, every Bamarian Council member and their immediate family was accounted for, all looking stunning and forming an aisle down the center of the hall thanks to Eathan's directions.

My father would be at the end, standing at the base of the stair-case. He'd be the final person the Emperor would greet after parading through our welcoming committee. I was to stand off to the side of the stairs with Morgana while Meera, Heir Apparent, would be just behind our father. Tristan squeezed my hand before he strode off to stand with his grandparents, just across the aisle from me.

Morgana, in a black dress with a deep v that also veered so low it tucked into her belt—the darker sister of my gown—stood by my side. She squinted and discreetly took my hand, squeezing it.

"His guard comes," Eathan announced. "Ready now."

All at once, my father's sentries shifted position. Two new rows formed, surrounding us. A sentry stood guard every two feet. Across from me was Rhyan, his mouth open as he took in my appearance. One eyebrow lifted as his gaze moved slowly up and down my body. Warmth spread over me before his jaw tensed, and he straightened, maintaining the cold, strong stance of a fortress guard.

Euston and Rhodes formally announced the Emperor's arrival and flung open the double doors, drawing in a freezing gust of snow-coated wind. One hundred soturi poured through the door, single file, marching in sync, and splitting in the middle of the hall when they reached our lineup. Each soturion alternated turning left or right. They wore perfectly pressed green cloaks, the material somewhat softer and shinier than our own. Their armor was made of a brushed gold, and most of the soturi, as they stepped under the lights, revealed they'd had the Emperor's sigil, a single Valalumir, tattooed in gold ink across their cheeks.

Within seconds, we were completely surrounded by the Emperor's army—the soturi loyal to the man who'd ordered Jules's execution, singlehandedly killed every last member of Ka Azria, and replaced them with the conniving members of Ka Elys.

An entourage of ladies walked through the doors, all of them dripping in white fur cloaks as they promenaded down the aisle, tipping their heads down in respect to me, Morgana, and finally Meera. The ladies of his court were followed by his consort, a middle-aged woman wearing a shimmering silver gown and a simple diadem. Then came the Imperator and the Bastardmaker, followed by Viktor. Naria perked up when she saw him, and as he walked by her, he grabbed her hand, tugging her forward to kiss her brusquely. The Imperator, swishing his black and golden cloak behind him, paused before me, his blonde eyebrows narrowed.

"Our little warrior," he said, voice mocking, "the reason we're all here." He gestured at the hundred soturi now guarding us. "Your grace," he spoke quietly, "I do hope you've been taking your training far more seriously since the last time."

I bowed and straightened, staring back at him with as much defiance as I could muster. He smirked and extended his hand to me. Protocol demanded I take it.

"I have taken my studies extremely seriously, I assure you, your highness," I said sweetly.

"Is that so?" he asked. "We wouldn't want to waste the Emperor's time, now would we?"

He tugged me forward, his fingers digging into my wrist, and I was in the center of the aisle, my hand in the Imperator's. Rhyan's eyes widened, his hands fisting at his sides, but he remained still. Tristan started to move forward, but Lady Romula placed a firm hand across his arm. I tilted my head back to my father, who stood still as a statue, his mouth tight. His only tell of emotion was a slight narrowing of his eyes. He took one step down, and then paused. Coming any closer could be seen as an act of aggression.

I pressed my free hand into my hip, sucking in breaths, praying to be as still as an arkasva, as unmoving. Phantom fingers pressed into my back, but my wounds were closed. This wasn't like before, when I'd been injured and at the Imperator's mercy. It was worse.

The Emperor was about to walk through these very doors, and his presence seemed to give the Imperator the freedom to act with a boldness he'd only toed the line of before. Aemon and Arianna had been unable to protect me then. No one could protect me now if things went sour with his majesty.

"Your grace," the Imperator drawled, twirling me away from him. I faced the double doors, the entrance to Cresthaven, where the Emperor would appear at any moment. "Did you ever replace that tunic?" he asked. "Soturion Hart?"

Fire danced in Rhyan's eyes, a cold fury brewing in his aura that the Imperator clearly felt, for his own feral energy seemed to push forward and surround me, making me feel sick to my stomach.

The Imperator grabbed a fistful of my hair and tugged it painfully before he tossed it over my shoulder. The entire Bamarian nobility watched me, their eyes wide, their expressions mixed between scandal and something like disdain, like they wanted to distance themselves from me. Distance themselves from this display. The Bastardmaker leaned forward, his cheeks coloring as his eyes dipped down the v of my dress.

But I held my head up high. I would not react. I would not cry.

"Your back has healed remarkably well," he said. "And I assume by this pristine state of your skin, you didn't require quite so many spare tunics." He turned me to face him again, his hand snaking around my waist and drawing me toward him, his body pressed to mine. One finger caressed my cheek, the blunt tip of his finger circling around my eye. "This also healed. Perhaps you'll get that dance with the Emperor after all."

He released me back into the line and walked forward to take his place to greet the Emperor while I fought to keep the tremors in my body at bay. Tristan cocked his head to the side, his eyes flicking to Rhyan before returning to me. I could feel the heat of his aura pulsing with anger, the combination of hot and cold leaving me slightly faint. Morgana rested her palm against my lower back.

"Easy," she whispered. "You're safe now. That was his only plan for tonight."

Right...now we just have to face the Emperor.

She rubbed my back, shifting her body closer to mine.

My father walked down the remaining stairs as the Imperator and Bastardmaker moved to the side, taking their official posts for his majesty's arrival.

The Emperor's sentries shouted at once, their voices harmonizing in a singing choir, chanting the Emperor's praise in High Lumerian. Their expressions remained blank and neutral as they all —at once—lifted their swords. The practiced perfection of the movement, the way they held themselves, and their facial expressions all suggested this was nothing more than a ritual to enact in which they were all players assigned their part, but their muscles told a different story. As I took in the exact positioning of their feet, the way they held their swords, the tension in their arms, and the way they carried their weight, I realized I'd had it wrong. They weren't on display for the Emperor or a show of his strength. This wasn't simply a ritual or performance, or even a line of defense. They were ready to attack. One word, one call, one breath from the Emperor would be all it took—and they'd have our heads on pikes. They could slaughter us all within minutes if they chose to do so.

Had it been the same with Ka Azria? Had they dressed in their finest, trying to make a good impression, with no idea they'd dressed for their deaths?

For a second, I felt panic, fear that this was all a set up—that the Emperor hadn't come to test me at all but to execute me, my family, and all of Ka Batavia because he knew that deep inside of Cresthaven, we were concealing vorakh.

"Formality," Morgana hissed in my ear. "It looks scary, but it's by design. A formality. I've seen this show before. Stay calm."

I swallowed, shifting my glance from my father, standing regally with the golden Laurel of the Arkasva atop his head, down the row of the stiffly waiting Bamarian Council. There in the doorway to my home, to Cresthaven, the fortress of Bamaria, stood the Emperor of Lumeria.

CHAPTER
TWENTY-ONE

"His Majesty, Emperor Theotis, High Lord of Lumeria Nutavia," cried the herald.

Like a wave crashing against the shore, we sank to our knees. Even the Imperator knelt. I stared down, fixating on the folds of my dress, the way the fabric rippled across the marble floor. My hands shook in my lap as I wrung them together.

I didn't dare look fully upon him as he made his way down the aisle in slow measured steps. The Emperor was undoubtedly an old man, with thick white eyebrows and a white beard trimmed short. Gold and purple velvet robes cascaded down his back with a train that flowed into the aisle. Golden Valalumirs had been threaded into the material, shining and sparkling with every step he took.

His tunic was tightly fitted to his body, revealing plenty of lean muscle. He was a killer in every way, even at his age. The Emperor's warlord, the warlord of the Empire, formally known as Arkturion Pompellus Agrippa, marched behind him. Like most arkturi, he too had been granted a nickname. Arkturion Pompellus was known throughout Bamaria as the Blade. I'd heard it had been his hand that had snuffed the life of the first member of Ka Azria, and that he himself had personally overseen or handled every execution. He hadn't used a weapon but his actual hand; hence he, like the akadim, had become a weapon.

The Blade was also ancient in appearance though I knew all too well from the stories that he was a fair match for the Ready in battle. The capital regularly hosted games in the Nutavian Katurium, and the Blade was famous for competing against soturi in the arena. Now, his gray eyes moved quickly as he marched, assessing each corner of the Great Hall and every Bamarian noble. A few of the nobles looked down from his gaze.

Every measured step of the warlord seemed to show some ripple of muscle, as he allowed his red arkturion cloak to flow behind him. The frown lines on the Blade's face deepened as though they'd been carved into his skin. A sentry, one of ours, coughed uncomfortably behind me.

I shivered as the Blade drew closer, noting each weapon he carried—the dagger sheathed in his leather belt, the sharpened Vala-lumir stars hanging from its seven straps, and the sword at his side. They all had blood on them—Ka Azria's blood—as did his hands.

I had to be perfect. I had to survive. One wrong move, and another Ka's blood could be on the Blade's hands or weapons.

It seemed like hours passed as I sat with my back stiff, my arms and hands placed just so in my lap, but the next thing I knew, Emperor Theotis and the Blade were before me, their ancient-look-ing, piercing eyes coldly assessing me.

"It's been some years, your grace," the Emperor said, "but that is the youngest Bamarian Heir to the Arkasva, is it not? All grown up? And training to be a soturion?" His voice was quieter than I remembered. I couldn't tell if it was due to my fear of his power that I'd been expecting his voice to be harder and louder, or if I'd simply thought he'd sounded louder when I was younger and all adults sounded loud in my ears. I'd been thirteen for his last visit and considered too young for this formal greeting. I'd remained upstairs, listening in the hall, curious about the Emperor of the Lumerian Empire.

"Your majesty," I said carefully, properly, as I'd been trained. "You honor us with your presence on Valyati."

He placed his hand before my face, presenting his golden Vala-lumir ring. I leaned forward to kiss it, the cloudiness of his aura more suffocating the closer I got. There was an overwhelming scent to it, something old and rotten.

"Rise, your grace," he said softly, his hand held out for me to take. "Let me look at you."

My ankles felt weak as I bore weight down on my feet, standing. My dress fell in loose waves from my hips, and my necklace felt as if it had gained ten pounds, pushing into my chest and warming against my skin.

"A girl of an ancient bloodline," he said, almost as though he was musing to himself. "And yet...." He frowned, flicking his finger in a circle.

I was to spin around. Again. I twirled and curtsied, praying to every God in Heaven my face was neutral, that I wore my mask that hid my fear and disgust.

He shook his head, sharing a small glance with his arkturion. "Not an ounce of magic."

"Akadim don't respond to magic," said the Blade.

The Emperor wrinkled his nose. "They still respond to strength. But do you have it?" He waved me off in dismissal before he greeted the Imperator, the Bastardmaker, and my father. I fell back to my seat on the floor, catching Rhyan's eyes across the room boring into me, his mouth hardened into a tight line.

Standing before the full Council of Bamaria, the Emperor lifted his arms, signaling everyone to rise. "Thank you," he said, voice suddenly booming, "for this wonderful greeting. It has been too many years since I've visited the jewel of the Empire, Bamaria. Here on the shores of the Lumerian Ocean, we have our deepest connection to our heritage, to our source of magic. I am always pleased to come to our capital of education and learning. We've seen Lumeria's finest mages and most powerful soturi arise from these shores. And yet, recent events have cast a shadow on our Empire's jewel."

The room darkened, his cloudy aura spreading within it. It was the strangest feeling, like a fog descending within the walls of fortress. He didn't sound particularly emotional—the usual mark of an aura—and he wasn't exerting any magic or strength.

He extended a hand to Meera, and she took it, walking to stand behind him. "We have high hopes for Ka Batavia to put such scandal behind them. Would you not agree, Lady Meera Batavia, Heir Apparent to the Arkasva, High Lord of Bamaria?"

Meera bowed her head, taking a second too long to pull it back up. She looked weak, sick, unfit to be Heir Apparent. Beside the ancient Emperor, it was even more obvious who held the energy and strength.

"We look forward to brighter days, your majesty," Meera said.

"The scandals go as far back as your mother not following the tradition of Bamaria and then her niece, your cousin the Lady Julianna," he said, not acknowledging Meera's words.

My chest tightened, and my throat went dry. The Imperator smirked, as did the Bastardmaker. And though I knew I shouldn't, I caught Tristan's eyes. His brows narrowed, his gaze on me full of the anger and vitriol he felt for vorkah. His eyes lost none of their fury as they flicked back to Meera and Emperor Theotis.

The Emperor smiled warmly at Meera and gestured for her to return to the line.

"And now, I see scandal continues." He pointed toward me.

Heat bloomed across my cheeks, down my neck. My heart hammered in my chest. Morgana's hand found the small of my back once more, her touch solid and supportive.

"Nahashim who can find anything in Lumeria, in the world, searched Lady Lyriana's body and could not find a thing. Not an ounce of magic, of power, of strength."

Did you truly believe that mere nahashim could scent what you truly are? Could find the well of your power? No. For they've never encountered your kind before.

Mercurial's words played through my mind.

"Did you know," the Emperor asked casually, his voice soft once more, "that the Goddess Asherah, after she fell from grace for her evil seduction of Auriel, for convincing him to steal the Valalumir from Heaven, lost her power, too?"

I stilled. Had he read Sianna's writings?

"That after being given the highest honor—to be chosen to become a Guardian of the Valalumir, our most precious gift—she was left without her gift as punishment for the crimes that robbed Heaven of its light?" The Emperor turned to me. "I wonder, what sins have you committed, Lady Lyriana Batavia? And what sin have we, by allowing this training to go on?"

"She'll show us soon enough, won't she?" said the Blade.

"That she will," the Imperator said, his voice final and deadly. "Much against my preference."

The Emperor sighed. "Hmm. Well, either way, this experiment must come to an end. Now, shall we retire? A nice and quiet dinner before tomorrow's celebration. Valyati comes again, the darkness of Lumeria Matavia ended as soon as Auriel fell from Heaven, carrying the Valalumir with him. A hero, bringing us our greatest light. And so, as the days have been so dark, light will return again. Let us hope. For akadim have been multiplying, and unrest lies in the jewel of the Empire. I do not like to see it. But for now, let us eat."

I tensed at the warning in his words. He was unhappy with Ka Batavia, with what had happened to me, with my father's rule, with Jules—even though all of those things were on some level his fault. It seemed he'd been displeased with everything Ka Batavia-related for the last twenty years. And I was unlikely to make the situation any better.

Dinner was tense and silent. I sat with Meera and Morgana, carefully observing their faces for any signs of discomfort, of a coming vision, of Morgana's thoughts growing too loud and painful. Tristan had also been seated at our table and held my hand, trying to be supportive. For once, I had an excuse for my nerves, for my lack of desire for him.

I downed the wine before me, and the moment custom dictated, I retired, whisking my way to bed. We'd survived one night of the Emperor's presence.

But I still had two more.

CHAPTER
TWENTY-TWO

The day of Valyati, the winter solstice, was somber. It was the longest night of the year in terms of darkness, but it was also going to be the longest night of my life, as I was forced to dance before the Emperor, to pretend everything was fine, Ka Batavia was strong, and my courtship with Tristan remained unblemished.

The snow that began the day before had fallen steadily without pause all day. The flakes were fat and fluffy, coating the ground outside the Temple of Dawn in a sparkling white. I emerged from my seraphim carriage on a sparkling waterway, the glass cleared of all snow. The water underneath the waterway continued to run, the temperatures not quite cold enough to freeze it, though small crystalized pieces appeared within it, quickly floating past and sparkling red beneath the torches lighting the way to the ball.

Beyond the path, my escorts stood in the snow, their boots sinking. Rhyan was not among them. I hadn't seen him all day.

The wind picked up, spurred on by the flapping of wings as a half dozen seraphim flew overhead, preparing to land. Meera and her escorts and Morgana and hers stood before me on the waterway. As my father emerged from his carriage, a dozen more guards appeared, along with the Ready and Turion Dairen, all dressed in their finest leathers and cloaks. Boots shined and sword hilts gleamed. The Valalumirs on the seven leather straps of their belts looked recently sharpened to deadly precision and glittered as they hit the light.

For the night of Valyati, the temple was always transformed from a place of ritual and contemplation to one of revelry. The pews had been replaced by dinner tables with place settings full of crystals and candles. A dance floor stood in the center of the temple, shaped like a seven-pointed star jutting into the seating areas of the seven rays.

We took our places in the middle of the dance floor, standing in waiting to greet the guests as they arrived. Noble Kavim, members of the Bamarian Council, the Soturi of Ka Kormac, and finally the one hundred members of the Emperor's personal guard entered, taking their places in every corner of the Temple. We all fell to our knees as the Emperor entered, this time holding hands with his consort. The Blade walked slowly behind them. The Emperor made his usual greeting, his voice still unnervingly soft-spoken but resounding. When his remarks came to an end, we waited patiently for him to take his seat at the table of honor raised on a dais besides Auriel's Chamber. He took his time sitting down and adjusting himself and then finally offered a wave of dismissal. We all rose to our feet, and the music began to play, a fast-paced drum beat to get the revelry started.

Tristan, who'd stood with the Bamarian Council, walked forward and took my hand to lead me to the dance floor. I wore a white gown, identical in cut and design to the one I'd worn the night before. Morgana had helped me secure Ramia's necklace around my collar and shoulders. Beneath the torchlights floating across the ceiling of the Temple of Dawn, flashing and crackling their light alongside the eternal flame, my necklace was alight in every color of the rainbow. The torches had been spelled to mimic the shifting shades of the flame, and with every step taken on the dance floor, every swerve of my hips or spin on my heels, the room changed colors.

The fast songs continued until a slower tune was called, somber and heavy, the notes signaling the ritualistic moments of the celebration. The dance floor cleared, and Arkmage Kolaya walked into the center, her long white robes trailing behind her. All seven Watchers of the Light emerged from each of the temple's seven rays. Their ceremonial robes had been pressed and trailed behind their feet. Their faces remained veiled, each in the color they served. As they joined, forming the shape of a star, a flurry of movement rained down from the high ceilings. Masks floated across the dance floor, dropping into everyone's hands, along with glasses of white wine spelled not to spill over.

Cheers erupted amidst gasps of delight as every guest began grabbing for the masks that now fell in a dizzying frenzy. Shouts of triumph sounded, rising above yells of annoyance and small fights and skirmishes breaking out as everyone tried to acquire a mask in a style that complimented their Valyati attire.

I had my eye on a white mask with gold Valalumir jewels sewn along the eye cut-outs. Sparkling golden ribbon trailed along either side. The mask looked as if it had been specially tailored to match my dress. Tristan eyed it as soon as I did and winked, rushing forward and leaping for it. He'd been catching my mask for me at Valyati since the year before we began courting. The first time he caught my mask for me was perhaps the moment my crush began.

He drew his stave, blasting back another mage reaching for it, and thrust its point through the eyehole of the mask before he landed. A crowd of onlookers, all eager for their own preferred mask, rushed at him, ready to attack. Tristan turned back to look at me, a silly smile on his face before he accepted his fate and vanished into the crowd.

I laughed, stepping back to avoid getting myself lost in the fray. Mine had been won. Tristan would return with it at any moment. I tried to find him in the crowd. It was all in good fun, but the fight for one's desired Valyati mask had been known to break an arm or twist an ankle from time to time. One year, when a certain shade of purple masks had been on trend, Jules had broken her middle toe.

Mages emerged from the crowd, their hair mussed and robes

askew, clutching the masks of their partners in hand. Still, Tristan did not emerge.

For a moment, everything had felt safe, comfortable. I supposed holidays and traditions had a way of bringing one back in time, to earlier versions of the event and earlier versions of oneself, to times when loved ones were still alive, when things were still simple.

But the Emperor's sentries stood out against the wall, their brushed golden armor easy to spot, and I was immediately reminded of the present and what was at stake.

I found my eyes wandering away from the skirmish and around the room—wandering in search of a pair of emerald eyes, a silvered scar through the left.

He was here. Somewhere. I suspected he'd be in the shadows, guarding, watching, not hunting for a mask.

"You seek him out even now. Even with the young lord of silver warming your bed. Oh, but he has been leaving it cold lately."

I froze. Mercurial stood beside me. His skin had returned to its blue tinge. A golden cape fell in elegant folds over his shoulders, linked together by a chain of shimmering diamonds. A golden skirt covered him from waist to knees, and golden sandals laced up the lengths of his calves.

"Happy Valyati, Mercurial," I said. "I did not know the Afeya celebrated."

"Your grace." He bowed low. "The Afeya celebrate anything that calls for a party. Especially if it can lead to debauchery. Then we are particularly fond of it in the Star Court." As he rose, his eyes flickered over my body, pausing on my chest where my necklace sat, covering me as completely as armor.

My cheeks heated with embarrassment. This damned necklace. Everything about it made me uneasy, and yet I'd worn it again tonight willingly, wanting to cover myself, to not feel exposed before my enemies in the cut of my gown.

"You took my advice," he said. "Very good."

"It complimented the dress," I said carefully.

"Of course." He smirked. "And where is my humble not-lord? This is the first I've seen you without him by your side."

"Perhaps if you came around more often, you would find that there are indeed quite a number of times he's not by my side," I said, heart pounding. From the corner of my eye, I spotted Morgana watching us wearily. Black eyebrows narrowed as she slowly shook her head. A warning. *Get away from him.*

"I'm around plenty."

"Around to meet with my father," I said, feeling cold inside. "Collecting on debt, I presume?"

A cruel smile spread across his lips, catlike and predatory. "All debts eventually must be paid."

"I suppose it depends on the price whether or not it's fair."

Mercurial laughed, the sound so alluring I leaned forward as he said, "You seem very interested in understanding my prices. In the market yourself?"

"No," I said, pulling myself back.

Mercurial shook his head, holding out his palm. A glittering Valalumir spun within it. "This is where the First Messenger first met Lady Lyriana," he said. "When you had so many questions. And I can see now that you only have more."

"Perhaps if the scrolls in the Library remained untouched, I'd have less questions to ask."

"Sweet, sweet child. The answers you seek are not written or recorded. They only exist in living memory."

"Then—" I bit my tongue. I'd been about to ask why he'd destroyed the scrolls of Sianna if they held no answers, but I already knew why. He'd done so to manipulate me—to force me to bargain.

"You want something from me," I said.

Mercurial laughed. "You think you've just made some clever observation. But I told you as much in as many words. And I tell you this now, just as plainly. I intend to get it. One way or another, Mercurial always gets his way."

Before I could react, he vanished into a puff of smoke that I suspected only I could see as Tristan walked unbothered through the wisps. He held my mask before me, bowing as if he'd been on some noble quest to bring me a rare gift.

"I fought a hard battle, but I have emerged victorious. Your mask, your grace," he said formally before stepping behind me to help tie it over my eyes.

Mercurial reappeared across the temple, beside a set of curtains hung to close off various adjoining rooms and halls. He pulled the curtain beside him away from the wall, eyes still focused on me as he clothed his body with the drapes. Tightening the material around his waist, he looked like he was wearing one of Arianna's dresses. Mercurial winked, holding his palm to his head as though he were posing for a portrait. With a wave, he vanished.

Tristan finished tying the ribbons behind my head, then secured his own mask to his face. It was silver with a blue border that matched his mage robes.

"Nearly died for this one," he said with a laugh. "Is it just me, or is this night getting more brutal?"

I forced a laugh. "Considering present company…."

He stepped closer. "Are you doing okay? I saw your face last night, you looked so upset." Tristan squeezed my hand.

I sucked in a breath. Upset when Jules had been mentioned? Upset when the Imperator had humiliated me? Or upset when the Emperor had shown his disdain for my Ka?

"It's nerves about tomorrow. I'd rather not think about it."

His face darkened, but he nodded. "Of course."

One by one, the crystals hanging from the walls winked out, signaling the Valyati Dance of Darkness. The spelled torches flashed from Batavia red to a simmering orange to a golden yellow and on through every color of the rainbow before they blinked out. We were left with only the eternal flame, which was now glowing bright white.

The seven Watchers stood beneath the fire and held up banners made of soft winter velvet dyed in each of their sacred colors, blocking out the remaining temple light. There was just enough lightness seeping through for me to see silhouettes after my sight adjusted. My vision was just a little better than it had been the night of the Oath Ceremony. Valyati's Dance of Darkness was meant to be one of mystery, a fast choreography of swiftly changing partners spinning to and from each other until the song ended. Once that happened, a new song would play, and you were bound to dance with your last partner—no matter who it was.

Tristan blew me a kiss and vanished into the crowd. He'd managed to catch me at the end of the dance the last two years in a row. Everyone knew that to properly play the Dance of Darkness, the first part of the dance required a strategy—stay as far away from the person you truly wanted to dance with. This allowed you to make your way to them at the end. There were counts and beats to consider, as well as the number of partners across the floor. Being in the dark meant miscalculations were likely to happen, especially when the opening of the dance was a frenzied quick-step shared with strangers.

We began, taking our places across the dance floor. I noted Haleika nearby, recognizing the shape of her curly hair in the dark, and Galen's familiar figure seemed to be heading across the floor— as far from her as possible. But one more familiar silhouette glided in the opposite direction, and Haleika's head turned to follow. Leander.

A hushed silence filled the room, and then the music swelled, fast and upbeat. I stepped forward, performing the opening routine alongside the rest of the Lumerians in my row. We swiveled our hips, stomped our feet, and sauntered forward. A hand reached out for me, and I was pulled into a soturion's arms. I barely had time to process his appearance in the dark before I was twirled away and landed in the arms of a mage whom I thought to be one of the girls in Meera's friend group, but it was too dark for me to be sure, especially with her mask. She smiled widely at me, twirling me around until I ended up in the arms of another soturion woman, then a male mage, a bald male soturion, a mage with curly hair, and then a soturion again.

The beat quickened, and I traveled through more partners, losing track of whom I'd danced with and whom I hadn't. The masked faces all began to blur together. I was passed from one set of arms to another, some thin, some thick, some bursting with muscle, all dancing, swaying, stepping, stomping. I scanned the room while keeping the beat, undulating and twirling up to my new dance partners again and again and again.

The music intensified, new instruments joining the harmony, the volume increasing, the pace quickening. We were at the end of the song, the moment we'd be duty-bound to dance with whomever was before us.

I twirled away from my current dance partner, searching for Tristan. He had to be close. He always found me in this moment, had perfected his strategy. But when I caught a scent of mint and salt, its owner danced past me, taking the hands of a blonde girl in a red mask. Naria. Tristan was dancing with Naria.

My stomach dropped.

The Watchers held up black banners, hiding the eternal flame. I was cast in almost total darkness. I was alone. No dance partner. No Tristan. No idea where anyone was. A chilly air swept around me then warmed as the opening notes of the next song sang through the ball—the lover's dance, the ballad of Auriel and Asherah.

I crossed my arms over my chest, feeling alone and cold in the dark. Everyone around me was dancing with someone, was held by someone. And then there was me, standing alone on what was possibly my last night, sharing what had once been a beautiful holiday with Jules's killers. The killers who had their blades out for me and wouldn't hesitate to murder Meera and Morgana if they made one misstep.

I wasn't even sure I cared Tristan was with Naria. I'd always hated the way she openly coveted and courted what was mine, but I knew now my feelings stemmed from what Tristan represented for me—protection and salvation. Though I still loved him like a friend, like the friend I'd grown up with, any love I felt for him otherwise or had tricked myself into feeling was gone. And it had been that way for months. Maybe years. At least now I could finally see it.

I took a step back, my breath shaky as I scanned the room for a friendly face, but I only saw black shadows cast against the darkened walls. The music swelled around me, as did the feeling of loneliness, of being left behind.

Then a familiar scent wrapped around me, a cool cocooning aura kissed my skin. Musk, and pine.

Warm hands covered my eyes from behind, further plunging me into darkness, and a smooth voice with a northern lilt crooned in my ear, "Hello, lover."

CHAPTER
TWENTY-THREE

He was so close, his breath soft against my neck. He withdrew his hands, and I turned and came face to face with Rhyan.

The fires spit and crackled, and more complicated elements of the song began, the instruments joining together in harmony, each note rising.

Warmth rose from my toes to my belly. In the dim light, I could see Rhyan wore a black jacket beneath his soturion cloak, freshly laundered and pressed. His hair had been neatly trimmed, too short now to curl and pushed back from his forehead in loose waves. It was too dark for me to see the color of his eyes but not too dark to see the desire barely veiled inside them.

"What are you doing?" I asked.

"Couldn't help myself. I want to dance with you."

I shook my head. We'd be seen. The Imperator danced on this floor now, as did the Emperor, the Bastardmaker…Tristan.

"Rhyan," I said, voice barely above a whisper. My throat tightened.

"I know we can't." His lips quirked up. A small, sad smile. "But I didn't want you to be alone for this song." He was backing up, moving against the wall, deeper into the sanctuary's darkness, and I followed, maintaining a careful, respectable distance in case anyone looked over and managed to see through the shadows and recognize us.

The dance was in full swing. Bodies pressed together, spinning across the floor, one masked face indistinguishable from the next. We were completely covered by darkness, in our own private corner of the temple, away from the tangled limbs of the couples dancing in the temple's center.

"Can I keep you company?" Rhyan asked, stepping in front of me. His body angled to hide me from the crowd, as his hand moved behind his back. "Take my hand if yes."

I closed my eyes. No one could see us. And the way he stood— he looked like an escort on duty, nothing more. I lifted my hand, pressed my palm flush against his. The sensation sent a shiver down my spine as his calloused fingers entwined with mine.

"Did you get what you wanted for Valyati?" he asked.

"No," I said. With everything going on, there would be no presents this year. "Did you?"

"Enough for now."

"What's enough?" My eyes adjusted to the low light until I could clearly take in his features as he watched me over his shoulder—the open expression on his face, the sensuous curve of his lips beneath his Valyati mask. He'd chosen one that was simple and black like his armor.

"This," he said, voice low. "Lyr, I wanted to dance with you all night. For three years I've wanted to."

My heart felt like it would burst.

"I've been watching you out there, and it's been torture. You look like a goddess. And when this song came on, I couldn't resist. I know we can't be together. Or dance together. But holding your hand," he smiled, one of his rare, wide smiles, "it's the best Valyati I've ever had."

I tightened my grip around his hand. My heart swelled, but I couldn't find the words to respond.

"This was our first dance at solstice," he said, turning back to watch the ball. He shifted his stance, scanning the room, exactly as

I'd seen him and my other escorts do a thousand times. "The lover's dance."

My mouth fell open. I'd never thought about the song we'd danced to the night of our first kiss. I'd been so consumed by Rhyan, touching him, watching him, following the steps of the choreography, that I hadn't been able to hear the music over the sound of my heart pounding or the words he'd spoken. But I could hear it now in real time and feel the sound cocooning the memory, bringing another element to it. I remembered the feel of the wind blowing through my hair, the way his hand rested on my back, warm, strong, and sure.

Haleika's curls appeared in the shadows before us. Leander was her dance partner. They'd managed their stolen moment. My gaze fell to our secretly joined hands, his thumb rubbing small circles into my palm.

"If you could dance with me," I said, "how would you?"

He glanced over his shoulder, his eyes dipping low on my dress then back up to my eyes before he turned around, on guard once more save for our joined hands.

"I would spin you. Just once. Because I love to see you move. But then I'd pull you close, too close for the proper steps." He tugged on my hand, forcing me to step forward, closer. "One hand on your waist, pulling you to me, my fingers pressing into your hip, right where it curves."

I swallowed roughly. "And then what?"

His shoulders rose and fell like he was breathing heavily. "I'd run my hands down your arms, feeling how soft you are—and how strong. Then I'd turn you, and pull you against me, so I could whisper in your ear, so you could feel…." He took a deep breath.

"Feel what?" I asked, even as I knew the answer, even as heat pooled between my legs.

"How desperately I want you." He squeezed my hand.

My breaths were uneven.

"I'd turn you once more. And then I'd back you up, right against that wall behind you, and take you deep in the shadows, so I could...." He coughed.

"What?" I asked, my heart pounding.

"You know. Finish what we started...what I think about doing to you every day, and dream about doing to you every night."

The song was over. Rhyan's shoulders tensed, then he dropped my hand. After the last note of the song, he walked away. All at once, the guests seemed to speed up, moving through the room twice as fast as before—or maybe I was moving slowly.

"Lyr! Sorry!" Tristan called to me. The lights had also begun springing back to life, the flames crackling and licking toward the ceiling, each one shining in a different color so that a rainbow was cast across the temple. "I'm so sorry."

"It's fine," I said. "Dance of Darkness...doesn't always work." I shrugged. Haleika was running, holding the skirts of her dress in her hands, right into Galen's arms and laughing.

"Why don't we get a drink?" he said, his gaze narrowed. His brown eyes were scrutinizing me, searching.

"What?" I asked, not hearing the next part of his question.

"Did you dance with someone?"

I pushed my hair over my shoulder. "No. I just...waited here."

He cocked his head to the side, and sweat beaded at the nape of my neck.

"I think a drink would be good," I said.

He nodded, extending his arm for me to take before escorting me off the dance floor.

A new song began to play as the bartender poured our drinks. Standing off to the side, Morgana drank another glass of wine, as Meera danced with a noble, looking uncomfortable and attempting to keep her distance.

Arianna, wearing a black mask, twirled past me and ended up in the arms of the Imperator, her expression going from joyful to severe. Someone spun on the dance floor wearing a black mask made of feathers with a peaked nose just like a seraphim—a black seraphim.

The mask vanished along with the dancer. I blinked. Had I really seen that? Or had it been a trick of the light?

There was another turn by the dancers. Another black seraphim flashed. Then another.

I pulled out of Tristan's arms. The Emperor sat nearby in his Seat of Honor, his consort at his side sipping wine.

He narrowed his whitened eyebrows, frowning. The Blade stood behind him, head turning side to side, watching and observing every move made.

Three more black seraphim masks appeared and vanished.

Something was wrong. I wasn't imagining these masks. The Emartis were here. Even with the presence of the Council, the Emperor, the Ready...they dared to show themselves.

I sucked in a breath.

"Are you all right?" Tristan asked.

"I think I got a little dizzy," I said, scanning the room, trying to find the Ready. He was in the center of the dance floor, stoic and watching, looking everything like the God of Death. In every corner and in every shadow stood a soturion of Ka Batavia wearing freshly pressed green cloaks and golden armor sharpened into golden feathers at their shoulders.

But I couldn't stop this nagging feeling. Something was wrong. Something was happening.

A shadow loomed behind me. "About that dance you requested," the Imperator drawled. His hand was already on my waist. "The Emperor isn't in the mood."

"Well, I thank him for the consideration," I said carefully, trying to shift my body out of his reach. His fingers pressed into my skin, as I tightened my grip on Tristan's hand. "But I am otherwise with an escort."

"An Emperor's duty never ends. But he did not want you to be disappointed."

"I wish not to disappoint his majesty either," I said.

Tristan had gone still beside me, his eyes zeroing in on the Imperator's hand on me.

The Imperator's fingers pressed deeper, and I stifled a gasp, feeling not only his hand on my waist but his phantom fingers in my back.

"That is good," said the Imperator, "for he sent me to dance with you in his stead."

"Oh," I said. "Lord Tristan and I were—"

"Allow me to step in," the Imperator said, taking my hand from Tristan's and threading his fingers through mine. "How kind of you both. This is the Emperor's wish."

Tears burned behind my eyes. My hatred for this man made my physically ill, his touch was more than I could bear.

"I'll be right here, Lyr," Tristan said calmly. "As soon as you're done."

"Lord Tristan," the Imperator nodded and swept me out to the center of the dance floor, his boots moving so quickly that I stumbled to keep up.

We were in the center of the temple, in clear view of the Emperor, nearly beneath the eternal flame.

The music swelled, and the Imperator began to spin me around, one hand firmly gripping my hip as if I'd run away.

"You are quite the lovely dancer," he said, watching me carefully from behind his mask. He'd found one in silver with clawed edges.

"Thank you, your highness," I said, stiffly.

"And you really have mastered the art of moving these." He squeezed where he gripped me below my waist.

I stared ahead, the backs of my eyes burning.

"Are you prepared for tomorrow?" he asked.

"As prepared as I can be," I said. My heart was pounding, my skin crawling, but still I smiled and held my head up while his palm was against mine.

He smirked. "Doubtful. I will say this, though. Batavia women, you are made of something feisty."

I caught the Emperor watching me over the Imperator's shoulder as well as the Blade peering at us carefully. Beside us on the dance floor, the Bastardmaker grabbed a young female mage.

The Imperator stared down at me, a questioning look in his eyes, and I realized I'd never responded to his last statement. I swallowed, my throat dry. "You find us feisty," I said, keeping my voice neutral. "Is that Ka Kormac's way of admitting we're strong?"

"I was there, you know," he said, voice low. His arm wrapped around me, pulling me closer. "With the Lady Julianna in Lethea."

I froze.

The Imperator shifted roughly, taking the next step quickly to jolt me back into the dance. His grip on my hand tightened.

"You will not mind my saying this," he said. "After all, you've renounced vorakh."

My eyes burned. "Of course. I am a loyal daughter of the Empire."

The Imperator smirked again. "My uncle will be pleased to hear. Because you never know what secrets a family member is willing to hide."

"Not if it involves vorakh," I said darkly. The ceiling looked unstable above me. Was it moving closer?

"That is how I came to my opinion of your feistiness," he said lightly. "How hard the Lady Julianna fought back. Scratching and clawing until her power was completely stripped, removed from every inch of her body."

The Bastardmaker laughed beside us. "Love the feisty ones," he said, his black, beady eyes on me as he lowered his hands on his dance partner.

"If you should wish…." the Imperator started, leaning in, his bristly cheek pressed to mine.

I was going to faint. By the Gods, I was going to faint.

"…not to be tested tomorrow, we can find you a place to serve in the capitol."

The Emperor's eyes were on me as the Imperator spoke. He licked his lips before turning to his escort.

"Respectfully…" My voice shook. "Must decline."

He pulled back, his predatory smile spreading across his face, more wolf-like than human. "Julianna was a fighter, too. But it didn't make much difference in the end. Thanks for the dance." He released me, shoving me backwards. I stumbled, my vision foggy.

I needed air. I needed to get out of here, off the dance floor, away from prying eyes.

I spun on my heels, only half-seeing where I was going, tearing across the dance floor, pushing through the dancing couples and servers with floating trays of wine and fruit platters.

A door. I needed to find a door and get outside. But there were people everywhere and guards at the door loyal to the Emperor.

My vision was going in and out of focus, my stomach twisting. I slid into a corner and bumped right into Haleika. And Leander. Before I could react, he'd taken her hand, rushing them through a door, leaving me all alone, terrified and panicking. I stumbled back, clutching my chest and gulping for air. I needed to get away from what I'd seen, what I'd heard, away from myself. I ran right into a soturion with light brown hair that curled at the ends. He was older, with a few specks of gray mixed in.

A tear fell from my eye.

"Your grace," the soturion said, startled. "Are you unwell?"

"I-I'm fine." I sucked in a breath, searching for another place to go. I couldn't leave. But I couldn't stay here. I needed to calm down. To find my footing.

"Your grace, you look faint." He had a slight lilt to his speech, his accent familiar.

I looked up and found familiar green eyes and a kind face.

"Apologies. You must not recognize me," he said, seeing the confusion in my eyes. "I'm Rhyan's uncle. Sean. At your service, your grace."

"Sean?"

"Yes."

"Get me out of here."

He gave a curt nod. "Come." He took hold of my arm, guiding me back out to the dance floor. The music blasted in my ears alongside the sounds of laughter and feet stomping, glasses clinking, drinks pouring, silverware scraping against porcelain. I felt a hundred curious eyes on me trying to see through my mask. Sean's hand was light but firm on my arm as he led me to the other side of the temple out into a hallway.

Someone new took my arm, and warm, calloused fingers wrapped around me. "I've got her, Sean," Rhyan said. "Thank you."

"Be well, your grace," Sean said with a bow.

"Lyr, what happened? What did he say?" Rhyan asked.

Sean slipped back into the ballroom after offering Rhyan a quiet nod.

This was the hallway. The entrance to the red ray—the entrance that was always specific to Ka Batavia. The one I'd thought sacred to my family, to my Ka, until the Bastardmaker had picked up Jules, slung her over his shoulder, and carried her through here. This was the hallway I'd stopped using unless forced to since that night.

I could still feel the terror consuming my body, my fear for Jules. I could still hear the slaps of Markan's sandals against the floor as I tore off my diadem and flung it at him. I could still feel the way my scalp burned and my chest pounded and the sudden impact of Markan's brutish body against mine as he caught me. I could still smell the sharp scent of the cloth as he drugged me.

My knees buckled. White spots appeared in my vision, then blackness. I was going to be sick. I clutched at my stomach, sinking down.

My feet lifted off the ground. Rhyan had swept his hand under my knees, had scooped me into his arms.

"You're all right now, partner. It's just me." He pulled my mask off my face, letting it drop to the ground.

Waves of dizziness washed over me. There was a painful tug on my stomach, and the next thing I knew, we were at the other end of the hall. Rhyan kicked open a door and walked through it. We were in a small spare room full of Valya scrolls in need of repair.

"Down!" I shouted. I was going to throw up; my stomach felt like it had been ripped raw.

I rushed toward a table, my fingers grasping the edge, while I coughed and breathed until the wave of nausea passed. Dizziness and exhaustion took hold of me, and I sank to the floor.

Rhyan shut the door. The lock clicked into place. Seconds later, he sat down behind me, his arms gently encircling my waist. "Do you need a bucket?"

I exhaled sharply, closing my eyes as I tuned into the feeling inside my belly. "No. I'm not going to throw up. Just need to sit."

Rhyan drew me closer, settling my back against him. I clutched my chest as if I could reach through to my heart and make it beat properly.

"Lean into me," he said, positioning himself on the floor so I sat between his legs. His arms wrapped around me, one palm flattening across my belly, the other over my heart. "Just breathe. You're okay."

Tears burned paths down my cheeks. "Why does this keep happening?" I sobbed. "I should be stronger by now. I shouldn't be falling apart like this. I-I thought I was doing better. Getting over all these…attacks." I wiped my eyes in frustration.

"You're not falling apart. You're getting stronger," he said, breath hot on my neck. His arms tightened. "You're the strongest person I know."

"No, I'm not. I'm sitting on the floor, barely fighting back a panic attack. Because of Jules. Because of the Imperator. I'm tired of feeling like this. It's been over two years."

"Did he say something to you?" Rhyan asked darkly.

My shoulders shook. "I can't…I can't…" He'd said nothing new, nothing I hadn't suspected. But to hear it from his mouth, to hear it spoke so boldly….

"Bastard," Rhyan swore. "Lyr, listen to me. It's not your fault. Awful things happened to you here. To people you loved. And the people who did these awful things are here right now—rubbing it in your face—because they're evil, because they want to upset you. And you're feeling it because you're finally facing what happened, instead of burying your feelings in some forgotten box. That's why.

Do you hear me? This is not your fault. It doesn't make you weak." He pressed his hands more firmly against me.

I sniffled, leaning back into him. "I feel so weak. Like I'm right back where I was two years ago. With all our training and meditating, I really thought I was getting better."

"You are getting better. And you're not weak," he said. "You're healing. It's not a linear process. You don't get to graduate or cross some threshold without looking back and never feel pain again. It's messy and ugly. The grief can hit at any time. Some days it's gone. Some days the pain chases you morning to night. But it doesn't make you weak. Remember who you are—all you have survived. The pain is not your fault. It's only here because you've had to be strong for far too long. Your strength is not determined by the pain, by the doubts or fears that they forced you to relive. What matters is what you choose to do with them. And all I see is a warrior, fighting back. Fighting through the pain. When I look at you, Lyr, I see strength."

A sob wracked through me. Something inside of me registered the truth in his words, and somehow that was more painful than anything else I'd felt tonight.

"I know," he said gently. "I know. I feel it, too. Every day. Just catch your breath. You're safe here with me. You're always safe with me. It's all right." He rocked us side to side. "It's okay. You're allowed to sit down sometimes." His arms tightened around me, and he continued his slow, even breathing. The rocking slowed, and as the minutes passed, I felt the panic washing away. We stilled, but he kept his hands firm against me, one still on my belly, one over my heart, steadying me.

"I shouldn't have dragged you into this," I said, wiping my eyes. "You should be back at the ball, enjoying yourself."

I felt him shake his head, his face brushing against my hair. "I'm right where I'm supposed to be. Where I want to be." He removed his hand from my chest, letting it join the other at my waist. "Better?" he asked.

I nodded and felt his hold loosen from around me as his body strained back, creating space between us.

"Don't go." My hands closed over his.

"I'm at your command, your grace." Rhyan's voice was hoarse. His hands flattened against my torso, his palms searing through my dress. I felt my breath shorten, but for a different reason than before. His fingers splayed across my stomach, touching the bared skin.

My nipples were sensitive against the rough material of my dress. My breasts felt heavy, dying to be touched, sensing his fingers so close yet so far away.

"I can't stop thinking about you." I writhed against him as if I could shift his hands higher to where I wanted them. Where I needed them. "I try not to, but I can't help myself."

"What are you doing?" he asked, even as his hands moved higher.

I arched against him, leaning my head back to watch his face. The muscles in his jaw worked, and his gaze was fixed to my necklace, my body, my exposed skin. "What are you doing?" I asked. I didn't sound like myself; my voice was low, almost hoarse. I was so full of desire.

He blinked slowly as he bit down on his bottom lip. "Lyr, please. I'm about to break. I want you. So fucking bad." His hands inched higher, and heat bloomed low in my belly, searing through my core.

I could feel his chest rising and falling behind me. His once steady breath, my anchor in the storm, was uneven, erratic, and heavy.

"You must tell me. Command me," he said, voice desperate. "Order me to leave. Order me away." His voice was husky, his breath on my neck leaving shivers up and down my spine.

"I thought we followed the chain of command. Apprentice." I writhed back into him, feeling just how badly he wanted me, and he tightened his grip, his fingers pressing into my bared flesh, his hands rising even higher. "Novice." I pushed my head to the side, exposing the length of my neck.

"Lyr, you must," he said desperately, even as his hips lifted, his arousal pressing against my backside. "Tell me to leave."

"Don't the apprentices give the orders? Don't the bodyguards command the ones they protect?"

"Not right now," he growled. His lips brushed against my neck. The tips of his fingers teased my curves. Back and forth. "Not when I have you in my arms, not when you feel so fucking good I can't remember my role, or duty, or any Godsdamned oaths I swore. I can barely remember my name. All I can think about is how I want to flip you over, splay you out beneath me, and drink my fill of you."

His cheek pressed against mine from behind. My chest heaved, and his hands moved up and up my torso, slowly, purposefully, sensually. My head fell back on his shoulder. Higher and higher his fingers spread, tucked under my necklace, until his hands cupped my breasts.

He sucked in a breath just as I gasped. Gods, he felt so good. But he was no longer moving, just cupping me, holding me. I arched my back, needing him to do more. But he was still, waiting. Waiting for me. For permission.

"Lyriana," he said. His breath was heavy and uneven, his hands hot enough to brand me. I reached behind me and gripped the back of his neck, my fingers tangling in his hair, pulling him closer. His chest heaved against my back. His fingers pressed into my flesh, and my nipples felt almost too sensitive against his palms. "Gods. You're perfect," he murmured. "Do you want me to stop?"

"No. I want you."

"Want me to what?" he asked.

"Touch me."

Rhyan moaned. His mouth was on my shoulder as he pressed his body against mine, thumbs brushing against my nipples through my dress. I cried out. He kneaded my breasts, his mouth hot on my neck and kissing its way up, his tongue flicking against my skin and sending shivers down my spine. I turned toward him just as his lips sought mine. The instant our mouths made contact, his felt like a searing brand. There was no softness like the last time, no tentative start. We weren't dancing around each other anymore. We'd made our choice.

His tongue swept across my mouth, opening me to him, lighting me on fire. I lost control, biting his lower lip, groaning. His own groan answered mine, as he tasted my lips, one hand rising to cup my chin and tangle in my hair.

He deepened the kiss, his tongue wrapping around mine as he continued to squeeze and caress my breasts, drawing ripples of pleasure down to a rising surge between my legs.

I turned in his arms, straddling his lap. He held my hips, helping me turn, the kiss unbroken. He cupped my chin, angling my face, sliding his hand through my hair to the back of my neck, undoing the clasp of the necklace. I felt its weight immediately release from my shoulders as he set it on the ground. I tangled my fingers in his soft waves, brushing them back from his face, kissing my way across his jaw and cheek, desperate to drink in as much of him as I could.

Without breaking the kiss, he lowered me to the ground, pushing the straps of my dress off my shoulders. I grabbed his belt, pulling him down on top of me. As he settled himself between my legs, I tore open his jacket, sliding my hands inside to push it off his shoulders. He pulled back just long enough to toss it aside while I furiously tugged up his shirt from his belt and slid my hands up his bare back, over his blood oaths and tattoo. His hands slid down my legs, sliding my dress higher and higher, our hips pressing together in a frenzy.

I couldn't stop. I couldn't stop touching him, kissing him, pressing against him. I felt half-mad, like I'd claw through his skin just to get closer.

He trailed kisses down my neck, nipping and licking until his face was buried between my breasts, where he pressed soft kisses over my heart that left me shuddering. Then he lifted himself up and gently, reverently pulled my straps down my arms, baring my breasts. His jaw tightened. My hands tangled in his hair as his mouth replaced his hands on my bared skin, and he sucked deeply, drawing a hardened nipple between his lips, pausing only long enough to look up at me, eyes hooded and drunk with desire.

He closed his mouth over me again, and I arched and writhed beneath him, pulling at the hair at the nape of his neck.

Waves of pleasure washed through me, ebbing and flowing again and again. I was burning, sinking, floating, and flying.

"Do you know how much I love your breasts?" he asked.

"I thought," I gasped, "I thought you hadn't seen them."

After I'd slept in his bed, topless after being lashed, I'd accidentally let the blanket slip in the morning, and he'd sworn he hadn't seen anything at the time.

He smiled wickedly against my skin before closing his mouth around my other nipple, kneading the first between his thumb and finger. I bucked, the sensations almost too much—too much coming from him.

"Do you want to know a secret?" he asked.

"Mmmhmmm."

"I'm a terrible liar."

I started to laugh before he lifted himself up and claimed my mouth again, and the frenzy started anew, like I needed to kiss him to breathe.

Rhyan growled low in his throat, as I reached for his belt, this time to remove it. My fingers worked furiously to undo the buckle until at last, I unclasped it, and the belt slid off his hips and fell to the ground with a clang.

"Lyr," he gasped.

The door slammed open.

CHAPTER
TWENTY-FOUR

Rhyan shot across the floor so fast, he crashed against a table full of scrolls. With a small rumble, they fell to the ground, rolling beside him as I turned away, fiddling with my dress to cover myself. The straps of the dress wouldn't rise. I was able to get the material up enough to cover my nipples, but that was it. No one who saw us could doubt for a second what we'd been in the middle of doing, what we'd been furiously on our way to doing.

The door closed and footsteps sounded.

I turned slowly, willing my eyes to stay open. Heart pounding as dread became a living body inside me, my eyes made contact with our intruder.

A grin, more sinister than any I'd ever seen, spread across Mercurial's face. His eyes darted from Rhyan, sitting on the floor with his shirt half open and untucked and his buckle on the ground, to me and my nearly fully exposed breasts. He laughed.

"Mercurial," Rhyan snarled.

"Ah, ah, ah. Mercurial, First Messenger of Her Royal Highness, Queen Ishtara of the Star Court, Lady of the Night Lands. When you are not fully clothed, you do not get to minimize my full title." He bowed. Straightening, he pressed his finger against his chin, looking up as though deep in thought. "Now, I do believe I once foretold of a certain forswearing between you two. It seems as though I were in fact...prophetic." He stalked closer. "Although I am already in possession of the knowledge that this was not your first-time foreswearing."

"You want something," Rhyan said, his voice deadly.

Mercurial's hand snapped up, his fingers pointing at us. "No! You do not get to take that tone with me." Afeyan magic, ancient, powerful, made of a terrifyingly bright light, and bound by a color I'd never seen before, pulsed around him. As quickly as it had been unleashed, it vanished, and he smiled sweetly.

"What do you want?" Rhyan asked.

"What do I want?" Mercurial asked. "What do you want?" His eyes slanted, taking in our state of undress and dishevelment. "Clearly to continue on with each other. What was the next piece of clothing to come off? What part of her grace's body was your slippery tongue hoping to taste next? Her belly button? Her thighs? Somewhere in between?"

"Get out," Rhyan said. He glanced back at me, seeing me still struggling to pull my dress up fully. "Or at least turn away, allow her grace to finish dressing. Now!"

"You have mocked the very oath you swore," Mercurial said, "the oath you swore in blood. You are Godsdamned lucky that kashonim doesn't operate the same as blood oaths, or the two of you would have been struck by lightning just now. Make no mistake—the magic is angry with you two, and a price will be paid. But I am who you need to be more concerned with. Well, me and the other man who I believe would be very interested in the activities happening in this room."

I stilled, hearing footsteps in the hall.

"Lord Tristan," Mercurial said. "He's on his way over here right now."

Right on cue, Tristan's voice carried itself into the room. "Lyr! Lyr? Are you back here?" He sounded frantic, his voice full of concern. The last time he'd seen me, I'd been escorted to the dance floor by the Imperator, and then I'd run off. How long ago was that? Fuck!

"He's coming in here. He'll find you. Not exactly what you want, is it?" Mercurial asked, his hips snaking sinuously side to side as he continued across the room. He reached into his long locks and produced a glittering Valalumir, which spun in his palm. He'd carried it the day we'd first met and had nearly hypnotized me with it. "I can easily redirect him. But you must do something for me first. Make a deal. Now. Go on. Ask me for my silence. I know you want to. I know you need to."

"Is this how you forced my father into a deal?" I asked. "You blackmailed him!"

Mercurial laughed. Even now, the sound was tantalizing and musical, drawing me in even as my entire body felt repulsed.

"He came to me on his own. As I knew he would after so foolish an act."

"I'll ask it," Rhyan said defiantly. "I'm ready to deal with you. I, Lord Rhyan Hart, ask for your silence, Mercurial. I beg it of you. Name your price."

Mercurial laughed. "Lord, now? How convenient. No," he said. "You don't have anything I want. Not yet. But you, your grace. Ask me." He held his hand out to me, and the star rose, turning slowly, hypnotically. Stars danced across my vision, and I swayed.

I pulled my gaze up to meet his eyes. "What's your price?"

"No!" Rhyan said. "Lyr, don't. I'll pay. This is my fault. I should be the one."

"Lyr?" Tristan called, his voice louder. He was closer. "Lyr!"

"The noble lord of silver is desperate to find you." The Valalumir in Mercurial's palm spun faster. "Ask me. Ask me for my silence. And when the time comes, I will find you. And you will pay the debt. Whatever it is. Refuse me, and your boyfriend walks through these very doors in the next minute. He'll find you two, report you—he's such a good little boy, following all the rules of the Empire. You know his mind, your grace, you know he will. And then, such a shame, tomorrow you'll both be in the arena on the stripping pole. No waiting, your judge and executioner sit jovially in the next room."

"Lyr? Are you in here?" The door knob jiggled.

"Ask me." Mercurial's nostrils flared. "You have, at most, fifteen seconds remaining before his stave unlocks the door. You've seen it before. He can do it."

Rhyan looked ready to fight, to tear Mercurial to pieces. But he had no weapons on him. And fighting an Afeya was a battle not even soturi prepared for.

"Mercurial," Rhyan said, "let me ask you for your silence. I'll pay double."

The Afeya sauntered over to Rhyan, bent down to where he still sat on the floor, placed a finger over Rhyan's lips, and slowly, seductively traced them until Rhyan snapped them shut. "So soft," he said.

Rhyan wrenched back. "Deal with me. Or I'll make sure you regret it."

"Must have been quite the kiss between you two." He sniffed at the air and frowned. "No. Kiss isn't the word for what just happened here. It smells like...hmmm, you know what it smells like between you two." His voice was light and flirtatious, but his eyebrows narrowed, and that anger he'd directed at us the first night returned. "My lord, do not dare threaten an Afeya of the Star Court, or even you will regret it!"

"Lyr!" Tristan yelled. The lock began to shift, the gears twisting and turning. He was breaking through it.

"Out of time," Mercurial said. "Should I let him in? It's rude to ignore guests so persistently knocking on the door." He pouted. "Very rude indeed."

"No," I shouted. "Don't let him in. I'll do it. I'm asking for your silence, Mercurial," I said. "Now! Please. I'll give you whatever you want."

"Lyr, no!" Rhyan cried, his voice full of anguish. "It was my fault!"

A slow smile spread across Mercurial's face, and his eyes

gleamed with joy like those of a cat who'd just found his prey and knew he had all the time in the world to play with it.

The door stilled, the lock clicking back into place. Footsteps echoed, moving away from the room.

"What did you do to him?" I asked.

Mercurial tossed his hair over his shoulder. "He just remembered he already looked in this room." His eyes narrowed. "You weren't here. You can get dressed now."

The straps of my dress moved up my arms, and my necklace floated off the ground, draping itself across my shoulders and chest. The clasp sealed itself with a loud snap as my hair was swept aside. Rhyan seethed as his own clothes were put back in place and neatened, his jacket buttoning up, his belt sliding around his hips and buckling. Mercurial even added a little muss to his hair.

"Now to sign the contract." He held out his palm, and his sparkling, golden Valalumir appeared, spinning. It was beautiful, mesmerizing. Mercurial twisted his arm, his hand undulating as the star rolled up and down his palm. It started to spin faster and faster. "Rise, Lady Lyriana Batavia, Heir to the Arkasva, High Lord of Bamaria. And stand before me."

I did, walking slowly to him, my hands pressed to my sides to keep from shaking. Mercurial's arm shot out, and Rhyan groaned, slamming into a wall. Valya scrolls crashed to the ground and rolled in every direction. "This contract is between me and her. Not you. Stop interfering." His fingers snapped. Rhyan's head smacked the wall. "Stop hurting yourself."

Rhyan groaned.

"Leave him alone, Mercurial, and deal with me," I said. "Where do I sign?"

Mercurial chuckled. "You child. We are not so uncivil as that in the Afeyan courts." He held the Valalumir out before me. "There's no ink in our contracts. No names. You mortals barely hold onto them. You won't even have to bleed this time, your grace." He laughed. "For one contract to end, as another begins, it's simply… this." He jerked his chin to the flowing Valalumir. "A little bit of my soul wrapped up in a speck of light from the original Valalumir. It goes into your heart."

My heart pounded in response, the beat so fast and hard my knees weakened.

"Lyr, no!" Rhyan yelled. "Don't do this. I'll take the blame. I'll say I forced you. You're innocent."

"They'll kill you," I said. "I'm doing this."

"Smart girl," Mercurial said. "It will be fast. It doesn't hurt… much. You will always feel its presence. Feel its weight in there. You'll be reminded of what is owed to the First Messenger day and night until the debt is paid, and then, and only then, will I extract it."

"And if I fail to pay the debt?" I asked.

"Fail to pay my debt, and the star inside your heart will catch fire, burning you to cinders from within."

"No!" Rhyan yelled.

"Fine," I said, squeezing my eyes shut. "Do it." I braced myself, grabbing hold of my belt, desperate for something to hold onto. My chest rose and fell, unable to remain calm. I braced for the pain.

But the sensation never came.

Bells began to ring—not the hourly bells. The warning bells. Once. Twice. Three times. I'd only ever heard those bells ring once before. At the end of summer, a week before my birthday. These bells rang for one reason, and one reason only.

Akadim.

TWENTY-FIVE

"That would be my cue to leave," Mercurial said, slinking toward the door. He kicked a scroll on the ground out of his way, letting it roll to my feet. "You would not want to fight an akadim who was once Afeya if I should fall. And I am not in the mood to brawl tonight with lesser soulless beings." The Valalumir spinning in his hand vanished. His dark eyebrows furrowed in annoyance. "The next time I see you, your grace, you will sign the contract."

"What about our deal?" Rhyan yelled. He tried to push himself off the wall against Mercurial's spell that was trapping him there.

"Not *our* deal, my not-lord," Mercurial seethed. He snapped his fingers, and Rhyan—still struggling to move from the wall—was freed. He stumbled forward. "Hers. And mine. Not yours." His eyes narrowed, fixing on Rhyan. "Not this time." Mercurial swiveled his head, looking back to me. "Fear not, your grace. No one will see or suspect you two. If you're seen together, if you go missing, all of your behavior will be excused for the next three hours, though I wouldn't push things too far. Consider it an act of good faith on my part. I do want to collect payment, after all. Do me one favor—try not to die out there. Too soon for that."

"I'll get you to Cresthaven," Rhyan said, facing me. "You have a whole team ready to protect you. You'll be safe."

"It's too late for that," Mercurial said, tapping his chin. "They're not at the border. No, no, no. They're here—surrounding the building. Three of them, if my senses are still intact."

The room shook as if something had crashed into the temple walls. Screams sounded beyond the door, yells of panic and fear erupting as another round of bells sounded off, echoing into the night. I'd never heard those bells used before. They were a specific three-part combination—a code I'd memorized as a girl in case the day came that they were ever to be called. And today was that day. The akadim hadn't just breached the border, they were deep into the heart of Bamaria.

Mercurial's eyes slit into two thin lines, and his lips widened into a smile. "Until next time." He looked up to the ceiling and vanished.

"They were just in Elyria," I said. "How did they get to Bamaria?"

Rhyan had returned from a hunting expedition only a week before.

"I don't know," he said, lips drawn.

I started pacing the room. "Three? Here? How, with an hourly patrol? With the hunting parties?" I asked, frantic. "We've never had them breach the borders. For them to get so deep into the city undetected, it's not possible. They would have been caught, they would have been seen. It's almost like…it's like someone let them in…Gods!" My eyes widened. "Ka Kormac! Rhyan, do you know the schedule? Were they patrolling the border tonight?"

Rhyan shook his head. "Lyr, come here to me." He took both my hands in his. "Listen. How they got in doesn't matter now. That's a future problem. Right now, we know they're here. So we're worrying about one thing, and one thing only—getting you to safety."

I heard a roar in the distance and the sounds of glass crashing and screaming.

"Your escort will be searching for you. We want to find them first."

My escorts probably had already been looking, but whatever Mercurial had done to steer Tristan away must have concealed us from them as well.

"Hart!" The call came right on cue from his vadati stone, muffled in the pocket of his belt—the belt I'd just removed from his waist. It was Markan. "Have you seen her grace? Location?"

Rhyan pulled the glowing stone out. "Secured. Temple back room," he said.

"Get her out," he roared. "Temple breached." Terrified screams sounded from the stone, echoing and reverberating against the halls outside our room.

The communication stopped, and the light vanished from the stone, leaving behind a milky white haze.

This couldn't be happening.

"Lyr," Rhyan said, "the best soturi in Lumeria are out there now. We're going to stop the threat. Nothing's going to happen to you."

"What about my sisters, my father?"

"They're protected. Remember? More protected than anyone out there. There's a protocol to keep you all safe." He exhaled sharply, a haunted look in his eyes, and I knew why; having me back here, alone, away from everyone, had broken that protocol. "Don't worry about them. Priority is always on the ruling Ka. That includes you." He squeezed my hand then withdrew his sword, the blade scraping against his sheath.

I reached down, pulled up the silvery white fabric of my gown, exposed my thigh, and unsheathed my own dagger.

Rhyan nodded in approval. "Stay close to me. If I say run, you run. Hide, you hide. No questions." His voice had roughened, taking on an air of power. The chain of command that had dissolved just moments ago as every line between us had blurred was now back in full force. "I'm getting you out of this."

He stepped forward and pressed his ear to the door. He unlocked it, turned the knob, and swung it open, his sword pointing forward, his stance protective and angled in front of me.

Screams carried through the temple hall as masked Lumerians

rushed past us without looking, their mouths drawn in horror. More came rushing by until Rhyan couldn't even step outside the door.

"Hart!" Aemon called through the vadati. "Seraphim carriage behind red ray. Blade slaughtered one akadim in sanctuary. We're tracking the other two. Go now!"

I stared at the hall. We were behind the green ray. I blinked. When I'd panicked earlier, we had been in the hall of the red ray, where Markan had chased me down, where I'd last seen Jules....

"Come on," Rhyan said, grabbing my hand, running against the crowd.

Together, we headed back through the hall out into the sanctuary where the Valyati ball had been.

I gasped. It looked like a hurricane had torn through the hall. Scrolls were lying across the floor, scattered and torn apart, amongst shattered glass. Some were on fire. Soturi of different Kavim littered the floor in what I prayed were moments of lost consciousness and injury...not loss of life. Tables had been overturned, and the final remnants of the party dwellers were all pushing and scrambling over each other to reach the various temple doors.

In the center of the sanctuary, across Auriel's Chamber, its body turning colors from the eternal flame, was the corpse of an akadim.

I froze. I'd never seen one before, only pictures or crude statues and puppets. Nothing prepared me for how truly massive the demons were. Blade stood over it, wiping blood from his forehead as he lifted his sword, the steel catching the firelight above.

"Ah!" he yelled as he slammed his blade down, severing the akadim's arm from its body—an arm that was the length of my entire body. The skin was pale and full of jagged red lines crossing each other.

The akadim's foot twitched as Blade pulled up his sword.

"Lyr," Rhyan hissed. "Let's go." He squeezed my hand, leading us forward, rushing past the overturned tables and chairs and the wreckage of food, plates, cups, and...more bodies. More bodies.

Please...please let them be alive.

Even though I knew they had to be gone by now, that Aemon

was on top of it, I still searched the hall for any sign of my sisters, of my father, of Eathan, Arianna, and Tristan...but all that seemed to remain now were the Emperor's soturi. He was gone, of course, as was his consort.

The red ray's hall came into view, and Rhyan led me through the door. We stepped outside into a blackened night sky and snow-covered ground. Our seraphim waited a few yards away. Two port attendants kept their staves pointed at her, trying to keep her down, but she was clearly agitated, cold and unhappy in the snow and sensing the danger nearby. Her golden wings struggled violently against the port mages' spells, and her feathers glowed under the sparsely lit torches outside the temple. She opened her beak, releasing a high-pitched shriek of fear.

I swallowed hard, my hand squeezing Rhyan's. The last time we'd ridden a distressed seraphim, it hadn't gone well.

Several Soturi of Ka Batavia stood guard on the outer perimeter. Snow fell in thick clumps as screams continued to sound from the fields.

"Ready?" Rhyan asked, his grip on me firm. "We're going to make a run for it."

He stepped forward as I prepared to run at his speed, my boots already sinking into the snow. I could feel him tensing, ready to sprint, when he froze, releasing my hand. His entire body moved before mine as I saw past his shoulder, in the shadows of torchlight, an akadim approaching.

The demon had to be at least ten feet tall, growling and naked save for the scraps of clothing around its waist that barely covered its male organs. Red lines cut across the akadim's pale skin. Its muscles flexed as it extended its elongated arms, claws out, eyes reddening, and sharpened teeth bared into a snarl that turned my stomach.

The soturion nearest the monster charged forward, his sword out. I recognized him as one of the soturi from Brenna's legion, Hector. After he managed one swipe at the akadim's arm, its claws sliced through Hector's face. He stumbled back, blood gushing as the akadim wrapped its hand around his waist, picking him up and hurling him at the two soturi coming to his aid. Hector's body hit them both with such impact that all three soturi fell unconscious in the snow.

I bit back a scream as the akadim lunged, picking up Hector's limp body, his face barely recognizable. The akadim ripped through his armor in one simple, motion, tearing away his cloak and shirt.

Myself to fucking Moriel. It was going to eat Hector's soul. Turn him forsaken.

Hector's armor landed in the snow, useless now. The akadim's clawed hand hovered over his bared and convulsing body before the monster leaned forward, licking the blood from his face.

"In the carriage," Rhyan ordered. "Now."

Two more soturi charged at the akadim, trying to distract it, as a third came from behind and jumped on the beast's back. It roared, blood dripping down its chin as it wrapped its hands around Hector's legs. The monster swung him about like a club, swatting him at the third soturion—Caius. Caius was Hector's cousin, and both were Ka Corra like Brenna. With another swing, Hector's body smashed into Caius's, and the cousins fell into the snow.

I ran, heading straight for the seraphim, keeping my eyes ahead, my feet moving. I saw myself on the carriage. I saw myself closing the door, flying to safety. But I hesitated. I couldn't fly off by myself. I couldn't leave Rhyan behind.

My seraphim's feathers were now standing on edge, the tips sharpened from her fear. She turned her head violently from side to side, squawking wildly, her beak opening and closing ready to bite anyone who approached.

Then she stood, suddenly freed from the spell that had kept her frozen. I realized the port mages had taken off the moment the akadim had appeared. I was nearly at the carriage, only a few feet from the stairs to climb aboard, when she stood, pushing gusts of freezing snow into my face. Her wings flapped powerfully, creating a cyclone-like effect as she took off, vanishing faster than I'd ever seen a seraphim fly.

"No!" Rhyan yelled, his eyes finally betraying his fear.

The soturi who remained had encircled the akadim, attacking the way we'd been taught in a five. But each one failed, the akadim too strong, too violent, tearing through their cloaks, their armor, their arms. The pristine white snow that had fallen all day was now littered in blood...and evidence that another soturion had lost control of his bowels in the fight.

Suddenly, it was just Rhyan and me against the akadim.

Its red eyes were on us as it kicked the fallen soturi and blood-and-fecal-matter-stained snow out of its way as it charged forward.

"Mine," it roared, red eyes fixed on me as it extended its claws again.

"Stay back," Rhyan said. "Lyr. Dagger ready."

Rhyan charged, racing for the akadim. He leapt forward, brandishing his sword and slicing the akadim's arm. Blood spurted from its arm. Rhyan landed behind it, his boots crashing into the snow only a few feet away from the fallen soturi. He turned and raced back at the akadim, this time running past it while his blade cut through the akadim's thigh.

Rhyan spun and charged at the beast again. It roared in anger but was clearly distracted by Rhyan's movements—a tactic I realized he was using to take the akadim's attention off me. He was refocusing it, turning it around with every hit, retreat, and charge. Each time he came at the akadim, he switched up the side he attacked from, sometimes jumping and hitting its arm while other times staying low to attack its leg.

The akadim growled, losing interest in Rhyan and moving its attention back to me.

Its lips vibrated as it roared, charging forward.

I held up my dagger, wishing I'd brought my sword.

Rhyan slid under the beast, his sword slicing between its legs. The akadim fell to its knees, as Rhyan leapt to his feet, spinning back and swinging his sword at the akadim's neck. He hacked again and again as the akadim screamed in agony—until it stopped screaming, and its head hit the snow, a bloody heap of gore amidst the remaining white flakes.

"Lyr!" Rhyan roared, racing back for me, his sword still out.

I started toward him, desperate to reach him, to touch him, to hold him. When pain erupted like fire in my belly, I gasped, unable to breath, my feet no longer on the ground.

My body went numb, cold seeping through my fingers and legs and up my arms. It was the sensation of shock, the haunting calm that came over me when I was too scared or horrified to process the world around me. It had happened when I'd learned Jules had died. It had happened when the Emartis had attacked the arena. And now my world slowed down as I realized that the third akadim had found us, had come up behind me, had wrapped its clawed hands around my body, and was lifting me higher and higher away from the ground. I tried to kick my legs, but its grip was too all-encompassing, too tight.

My breathing was restricted. I was going to pass out. My terror was almost paralyzing.

"LYR!"

I gasped for breath, my chest rising and falling. Rhyan's cry had pulled me back into the present.

"LYR!"

The akadim turned me in its hand, revealing what had once been the face of a Lumerian woman. Its head was three times the size of mine, its teeth pointed to delicate tips as it sniffed me, its nostrils flaring, its mouth hanging open in unconcealed hunger. I could smell its breath, like death and decay and something metallic. Blood.

I leaned back in horror, trying to free my arms from its grasps as a spiked finger protruded, poking at my necklace. It poked again, pushing the gold into my chest, then pulled its finger back and hissed, her cruel eyes widened in surprise. In that moment, I was able to free my blade, cutting the inside of its hand as I did so.

It screeched in pain, and I used the opportunity to stab its hand again and again and again, hitting that one spot—just like Rhyan had taught me. My strength might not have been enough to take a soturion down in one hit, but bang into a wall enough times, and it would eventually crumble. On my last stab, blood spurted from its hand. I'd hit an artery.

The akadim cried out, its scream deafening as its grip loosened just enough for me to slip through until I was falling.

"Lyr!" Rhyan screamed.

A second later, I was in his arms, shaking as the akadim charged forward, its claws inches from my face.

Rhyan tightened his grip on me. "I'm getting us out of here. Hold onto me," he ordered. "Close your eyes."

I gasped in pain. It felt like my stomach had been tugged at, like the akadim had gotten its claws into my belly and was trying to rip my guts out, to pull me away from Rhyan forever. The akadim screamed as Rhyan raced forward. I could smell its breath, feel its body close behind. I struggled to free myself from his arms. He'd run faster if he didn't have to carry me.

"I said hold on," he ordered, something almost feral in his voice. The command came with more force than he'd ever used on me. "Don't let go!"

His hands pressed almost painfully into me while the snow bit my cheeks as he ran. Then he jumped, and my heart dove into my stomach as we fell...until his boots thudded against hard, sturdy ground, and my heart lurched.

Warmth rushed against my body, and I felt Rhyan take a slow step forward, almost stumbling, his grip on me loosening before tightening again. He straightened.

I couldn't feel the cold anymore, or the wind or snow. The screams of the akadim had vanished. There was a slight popping sound in my ears, then a calming trickling sound—water.

"Lyr? You're okay?"

I nodded, unable to speak.

"You're safe now," Rhyan said. His voice sounded odd, nervous, shaky, and tired. There was also a slight echo to it, and I could sense that walls now encircled us even though we hadn't entered any

GUARDIAN OF THE DROWNED EMPIRE

building I was aware of, hadn't even been running in the direction
of one. Shakily, he set me on my feet.

My heart pounded as I slowly opened my eyes, finding myself
surrounded by darkness. Rhyan shuffled beside me, and within a
second, a flame erupted from a set of matches he kept in his belt.
His face was lit by the flames, as he walked away from me, every
step echoing until the flame touched a torch nudged into a crack of
rock. Cavern rocks. And at last I saw exactly what had caused the
change in temperature and sound.

We were no longer in the Urtavian fields outside the temple, and
there was no snow on the ground. We were in a cave, standing on
solid rock just beside a pool with pristine blue water.

There were no caves near the temple. We had several cave
formations near the Elyrian border, but the biggest ones, the ones
that looked like this…. I shook my head, not sure I believed what I
was seeing.

"Rhyan?" I asked.

He stumbled forward, his hair lit up by the flames behind him.
"I'm sorry. I'm always tired after…." He swept his hand across his
forehead where sweat had started to bead, dampening his hair. "Are
you hurt? Are you sure you're okay?" Concern flashed through his
eyes, as his hands reached for me. "Gods, Lyr," he said. "The last
one, when it grabbed you, it went right for your heart."

"I'm all right," I reassured him. I took his hand, placing it over
my necklace, over my heart. "I'm not hurt. Thanks to you."

His breathing was still heavy, erratic, and his eyes were on our
hands, over the place where the akadim would have sucked out my
soul and devoured it. But it hadn't. We were safe. And we were
definitely somewhere else completely.

"We're in a cave, right?" I asked.

Rhyan's hand against my chest shook a little. "We are." He still
had that nervous edge to his voice, that uncertainty.

I steadied my hand over his. "We're not in Urtavia, are we?" I
asked.

"No," he said. "Gryphon Island. In the caves behind the

Guardian of Bamaria." He was breathing roughly. A large rock stood behind us, almost like a bench, and Rhyan stepped back from me, slid onto it, and leaned his head against the wall.

I sat down beside him and took his hand in mine, threading our fingers together. The vulnerability in his eyes almost killed me as the truth about Rhyan became totally and utterly clear. We'd moved from the city to an island in seconds, an island that had taken half an hour to fly to by seraphim when we'd come here on Days of Shadows.

I squeezed his hand. "So that's how it feels to travel?"

"Yes. That's what it feels like when you have the third vorakh."

CHAPTER
TWENTY-SIX

The cave was spinning around me. Jagged rock formations jutted from the walls and ceilings, and over the trickling of the pool was a dripping sound. The single torch offering light cast dancing shadows across the walls.

I took a deep breath, my mind reeling. Rhyan had a vorakh. All this time, his sympathy toward Jules, his quick promise to protect and keep Meera's and Morgana's secret—it was all because he knew what it was like, because he had it himself, because he'd lived with it for years, hiding it, learning to control it…fearing its consequences.

The pit that had formed in my belly when Jules's vorkah had appeared, then Meera's, then Morgana's, enlarged. Gods, not him. Not him, too.

I looked back at him. "Are you hurt?" He was still leaning against the wall, his breathing more shallow than usual.

"No," he said, rubbing between his eyebrows. "Just tired." His green eyes focused on me with a fiery intensity. "I almost lost you."

"But you didn't. You saved me." I placed my other hand over his, trying to help him calm down.

He closed his eyes, looking embarrassed. "I should have used it sooner. I'm sorry, I cut it too close, I was just—fuck. I was trying to do the right thing, to stop the threat, to get us out of there the right way, the soturion way. But when it came down to it, when it grabbed you...I lost it. And I knew then, I'd risk everything to save you."

I leaned in toward him. "Thank you."

"Fuck. I don't know what I'm doing. I had to keep you safe but..." He shook his head.

"It's okay," I said. "It's all right. Just take a breath. We're both okay."

He nodded, watching me as I helped him calm his breathing.

"Did you ever do that with me before?" I asked, more curious than anything, but also knowing I needed to distract him, to refocus his attention so he could calm himself down. "Earlier, when I was having a panic attack, we were in the red ray's hallway, but after, we walked out into the green. Did we...?"

He closed his eyes, his hand reaching for my face. "I'm sorry I didn't tell you." He swallowed and leaned forward, looking pale.

"Rhyan, it's okay. I understand why. Were there other times?" I asked.

He nodded slowly. "Yes." He sat back, staring at our joined hands. "I never meant to though. I was *trained* to control it."

"Trained?" I asked. He'd used an odd affect on the word, like it didn't mean what I thought. And as far as I knew, no training for vorakh existed anywhere in the Empire.

He looked away, his gaze distant. "The beatings, the reason my father bound me, it was partly his attempt to suppress my vorakh." He bit his lip before turning toward me again. "He seemed to think he could beat it out of me—although he'd been beating me long before. At least then, he had an excuse. And when he couldn't, he tried to torture it out of me."

Gods. "That's why he bound you?" My throat tightened.

His fingers twitched nervously in my hand. "I couldn't," he started helplessly, "I couldn't control it at first." He sounded so small and vulnerable in that moment. Like a much younger Rhyan was speaking, the one who'd been hurting, and lying, and covering up his bruises, doing all he could to protect his Ka. Like I had been. "I'd be walking through the fortress, some random hall one second, and then the next, I'd be on a different floor. In a different room. Accidentally finding myself in the kitchens and scaring the cooks, or disturbing someone in the bathroom. He beat me. Every time. He always knew, every single time it happened. He sensed it somehow. And he'd punish me along with whoever was unfortunate enough to see me. And when his punishments didn't take effect the first few times, he decided to beat her instead. My mother. Make me watch."

I cupped his cheek, stroking my thumb against his skin. He looked so bone-weary as he leaned his head against my hand.

"I tried to control it," he continued, "for her sake, for mine. The only thing I could figure out was it happened during moments of intense emotion. If I was feeling particularly angry or sad or just... Gods, if I laughed too loud, it happened. And he'd come for me. Come for her. Come for any witnesses. I'd spend the following morning running our arena bound, training in fives without being able to touch my power—lest I travel by accident. It went on and on until I'd been beaten so much, helped her clean up so many times, watched so many of the servants...." He blinked back his tears. "I had to stop feeling. I kept everything cold and buried. I did all I could not to feel. But sometimes," his eyes were red, "sometimes I couldn't help it." A tear fell against my hand.

"Rhyan." I leaned forward, wrapping him in my arms. I cupped the nape of his neck, pulling him closer, holding him tighter. His chest shook against mine. "I'm sorry. I'm sorry all that happened to you. He's a monster. You should have been protected, you should have been allowed to feel everything you did. You should have been made safe when your vorakh acted up, not punished for it."

He buried his face against my neck, more tears fell, warm against my skin.

I felt my own tears welling behind my eyes. "I wish I'd been there, I wish I could have protected you, made you safe." I wanted do everything for him I'd done for Meera and Morgana. He'd been alone the whole time, dealing with everything by himself.

His chest heaved against mine. "I know," he said against my neck. His hands pressed against my back. "Those, um," he cleared his throat, "those were the moments I used it with you."

"When you were emotional?" I asked.

Rhyan nodded and sat back, taking my hand back into his. "After you were lashed, that was the first time it happened. You were bleeding so much. I didn't want to waste time. I was terrified of you getting an infection, of what those whips would do to you. So when you closed your eyes in my arms, I traveled to my apartment. I did it again the following morning to yours. And tonight, I knew you needed somewhere private to fall apart, a safe place to put yourself back together. And that room was a good option—so."

"You were using it the right way then, every single time."

He laughed, the sound mirthless and bitter. "If he could see me now."

"Fuck him," I snarled.

Rhyan nodded, his face still pale.

"Is this an effect of the vorakh?" I asked. "How tired you are?"

"It's...." He took a deep breath. "It's based on distance. If I travel, say, from the Katurium to my apartment—a distance I'd easily cross—I feel every step at once when I get there. Kind of like I speed walked or finished a sprint. It winds me, but I usually don't show any signs, and I recover quickly, my power doesn't really change. Coming here," he laughed, "we went a bit farther."

I laughed, too. "Just a bit. So this is like covering the distance all at once?"

Rhyan sighed. "It's going to take me a little longer to recharge. I just," he exhaled and pinched the bridge of his nose, "I just carried you across Bamaria and across the water to get here. It's all hitting me now at once. I just need to rest a little, and I'll be at full strength. I'll bring us back."

"Back?"

"Got to get you home to Cresthaven. Every soturion in Bamaria will be looking for you soon. Which...." He fumbled through his belt pocket and pulled out the vadati stone. "Let me report in. By now, they should have realized your seraphim carriage hasn't arrived."

I sat back as he cupped the stone in his palm, bringing it to his mouth.

"Aemon," he said, speaking into the stone.

"Hart, on the way?" he asked, the stone filling with bright blue light.

"We were attacked. Killed an akadim." He bit his lip, one eyebrow furrowed in concentration, and it dawned on me.

Rhyan hadn't just used vorakh to save me. He'd broken the first rule of being a soturion—stop the threat. He was supposed to kill the akadim no matter what. And instead, in his fear for me, in his concern, he had let the monster go. He had let it live in favor of saving my life.

My stomach twisted.

Rhyan looked away from me, guilt in his eyes. "Seraphim left us behind. Had to take her grace into hiding. She's safe," he said, voice shaking.

"Good work," Aemon said. "All three dead now. I'll be sure to credit the second death to you."

"Who killed the third?" Rhyan asked.

"We'll discuss it when you arrive. Keep her grace well hidden."

"Yes, Arkturion." The stone turned white, and he replaced it in his belt. "Fuck." He shook his head. "Fuck."

"Rhyan," I said. "It's dead. You did what you had to do."

"I know," he said, turning back to me. "I just…Gods. I never thought I'd break that oath."

I squeezed his hand. "Maybe that oath is wrong to begin with."

He stared ahead, nostrils flaring, jaw tensed. "I've been thinking about that a lot. All the oaths I've sworn over the years—the ones I kept, the ones I broke, and if I made the right choice." He turned back to me. "There's only one thing I'm sure about. Right or wrong, I'd break my oath a thousand times for you." His eyes darkened, blazing with the intensity of his words.

His lips were on mine before I could react, and we were kissing like we'd never been interrupted. Like we hadn't just faced the mouth of death and barely escaped it, like we weren't miles away from danger, from everyone in Bamaria who was worried and searching for me, like it wasn't urgent that we get back immediately.

If anything, knowing we'd just barely escaped danger seemed to have lit a new fire within me. This wasn't the time, and he needed to rest, and yet I couldn't stop kissing him or touching him, and I knew from the way he moaned against my lips that he was under the same spell—that he had the same need to feel alive after facing death.

His hands cupped my face as he drew me to him, the kiss deepening. I shifted forward, sitting up on my knees to straddle him. He gripped my waist, pulling me in tighter, rocking my hips. He was rock hard beneath me.

I pressed my breasts to his chest, loving how firm he was everywhere I was soft, sucking his tongue into my mouth.

His fingers dug into my hips, and I ground down harder against him, growing slick between my legs, feeling like I was already on edge.

"Gods," I said, threading my fingers through his hair. "You feel so good."

He sucked on my bottom lip, giving me a playful bite before trailing his lips, hot and demanding, across my cheek to my neck, sucking and biting and kissing.

He moaned as I pressed down on him, rolling back and forth against his length.

He jerked beneath me, his mouth open, skin flushed, and he stilled.

I kissed his forehead, placing my hands on his face as I tried to catch my breath. "Did you...?" I asked.

"Fuck," he grunted. "No." He looked a little embarrassed. "Almost. Gods, I'm so fucking close." He pressed his forehead to mine, his eyes closing as he caught his breath.

"It's okay," I said. "There's been a lot of strain on you tonight."

"I've been ready to explode since that morning with you. But that's not it," he said, voice hoarse and pained and desperate. He swallowed, pulling back just enough to stare into my eyes.

"We can stop," I said. "We probably should—I doubt this is helping you get your energy back."

Rhyan's shoulders were rising and falling with his breaths. His hands ran up my back, and he pressed a soft kiss to my lips. He held me there for a moment, just breathing, calming down. Our eyes met, and he kissed me again, slower this time, his lips moving sensuously and languidly against mine.

When we pulled back for air, his eyes searched mine, and he took my hand, threading our fingers together before placing them over his heart.

"Lyr, I…" He squeezed his eyes shut, like he was in pain.

"What?"

Green eyes bore into mine with an intensity that made me shift on his lap.

Rhyan squeezed my hand. "I know," he said slowly, "I'm not supposed to, and I tried, I really did. I tried to stop. Tried not to. Because I knew it was wrong. Because I knew it would only complicate things. Because the way I felt…because of what had happened to me, feeling had been…something dangerous. Something awful. And it scared me. But I've known for a while. I think I knew when I made the decision to come Bamaria."

I stilled, wrapping my arms around him as his eyes searched mine.

He swallowed. "I knew I needed refuge. I knew I didn't want to swear to a new arkasva. And so I'd need family to vouch for me, but because of my father, most wouldn't. That left me with three options. An aunt and uncle in Hartavia. A cousin in Payunmar, and Sean, here." He shook his head. "I didn't even consider who my best choice was, or that it made more sense stay in the north. The moment I decided to leave, I headed south. And I know now, it's because of you. If I'm being honest, I knew it from our first kiss." His chest heaved.

"Knew what?" I asked, heart pounding.

"That I'm in love with you. And no matter how wrong, or how much it scares me, there is no oath in Heaven or Lumeria that could stop me. Lyr." He practically breathed my name. "Lyriana, I love you."

Tears welled behind my eyes, as my heart swelled. "I love you."

He sniffled and smiled, laughing lightly as he said, "Good." He leaned his forehead against mine and shook his head. "Otherwise, this could have become very awkward."

I released a shaky laugh, sniffling at the end.

He laughed, wiping the tears from his eyes, and then mine, before his jaw tightened, his face serious again. "After everything tonight...all that happened, I just...wanted to tell you."

"I'm glad you did." I shifted on his lap again, the movement causing me to brush against him in such a way, the heat was instantly rekindling between us.

Carefully watching me with hooded eyes, Rhyan asked, "Are you now?" His voice was laced with desire.

"Very."

He growled, low in his throat, his forehead pressed to mine as he inhaled through his nose. "It's too bad I can't...take you in this cave."

He kissed me again, softer, slower. It was a kiss full of intention, of promise. It made me wish he would take me right there on that rock.

"What's the problem?" I teased. "Can't work without a bed?"

He grinned, a wicked glint in his eyes. "Mmmmm." He inhaled again and shook his head. "I don't need a bed for all the things I plan to do to you, partner." He shifted me on his lap so we could lay down together. Back settled against the rock, Rhyan tucked me into his arms.

"Care to elaborate?" I asked, stroking his hair as I snuggled closer to him.

He kissed my cheek, my jaw, my neck, each kiss more tender than the last. "If we had all night here, maybe. But I am not going to rush through our first time, nor am I prepared to let you leave my arms right after. I'm going to need hours, days, weeks to bed you properly." His kisses returned to the corner of my mouth before he slanted his lips over mine.

"And what exactly are you going to do during that time?" I asked, voice low.

He grinned, pulling me closer, his arms like a metal cage around me, his lips against my ear. "Show you the real meaning of stamina, not speed."

I shivered, feeling heat flame through my body. "Promise?"

"On my soul." He swallowed, his hand threading through mine, his expression serious. "And on that note...I don't know if the akadim attack tonight will change anything, but assuming your test tomorrow is still on, I need to say something."

I squeezed his hand.

He pressed his forehead to mine again, his hand wrapped around the nape of my neck, his thumb stroking up and down. "I am so fucking proud of you. All the work you've done, all your training. You are a warrior. Magic or not, I trust in your strength."

"Thank you," I said. And seeing how serious he looked, I added, "But?"

He sighed. "But I don't trust the Emperor or the Imperator. Tomorrow, if things go awry, know that it has nothing to do with your strength or your skill. There are a fair number of soturi I could list right now who I believe you'd take easily in a fight. But we know they won't play fair. So, if it comes down to it, your life or mine—"

"Rhyan, no."

"If they play dirty tomorrow, if they have you cornered, I will be in that arena before you can blink. And we'll be gone."

I caressed his cheek, catching a tear. I dried it with my thumb and kissed his eyelid, and then his scar, only realizing then my own tears were starting to fall.

"I won't lose you," he said. "Of all the oaths I swore, this one I will hold. I will keep you safe."

I nodded. "Any more confessions?"

"I think we've reached our quota for the night," he said, squeezing his eyes shut. We lay like that, silent, cocooned in our own little world of the cave, watching the fiery shadows on the wall, both aware of the horrors we'd left behind and the mess we were minutes from returning to. At last, Rhyan sat up, stretching his neck from side to side.

"I'm going to take you back to just outside the fortress walls. I think, we should be safe. Enough time has passed that you could be believably hiding."

He was right. If we'd hidden from the threat and traveled back to Cresthaven by foot, we'd only be arriving just now. Plus—I exhaled sharply as reality began to sink in—I'd made a deal with Mercurial. And by his own show of good will, we still had another hour or so of being safe, of being free from suspicion if anyone saw us.

I didn't have my soturion cloak, so I wound my arms around Rhyan's neck as he wrapped the edge of his cloak around me.

"Ready, partner?" he asked.

I squeezed my eyes shut, not wanting to leave the warmth of the cave, not wanting to leave the warmth of this moment, and our confession. Knowing the moment we traveled, I'd be pulled from his arms, back into reality, back into the horrors of the night and our duties. But it was time. My stomach twisted as the tinkling water sounds of the nearby pool, and the final hiss of the extinguished torchlights vanished.

My feet touched down on the cold ground. Rhyan breathed in the scent of my hair, and then we separated. He paled, the traveling immediately catching up to him. He'd only just gotten some of his energy back. I reached for him, wrapping my arms around his waist as he leaned his head on my shoulder, catching his breath. I supported his weight for several minutes. We were just outside the wall of Cresthaven—a spot behind a tree where we were unlikely to be discovered.

I rubbed his back, so grateful to him, and wishing so desperately once more that I could give my own strength to him. But soon his breathing deepened, and he started to straighten. I kept my hand on the small of his back until I was sure he was steady. With a nod of his head, assuring me he could continue, I stepped away and we approached the fortress walls.

We were immediately let inside. The moment I touched the waterway path, I ran, racing to get inside, to see my sisters, to make sure everyone was alive and unharmed.

But when Euston and Rhodes opened the doors for me, they didn't greet me. Their faces were long and grim, and I found chaos inside the Great Hall. Auras full of fear and grief and anger were biting back and forth across the hall, so heavy and intense I felt I was sinking into the ocean.

"Your grace," Eathan shouted, racing through the crowd to get to me. "Thank the Gods." He pulled me into a tight hug, and my stomach turned as I saw that many of the Bamarian nobility were here, huddled in small groups, many openly crying. Some shouting. A mage stood a few feet away from me in shock. Tears filled her eyes but she stood completely still, staring at nothing.

"Eathan...." I swallowed, feeling my throat go dry. "What happened? Aren't all the akadim dead?"

He looked away, his jaw tensing.

"Eathan?" I turned to Rhyan, who stood a few feet behind me, a respectable distance, the distance one might expect between a novice and apprentice or a bodyguard and his charge. "Aemon reported all the akadim were dead."

Eathan cleared his throat. "The three akadim who entered Bamaria have all been killed." He spoke slowly, his words so obviously chosen with care that I knew he was hiding something from me.

"What aren't you telling me?"

In the corner, I caught Lady Romula. She leaned against Lord Trajan, her shoulders shaking. Beside them was Tristan. His face was red, his eyes puffy. When he saw me, he turned away, putting a hand on his grandmother's arm, reassuring her.

My stomach sank. "Eathan, what's going on?"

"Come," he said at last. "Not out here."

I narrowed my gaze but did as I was told, following Eathan to my father's Seating Room. It had been vacated recently—possibly after Eathan had announced whatever he was about to tell me. He held the door open for Rhyan, assuming I was not to be separated from my guard, and locked the door behind him.

"You should take a seat," Eathan said, his voice hoarse, and I saw then his eyes were red, his face drawn.

I looked to Rhyan and then back at Eathan, my heart starting to race. Had something else happened? To Meera? To Morgana?

Gods, my father wasn't here. What if...?

"Eathan, are my sisters here?" I asked.

"Of course."

"Safe? Unharmed?"

"They're safe upstairs. And your father is safe, too, as is Arianna and Naria." He coughed.

I nodded slowly, my stomach turning. "Okay," I said, uncertainty and fear washing through me.

Eathan's nostrils flared as he continued, "Three akadim entered Bamaria tonight," he said. "They managed to remain unseen, breaching not only the border but Urtavia. One of the demons even entered the temple tonight. That akadim was killed by the Blade. There were no casualties inside."

I nodded, waiting for the knot in my stomach to loosen. Thank the Gods no one in the temple was killed. But...outside the temple....

Eathan offered a small smile. "I hear, Soturion Rhyan, that Bamaria is indebted to you once again for slaying an akadim. You were responsible for the second and in doing so saved the lives of many of our soturi."

"Hector?" I asked. "Caius?"

"Injured," he said. "But all of the soturi stationed outside the temple are expected to make a full recovery."

"And the third akadim?" I asked.

My heart hammered. This was the one that had grabbed me, that

I'd stabbed, that had almost killed me, that would have killed me if Rhyan hadn't been there—hadn't traveled.

Eathan's eyes moved between me and Rhyan, like he was trying to delay his next words. "The final akadim was killed by Soturion Leander Abden of Damara."

Haleika's apprentice. I sucked in a breath.

Eathan's gray eyes were on me, watching me carefully, assessing me. "Soturion Leander made the killing blow, but he did not survive."

My mouth fell open. Leander...Leander was dead?

"Gods," Rhyan said.

"He was...." Eathan trailed off. "He was defending his novice."

"Haleika?" I asked. "Is she all right?" Oh, Gods. She loved him. She was probably heartbroken. I looked to Rhyan, and his eyes were red, his face full of anguish. My heart hurt just thinking of it, of the agony she must have been feeling. "Where is she?" I had to go to her. Comfort her.

Eathan shook his head. "Her body is being kept in the Shadow Stronghold overnight."

"What? Why?" I asked just as Rhyan cursed under his breath.

Rhyan caught my eye, his jaw tensing. He gave me the slightest shake of his head.

"Eathan, is she okay? Why would she be there?"

And then his wording sank into my mind. He hadn't said *she* was being kept in the Shadow Stronghold. He'd said her *body* was.

"She's being kept there," Eathan said, "because Leander was too late to save her. The akadim ate her soul."

"No."

"She's in the process of changing. She's forsaken now. In between. But by nightfall tomorrow—"

"No. No. No." I couldn't stop, as if I said it enough, I could undo it, make his words untrue. My chest heaved, my stomach twisting, tears falling from eyes. "Eathan, no. No."

He bowed his head. "As soon as the sun sets tomorrow night, Haleika Grey will become an akadim. And she will be killed."

CHAPTER
TWENTY-SEVEN

"I'm sorry to deliver such upsetting news. Now, I must," Eathan cleared his throat, "I must go back out there. Details to go over. People to talk to."

I stood frozen in place, my head swimming as Eathan walked away. Every footstep seemed to pound into the floor, too loud, too jarring. The door slammed shut behind him, the sound echoing in my ears.

Haleika, an akadim? Haleika dying, transforming, her soul gone —eaten. And Leander...Leander...Gods. I couldn't process this, believe this, accept it. I couldn't....

I sensed Rhyan moving across the room. His steps were slow and measured, almost as if he were walking in a trance as he approached me. He stood before me, not speaking, not looking at me, his aura leaping out in powerful gusts of cold, frosting my skin. Ice crawled over every exposed inch of my body, and when I exhaled, my breath was visible on the air. I felt numb and frozen inside. My hands shook helplessly in front of me, and I wanted desperately to reach out to him. I needed to touch him, to reassure him, to reassure myself, to take us out of the cold and the dark. Back to the cave. Back where it was warm, where we were safe.

But I didn't touch him. I couldn't.

His fingers tensed, knuckles whitening, the tendons on his fore-arms tight. His entire body stilled with tension. He didn't move, just stared ahead, his eyes red.

We remained like that, not talking, not moving as a minute passed and another. We stood together in the storm that raged in and out of our bodies, neither of us attempting to warm ourselves. The only sound was his heavy breathing, rough against the pained sound of mine, and then he sat, his eyes screwed shut, his hands fisted in his lap. A tear rolled down his cheek, and his lips trembled. I turned to him at last.

"Rhyan." My voice came out a tremorous whisper.

Another tear fell down his face, and then another as he swallowed.

"Go to him," he said, voice breaking. "She was his cousin, right?"

"She—" I cleared my throat, not sure I could speak. "She was." Was—past tense. She was Tristan's cousin. She was my friend.

"He needs you. Go to him. Comfort each other."

"And you? Are you all right?" I asked, my heart breaking. But I already knew. I knew Rhyan so well now. I knew the guilt he was internalizing, the blame he placed on himself for the role we'd played tonight. I knew he was consumed by the fact that he hadn't stopped the threat, the feeling that he could have done something more—moved faster, been stronger, kept Haleika and Leander from this fate. I knew he felt that it was somehow his fault, his respon-sibility.

I'd felt the same when I hadn't been able to save Jules. When I hadn't been fast enough to keep my blood oath to Meera. And now I felt it tonight—the guilt slicing me to the core of my very soul. Gods. The guilt....

Rhyan stood. "I have to get out of here."

"Rhyan, wait."

"I should have known," he said darkly.

"Known what?"

"There'd be consequences. There always are. Especially when I'm...." He clenched his jaw. "He's the one who needs you now."

Before I could respond, he was moving, his back to me, his shoulders tensed, and his aura retracting to nothing as he walked out the door of the Seating Room.

I swallowed, trying to compose myself, to find some inner ember of strength still blazing inside of me. He was right. I had to go to Tristan. I had to comfort him. And I had to appear strong before the Bamarian nobles. I had to be Lady Lyriana Batavia. I had to forget what I'd seen tonight, what I'd witnessed, what I'd done. I stepped forward, lifting my chin and pushing back my shoulders as I entered the crowd.

I searched through the overwhelming cluster of nobles with tears falling, sobs erupting, and hands wringing as accusatory and devasted sets of eyes landed on me. I steeled myself, pushing down every feeling and memory of Haleika: her laugh, the way she bounced on her feet when she was excited for food, the passion she expressed for the people she loved, for Leander....

I found Tristan. He stood stoically next to his grandparents, his eyes reddened with tears, his chin lifted in defiance of the tragedy. It was the same stance I'd seen him take dozens of times during memorial services devoted to his parents and how I imagined he'd looked as a toddler at their funeral—tiny and helpless, already carrying the title of Lord, and preparing to join the Bamarian Council one day.

Tristan rolled his shoulders back, stretching his head from side to side. He was holding back his tears, fighting to keep them at bay. When he saw me, his brown eyes, so full of loss and sorrow, seared into me. He crossed the room in quick, determined strides, meeting me in the middle of the hall.

I threw my arms around him, breathing in his mint and salt scent, the scent of my childhood, of my friend, of Haleika's cousin. "I'm so sorry," I said.

His arms tightened around me, his face buried in the crook of my shoulder. He bit back a sob, his mouth pressed to my skin, and the delicate dam I'd built inside myself to conceal my emotions and find the strength I needed to survive the night was gone.

I saw Haleika in my mind, imagined her fighting to protect Leander, neither leaving the battle against the akadim, refusing to allow the threat to continue for the next soturion to face. I imagined their fear and pain while fighting against death to save the one they loved. I imagined their horror in knowing what they were about to lose.

Guilt began to gnaw through my bones. I almost couldn't bear for Tristan to touch me. My skin felt prickly and hot—and for once, it was because of me, not him. He hadn't deserved this or any of what I'd done tonight with Rhyan. He hadn't deserved my betrayal—not just tonight, but during most of our relationship. I hadn't been there with him emotionally for a long time. I'd fooled myself for years, and that had fooled him, but now the truth was weighing on me. But the guilt was about more than Tristan. Maybe if I'd been faster, trained harder, stabbed deeper, or if we'd been more focused, less afraid of losing each other, Rhyan and I could have killed that third akadim, could have saved Haleika from a fate worse than death, could have saved Leander.

But we'd let the demon go. We hadn't stopped the threat.

Rhyan may have been the one to take me away, but I refused to let him shoulder the blame alone. I had been there, too. I had been in the cave, safe in his arms, kissing him, touching him, telling him I loved him while back here, Haleika and Leander's love had failed them. I squeezed my eyes shut, hot tears falling. A part of us had known, deep down, when we'd escaped the akadim, how close we'd come to death, to losing each other, and that was why we'd had to confess how we felt, that was why we'd had to do anything we could to feel alive.

Haleika and Leander's fate had been ours first. Our destiny. And we'd cheated our way out of it. They'd been good, so good. Leander had defended Rhyan in the habibellum, and Haleika...fuck. Fuck!

Tristan's arms tightened around me, and I started to shake. I wanted to hug him and comfort him, and I wanted to tell him to run away from me—that I didn't deserve to be in his arms, that this was my fault. That I'd killed them. I'd let this happen.

But I couldn't step away, I couldn't. I had to live with this, and I had to be here.

"They won't let us see her," Tristan said quietly, his voice weak, like the emotion was too close to the surface for him to speak without it drowning him. "She's all alone."

"I'm sorry," I whispered. "I'm so sorry."

"I know," he said, his hands running up and down my back. "So am I."

The doors to Cresthaven burst open, and the herald who'd announced the Emperor's arrival the previous night burst into the hall. His cheeks were flushed with exertion as he blew on his horn. "He comes!" he shouted.

The sobs and cries filling the room came to a halt.

The Emperor's sentries, adorned in their brushed-gold armor, their bodies poised for battle, and their cheeks glowing as the fire-light flickered over their golden Valalumir tattoos, rushed into the hall. They brandished their swords as they snaked their way through the crowd in a sort of organized chaos, ordering everyone to get in line.

Tristan let go of me. "What in Moriel's name?" he snarled. His nostrils flared. "What does he want now? Can we not fucking grieve in peace?"

I bit my lip. "That's not his way."

Tristan squeezed my hand, leaning in to kiss me quickly on the lips. I froze, unable to kiss him back, tasting only the salt of our tears that had mixed together. When he pulled away, I found Rhyan across the room, watching us, his expression schooled to indifference, to that of the cruel, cold high-lord-to-be of Glemaria. I felt the ice of his aura abruptly against my skin as it escaped him again, and then, just as quickly, he pulled it back.

"I must stand with Ka Grey," Tristan said, hand on his stave as his grandparents yelled at a soturion before marching with indignation to the same place they'd stood when we'd first greeted and celebrated the Emperor's arrival in the Great Hall.

"Of course," I said, heart pounding.

Tristan marched away, his back straight and his head held high, as he swallowed his grief and resumed his role as the future lord of Ka Grey.

I stood alone, unable to move, unable to find my place in the fray as nobles were pushed about in every direction, swarming back and forth across the hall. I looked for Rhyan again in the chaos, but he'd moved. There was no sign of him, no hint of his aura.

Meera and Morgana came down the steps, their hair unstyled and hastily brushed back, their diadems set on their foreheads slightly askew. I wasn't sure if Morgana had heard what was happening already or if they'd been summoned to appear for the sudden visit.

My father walked through the doors next, looking like he'd aged a decade, with more gray hair around his temples and a balding spot at the back of his head I'd never seen before. Within seconds, every member of the Bamarian Council along with their immediate family stood organized in two long lines in the Great Hall. Markan had appeared and pushed me to my place beside Meera and Morgana just before the Imperator walked through the makeshift aisle, followed by the Emperor.

At once, everyone fell to their knees, heads hung low. We rose from the ground on command, silent as Emperor Theotis paced back and forth, his thick white eyebrows furrowed.

"Tonight," he said in his unsettlingly quiet and calm voice, "was nothing less than a tragedy. A careless, pointless tragedy. On our holiest of holy days, on Valyati, a night to celebrate the return of light to this forsaken world, on the night we celebrate the Valalumir's power to heal and nurture. Instead of the promise of light, we saw darkness descend across Bamaria. We saw the Soturi of Ka Batavia fail in their duty to protect its citizens. To protect Bamarians. Lumerians. To protect the students attending the Mage Academy, the Soturion Academy. Three akadim roamed free tonight.

Three akadim were allowed inside these previously protected borders. Here they maimed and attacked Lumerians. The healing centers of Bamaria are full tonight, full of soturi many of whom are gravely injured, fighting for their lives."

The Imperator smirked his insufferable, wolfish smile. And I knew beyond a shadow of a doubt who had been at fault tonight. Who had allowed akadim to pass, who had been so lax in their duties to protect that they hadn't even attempted to use the warning bells until it was too late. Ever since Ka Kormac's presence had increased, so had the presence of akadim. It could not be a coincidence.

Never in all our years of patrol had an akadim breached Bamaria. Never—until a full legion of Ka Kormac had taken over protection duties.

And now our own soturi—the soturi who had fought back, who had done all they could to stop the threat, who had kept these borders safe for centuries—would be blamed by the Emperor. Blamed for his nephew's egregious fault. How many of our soturi were fighting for their lives in the healing centers now? And how many of Ka Kormac's men ran and hid like cowards, watching the chaos and tragedy unfold while doing absolutely nothing to stop it?

"When all of this mess is over," the Emperor continued, "I am appointing Imperator Kormac to remain in Bamaria. To lead a special task force to uncover how this could have happened."

Try looking in a fucking mirror! My hands balled into fists at my side. It was the Imperator's fault that Turion Brenna's soturi were injured. His fault we'd lost Leander. His fault—his fucking fault—that Haleika was…that she was….

I couldn't even form the thought. All I could do was bite back a scream and tense when Morgana reached over to take my hand.

"Still," she hissed in my ear. "Be still."

The Imperator bowed. "I look forward to uncovering this treachery. I will be working very closely with Arkturion Aemon to ensure that with the efforts and strength of Ka Kormac, this horrific event is never repeated. I promise you, my fellow Lumerians, Bamarians, we will make Bamaria safe again."

You won't even send your soturi to Elyria when there's akadim. You didn't even protect your own lands when the pack Rhyan hunted hid inside your hills. You fucking knew and you did nothing! It's your fault! And now we're paying the price!

Morgana's hand tightened around my wrist. "Lyr," she hissed under her breath. "You must be still." She tugged, and I took a step back. I hadn't realized I'd moved forward.

"Now," the Emperor continued, "three akadim entered Bamaria tonight, and three akadim were killed. I want to acknowledge the heroics of those soturi who slayed the beasts. For it is our soturi who saved us all tonight. It is my honor to begin by naming Arkturion Pompellus Agrippa, warlord of all Lumeria Nutavia, as the first to kill an akadim tonight. Arkturion, we are in your debt for killing the monster that defiled the Temple of Dawn with its evil presence."

The Blade stepped forward, his eyes narrowed, his expression drawn as he surveyed the room. I clapped along with everyone else because it was expected, because I'd been trained to do so. But I was numb as the Emperor's sentries cried out, "The Blade! The Blade!" They still surrounded us, their swords drawn, their bodies tensed to fight. My stomach twisted at the sight of them filling my Ka's fortress. Their proud screams sounded like an omen.

"Yes, yes," the Emperor said, his quiet voice somehow rising above the yells. "And we have confirmed that despite being forsworn, Soturion Rhyan Hart brought death to the second akadim who attacked tonight. He struck the final killing blow outside the temple, defending her grace, the Lady Lyriana Batavia. Soturion Rhyan, where are you?"

Rhyan stepped out from the back of the hushed crowd. His jaw was tense as he approached the makeshift aisle and walked slowly to the Emperor and Imperator. He did not make eye contact with me as he passed.

There were some cheers and claps for Rhyan, but the crowd was subdued, unwilling to show support for a forsworn.

"That's your second akadim kill this year," the Imperator said. He spoke with an air of disbelief, the accusation clear in his voice. He didn't believe him. "Too bad I missed it. Again."

"Were you not forsworn," said the Emperor, "you might have made a fine arkturion."

Rhyan stiffened but bowed and made his way back down the aisle, standing apart from the crowd. His chilled aura vanished with his retreating form.

"And finally, the third akadim was slain tonight by another apprentice of the Soturion Academy. Were he here, I would congratulate him. And were he a hero, I would name him as such," the Emperor said, anger rising in his voice.

I froze. Leander was a hero. He'd killed the demon. The Emperor should have been announcing Leander's full name and title as shouts of *Bar Ka Mokan* and "his soul freed" were cheered. How was he not a hero for his actions tonight? For losing his life in the fight against the threat? For stopping the threat—for doing the very thing we'd all sworn to do?

The Emperor stepped forward, his eyes scanning the hall. "A hero, I did not see tonight. What we saw, thanks to the piecing together of witnesses, was the breaking of the most sacred of oaths —the illicit relationship between a novice and apprentice, between two soturi of the same kashonim. Leander Abden and Haleika Grey swore to put the fight against evil above all else. They swore mere months ago that if they should put others before their duties, if they should love those whom they've sworn not to, then they would no longer be soturi. They swore they would gladly accept their death. That is the oath they swore—and foreswore when their relationship interfered with their sacred duty, with their ability to stop the threat. Tonight, they failed. Were they alive, had they somehow survived the akadim attack, these soturi would be standing trial tomorrow for breaking their oaths. But it seems justice has served itself tonight. And though Soturion Leander Abden killed the akadim, he is not named a hero. And though Soturion Haleika Grey lost her life, she will not be mourned."

My mouth fell open. I found Tristan, his entire face turning red, while Lady Romula's eyes filled with venomous hatred—but not at the Emperor. She was staring at me, at my family, hatred clear in her aura, which emitted a spicy, unsettling cloud of power. She blamed us. She blamed Ka Batavia for allowing akadim inside, for being weak enough to allow a foreign soturi's occupation. Ka Kormac had done this, but it was still our responsibility at the end of the day. It was our fault she'd lost a member of her Ka, her family. I couldn't bear to hold eye contact, not with my guilt. Not with my grief. And not with hers so freshly wrought.

"The shame of two soturi putting their feelings for each other above their duty and failing to stop the threat," the Emperor roared, "will be a taint on this academy for years. Had they upheld their oaths, they may have fought more precisely. Stopped the threat. Not suffered this fate."

I found Rhyan. His face was pale, his eyes hollow.

"Tomorrow," the Emperor continued, "knowing that the threat has been stopped, that Bamaria has been made safe once more, we will continue with the testing of Soturion Lyriana Batavia. Now that we know what comes of weakness in the fight against akadim—now that we know how easily tragedy can fall—it is more important than ever she prove herself, prove her strength. Tomorrow evening, we will meet in the arena at sundown. And we will know once and for all if this little experiment of her grace's and the Imperator's has proven fruitful or deadly for this country. The consequences have shown themselves tonight, and they will not be ignored. No one is above the law. Not even heirs."

I swayed on the spot. Of course, I'd still be tested. Of course, they'd use this against me, find a way to blame Bamaria, blame Ka Batavia, blame me.

They didn't know. Nor would they care. I was already blaming myself.

CHAPTER
TWENTY-EIGHT

I didn't come out of my room at Cresthaven for the rest of the night. Nor could I leave the following morning or afternoon.

I lay in bed, sometimes in a black, dreamless sleep, sometimes awake and staring at the ceiling. Sometimes hungry and sometimes racing to the bathroom to vomit everything my body could muster.

The timekeeper rang out the final hour of daylight. It would be dark by the next ringing of the bells. At that time, I'd be in the arena facing my final test from the Emperor. Deep in the Shadow Stronghold, Haleika would be losing her final connection to her life, her body, and her soul as the forsaken process was completed. Her limbs would grow, and her nails would extend into claws as she made the final transformation to akadim.

And I couldn't be there to ease her pain. Or support Tristan. Or do anything remotely useful.

There was a knock on my door. I pushed myself off my bed, hands shaking, knees wobbly. I was dressed in full soturion regalia. Morgana had come in at some point and warned me that the Emperor's soturi were on the way, that they would privately escort me to the Katurium, and I was to be dressed. And so I was locked into my armor, my boots laced up to my knees, my cloak pleated around my waist and cinched in by my belt with shined and sharpened Valalu-mirs, and my arm cuffs tightened just so.

Because it was there, because I seemed to associate the jewelry with meeting my doom, I put Ramia's necklace on top of it all. The effect was powerful as I braided back my hair—deep brown, as there was no sun to be seen at a time like this, not with the ringing of the bells indicating sunset had arrived.

I opened the door, finding two escorts in brushed-gold armor. I stepped back in surprise—we hadn't had any staff or servants in our bedroom wing in years, much less foreign soturi. They both sneered before offering slight bows of their heads, the slightest show of respect. I was marched downstairs through the Great Hall without ceremony, past the columns detailing the history and deeds of my ancestors, of the arkasvim of Ka Batavia who'd ruled for a thousand years. I felt the bloodline ending today, ending with me.

Meera and Morgana waited at the front doors, dressed in their finest dresses of Batavia red. Their blue mage robes were elegantly draped across their shoulders.

My father was stoic, silent, as we were all led across the prome-nade, away from Cresthaven to the port where our seraphim waited. There we were separated into our own seraphim carriages full of escorts. The guard was made of a blend of our own soturi and those of the Emperor.

Markan, of course, was paired with me, as well as two bearded soturi who seemed completely uninterested in acknowledging my presence.

Before I stepped into my carriage, my father appeared, pulling me back into a hug. His arms squeezed tight around me, his face buried in my hair.

"Me bat," he said. *My daughter.* He only used the High Lumerian term when he was truly feeling worried, or full of emotion. "I love you," he said quietly. "You're strong. Remember that."

I nodded, too choked up to respond as his guard escorted him back to his carriage.

I huddled into the corner of mine, trying to shake the sense that this was my last time flying away from Cresthaven. I couldn't think that. I didn't want to entertain the thought. I wanted to believe I was strong enough, that I would be given a fair chance, that I would survive. Or, at the least, if necessary, Rhyan would keep his promise. But I didn't want that, not for either of us. Not when so much had been lost already. Not when he was so devastated from last night. Not when exile wasn't what either of us desired. And not when my duties still bound me here.

But my father's sudden show of emotion left me full of fear and dread.

My fingers tightened around the hilt of my sword, sheathed at my hip. My dagger rested beside its scabbard, and beneath my cloak and belt, two more knives were strapped to my thighs.

The floor shifted beneath my feet, the wind blowing through the windows as our seraphim began her descent outside the Katurium.

Rhyan waited for me with a row of Bamarian escorts. A row of soturi who served the Emperor stood at attention behind them. The contrasting shades of gold were stark against the snow.

My eyes found Rhyan's, green and distant. As our gazes met, he looked away, assessing the soturi around him.

We were marched into the Katurium and deposited inside our training room. Only Rhyan, as my apprentice, was permitted to enter, while the rest of the soturi guarding me—perhaps to keep me from fleeing—waited outside the door.

"Give her a minute," Rhyan snarled, slamming the door shut.

It burst back open, revealing an angry guard. "She's due on the field before the bells ring again."

"I know," Rhyan yelled. "You think she's going to escape? Or has your tattoo gone to your brain? How far do you think she'd get when the city's infected with your kind?"

The soturion glared. "Five minutes. I hear anything funny, I open the door. And you'll both be taken in."

"Fantastic." Rhyan slammed the door in his face, his chest heaving, aura cold.

Hands fisted at his sides, he exhaled sharply before coming to stand before me, his eyes assessing my body, studious. His expression softened as he took me in, took in my fear and nerves. I had no aura without magic, but I knew he could feel everything I did from the way he watched me. He reached out before abruptly fisting his hand back at his side.

"You have your knives?" he asked, his voice detached and cold. "Blade? Sword?"

I swallowed, my mouth dry. "Yes."

"Armor tightened and buckled?" he asked.

My stomach twisted. "Do you want to check?"

I'd only put on my full armor a few times, and Rhyan knew this. His eyes darkened as he closed the space between us, his hand brushing against each buckle, latch, and notch that sealed me into place. Slowly, he circled me, his touch firm against the golden seraphim wings at my shoulders, on the belt at my waist, and on the sword seated in its scabbard at my hip.

He sucked in a breath, still standing behind me. On instinct, I closed my eyes and leaned back, resting my head against his chest, feeling his warmth as his arms moved, his hands pressing against my hips, hot even through my layers of armor and protection.

"Lyr," he breathed, and his hands rose to my armored vest, his arms tightening around me. "How are you doing?"

"Not good. You?"

His nose brushed against my hair. "Not good."

I closed my eyes, inhaling the scent of his musk alongside the faded scent of the coffee and cakes we had enjoyed so often these last few months.

"They haven't told me what to expect," he said, "or offered any advice on the test's nature. I just heard there was a change of plans —not sure what that means."

I tried to keep from shaking. "Do I stand a chance?" I asked.

"You do," he said firmly. "Do not doubt the strength you've worked, fought, and bled for. Last night, you faced down an akadim, and you survived. Not many do."

"Survived?" I closed my eyes. "I let it live."

"No. That's my sin," he said, his breath hot against my neck.

I shook my head, and his hands rose to my shoulders, his fingers slipping into the edge of the armor and necklace at my collar. "It's mine, too."

"The point is you fought back. You didn't faint. You didn't freeze, you freed yourself before I got to you. Remember, you did that."

Sweat beaded at the back of my neck despite the winter chill swirling with Rhyan's aura.

"Freer than a seraphim," I whispered.

"Stronger than a gryphon," he said, repeating the words he'd said months ago, the words that had finally convinced me that I could train, that I stood a chance. His fingers ran down the sides of my neck, and I arched into the touch.

"What do I visualize?" I asked.

"The end. You in the arena, hearing the Emperor say only this—the test is over, and you passed."

"Where will you be?"

"Watching," he said. "Waiting for you."

"To fail, or succeed?"

"You only have one option." He dropped his hands from me, stepping back, leaving me cold.

I turned to face him. "Do you regret last night?"

His lips tightened. "What part?"

"You know what part," I said, voice hushed.

His nostrils flared, and at last he looked at me, really looked at me, his eyes filling with far more heat and love than I'd have thought possible with all that was happening, all that had happened, and all that was about to.

"No." He pinched the bridge of his nose. "I wish—I wish it had ended differently. I wish the choice hadn't had to be made." His eyes bore into mine. "But if I could relive last night, do it differently, make another decision, even if I knew the outcome, knew what would happen, knew the horror—I would still save you. Every time. I would save you a thousand times over, knowing exactly what would happen, knowing even worse was possible. I would have never, not in one scenario, not come for you, not taken you from there." His lips trembled. "But I don't know how to live with that."

"That you love me?" I asked.

"No." He tossed his head back and sighed. "Knowing what kind of monster I could become because of that love. Knowing the destruction I left behind. Knowing all the oaths I would break a thousand times over. Just for you."

There was a knock on the door. Rhyan blinked rapidly, coughing and stepping back.

"The plan hasn't changed no matter where we stand," he said quickly. "If need be, I will come for you. But first, Lyriana, remember who you are. Remember you can do this. No ropes can hold you. No cage can trap you. You get scared—you see that rope in your mind. And you tear that fucking rope apart."

The door burst open.

The two bearded soturi of the Emperor's guard crossed the threshold, followed by three more, all wearing the sigil of the Emperor. The bearded soturi flanked me, each grabbing an arm, but before I knew it, the remaining soldiers surrounded Rhyan.

"What are you…?" I asked.

There was a punch, the sound of skin slapping skin, as I tried to turn back. Rhyan's arms had been held wide open, a soturion needed for each arm, while a third had punched him in the face. Rhyan's scar was red and irritated, and blood dripped from the corner of his mouth that he spat onto the soturion who'd hit him.

"Fuck you."

"Forsworn mongrel," the guard cursed, grabbing the hem of Rhyan's cloak to wipe the blood from his own golden armor.

The other guards pulled his arms back—too far. They were going to break his arms if they pulled any farther. Rhyan grimaced but didn't move, didn't try to fight back.

"What are you doing?" I asked. "Answer me."

"You're in no position to ask questions, your grace."

A mage bearing the golden Valalumir sigil strolled into the room, his blue cloak trailing behind him, his stave pointed. He barely seemed to notice my presence, as he strode past me, his dark eyes piercing. His attention was focused wholly on Rhyan.

I struggled against my captors, trying to turn around to see what they were doing, when the mage began the incantation for a binding.

"No! Stop!" I yelled. "He's not being tested! I am!" I shoved and kicked against the soturi at my sides. They pushed my arms behind my back, their strength so forceful, I cried out in pain.

"Stop!" Rhyan roared as the magic began to unfurl from the mage's stave. But he wasn't speaking to the mage. He was glaring at my guards, his expression feral. "She has no magic, you bastards. Do that again, and you'll break her arms. Is that what your Emperor ordered? Is he so scared of a girl without power?"

I grunted in pain as they pulled harder on me in response. Exhaling sharply, I adjusted my posture to flow with their assault, leaning into the position they forced on me. Rhyan was right—one more forceful touch from either of them, and my bones would snap.

It seemed to work, and I could almost feel relief, but then their hands tightened around me to the point of pain. If I survived, I'd have bruises on my arms for weeks.

Rhyan snarled but remained still, his expression solemn, like he had resigned himself to his fate as the Emperor's mage finished his incantation. The black shadows transformed into ropes that glowed red as they wound their way across Rhyan's body, sealing him in place, cutting him off from his power and magic strength. The binding ropes turned black and glittering beneath the room's torch-light as Rhyan's jaw clenched.

I remembered their heat, the horrific feel of them against my body.

They were hurting him. Burning him.

He shook his head at me, the move subtle as he tried to give me a reassuring look, but I could see the pain in his eyes, the fear at being unable to access his power, unable to help me. They'd just effectively cut him off from traveling and rescuing me from the field. They'd also cut me off from any possibility of using kashonim.

But I didn't care about that. I cared about the look of anguish on Rhyan's face, that he was back in the ropes he hated so much—the ropes he'd spent years trying to break free from, the ropes he'd fought so hard to tear apart.

I wanted to kill them all. After I survived this test, I was going to hunt down these men, punish them for forcing Rhyan back into that place where his father had imprisoned him.

His mouth tightened, the lines on his face hard, but again he shook his head, still trying to reassure me.

"Time to go," said the soturion at my right. "Ready, your grace?"

I stumbled as my captors pulled me out of the room, down the winding halls, and outside where they released my arms and shoved me into the arena alone.

I caught my bearings and realized the entire Katurium was full. I turned in a circle, staring up at the stadium stands, the sections full of brushed-gold armor and silver. My enemies seemed to have taken every last seat, all here to watch my doom.

I looked back. Rhyan's guards were behind me, pushing him toward the pole. My body started to shake. What the fuck was happening?

They forced him to stand against it as the mage pointed his stave at Rhyan, freeing his arms only. The binding still glittered and burned across his body, shining across his leathered armor. Directing his stave, the mage tried to force Rhyan's arms up.

Rhyan grunted, his muscles tensed, keeping his arms down and completely defying the will of the mage. The mage's knuckles whitened as he tightened his grip on the twisting of sun-and-moon wood. He pushed his stave forward, the tendons in his arms taut, his teeth gritted, but still Rhyan's personal strength dominated the mage's magic. Even without access to his power, Rhyan was a force to be reckoned with.

The mage cursed and relented. He took one glance at the filled stadium before he sneered at Rhyan. "Either you do it my way, boy, or the Blade rips your arms apart."

Rhyan's eyes narrowed as he lifted his arms, his wrists twisting in a dramatic flourish to prove how willing he was in that moment. The mage moved his stave, directing the glittering ropes around Rhyan's body to snake toward his arms and wrists until he was bound to the pole.

"He comes!" the herald screamed, running out into the arena, his voice amplified by magic.

I had to cover my ears from the volume. Rhyan winced in pain, unable to move his arms or hands.

The entire stadium sank to their knees, the floors creaking, as the Emperor entered the arena.

I bent down, sinking onto the cold, frozen ground, my heart pounding. I took a quick glance behind me at Rhyan, bound and unable to bend a knee. Instead, he'd lowered his head, his chin pressed into his chest, his bronzed hair wild and wavy from his struggle.

The field of the arena quickly filled with the Emperor's men. They surrounded him along with the Imperator and the Blade. Aemon entered the field from a separate door. Turion Dairen and three soturi I recognized from the guard at Aemon's townhouse followed, their hands resting on the hilts of starfire blades. I braced myself against the Ready's dark anger blazing through the arena.

The Emperor's eyes fell on me, then with a look of disdain, they moved to where Rhyan stood bound behind me. He shrugged, his velvet cloak shining in the torchlight with every shift of his body, and then he turned, looking up at the filled stadium.

"Welcome." The Emperor's voice had also been spelled to amplify, but it still maintained that eerie, quiet manner. "On Auriel's Feast Day, we celebrated the God who brought the Valalumir to Lumeria. The God who saw his people suffering on the earthly plane, our ancestors who were losing battles under the leadership and weakness of the seductress Asherah, the goddess who fell, the goddess who wanted the Valalumir for herself. And on that day, as was tradition, we celebrated the Revelation Ceremony, welcoming a new class of soturi and mages, future Lumerians who would protect our Empire and bring us into a new age. Her grace, Lady Lyriana Batavia, Heir to the Arkasva, High Lord of Bamaria was amongst the initiates with plans of becoming a mage like the many esteemed arkasvim in her bloodline before her."

My chest heaved. So on top of my having to suffer through whatever this test was going to be, I had to be bored and humiliated by a long speech.

"Unfortunately for her grace, she was unable to produce any magic. A fact that was confirmed by nahashim. We desired to be fair and uphold the law of our lands, the laws that unite us, the laws that keep us safe, that keep us from reliving the mistakes of the past that led to an Empire drowned. And our laws clearly stated that her grace was to be exiled from Lumeria Nutavia. But," the Emperor turned to the Imperator, his nephew, his face suddenly full of indulgence, "Imperator Kormac has a soft heart and a deep respect for Ka Batavia—as do we all."

"Shekar arkasva!"

The shout came out of nowhere and was immediately silenced. I couldn't find the source in the overcrowded stadium, but a black seraphim mask appeared in the distance before vanishing. I narrowed my eyes, seeing another appear in the corner of my vision, though just as quickly, it, too, was gone.

"And in his kindness and intelligence," said the Emperor, "he foresaw an opportunity. A chance for her grace to prove herself. Not as a mage, for she was without magic. But with her own hands, her own strength. After all, akadim remain the greatest threat to our safety, and yet are the one aspect of Lumeria impervious to magic, a fact her grace was eager to remind everyone of during that fateful meeting when she convinced us to allow her this indulgence. And so tonight, the perfect opportunity has arisen. Her grace may prove herself as a soturion once and for all. And tonight, we shall put to the test just how impervious akadim are to mage magic."

I turned back to the Emperor. *What?*

The sky darkened, and snow began to fall anew as the arena was cleared of the Emperor's men and finally the Emperor himself.

I glanced back at Rhyan. He stared straight ahead as another door of the Katurium opened into the arena and a silver metal box was pushed through it. It stood over six feet tall with no visible opening in sight. What in Lumeria? Was it just solid silver? Four soturi were needed to pull it out, the box grating and creaking as it was pushed forward. Once it had fully cleared the door, they rushed back inside, and the familiar hum of a door being magically warded sounded in my ears.

The snow continued to fall, the frozen ground starting to dampen beneath my boots as the Emperor took his seat, surrounded by his men.

"Fear not for our bound guest," said the Emperor, now seated high the stands. "We've all heard the rumors of Soturion Rhyan's strength. Despite his reputation and past crimes, Soturion Rhyan has killed two akadim in the past four months alone."

Rhyan seemed unmoved by the underhanded praise and insults. Instead, his face had gone white as his gaze remained fixated on the silver box. His good eyebrow had lifted in alarm.

"If Soturion Lyriana is unable to stop the threat tonight the way a proper soturion should, then, Soturion Rhyan, your bindings will be released so you might finish the work. My personal mage is on standby to free you on my command."

"One hopes," Rhyan yelled into the crowd, "your command is swift."

The Emperor chuckled. "And we hope your binding doesn't chafe too much, but we couldn't risk Soturion Lyriana calling on kashonim, now could we? That would hardly be fair. This test is to assure us that she has soturion strength acquired through sheer will and muscle, and not a simple siphoning of the power of her apprentice."

My entire body began to shake as realization dawned. They

knew. They knew Rhyan had given me kashonim before the habibellum, they knew we had cheated.

"If Soturion Lyriana fails her test, then tonight, at least, we shall finally bear witness to Soturion Rhyan's ability to slay an akadim."

The crowd roared, and a blue spark of mage magic shot from the stands, hitting the front of the silver box. Flames of red and blue hissed their way around the border, creating the outline of a rectangle. A door.

The flames vanished, and the door began to slide off the box, slowly, the sound metallic and grating until it finally fell with a heavy thud on the arena's snowy ground.

"No!" Rhyan yelled as the crowd filling the arena cried out in horror and disgust.

I stepped forward, my heart pounding, as tears filled my eyes.

A shadowy figure emerged from the darkness, a figure with far too familiar curls of brown hair, the exact shade that adorned the heads of those in Ka Grey.

Haleika. Haleika in her forsaken form.

The bells rang, the sound vibrating through my body as the ashvan soared into the sky above the flame-lit circle of the arena, their jewel-toned bodies alight only by the blue streaks of magic carrying their hooves as they ascended into the blackened sky. Snowflakes kissed my face, landing in my lashes.

Haleika stepped out of the silver box, her feet unsteady as she walked across the metal door beneath her. She was my test. My chance to prove myself as a soturion to the Emperor, to stay in Bamaria, to claim my birthright and protect my sisters. It all came down to me fighting and killing my friend.

She looked up at me, her head cocking to the side with curiosity, the gesture so like Tristan's, and yet not. A moment passed before she moved, shifting her body preternaturally slowly. It was the movement of a predator. As the bells softened into faint echoes of the night, only seconds remained before Haleika completed her transformation from forsaken to akadim.

CHAPTER

TWENTY-NINE

I staggered back as Haleika took another step forward. The reality of what was about to happen and what I had to do crashed down on me. "No. No. No."

The horror of this test. The cruelty. My hands shook at my sides.

Outside of her box, her form was now recognizable by the audience filling the stadium. She glanced up, her movements oddly precise, hinting at the monster lurking beneath the surface.

Horrified cries rang out from the arena as she was recognized, the sound deafening and full of pain.

This was no test. A test would be a Bound Five. An obstacle course. An opportunity to show my skill with different weapons or to answer questions about combat theory, soturion history, or fighting sequences. Not this. This was torture. Cruel and evil. Not just for me, but for Haleika, for her family, for all of Ka Grey. It was cruel to force them and all of Haleika's friends in the academy to watch. It was a cruelty disguised once more as a lawful punishment by the Emperor.

I saw through the façade. This was nothing less than a direct assault and attack on Bamaria.

Someone shouted Haleika's name. The last syllable hung in the air as there was another shout of "Haleika!" followed by a round of insults at my father. Curses aimed at Ka Batavia threaded their way through the verbal assault. They called us cruel, barbaric, and savage, as if this horrid display had been our idea. As if we were responsible, as if we'd killed her on purpose.

My heart sank. In the end, it was my fault she was forsaken, my fault she'd transform into an akadim—my fault she was about to die.

Unless she killed me first.

Gods. If it came down to that, I hoped that was all she did to me.

The sudden fear and possibility that she truly could kill me— and not just kill me but brutalize my body publicly and tear my soul away—left me shaking.

The roars and screams of anger and disapproval increased in volume. The fury in the stadium was unlike anything I'd heard before: pure unbridled hatred and disgust at my family, my Ka, along with fear over what they were about to bear witness to.

This was wrong on every level. We didn't kill for sport. We killed for necessity. And the Emperor had just turned a tragedy and loss of Lumerian life into a game, into entertainment. Those present were rightfully angry. But the anger was misdirected. Just as the Imperator had planned.

"Shekar arkasva! Shekar arkasva!" The chant sounded once, then again, until within seconds the insults were being thrown back and forth across the stands. There was the sound of a punch, of flesh hitting flesh, and a scurry of movement, of soturi in brushed-gold armor moving through the stands to make an arrest. Another shout, another curse against my father, and a second brawl erupted on the other side of the arena.

"Shekar arkasva!"

My body was numb.

No. I couldn't allow that. I couldn't panic. Not here. Not now. I had to survive. First, I had to survive.

Survive an akadim. On my own. And not just survive, but kill. Kill the akadim that had once been my friend.

She still looked human as she stared up above the arena, her face turned to the blackened night sky before moving methodically as her attention returned to me. She was still Haleika. Haleika's size with Haleika's face. My friend I'd known my entire life.

Her Ka-Grey-brown eyes were gone. Black, empty orbs stared into the expanse of the field. Not even the whites of her eyes remained.

Across her heart, a black mark marred her skin—the signifier of her death, the place where the monster had sucked out her soul to eat it. Someone had changed her from her Valyati ballgown to what at first appeared to be a dress but was in fact a simple white tunic. The frock was extremely oversized and loose on her body, far too big for her lean frame. The collar hung low over her chest, showing the blackened mark across her heart.

In her current form, I could kill her. I should kill her now—this was when she was at her weakest. In the in-between, not living, not dead. Not human, not yet akadim. Forsaken. But I couldn't. Just the thought made me ill.

I had never killed before. Not with my own hands.

Something that smelled of death and decay whispered past me— the dying breath of Haleika's aura. It moved through my armor, my body, leaving me chilled to the bone.

"Lyr! LYR!" Rhyan called. I was too terrified to look at him, fear and guilt gnawing at me. My body tensed, and I found that some inner part of my mind attuned to survival would not allow me to turn away from the monster, but the urgency in Rhyan's voice tore through me. Slowly, I backed up, one boot sliding through the snow, shifting me closer to the pole.

"Her transformation will complete in seconds," he said quickly. "She'll remember you. Akadim keep their memories. But she'll be disoriented. Not used to her strength or her size. Use that to your advantage. You know how."

I nodded, keeping my gaze fixed on Haleika as she stumbled forward, uneasy on her legs. She wasn't moving with purpose, yet at the same time her pace was picking up with unnatural speed. She appeared to be walking, almost aimlessly, yet her feet were carrying her with the speed of a running soturion. I blinked at the odd visual, unable to wrap my mind around it.

She froze. Her back arched, and a look of pure pain etched across her delicate features.

"It's starting," Rhyan said. "Stay calm. You can do this. She's just a rope, Lyr. She's just another rope."

I bit my lip, swallowing hard.

Her arms strained at her sides as she threw them out. Her hands opened and flexed in pain, her muscles straining and tensing. Haleika turned her face to the sky, and a cold gust of wind blew her hair back as a cry of absolute horror erupted from her mouth. It was a scream born of pure agony and pain—of the loss of her soul, the loss of her life, and now, at last, the loss of her body.

"HAL!" A cry just as full of pain reverberated across the arena. The voice was deep, anguished. Galen. "Haleika! No!"

Tears burned in my eyes.

"I can't watch," I cried.

"You must. Do not look away from a demon. She's not your friend anymore," Rhyan said quickly, his voice urgent. "She died last night. Whatever she remembers, there's no emotion behind it. Sword out. Lyr. Lyr! Sword! Now!"

I unsheathed my sword, watching the silver of my starfire blade catch the flames of the firelight around us. Haleika screamed again, her voice already changing, deepening, growing louder.

It was happening. There was no going back. Her limbs lengthened, and the expanse of her body grew. The loose tunic she'd been dressed in had been too big for her body, but within seconds she was filling it out. One second, it fit, the next it was too tight. The material stretched and pulled until it ripped down the center, tearing open from collar to waist. Rips slit open the sides of the material to make room for her thickened, elongated thighs.

While her body grew, the black mark over her exposed heart shrank smaller and smaller until nothing but pristine, pale white skin lay between the breasts that were straining against the tunic.

Her skin was splitting open with the force of the growth spurt, her veins openly bleeding across her barely concealed body. She pulled her lips back as her teeth sharpened into vicious canines. Her nails spiked into claws, and with a final primal scream of pain and violence, her head snapped from side to side. The transformation was complete.

Her black eyes reddened, focusing with predatory stillness on me and Rhyan. Horror filled me as I realized what was about to happen.

Akadim went for the easiest pickings. As a newborn monster, Haleika was going to be hungry, if not starving. She wasn't going to prioritize a fight. She'd want a soul to eat. And for once, the easiest opponent to defeat and conquer wouldn't be me.

It was Rhyan, bound and tied to the pole. Helpless. I didn't have to just fight and defeat Haleika—I had to protect him.

Knowing that, something inside of me snapped into place. A fierceness and a readiness. A knowing that Rhyan was tearing himself apart inside over saving me from this fate last night—and a knowledge that I would do no less for him. I would tear down anyone or anything that tried to hurt him, no matter the consequences.

My grip tightened on the hilt of my sword as I lifted it, my stance widening, knees bending, body angling. I surveyed our surroundings. Haleika's feral body-language intensified as her eyes shifted back and forth between me and Rhyan.

The cries from the stadium started anew, filled with hatred and anger. The fear of the Lumerians had formed a tangible aura that weighed down on me as the shouts of *"Shekar arkasva"* tried to undo me. At least three more fights had broken out, from the sound of it.

I blocked it all out. I'd finish this first. Then I'd deal with whatever was happening in the stands.

I weighed my sword in my hand, adjusting my grip like I'd practiced, until it felt like an extension of my arm. I took one deep breath, and then I ran, charging at Haleika as the crowd screamed, now with a hint of excitement.

Haleika's focus immediately jumped to me. If she wanted Rhyan, she'd have to go through me first.

I raced at the speed I'd worked so hard to build these last few months, my feet carrying me forward faster than I'd ever run before.

"Lyr," Haleika hissed, turning to swipe her claws out at me. "Your grace," she mocked.

I was ready, and with a thrust of my sword I sliced her hand, my blade drawing blood.

She screeched in pain. Her voice was that of an akadim, loud and dark. It made my skin crawl, and yet…Haleika was underneath it. I could hear her unique tone, her unique personality bubbling at the edges of her words. I would have known it was her with my eyes closed, and this knowledge pierced my heart.

No. No. It's not her. It's not her. Gods…forgive me.

I rolled my shoulders back, my fingers flexing to prepare for my next attack.

Haleika—no, the akadim who was Haleika—turned, her huge nostrils flaring.

I ran at her again, my eyes on the slit of her hand, on the blood dripping onto the snow. I needed to cut her again, and I needed to do it in the exact same spot.

She growled, moving closer, her movements ripping the remains of her tunic until she was barely covered by the white material.

I lifted my sword, seeing her eyes watching mine, and at the last second, feinted, changing the direction of my gaze. She shifted with me, and then I was back, eyes on my target, and with another swipe, I hit my mark.

More blood gushed from her wound as my chest heaved with exertion.

Stamina, not speed.

I turned, lifting my sword, seeing she'd shifted her gaze to Rhyan across the arena, her nostrils flaring as she sniffed him out.

"No!"

I ran back at her, but she knew my game now and protected her hand, feinting and shifting in mockery of my plan. No matter. I'd hit the other hand instead. But she was ready and swiped her claws at me, the sharpened edges crashing against my golden armor. I staggered back, the shock of the impact reverberating against my chest. I breathed in and out through my mouth, trying to ignore the pain in my side. I'd be bruised across my ribs if I survived. Again, her attention turned to Rhyan.

"Haleika!" I shouted.

She laughed. "Your grace." Her voice was gravelly, thick, like multiple voices threaded together. "Still trying to prove you're a soturion."

I snarled, trying to gauge her next move. Was I fast enough to hit her legs? They were thicker—I'd need to hit harder. Strike fast and precise.

I didn't think. I just ran. But she was faster. I sped up, my legs burning as I sprinted, and at the last second, she turned, running straight for me. I held out my sword, my hand shaking, but I was ready. She neared, and I struck. My blade sliced through her thigh. But the cut wasn't deep. I'd made barely a scratch against her newly thickened skin.

Before she could react, I hit her again and again.

I saw it in her eyes before she acted, her decision to grab me. My heart pounded as I watched her clawed hands reaching for my stomach, just like the akadim the night before had done.

I waited, holding my ground, and at the last second—my heart a drum in my ears as the crowd screamed and roared—I jumped back. Her claws missed me by barely an inch.

Snow was falling in heavy flakes, and sweat was dripping down my face, as she moved again. I wasn't fast enough this time. My armor protected me from her claws, but both her hands wrapped around my waist. Tightly. Too tightly. I gasped for breath, wheezing as my feet left the ground. I lifted my sword arm, my free hand digging for my dagger, my feet dangling helplessly.

"LYR!" Rhyan was roaring from the pole. His cry of anguish was echoed by voices in the crowd. My sisters. Tristan. My father.

I stabbed at her hands as they squeezed me, tighter and tighter.

My blades sank into her flesh, and blood gushed, spilling across my armor and the snow.

Another stab, and Haleika roared in my face, the sound monstrous and pained. She released me with a cry, and I crashed onto the ground, landing on my ankle at the wrong angle.

"Fuck!" I fell onto my back, the snow cold against my cloak and hair while my ankle screamed in agony.

My ears rushed with the sound of my heartbeat pounding furiously, blocking out everything else in the arena—the screams and cries from the stands; the fights, protests, and arrests; the worry from my sisters and father; the anger from everyone else; their hatred for my family; their grief for Haleika.

Haleika stood over me, roaring with such ferocity, the falling snow was blown across my face, blurring my vision. I couldn't breathe, I couldn't move. She swiped her claws at my dagger and my blade until both were spinning across the arena's ground away from me.

"Hungry," she snarled. Her foot stomped on my belly, her weight crushing me. I gasped, all the air rushing from my lungs. I coughed, trying desperately to breathe, to control my wheezing.

I had to get her off of me. I needed another weapon.

Reaching past my hips, I found what I needed—a Valalumir from my belt. It was stuck on the leather. She pressed harder on me, and with a cry of anguish, I tightened my grip on the nearest blade of the star, and with a grunt, ripped it free. I slammed the sharpened edges into her foot again and again and again until she stumbled back, releasing me from her weight.

I rolled over, sputtering and gasping for breath, my lungs in distress, my ribcage sore and bruised, my entire torso pulsing with pain.

"No more playing." Haleika smacked my hand with such force, I released the star and screamed. Something crunched, and blinding white pain flashed through my body, my vision blanking for a second. She'd broken my hand.

I pulled myself up to a seat, barely able to move my right ankle or arm. Leaning onto my left side, my right hand broken and against my chest, I scrambled back as far from her as I could get. She swiped, and I threw my head back. Too late. She sliced her claws through my cheek. Blood ran down my face, dripping onto my neck and down onto my necklace, my blood coating the red starfire diamonds in the center of each golden Valalumir across my collarbone, chest, and shoulders.

I leaned my weight onto my left elbow. I had to get up. I had to stand, but Haleika's large hands wrapped around me again, and I was hoisted back into the air, my heart plummeting into my belly as I soared up and then suddenly dropped down.

She held me by the back of my soturion cloak. My body dangled as her free hand shot forward, her claws aimed at my necklace. She was going to remove it, remove my jewelry, remove my armor, cloak, and tunic—undress me until there was a clear exit for my soul to leave my body, until only a black mark on my heart remained.

I was going to die. Worse. I was going to lose my soul and become a monster like her. It was too late. Even if they freed Rhyan, he couldn't get here in time—even if he traveled.

I squeezed my eyes shut. Rhyan was screaming my name; the sound of the crowd was deafening.

Haleika roared in hunger as I felt her clawed hands coming for me. There was a tug, her nails piercing through my necklace, the chain and clasp digging into the back of my neck. But the moment she made contact, she roared in agony, as if she'd just been burned by fire. Her grip on me faltered, and I fell unceremoniously to the ground in a heap, landing on my left hip.

I groaned in pain, watching the horror in Haleika's eyes as she stared at her hand.

Something similar had happened the night before when the other akadim attacked. I stared down at the collection of golden stars covering my chest and shoulders.

It was the necklace. Akadim didn't like it.

But before I could figure out what that meant or how to use it to my advantage, Haleika punched me square in the chest. Even with my armor on, I wheezed, the air knocked out of my lungs as I heard the sound of glass shattering. I fell on my back, dizzy, seeing flashes of white and gold before glancing down. It wasn't glass I'd heard breaking. It was diamonds.

My necklace. She'd broken three of the starfire diamonds, their precious centers spilling down my armor. The starfire ran into the blood dripping onto my body.

"LYR!" Rhyan screamed again. "LYR!"

In the stands were shouts of, "Free him! Free him!"

Haleika abandoned the fight against me, turned, and started racing for Rhyan. His arms were still pinned above his head to the pole, his body restricted by the bindings, his magic and strength cut off.

No. NO! I needed to get there first, between him and her.

But the moment I moved to stand, my vision blackened. Something warm was growing inside my body, a heat, an inner fire. I'd been freezing the entire time I was out here, but now my insides felt like they were singing with flames I'd only felt once before—when the nahashim had snaked their way inside of me.

I screamed. I was lying on the snow, my body bruised and broken, my necklace and blood spilling out across me. I felt like my insides were on fire.

"Help!" I screamed. "Help him!" But I was screaming at myself. At my body. To get up, to find strength, to do this one final thing. Protect Rhyan.

Red flashed in my vision, and I saw a glimmer of gold before the flames within me increased. My entire body seized, my arms and legs stretched out like I'd been blasted back by some unknown force. The pain in my hand vanished, and I knew without looking it was no longer broken but healed. My ankle righted itself, and a surge of power burst inside of me.

You're the fire. Rhyan had told me, both in my dream and asleep in my arms. Mercurial had said the same.

And though I saw no flames anywhere, their words had become truth. I was fire.

Some inner strength, some inner power, blazed inside of me. I felt strong. Energized. Full of light. Ready to end this, once and for all.

A mage who served the Emperor leaned over the wall of the stadium, his stave pointed at Rhyan. But he made no movement to undo the spell. He was waiting on a command from the Emperor that was not coming. Rhyan's eyes were on me, his face torn in anguish, and with a cry of my name, he released his arms from their bonds.

Gods, he was freeing himself.

But not fast enough. Haleika was going to get him. Unless I got there first.

And I would get there first.

Flames licked me from the inside, singed around my heart. I didn't care. I rolled onto my side, coughing blood, and jumped to my feet, my eyes on Haleika's back as I tore across the arena, running at a speed that shouldn't have been possible. Power surged through my veins, and I picked up speed, my feet barely touching the ground, some inner wind carrying me forward.

She would not lay a hand on him, not when I still had breath.

"HAL!" I screamed. "HAL!"

I reached for another Valalumir, ripped it from my belt strap. My fingers tightened over the sharpened blade, and my arm pulled back before I swung it forward, releasing the golden star with a force I hadn't known I could possess. Time seemed to slow, and my vision cleared, my body free of pain as I watched the star fly. The Vala-lumir spun and shimmered across the arena, a hum of magic sounding as it flew and hit my mark, slicing through her back.

Haleika shrieked and turned from Rhyan just as he freed himself from the bond, the black ropes around his body dissolving into black shadows disintegrating at his feet. All at once his aura surged, a coolness in the air I'd been missing while he was bound.

The Emperor's mage cried out in protest. Rhyan had torn the ropes apart himself. Even without his magic, without his power.

But now Haleika was racing for me. My heart pounded. Good. I was ready.

She charged forward, but I moved faster, reaching down for another star. I assessed the distance between me and my blade and sword. Too far. And a throwing star wouldn't end her life. I still had my knives, but I needed something more, something bigger.

My mind raced through the three ways to kill an akadim. Cut off their head, stab their heart, or.... I eyed the flames above me, the torches circling the stadium. I swung my arm back, my eyes on the torchlight, and threw the star at the flame, its magic singing out to me as it soared.

The star sliced cleanly through the wooden stake, and firelight fell into the arena as the stake landed right in my hand.

I gripped the wood like a stave, as Rhyan ran and brandished his sword. Before he reached her, I took off, pressing my heels into the ground, bending at the knees, and leaping forward, catapulting myself until I was flying through the air.

Haleika's red eyes widened with fear, her expression crumbling just like it used to when she'd been human. I slammed into her chest, grabbed hold of her tunic with one hand, and staked the fire-light through her heart with the other.

Haleika roared in pain, the flames licking and dancing across her chest. I swung my legs back and forth, picking up enough momentum to kick her and propel myself away. I hit the ground with a sharp thud. Rhyan was at my side in an instant, helping me to my feet, his arms wrapping around me as he pulled me away from Haleika, now running toward us, fire spreading through her body and black smoke misting into the falling snow above her head.

She sank to her knees. I'd hit her heart but not deep enough to kill her. The flames would do the rest, but they weren't moving fast enough. She was suffering. Greatly. And with her akadim strength, the process would likely last for an agonizing length of time. She dropped to the ground, to the snow, but the fires were spreading.

"Is this enough?" Rhyan yelled. "Was that enough for you?" he roared at the Emperor.

Tears burned in my eyes, my actions catching up to me now that the threat had been stopped. The surge of energy, power, and strength I'd felt, that I'd needed and called up to protect Rhyan, was quickly ebbing, leaving me feeling entirely drained. My eyesight was going in and out of focus, my heart pounding too fast, exhaustion overwhelming me.

The Emperor leaned forward in his seat, his brows furrowed in disgust as he held out his hand, shifted his fingers into a fist, and pointed his thumb up.

I'd passed. I'd done it.

And I felt like total and utter shit.

My heart squeezed. A new pain erupted inside as the exhaustion finally swept through me. I felt my eyes beginning to close, and I sank to my knees, no longer having the strength to stand.

It was like I'd gone through Rhyan's kashonim ten times over. But I hadn't. He'd been bound; his magic had been cut off from me. I couldn't make sense of where the energy and strength had come from.

Haleika roared, her arms flailing and covered in flames.

"Lyr," Rhyan stared down at me. "Are you...?"

"Help her," I croaked. "End it."

His nostrils flared, jaw tightening as he nodded once and ran forward, sword drawn before he leaped. He spun across Haleika's front, his body far enough from the flames to keep from being burned, as his sword sliced through her neck.

His black boots crashed into the reddened snow at the same moment her head hit the ground.

I clutched my chest. It was done. I'd survived. We'd survived.

That was the moment the arena exploded.

"Ka Batavia kills its own people!" someone shouted.

"Murderers."

"Justice for Haleika Grey!"

"Fuck Harren Batavia."

Something shot forth from the stands and landed by my foot. A black rock. I picked it up. The sigil of the Emartis stared back at me as another rock fell.

"Shekar arkasva. Shekar arkasva. Shekar arkasva!"

"LYR!" Rhyan screamed, running back to my side. His arms wrapped around my waist as he began hauling me away from the center of the arena.

I collapsed into Rhyan's arms. I couldn't hold myself up. There was no energy left inside me, no strength. I felt like I'd used a lifetime of power in minutes. The shouts continued, and more rocks were thrown, some only narrowly missing me by a few inches.

"Lyr," he said. "Lyr! Gods!"

"What's happening?" I asked, not sure if I was referring to me or the arena. "Rhyan?"

The wind picked up speed, the sky seemed to blacken, and the aura of the crowd took on a fiery, violent feel.

A black, shimmering seraphim appeared in the sky, and screams filled the stadium as every torchlight went out.

I clutched at Rhyan, only able to see his outline from the flames that still torched the remains of Haleika's akadim body. Screams sounded from every side of the stadium. Feet shuffled, bodies pushed against each other as curses were flung, and starfire blades sang out as they were unsheathed.

"Rhyan? What's…?"

He'd lifted me into his arms, still hauling me back, searching for a door.

"Lyr," he said, panic in his voice.

Screams erupted from everywhere, but one rose above all the others. It was a cry of horror, of pain, and in response came two more voices. Voices I'd know anywhere. Voices I'd always pick out, even in a crowd, even in a mob.

Meera. Morgana.

"Shekar arkasva! Emartis!" The cry was spelled to amplify, the chant made up of hundreds of voices.

There was a crack of thunder. A scream. A loud thud in the

center of the arena as Meera and Morgana's voices rose to an alarming pitch of horror.

"Lyr, we have to go. Right now!" Rhyan said.

"What—" I clutched my arms around his neck, my eyes starting to close. My energy was nearly gone, and I could barely keep my eyes open.

A cold yell pierced through the arena, "Victory!"

All at once, the torchlights returned, flaming back to life in one burst of power.

I blinked, barely able to keep my eyes open. They took a moment to readjust to the light, but then they did.

Lying in the center of the arena, his body only a few feet from Haleika's burning remains, was my father.

His limbs were unnaturally twisted, his body broken, his eyes open in horror, focusing on me as he exhaled his final breath.

His eyelids closed, and his chest stilled.

"NO! NO!" I screamed, trying to race forward, to go to him, to save his life, but Rhyan gripped me harder, taking me away.

"Father!" I yelled. "FATHER!"

My strength, my power, all the energy I'd summoned in the arena had been vanquished. I knew nothing more but that Haleika was gone. My father was gone. Screams sounded. Inside me. In my heart. In the arena.

Rhyan's arms tightened around me.

My eyes shut.

CHAPTER
THIRTY

Golden light flashed before my closed eyes. Everything ached. My head. My body. My mouth was dry, and it hurt to swallow. Slowly, I began to blink my eyes open. Light streamed in through a window beside a Cresthaven bed. But it wasn't mine. My window was on the other side.

Fuck. What time is it? What room am I in? What just happened?

"You're in Meera's room," Morgana said dully. "Thank fuck you're awake."

I turned my head, finding a ghostly pale Morgana, her black hair wild in her face, sitting at the foot of Meera's bed. Behind her was Meera's mural of visions. A painting of myself with my hair red and my body transforming into a black seraphim stared back. The Emartis.

The Emartis had....

Tears welled in my eyes. My lips trembled as my eyes focused on Morgana, the question on the tip of my tongue, but I couldn't bear to ask it aloud.

Morgana bit her lip, her black eyes rimmed in red. "They killed him."

I shook my head. "Father's...." I couldn't speak. I was going to be sick, yet I didn't have the strength to even turn to my side.

What's wrong with me? What happened? What time is it? I'd been on the field of the arena. It had been night. Rhyan had just cut off Haleika's head after I'd set her on fire. And then the screams had come, and Father...Father...his body...his eyes...the twisting of his limbs....

"That was last night," Morgana said, her voice clipped. "It's," she coughed like she was trying to hold back some of her emotion, "it's nearly three."

"In the afternoon?" *How long have I been asleep?*

The bells rang, louder and harsher than I'd ever heard them before. The tone was shrill, almost painfully so.

"They're not the normal bells," Morgana said quietly. She wrung her hands together in her lap and leaned forward so more hair fell over her face. "They ring them only for the passing of an arkasva. I heard them when mother...." She shook her head. "They sounded like gryphon-shit back then, too. They'll switch back to the normal bells when the new arkasva is consecrated."

The new arkasva. Not Father. Because Father was....

"I think you've been out for almost twenty hours," Morgana said. "The moment the," she paused to clear her throat again, "*test* started, the Emartis made themselves known. They were shouting, flashing black seraphim masks and their sigils in random patterns across the arena. Fights were breaking out. Mobs forming. The Emperor insisted the test continue despite the insanity taking place. And when it was over, when you'd killed Hal—the akadim—and Rhyan finished her, I don't know. The soturi were scattered. Father's guard remained at his side. It was so chaotic. I don't know how it could have happened. We were surrounded, protected, and somehow, with all the fighting, all the displays of treason, the Emartis managed to break through our defenses. He was lifted—it was magic. Our soturi weren't fast enough. His guard, they—they tried to grab him, to save him. Our mages were throwing out protective shields from every direction, and I tried...I tried to listen, to find out who it was. But...." She hissed out a breath. "There were too many voices, and I couldn't—I couldn't. I'd been so worried about losing you, so scared for you, and then, just like that...he was gone. They flew him up, higher and higher, and then.... They let him fall." Tears streamed down my sister's cheeks.

"I passed out," I said in horror. I'd seen him fall, seen his body broken. I'd seen his eyes close. And I'd passed out. I'd retreated. I'd left.

"No," Morgana said. "I don't think that's what happened. I don't know what, but I know you didn't use kashonim. You seemed to— to have tapped into something else. Something bigger."

"My power?" I asked.

Morgana shrugged. "I don't know. Do you feel like you have it now?"

I shook my head. I couldn't move.

"It was good you were with him. When the mob broke out."

I blinked. "With Rhyan?" I asked.

Morgana swallowed and straightened, pushing her hair behind her ear. A long cut ran across her right cheek. "They weren't done," she said. "They tried to get me."

"Where's Meera?" I sat up.

"She's fine," Morgana said quickly. "Downstairs. In the Seating Room. Eathan is, um, Eathan is the acting arkasva. Meera's talking to him and the Council, making plans."

"She's going to be High Lady," I said, a pit forming in my stomach. *She won't survive—she'll never be able to hide, not with all the extra scrutiny she'll receive.*

"I know," Morgana said. "But we have a month to plan. They'll set a date to coincide with the next full moon and to give the other eleven arkasvim time to arrive in Bamaria."

My eyes widened. "The other arkasvim?" Rhyan's father. The Imperator of the North, he'd be here. Then we'd have two Imperators in Bamaria.

Bells rang again. Not the bells of the timekeeper. Warning bells.

"They're still fighting in the streets," Morgana said. "Rounding up every suspected member of the Emartis. The Shadow Stronghold is already full of traitors. It's a miracle we all made it home.

We had to be evacuated with ten escorts each. I'll be in Rhyan's debt forever for him getting you here safely. Fuck. That reminds me." She reached into her belt pocket and pulled out a small vadati stone.

My vadati stone. The one Rhyan had given to me. My nostrils flared as she held it to her mouth and said, "Rhyan."

White smoke swirled, filling the nearly clear stone until it burned with blue light.

"Morgana," Rhyan said through the stone, his voice strained.

"She's awake," Morgana said.

There was a gasp and then a long pause on Rhyan's end. "Thank the Gods," he said, relief flooding his voice. "Is she in pain?"

Morgana narrowed her eyes at me before saying, "She's a bit sore and aching. Mostly tired."

"Thank you," he said. "I'll be in touch as soon as I can."

The stone went white as she leaned forward, placing it back in my hand.

My fingers closed tightly around it. I didn't like anyone else touching it. I'd been keeping it inside a small golden charm that I'd strung through a necklace. But, of course, Morgana knew that.

"He stayed with you," Morgana said. "Half the night. But he's been pulled into guard duty. He's outside the fortress now, patrolling. He begged me to contact him the moment you woke."

I was silent, sitting up and curling my knees to my chest. Morgana went quiet, and we sat there as time passed. The grief for my father covered me like a too-heavy blanket. Suffocating.

Morgana sniffled but remained in her seat, staring out the window.

I tried to breathe. To process that he was gone. And Haleika, too. And Leander. But instead, I just felt numb. My stomach tightened with fear and uncertainty.

As the sky began to gray once more and sunset seemed imminent, Morgana shot out of her chair, her eyebrows furrowed in concentration before she yelled out, "Fuck! Fuck!"

"What? What happened?"

"The Council's ended their session. Meera's on her way upstairs to talk to us."

A few seconds later, the door opened, and Meera's frail form appeared in the doorway. She looked completely deflated, her hazel eyes downcast.

"You're awake," she said softly, as she collapsed onto her bed.

Morgana was beside her in an instant, gripping her shoulders.

"What the fuck!" Morgana shouted.

"Morgs!" I yelled. "What are you doing?"

"How could you? What the fuck, Meera?"

"What?" I asked. "Meera, what is going on?"

"Stop it," Meera commanded, her voice icy. She shook Morgana off her and swept to her feet, moving across the room. Her chest rose and fell with heavy breaths as she rested her hands against her dresser, staring back at us in her vanity mirror. "What else would you have me do? How else do we solve this problem?"

"I don't know," Morgana said through gritted teeth. "But this wasn't fucking it!"

"You have no right," Meera said, a tear rolling down her cheek.

"You should have gotten me, brought me down into the Council. Consulted me. Consulted us!" Morgana snarled.

"You're not on the Council. Now stop it. You have no right to speak to me this way."

"Maybe I wouldn't if I was talking to my future High Lady. Maybe if I were speaking to the next Arkasva Batavia. But I'm not! Do you understand what you've done?"

Meera turned around as I sat forward, my stomach sinking.

"Done what?" I asked.

Meera and Morgana were both seething, staring at each other, their auras pulsing in a silent battle, thunder and lightning.

"Done what?" I yelled.

"I did what I had to do. For Bamaria."

"For yourself," Morgana said.

"And for you! And Lyr. We all knew. We all knew I wasn't going to rule. Not if we're going to keep our secrets. Not if we're going to quell this rebellion. Do you understand just how angry the people of Bamaria are? How last night looked to them?" She shook her head. "Of course, you do, your vorakh told you. So you know. You know there was no other choice. I need some air." She grabbed a shawl from her closet and wrapped it around her shoulders. "We have one hour. One hour until we're to appear downstairs in the Seating Room. And then it's all over."

She walked out of the room, as I turned to Morgana.

"Morgs! What in Lumeria is happening?"

Morgana's nostrils flared, her eyes darkening. "She's abdicating the Seat of Power."

I felt like I'd been punched in the gut. Of course, she was, she had to. She was too frail to rule. Too vulnerable with her vorakh. But hearing it was happening now...I wasn't ready. Father wasn't even cold or buried yet, and already Meera was abdicating.

I stared at Morgana carefully, my gut twisting, as I tried to bury the desire I'd always had, always carried. My own desire to rule. My own desire to become arkasva because I'd known it couldn't be Meera since her vorakh had appeared. And I knew it couldn't be Morgana for the same reason. But I...I wasn't ready. Not now. Not yet.

Morgana's gaze narrowed on me, and she shook her head, a mirthless laugh on her lips, almost cruel. "She's not abdicating to you," she seethed.

"To you?" I asked, my gut twisting.

"No. She's removed us from the line of succession. Enjoy your diadem while you can, your grace. In one hour, she's going to make the formal announcement. Aunt Arianna will be the next Arkasva Batavia, High Lady of Bamaria."

CHAPTER
THIRTY-ONE

I stood in the Seating Room, which was now filled with every member of the Bamarian Council and their family members, the most important nobles of Bamarian society. The Imperator remained, and Viktor had been allowed to attend the announcement as well.

I'd been informed that the Emperor and his men had left in the middle of the night, retreating to the capitol where it was safe and civil. He'd left a small scroll behind for me.

Congratulations, Soturion Lyriana Batavia. You may continue to train so long as you may survive. Be warned, one akadim fight does not a soturion make. Tovayah maischa, as you continue on this quest. You'll need it.

And my deepest sympathies on the loss of your father, Harren Batavia. Bar Ka Mokan.

Emperor Theotis, High Lord of Lumeria Nutavia

I crumpled the scroll. *Bar Ka Mokan.* His soul freed. Because he was gone. Dead. And I was standing here in a pretty dress, expected to celebrate his replacement.

Arianna stood across the room with Naria, Viktor, and the Imperator at her side.

I loved Arianna. Arianna made sense as ruler. She would be a good arkasva. Meera couldn't do it. Morgana couldn't do it. But every time I looked at her, I felt a knot in my stomach.

She had been the Emartis's chosen ruler. She had been whom they'd fought for, whom they'd died for. Because of them, Father had walked for most of my life with a limp. Because of them, unrest had brewed in Bamaria, made the streets unsafe, and allowed the occupation of Ka Kormac in our streets.

Because of the Emartis, Father had been murdered. Because they wanted her to rule. Because of the Emartis, I'd never see him again, never speak to him again.

I blinked back tears. I had to appear strong, to show my solidarity over the transfer of power. But I couldn't stop imagining the traitors celebrating in the streets, toasting and drinking to Father's dead body. I wanted to be happy for Arianna, for her being given this opportunity to rule, to do good in Bamaria, to be recognized for her strength and intelligence.

But not at this cost. Not at this price. Not when it made my father's murderers happy.

Familiar mage escorts entered the Seating Room—Bellamy and those employed by Ka Grey. Lady Romula walked through the threshold wearing a black and silver gown, her hand resting on the arm of her husband Lord Trajan. Bellamy, whom I was still paying to keep silent from Tristan about anything he witnessed while on my guard, gave me a curt nod, sorrow in his eyes. I didn't see Tristan, but upon seeing me, Lady Romula left her husband's arm and walked faster than she usually pretended she could to reach my side.

"My poor dear," she said. "Your grace, you have my greatest sympathies on the loss of your father. *Bar Ka Mokan.*"

My eyes welled up. I couldn't be here. I couldn't do this. I couldn't breathe.

"His soul freed," I said, voice barely above a whisper.

She shook her head, one ancient, withered hand reaching forward to brush a tear from my cheek. She grimaced but took my hand and placed it on her arm, patting it gently and leading me away from the crowd, away from the noise.

"There, there," she said. "Away from all that. It is cruel for them to have you here. For you to bear witness to the transfer of power not even a full day later. But such is the burden of the lords and ladies of Lumeria. Such is the burden of being an Heir to the Arkasva. Life must go on even in the face of death."

I nodded, knowing she spoke somewhat of herself, of Ka Grey and Haleika. "Thank you. And, Lady Romula, I am so sorry...." Tears were falling freely down my cheeks, and she frowned, her dried lips pursed together. "I am sorry for...for...."

"Do not mention her name to me. She is dead. You killed her."

"I...." I swallowed. I had. I had killed her. I'd had to do it. But I was still sorry, I still wanted to offer my sympathies, to grieve Haleika with her family.

"You will not speak to me again on this matter. I am sorry for your loss," she said. "I know what it is to grieve a loved one. To suffer their murder, to suffer the pain of their leaving their bodies too soon and in such a violent manner. I am no stranger to the grief you feel, to the pain in your heart. I do mean it when I say I am sorry for your loss. Ka Grey's suffering has been unique to position us in a place of sympathy that nobles rarely achieve."

She held out her hand, and I took it.

"That being said," Lady Romula continued, her shrewd eyes taking me in, "after tonight, a countdown begins. A month until your Aunt Arianna's consecration. She will become Arkasva Batavia, High Lady of Bamaria. And order will be restored to the country at last. However, it cannot be ignored that when this happens, Lady Naria will become Heir Apparent. And you, your grace, will be referred to as such for the very last time."

I blinked. "Yes," I said, unsure where she was going with this.

"The Emartis may be pleased for the moment," she said. "Their champion is coming to power."

"Do you think that means they will go away now? Because they won?"

Lady Romula's eyes darkened. "I thought you more intelligent than this. They won, and winning has a way of making one want more. They will believe their tactics were successful. So, no. They will not go away," she said with disdain. "They will become louder. And now, without your title, what benefit is it to Ka Grey for you and Tristan to wed?"

My mouth fell open. Was she really doing this now?

"Lady Romula," I started, but she held up her hand.

"My dear. I have always cared for you. And I do wish you the best. But I must look out for my family. My Ka comes first. I told you, I didn't like their presence. And now, they have essentially placed themselves in a position of power and authority from behind the scenes. The restoration of order to Bamaria will be a façade, and it will be brief, and I will not risk Ka Grey. You passed your test, congratulations. But you still remain powerless. You still remain the blood of a vorakh."

I stepped back, my throat going dry. Tristan stood with Naria across the room, watching us, his eyes full of guilt.

"So you intend to break apart our engagement?" I asked.

She stepped forward, retrieving my hand again, her bony fingers running up and down my ring finger. "This remains empty," she said. "I cannot break apart that which does not exist."

I pulled my hand away. Spiteful old crone. Things were over with me and Tristan. I'd known that for months. I suspected on some level he might know it, too. But this was not the day. This was not the way to go about it. Before we'd courted, we had been friends. In the scope of a day, he'd lost his cousin, I'd lost my father. Whatever else was wrong between us, whatever complications existed, we both did care for the other and it was cruel for us to lose each other as well.

"Even if," she said, "I could look past your magic status, your family history, your lack of station…." she trailed off, her mouth tightening and twisting as if fighting to keep back her own emotions. "Do you think I will ever forget the image of you murdering my Haleika? I know what happened. I know what she was. I know you only did what you had to do. But sometimes, logic isn't enough for forgiveness. Ka Grey will never forget. And though

Tristan may be more romantic than I ever was, I do not believe he will be able to look past this either."

"He loves me," I said. Even though I knew she spoke the truth, I couldn't allow her this. The hateful hag had no right to come to me now, to tell me this. Not when my father's body wasn't even in the ground. "And if you end things between us now," I seethed, "in this manner, I will not forget."

She bowed her head. "I don't expect you will. But soon your reach for revenge will be quite small. *Bar Ka Mokan*. He did the best he could. May our next arkasva finally bring peace." She turned her back on me and strode across the room, waving to Arianna, who looked resplendent and queenly despite wearing a black mourning dress. She had styled her red hair in braids that crowned her head. Golden jewels had been threaded through the braids, giving them the appearance of a red-and-gold diadem or laurel. In one month, she'd wear it—the Laurel of the Arkasva.

My chest tightened. Beside her was Lady Romula and Tristan, who was whispering something to Naria. The Imperator gazed my way, his black eyes predatory and feral.

I couldn't face him. I was out of all energy, all courtesy, all caring. The ceiling was starting to cave in, and I just needed to get out of there, to go outside, to breathe, to....

A cool breeze caressed my skin, and a warm hand glided past the crook of my elbow.

"Partner."

"Can you get me out of here?" I asked, still facing the Imperator.

"Walk to the opposite corner of the room. The tapestry behind the column is well concealed. Stand behind it. When no one is looking, move behind the tapestry. Go. Now."

Rhyan's back retreated, heading for the room's exit, and I turned in the opposite direction, my stomach twisting to the point I thought I'd be sick all over the floor. Several nobles looked at their feet as I walked by, and I clutched my stomach, realizing for once, no one wanted to look at me, talk to me, or gain my favor. Now they needed Arianna and Naria's approval.

I reached the other side, leaned against the column, waited a beat, and stepped behind the thick tapestry. Rhyan was there, waiting. His arms wrapped around me. There was a tug in my stomach, and my feet hit the ground behind Cresthaven. We stood before the pools, their waters shimmering in the starlight and fires of the fortress. It was the place where I'd first kissed Tristan.

We were alone, not a soul in sight. Everyone was either in the Seating Room or standing outside the front gates, guarding against the Emartis.

Rhyan wrapped his arms around me, and I leaned into him, finally letting the tears fall.

"I'm so sorry," he said.

I could only cry in response.

After a minute, I sucked in a breath and pulled my head back. He reached for my face, wiping the tears away. A bandage covered half his neck, and I saw then he was holding his head stiffly.

I reached out, my fingers gently tracing the edge of the bandage. "You're hurt."

Rhyan grimaced, pushing my hand down. White bandages poked out from beneath his leather arm cuffs. Burns. He'd been burned by the fucking ropes last night. He shook his head following my gaze.

"It's all right. It's healing. And this…" he gestured to his neck, "was from fighting to get you home. Don't even think of it. Worth it to keep you safe." His eyes blazed into mine. "I wish you had time to grieve. For him…and for Haleika. And Leander."

"And for me," I said. "And what I did. My role in this. And…." I looked back at the fortress.

"You're going to get through this," he said. "I'll help you."

"My heart literally hurts. And all anyone in there cares about is the politics."

"I know." He pulled me into his chest again. "But you will get through this."

"How?" I asked. "I don't even know what tomorrow's going to look like."

Rhyan sighed. "It will look different." He squeezed my hand. "You won't know how. You won't ever know. But there's a freedom in surrendering to that. In knowing everything is going to change."

I pressed my hands to my eyes, trying to swallow back a sob. "Everything already changed."

"And you fought back when it did, and you survived. Your heart won't hurt forever." He placed his hand on my chest, his skin warm, his eyes focused on the skin between my breasts, on the place where the akadim had tried to suck out my soul. The place Halieka had tried to expose before my necklace had gotten in her way. "Remember who you are. A title change does not change you."

"I don't think I can do it."

"You can, and you will. It's all going to change, and the sooner you accept that, the easier it will be. And," he bit his lip, his green eyes still on his hand between my breasts, "just remember that one thing remains constant. My love."

I placed my hand over his, remembering our last conversation before the arena. "But you can't live with it?"

"Can you?" he asked.

I closed my eyes. I had been there when we'd left the akadim alive. And I had been the one to end Haleika's life, even if Rhyan had dealt the final blow. The guilt of knowing I'd caused her pain and had some role to play in the end of her life felt as awful as the loss of my father did.

And yet....

"You told me if you could do it again, if you could relive that night, you'd still save me. I feel the same. When I realized you were in danger, some force awoke inside me. I don't know what. But it got me up, and it made me act. I can barely look at myself in the mirror for what I did. And yet," I squeezed his hand, "I would kill her every day for the rest of my life if it meant you got to live." My voice broke. "I don't know how to live with that knowledge."

Rhyan sighed. "I think we live in a world that's given us terrible choices. And we've had to choose as best we could." His jaw tensed. "Lyr, I love you. But I think," his lips quirked up, a sad smile ghosting across his face, "I think we need time. To heal. So, we'll take it. As much as we need. We'll do what we must to get through this. To learn to live with choices we never wanted to make. And then, when it's time, we're going to do what we know best. We're going to fight. We're going to tear that rope apart. And we're going to find our way back to each other."

"Do you swear?"

"*Me sha, me ka.*" He fisted his hand around mine, still pressed to my heart, and tapped it twice against my chest before flattening our hands together over my skin. He leaned forward, pressing a kiss to my forehead. "We're going to be okay, partner. I promise." He shifted his weight like he meant to step back, his hand pulling from mine, but then we were kissing, his arms wrapped around me as he pulled me closer to him.

"How does it come to be," drawled a voice, "that a messenger always stumbles upon you two, not just together, but in so compromising a position?"

Rhyan's arms tightened around me, lifting me off the ground and placing me behind him before he brandished his sword, pointing it straight at Mercurial. "I think you know the answer to that," he snarled. "You always wait, trying to find the most opportune moment to satisfy your perversions."

"That is quite an accusation to make, my not-lord. Perhaps the simpler answer is the truth—that I seek her grace, soon to be her former grace, when she is alone. And for some reason, you have a habit of getting her to be so. Oh, but I forgot," he laughed, "this is because you are a forsworn oath-breaker. Isn't that right?"

"Leave," Rhyan said. "Now."

"Unfortunately, I cannot." Mercurial's hips snaked as he sauntered closer to us. He wore a loincloth of Batavia red. The diamonds in the whorls painted across his body glowed red, like starfire. "Magic has its rules. We have a deal, her grace and I. I gave you a full two days' reprieve, did I not?" He held up his hand, and a gust of wind pushed Rhyan aside. "Put your sword away, my not-lord. I am weary and running short of patience. Next time you threaten the First Messenger, I will fight back."

"I'm not leaving her side. I'm sworn to protect her."

Mercurial chuckled. "The one oath you won't break." His hair flew over his shoulders in soft shimmering waves that reminded me of the ocean. "How valiant. But on my honor as an Afeya, I will not harm her. I'm merely here to offer my condolences and acquire her grace's signature on our contract. It's just business. I'll note that neither of you have stood trial for your oath-breaking. That's because of me. And she has not paid yet. So rest assured, no harm will come to her—not from me. Not until the debt is paid."

Rhyan's nostrils flared, and his body tensed.

"Hart." The voice called from Rhyan's belt pocket. His vadati stone.

Mercurial grinned conspiratorially at me, placing a finger over his lips for silence as Rhyan retrieved the blue stone.

"Yes, Arkturion." Rhyan stepped back, cupping his hand around the stone, pulling it closer to his mouth, his good eyebrow narrowed on Mercurial as if daring him to speak.

Mercurial shrugged innocently in response.

"Changing of the guard," Aemon said. "They want you at the fortress gate."

"The gate?" Rhyan asked. "I thought I was to remain in the Seating Room."

"Change of plans," Aemon snarled. "Go."

"At once, Arkturion." Rhyan replaced the stone in his belt.

Mercurial grinned, his smile feral yet feline. "Looks like someone isn't where they're supposed to be."

"If you hurt her...."

Mercurial's aura exploded from him, casting us in complete darkness. There was no starlight, no torches, only the fire in his eyes like two flickering flames. I sucked in a breath before he pulled his aura back, and the lights returned.

"If I hurt her, I do not make back my investment. You'd be

foolish to linger here and insult me again, no what matter what lies in your blood and soul! Go to your post, soldier."

"If you need me, Lyr," Rhyan patted his belt, glared once more at Mercurial, and retreated.

Mercurial waved back, fluttering his eyelashes. Then he whipped back to face me. "Now," he purred, "I have you. At last."

"Let's get it over with," I said dully.

"So quickly you want to get down to business. Might we chat a little? First, I truly must offer my condolences on your father. I am so sorry for your loss."

I bristled, willing my tears to dry. "I didn't think the Afeya were concerned with the short lives of mortal Lumerians."

His eyes brightened. "Come now, loss is loss. Do you not sorrow when a day ends or a flower wilts?"

My hands fisted at my sides, anger and hatred suddenly burning through me. "Or maybe you took a greater interest because last night, his own debt was paid. Is that what happened? He paid his debt, so now he could die!"

Mercurial bowed. "Releasing one from a blood oath," he clicked his tongue, "messy business. The magic does not appreciate when its debt goes unpaid. And to release three blood oaths? But, of course, he paid with his life."

"You killed him!" I shouted. I lifted a hand to punch him, but a powerful force pushed my arm down to my side.

Mercurial snarled. "He killed himself when he broke the bonds of the oath. I let him choose the language. He didn't offer his life. He offered to leave the Seat of Power. The magic chose the way it happened."

"You bastard!"

"Now, now. No time for that. I am only the messenger in this case. Enough about death. Something rather extraordinary happened last night. I fancied a chat about it." He came closer, his hand shooting for my heart. "Something happened when you wore your golden stars around your neck."

"My necklace," I said, stepping back from his touch. "The akadim, they didn't like it. It hurt them."

"A piece of jewelry hurting an akadim?" Mercurial shook his head. "I've never heard of such a thing. Unless the monster was previously an icon of fashion and found some offense in the design."

I narrowed my eyes at him, anger pulsing through me. "I think you have heard of such a thing. Why else were you so intent on me wearing it?"

"I had my reasons," he said. "But like I said, I never heard of *jewelry* hurting an akadim."

"Then what did?" I asked. I no longer cared to avoid asking questions. I was bound to him, about to sign my contract, sign away my soul—what was one more question asked?

"Not the gold," he said. "Not the shape of the star." He held out his hand, twisting his wrist with flourish, and my necklace appeared, the starfire diamonds glittering and gleaming red in the firelight. Three of the diamonds had been destroyed in the fight last night, but with a wave of his hand, the necklace was clean and the diamonds restored. Each star gleamed, each diamond whole and glittering red except for the three in the center, the three that Haleika —that the akadim—had broken. Those were clear.

I eyed them suspiciously. "You're almighty and powerful," I mocked. "The First Messenger of Her Royal Highness, Queen Ishtara. And you can't fix the starfire diamonds?"

Mercurial turned the necklace in his hand, and with a snap, it floated to my neck, clasping itself at my nape. "Of course, I can fix starfire. These diamonds, however, do not contain the material you speak of."

I blinked. "What?" The diamonds were red; only starfire turned red.

"Let me ask you a question, your grace," he said. "What happened the first time you wore this magnificent design?"

I felt the weight of my necklace against my chest. It had instantly warmed to my skin, molding itself to my shape. Like it had been mine from the start. Meant for me. Designed for me. Worn a thousand times before. I shook my head. I didn't want to tell him. To admit it. It sounded stupid. It was private.

But he swayed his head side to side, hypnotic, his eyes mesmerizing and drawing me in, and soon the answer was bursting from my tongue.

"I saw a beach. A golden beach."

"Lumeria." He grinned like a cat. "Lumeria Matavia. What else?"

"My hand," I said, remembering the vision. "But it wasn't my hand." I'd never told anyone this before. My fingers had been longer, my skin darker.

Mercurial eyed me carefully. "And what do you make of that?"

"I don't know," I said angrily, heart pounding. "You seem to know my thoughts. My dreams."

He smiled wider, his eyes narrowed.

"Why don't you tell me for once?" I said, hatred for this manipulative monster burning inside me, almost as fiercely as the fires had last night. I was tired of his questions, tired of his games.

"Last night, after the akadim broke the diamonds, what happened?" he asked.

I squeezed my eyes shut, not wanting to relive the moment. "I was bleeding," I said. "She cut me with her claws. And then she went for Rhyan. And I felt…fire inside of me. And power. My hand was broken, my ankle twisted, but then it wasn't. I was healed. I got up, and I chased her."

"I suppose you think it was love that motivated you?"

"What else could it have been?" I asked carefully.

"When the akadim broke these three diamonds last night, she released what was held inside them. Not starfire, but another common red substance. Blood. And you, your grace, were also bleeding. Do you know what that means? It means some of the blood you released from the stars mingled into your bloodstream. And some of your blood went back into the stars."

My mouth fell open. "There was blood in the necklace?"

Mercurial growled. "For Lumeria, do you not understand yet? This is no necklace! It's armor!"

I stared down, my chest heaving. "Armor. But...." My mind whirled.

"Yes. Armor from Lumeria Matavia. Why else could you not find the necklace in the Museion's jewelry exhibit? You were looking in the wrong place." He sneered. "And can you think of the last time you mixed your blood with another's? Mixed your blood with armor?"

I gasped. "With Rhyan at the Oath Ceremony. When we formed our kashonim. But I didn't—" I shook my head. "You're telling me I now have kashonim with the owner of this armor?"

"That's what lit the fire inside you. That's what gave you energy, strength, power. What allowed you to slay an akadim. What saved your precious Rhyan's life. Why else do you think it burned through you, left you sleeping for almost a day after?"

"Whose blood?" I asked, staring down at my arms. Whose blood ran through my veins?

"You may have heard of her. She was once an arkturion of the old world. A Guardian of the Valalumir in Heaven before she fell. The most powerful soturion in history. The Goddess Asherah."

I stumbled back. "Asherah? No. No. That's—That's not possible. How...how could I have a lineage with Asherah? Kashonim doesn't work like that. It only connects you to the part of your lineage that lives. And Asherah's dead."

Mercurial raced forward, his face inches from mine, his mouth pulled back in a feral sneer. Fire exploded around us, its flames licking my skin with a scalding heat. "You stupid, foolish girl!" His hand wrapped around my neck, his fingers squeezing, his chest rising and falling in rapid succession. "Goddesses. Never. Die." He pushed me back with such force, I fell to my ass, and crawled back onto my knees. Mercurial leaned forward, his hand gripping my chin, forcing my gaze upward. "They are reborn."

The fires vanished, and I rose to my feet, my heart pounding with what he'd said.

"Reborn?" I asked. "Are you saying…?"

"You are not human. You are no one's daughter. No one's sister. No one's friend. No one's lover. No one's slave. You are a goddess, made of the very essence of life itself. You are the sun, you are the moon, you are the stars. You are the water of the ocean, the dust of the Earth, the very air you breathe. And you," his lips curled, "you are the fire." He grinned. "And now, Goddess, you are in my debt."

"No," I said, still not daring to believe him. It was impossible. Unthinkable. I was Asherah. I was the Goddess reborn.

Mercurial rolled his eyes. "A goddess, a guardian, the fire at the center of the Valalumir, and the war, the drowning of the Lumerian Empire. Did you really think that Asherah could just die and her part in this was done? No. She's only getting started. *You're* only getting started. Now, let's finish the paperwork, shall we?"

He held up his opened palm, and the sparkling Valalumir he'd taunted me with for months spun and glittered. He blew at the star, and it burst into flames, flying straight for me, bypassing Asherah's armor, burning straight into my heart.

It was like the nahashim entering my body. Burning hot, invasive, burning me up from inside.

I screamed, as my insides turned to flames once more. My eyes closed, as I sank to the ground. The weight of it inside me almost too much to hold, to carry. And then, I was gone.

I woke beside the fortress pools. I was alone and shivering as a fresh bout of snow began to fall. Mercurial was gone, and I guessed if no one had come to find me, including Rhyan, I couldn't have been unconscious for more than a few minutes. I stared down at my armor, pulling it back to see my chest. The faintest outline of a golden Valalumir had been branded between my breasts. The mark of the star's entrance. The star that would bind me to Mercurial until I paid my debt for his silence.

I touched the stars again. Asherah's armor. My armor.

I felt dizzy.

Taking a deep breath, I picked up my skirts and started to run. I couldn't think about Mercurial's words yet. I needed to get back inside for the announcement, for the moment Meera abdicated to Arianna. But as I turned a corner, I spotted silver armor and immediately retreated.

Ka Kormac. Armed and inside our fortress? I flattened my body against the wall and peered back around the corner. Half a dozen of the Imperator's soturi marched forward. In the distance, two women appeared.

Arianna and Naria.

"Help me with this," Arianna said. Then she froze, noticing the soturi who surrounded her. "At ease," she said with disdain. "I don't require protection. I am quite safe."

"We're under the Imperator's orders," said one soturion.

Arianna scoffed and returned her attention to Naria. She presented her arm to her daughter—my horrible cousin. "It's chafing, but I need it in place. I must look perfect for your cousin's announcement."

"Yes, Mother," Naria said, her voice small and filled with more obedience than I'd ever heard her exhibit. She reached for the golden cuff around Arianna's bicep, the one in the shape of seraphim wings she'd been wearing for months.

"Pull," Arianna commanded. "Harder. Then I can adjust it properly."

Naria grunted, and with both hands, slid the cuff free from my aunt's arm.

"Thank you, my dear," Arianna said, massaging her arm and moaning in relief. With a sigh, she dropped her arm beside her, revealing the flash of skin that had been concealed under the cuff she'd worn for months.

Aunt Arianna had acquired a tattoo. One I'd seen before. The sigil of Ka Batavia. Seraphim wings under a full moon.

Black seraphim wings.

CHAPTER
THIRTY-TWO

The black seraphim.

My heart pounded. My vision went in and out of focus.

The Emartis hadn't just gotten their way. Arianna had. She'd been their leader. This entire time....

I saw Meera's mural in my mind. A girl with red hair who looked like me, exactly like me, turning into a black seraphim.

When Aunt Arianna was younger, she had been my spitting image. I looked more like her than my mother at my age.

The Emartis. The black seraphim. The vision. It had always been Arianna.

I didn't think. I couldn't think. It was too much.

I reached down the length of my leg, hiking up the hem of my black dress, revealing the hilt of my dagger—the dagger I'd earned when Arianna had snapped my stave in half and expelled me from my own Ka's academy. I closed my fingers around the smooth hilt and unsheathed the blade from my thigh.

My arm raised, my skirts flowed down to my heels, and I started forward.

Another half dozen soturi of Ka Kormac emerged from the shadows, and I stepped back, my chest rising and falling in rapid succession.

I couldn't kill her. Not like this. Not if I was going to survive.

Slowly, I stepped back, silently replacing my blade and clutching my chest, sure my heart was pounding as loud as a drum.

I turned the corner and found myself once more in the safety of the shadows. But I was not alone.

Mercurial stood there, his arms folded across his chest. He leaned his head forward, sniffing me with a grin. "Very good," he said. "I'm glad to see my goddess has allowed her mind to think before her body reacts."

I snarled. "Did you know? Did you know it was her?"

"And to think only moments ago, you were blaming me for his death. How the perception of the world around you changes. Though I admit, it brings me pleasure to see you placing the blame where it rightly belongs. One day, you and your little not-lord might do the same for yourselves, for all the guilt you carry for deaths that were orchestrated before you were even born."

"I have to stop her. I can't let her go into power."

"You can, and you will. But not tonight. Because we're about to play the long game, Goddess. Bamaria isn't stable. But soon it will be. Before you can find justice for your father and justice for your mother...."

I gasped. For my mother. By the Gods...there had been a reason why power had gone to my father instead of the next woman in the bloodline. For the first time ever, I considered that my mother hadn't just gotten sick, she'd been murdered. And most likely, by my aunt. My mother had known...known not to trust her.

Mercurial licked his thumb then pushed back my hair over my forehead and flounced some of my locks across my shoulder. I flinched.

"First, you're going to find your magic power. I will ensure it. For that is the only way you will pay your debt to me."

"My magic?" I asked.

"My remembered goddess, did you truly think you had none? No, you just have to come by it through a different path. Luckily, I have a map. Now go in there and play dumb, forget what you've seen. And when the time is right, you will strike and have your revenge. And then you will retake the throne of Bamaria."

"We don't have thrones here," I said, dully.

He pressed his hand to my armor, the gold warming to my chest, igniting the fire inside my heart and the Valalumir of our contract.

Mercurial vanished, leaving behind only his feline grin. "You will."

SOLSTICE OF THE DROWNED EMPIRE

Before you read Lady of the Drowned Empire, dive into Solstice of the Drowned Empire, a novella from Rhyan's POV with all the details of that one summer and their first kiss…

LADY OF THE DROWNED EMPIRE

THE STORY CONTINUES IN THE DROWNED EMPIRE
SERIES, #3

Lady of the Drowned Empire

THE EMPIRE OF LUMERIA

There are twelve countries united under the Lumerian Empire. The 12 Ruling Kavim of Lumeria Nutavia.

Each country is ruled by an Arkasva, the High Lord or Lady of the ruling Ka.

All twelve countries submit to the rule and law of the Emperor. Each Arkasva also answers to an Imperator, one Arkasva with jurisdiction over each country in either the Northern or Southern hemispheres of the Empire.

In addition to the Emperor's rule, twelve senators, one from each country (may not be a member of the ruling Ka) fill the twelve seats of the Senate. The roles of Imperator and Emperor are lifelong appointments. They may not be passed onto family members. Imperators and Emperors must be elected by the ruling Kavim. Kavim may not submit a candidate for either role if the previous Imperator or Emperor belonged to their Ka.

Imperators may keep their ties to their Ka and rule in their country. An Emperor will lose their Ka upon anointing and must be like a father or mother to all Lumerians.

EMPIRIC CHAIN OF COMMAND
EMPEROR THEOTIS, HIGH LORD OF LUMERIA NUTAVIA

The Emperor rules over the entire Empire, from its capitol, Numeria. The Emperor oversees the running of the Senate, and the twelve countries united under the Empire.

Devon Hart, Imperator to the North

The Imperator of the North if an Arkasva who rules not only their country, but oversees rule of the remaining five countries belonging to the North. His rule includes the following countries currently by the following Kavim:

Glemaria, Ka Hart
Payunmar, Ka Valyan
Hartavia, Ka Taria
Ereztia, Ka Sephiron
Aravia, Ka Lumerin
Sindhuvine, Ka Kether

Avery Kormac, Imperator to the South

The Imperator of the South is an Arkasva who rules not only their country, but oversees rule of the remaining five countries belonging to the North. The sitting Imperator is also nephew to the

Emperor. His rule includes the following countries currently being ruled by the following Kavim:

Bamaria, Ka Batavia

Korteria, Ka Kormac

Elyria, Ka Elys (previously Ka Azria)

Damara, Ka Daquataine

Lethea, Ka Maras

Cretanya, Ka Zarine

The Immortal Afeyan Courts*

The Sun Court: El Zandria, ruled by King RaKanam

The Moon Court: Khemet, ruled by Queen Ma'Nia

The Star Court: Night Lands, ruled by Queen Ishtara

Afeyan Courts are not considered part of the Lumerian Empire, nor do they submit to the Emperor, however, history, prior treaties, and trade agreements have kept the courts at peace, and working together. They are the only two groups to have shared life on the continent of Lumeria Matavia.

THE BAMARIAN COUNCIL

Each of the twelve countries in the Lumerian Empire includes a 12-member council comprised of members of the nobility to assist the Arkasva in ruling and decision-making.

The Bamarian Council includes the following:

Role, Name
Arkasva, Harren Batavia
Master of the Horse, Eathan Ezara
Arkturion, Aemon Melvik
Turion, Dairen Melvik
Arkmage, Kolaya Scholar
Master of Education, Arianna Batavia
Master of Spies, Sila Shavo
Master of Finance, Romula Grey
Master of Law, Kiera Ezara
Naturion, Dagana Scholar
Senator, Janvi Elys
Master of Peace, Brenna Corra

TITLES AND FORMS OF ADDRESS

Arkasva (Ark-kas-va): Ruler of the country, literally translates as the "will of the highest soul."

    Arkasvim (Ark-kas-veem): Plural of Arkasva

    Arkturion (Ark-tor-ree-an): Warlord for the country, general of their soturi/army.

    Imperator: A miniature Emperor. The Empire always has two Imperators, one for the Northern Hemisphere, one for the South. The Imperator will also be the arkasva of their country, they have jurisdiction over their hemisphere but also act as a voice and direct messenger between each Arkasva and the Emperor.

    Emperor: Ruler of all twelve countries in the Lumerian Empire. The Emperor is elected by the ruling arkasvim. They are appointed for life. Once an Emperor or Empress dies, the Kavim must elect a new ruler. The Emperor must renounce their Ka when anointed, but no Ka may produce an Emperor/Empress twice in a row.

    Heir Apparent: Title given to the eldest child or heir of the Arkasva. The next in line to the Seat of Power or First from the Seat.

    Soturion: Soldier, magically enhanced warrior. A Lumerian who can transmute magic through their body. May be used as a form of address for a non-noble.

Turion: Commander, may lead legions of soturi, must answer to their Arkturion.

Mage: A Lumerian who transmutes magic through spells. A stave is used to focus their magic. The more focus one has, the less a stave is needed, but the more magic one can use, the larger the stave may need to be. Arkmages (the high mages) tend to have staves as tall as them.

Novice: The term used to describe a soturion or mage who is in the beginning of their learning to become an anointed mage or soturion.

Apprentice: The term used to describe a soturion or mage who has passed their first three years of training. As an apprentice their time is divided between their own studies and teaching the novice they are bound to. This is done to strengthen the power of Kashonim, and because of the Bamarian philosophy that teaching a subject is the best way to learn and master a subject.

Lady: Formal address for a female, or female-identifying member of the nobility.

Lord: Formal address for a male, or male-identifying member of the nobility.

Your Grace: Formal address for any member of the ruling Ka. Anyone who is in line to the Seat of Power must be addressed so, including the Arkasva. A noble may only be addressed as "your grace" if they are in line to the Seat.

Your Highness: Reserved as formal address only for the member of Lumerian nobility serving as imperator. The term of address has also been adopted by the Afeyan Star Court.

Your Majesty: Used only for the Emperor or Empress. Previously used for the kings and queens of Lumeria Matavia. This can also be applied to the King and Queen of the Afeyan Sun and Moon Courts.

GLOSSARY

Names:

Lyriana Batavia (Leer-ree-ana Ba-tah-via): Third in line to the Seat of Power in Bamaria

Morgana Batavia (Mor-ga-na Ba-tah-via): Second in line to the Seat of Power in Bamaria

Meera Batavia (Mee-ra Ba-tah-via): First in line to the Seat of Power in Bamaria (Heir Apparent)

Naria Batavia (Nar-ria Ba-tah-via): Niece to the Arkasva, not in line to the Seat

Arianna Batavia (Ar-ree-ana Ba-tah-via): Sister-in-law to the Arkasva, previously third in line to Seat, Master of Education on the Council of Bamaria

Aemon Melvik (Ae-mon Mel-vik): Warlord of Bamaria, Arkturion on the Council of Bamaria

Rhyan Hart (Ry-an Hart): Forsworn and exiled from Glemaria. Previously was in first in line to the Seat of Power (Heir Apparent)

Haleika Grey (Hal-eye-ka Gray): Tristan's cousin, and one of the few friends and allies Lyr has in the Soturion Academy

Auriel (Or-ree-el): Original Guardian of the Valalumir in

Heaven, stole the light to bring to Earth where it turned into a crystal before shattering at the time of the Drowning

Asherah (A-sher-ah): Original Guardian of the Valalumir in Heaven. She was banished to Earth as a mortal after her affair with Auriel was discovered.

Mercurial (Mer-cure-ree-el): An immortal Afeya, First Messenger of her Highness Queen Ishtara, High Lady of the Night Lands

Moriel (Mor-ree-el): Original Guardian of the Valalumir in Heaven. He reported Auriel and Asherah's affair to the Council of 44 leading to Asherah's banishment, Auriel's theft of the light, and its subsequent destruction. He was banished to Earth where he allied with the akadim in the war that led to the Drowning.

Theotis (Thee-otis): Current Emperor of Lumeria Nutavia. Theotis was previously from Korteria, and a noble of Ka Kormac. His nephew, Avery Kormac, is the current Imperator to the Southern hemisphere of the Empire, and Arkasva to Korteria.

Avery Kormac (Ae-very Core-mac): Nephew to the Emperor, as Imperator, he rules over the six southern countries of the Empire, as well as ruling Korteria as the Arkasva.

Afeya (Ah-fay-ah): Immortal Lumerians who survived the Drowning. Prior to, Afeya were non-distinguishable from other Lumerians in Lumeria Matavia. They were descended from the Gods and Goddesses, trapped in the mortal coil. But they refused the request to join the war efforts. Some sources believe they allied with Moriel's forces and the akadim. When the Valalumir shattered, they were cursed to live forever, unable to return to their home, be relieved of life, or touch or perform magic—unless asked to by another.

Places:

Lumeria (Lu-mair-ria): The name of continent where Gods and Goddesses first incarnated until it sank into the Lumerian Ocean in the Drowning.

Matavia (Ma-tah-via): Motherland. When used with Lumeria, it refers to the continent that sank.

Nutavia (New-tah-via): New land. When used with Lumeria, it refers to the Empire forged after the Drowning by those who survived and made it to Bamaria—previously Dobra.

Bamaria (Ba-mar-ria): Southernmost country of the Lumerian Empire, home of the South's most prestigious University and the Great Library. Ruled by Ka Batavia.

Korteria (Kor-ter-ria): Westernmost country in the Empire. Magic is least effective in their mountains, but Korteria does have access to Starfire for Lumerian weapons. Ruled by Ka Kormac.

Elyria (El-leer-ria): Historically ruled by Ka Azria, rulership has now passed to Ka Elys, originally nobility from Bamaria.

Lethea (Lee-thee-a): The only part of the Empire located in the Lumerian Ocean. Ruled by Ka Maras, this is the country where criminals stripped of powers, or accused of vorakh are sent for imprisonment. The expression "Farther than Lethea" comes from the fact that there is nothing but ocean beyond the island. Due to the Drowning, the idea of going past the island is akin to losing one's mind.

Damara (Da-mar-ra): A Southern country known for strong warriors, ruled by Ka Daquataine.

Glemaria (Gleh-mar-ria): Northernmost country of the Empire, ruled by Ka Hart. Imperator Devon Hart is the Arkasva and Imperator to the North. Rhyan Hart was previously first in line to the Seat.

Prominent Creatures of the Old World Known to Have Survived the Drowning:

Seraphim (Ser-a-feem): Birds with wings of gold, they resemble a cross between an eagle and a dove. Seraphim are peaceful creatures, sacred in Bamaria, and most often used for transport across the Lumerian Empire. Though delicate in appearance, they are extremely strong and can carry loads of up ten people over short distances. Seraphim all prefer warmer climates and are rarely found in the northernmost part of the Empire.

Ashvan: Flying horses. These are the only sky creatures that do not possess wings. Their flight comes from magic contained in their hooves. Once an ashvan picks up speed, their magic will create small temporary pathways to run upon. Technically, ashvan cannot fly, but are running on magic pathways that appear and vanish once stepped upon. Residue of the magic is left behind, creating streaks behind them, but these fade within seconds.

Nahashim: Snakes with the ability to grow and shrink at will, able to fit into any size space for the purposes of seeking. Anything lost or desired can almost always be found by a nahashim. Their scales remain almost burning hot and they prefer to live near the water. Most nahashim are bred on Lethea, the country furthest out into the ocean, closest to the original location of Lumeria Matavia.

Gryphon (Grif-in): Sky creatures that are half eagle, half lion. Extremely large, these animals can be taken into battle, preferring mountains and colder climates. They replace seraphim and ashvan in the northernmost parts of the Lumerian Empire. They may carry far heavier loads than seraphim.

Akadim (A-ka-deem): The most feared of all creatures, literally bodies without souls. Akadim kill by eating the soul of their victims. The demonic creatures were previously Lumerians transformed. Akadim grow to be twice the size of a Lumerian and gain five times the strength of a soturion. Immortal as long as they continue to feed on souls, these creatures are impervious to Lumerian magic. Akadim are weakened by the sun and tend to live in the Northern Hemisphere.

Water Dragon: Dragons with blue scales that live deep in the Lumerian Ocean. Previously spending their time equally between land and water, all water dragons have taken to the Lumerian Ocean and are usually spotted closer to Lethea.

Agnavim (Ahg-naw-veem): Rarely sighted in Lumerian lands. These red birds with wings made of pure flame favor the lands occupied by the Afeyan Star Court. Lumerians have been unable to tame them since the Drowning.

Terms/Items:

Birth Bind/Binding: Unlike a traditional bind which includes a spell that ties a rope around a Lumerian to keep them from touching their power, or restricting their physical ability to move a Birth Bind leaves no mark. A Binding is temporary, and can have more or less strength and heat depending on the mage casting the spell. A Birth Bind is given to all Lumerians in their first year of life, a spell that will keep them from accessing their magic power whenever it develops. All Lumerians

develop their magic along with puberty. The Birth Bind may only be removed after the Lumerian has turned nineteen, the age of adulthood.

Dagger: Ceremonial weapon given to soturi. The dagger has no special power on its own as the magic of a soturion is transmuted through their body.

Ka (Kah): Soul. A Ka is a soul tribe or family.

Kashonim (Ka-show-neem): Ancestral lineage and link of power. Calling on Kashonim allows you to absorb the power of your lineage, but depending on the situation, usage can be dangerous. For one, it can be an overwhelming amount of power that leaves you unconscious if you come from a long lineage, or a particularly powerful one. Two, it has the potential to weaken the mages or soturi the caller is drawing from. It is also illegal to use against fellow students.

Kavim (Ka-veem): Plural of Ka. A Ka can be likened to a soul tribe or family. When marriages occur, either member of the union may take on the name of their significant other's Ka. Typically, the Ka with more prestige or nobility will be used thus ensuring the most powerful Kavim continue to grow.

Laurel of the Arkasva (Lor-el of the Ar-kas-va): A golden circlet like a crown worn by the Arkasva. The Arkasva replaced the title of King and Queen in Lumeria Matavia, and the Laurel replaced the crown though they are held in the same high esteem.

Seat of Power: Akin to a throne. Thrones were replaced by Seats in Lumeria Nutavia, as many members of royalty were blamed by the citizens of Lumeria for the Drowning. Much as a monarch may have a throne room, the Arkasvim have a Seating Room. The Arkasva typically has a Seat of Power in their Seating Room in their Ka's fortress, and another in their temple.

Stave: Made of twisted moon and sun wood, the stave transmutes magic created by mages. A stave is not needed to perform magic, but greatly focuses and strengthens it. More magic being transmuted may require a larger stave.

Vadati (Va-dah-tee): Stones that allow Lumerians to hear and speak to each other over vast distances. Most of these stones were lost in the Drowning. The Empire now keeps a strict registry of each known stone.

Valalumir (Val-la-loo-meer): The sacred light of Heaven that began the Celestial War which began in Heaven and ended with the Drowning. The light was guarded by seven Gods and Goddesses until Asherah and Auriel's affair. Asherah was banished to become mortal, and Auriel fell to bring her the light. Part of the light went into Asherah before it crystalized. When the war ended, the Valalumir shattered in seven pieces—all lost in the Drowning.

Valya (Val-yah): The sacred text of recounting the history of the Lumerian people up until the Drowning. There are multiple valyas recorded, each with slight variations, but the Mar Valya is the standard. Another popular translation is the Tavia Valya which is believed to have been better preserved than the Mar Valya after the Drowning, but was never made into the standard for copying. Slight changes or possible effects of water damage offer different insights into Auriel's initial meeting with Asherah.

Vorakh (Vor-rock): Taboo, forbidden powers. Three magical abilities that faded after the Drowning are considered illegal: visions, mind-reading, and traveling by mind. Vorakh can be translated as "gift from the Gods" in High Lumerian, but is now translated as "curse from the Gods."

LUMERIAN RITES OF PASSAGE

Revelation Ceremony: All Lumerians are given a Birth Bind in their first year of life, a spell that will keep them from accessing their magic power whenever it develops. All Lumerians develop their magic along with puberty. **The Birth Bind** may only be removed after the Lumerian has turned nineteen, the age of adulthood. Any Lumerian who is nineteen may participate in the Revelation Ceremony that year, celebrated on Auriel's Feast Day. At this time, their binding is removed by an Arkmage, and they may choose whether they will become a mage and be offered a stave, or a soturion and receive a dagger. The Arkmage will cut each participant to begin an oath that completes itself in the Oath Ceremony. Participants traditionally wear white robes which are discarded after their choice is made. A cut is made to the left wrist for a soturion, and their oath is made by dripping their blood into fire. A cut is made to the right wrist for a mage, and their oath is made by dripping their blood into water.

Oath Ceremony: Following the decision to become a mage or soturion, every Lumerian will become part of a Kashonim, or lineage. This allows them greater access to power in times of need, as well as continues to establish bonds across the Kavim and keep the Empire united. During the Oath Ceremony, every mage and soturion becomes a novice, and is bound to an apprentice. Once the oath is sworn, the novice has access to the powers of the apprentice's entire living lineage. The apprentice is also duty-bound to teach the novice all they know. Romantic relationships are strongly discouraged between mage apprentice and novices.

Romantic relationships are strictly forbidden between apprentice and novice soturi as this can cause interruptions to their duties to fight and protect. Participants traditionally wear black robes which are burned before their apprentice dresses them in their new attire.

Anointing: After an apprentice completes their training, they will be anointed, and become a full-fledged member of Lumerian society. An anointed mage or soturion is one who has completed their training. Anointing ceremonies will also be performed anytime a Lumerian rises in rank, for example an Heir becoming Arkasva, or an Arkasva becoming Imperator or Emperor. Anointings signify a life-long role.

ACKNOWLEDGMENTS

I still feel like I was just publishing Daughter of the Drowned Empire, but here I am again only a few months later, and it's time for some acknowledgements. Creating Guardian was a very different process from Daughter in some ways, and in others, not much changed. The biggest thing to know is that originally, the events of Guardian were meant to take place in Daughter, but the manuscript was becoming too long, and after a certain someone decided to break the book in half (twice) *cough* Marcella *cough*, I could see there were two stories here, though they are very much meant to be read together. So when I sat down after Daughter was out, I thought I had half of Guardian already written.

Dear reader, I was wrong. SO wrong. I threw nearly everything I wrote away, and started again. The bones of the story still existed, but...not much else. And I am so proud of the result.

But, I would have never gotten to that point ever if it were not for a little club known as the First Novels Club. Okay, we were never a club, just friends who met in a creative writing class in grad school, but that was our blog name, and so...

Donna, seriously, my wifey, what can I say. You have been there every step of the journey, read every horrible draft, and listened to me go on for hours and hours...probably years at this point about this book. I am so grateful for your critical eye, and the fact that you never let me get away with anything, even though it's not that fun in the moment to take all your notes—yet I wouldn't have it any other way, your notes are gold. You really have been such a guiding force for my writing. And of course thank you, thank you, thank you for reading the whole draft, and sending your voice-messages from vacation as you read. Thank you!

Sara, again, how many Sundays did we spend in our "office" scrawling plot points and character motives on the giant whiteboard. It's been years, but without those whiteboard sessions, I wouldn't have figured out the underbelly of Guardian.

Janine, all of your gentle encouragement over the years and reading has meant the world to me.

Marcella (not a part of the FNC), thank you for being the one to talk me down over and over and be my mentor (when did our roles switch?) and remind me that I could actually do this, and also that despite all of my doubts, I did know what I was doing the whole time. Oh yeah, and thanks for forcing me to take breaks and celebrate and enjoy the moment—still learning to do that!

Asha, you have no idea how grateful I am to you for beta-reading, and reading so quickly! Also, thank you for letting me spew the entire ending on you for several hours before I actually wrote the thing.

Mom, thank you for constantly supporting my efforts to run after my dream.

Elissa, seriously, thank you! Data Analyst God! And being an amazing and crucial support system for letting me get this done.

Julie, your help for this round was absolutely necessary and amazing! You know what you did!

Eva, thank you for reminding me to take breaks and feeding me lunch.

Michael, thank you for the constant support you give.

Dylan, Blake, Hannah, and Dani, really just you all existing makes everything better.

Aunt Simone, for being an actually amazing aunt (not an evil one)!

Nina, thank you thank you for allowing me to actually see and reflect on all the things that made its way into the story. I don't think I could have pulled this out of myself or my psyche until this year, and the timing in the end was exactly as it should be.

Steve, thank you for being the defender of the realm, and guardian of the virtual empire.

Stefanie, for another exceptional cover design, and for not killing me when I almost destroyed it. Thank you for accepting my resignation from the design team. I just write the words, you have the vision.

Danielle, once again, amazing editing! Thank you.

The Drowned Empire ARC Team, I love you! You'll never know how much your enthusiasm and support energized me through finishing Guardian. I am forever grateful you all took a chance on me and my book, and have trusted me to continue telling the story.

A very special thank you to the Drowned Empire Street Team: Jade Lawson, Kiah McDaniel, Iliana Katana, Sandra Glazebrook, Joyce Fernandez, Jennifer Sebring, Alina Heras, Erin Smith, Katie Hunsberger, Heather Corrales, Sam Love, Emily Kordys, Priscilla Osorno, Quinn Shing, Jess Murphy, Katie Mazza, Christine Stewart, Andrea Morgan, Brittany Crain, Audra Jones, Meg Hughes, Kayla Reneau, Kelsey Rhodes, Emma Reece, Lauren, Tifany Ness, Céline Yzewyn, Alexandra Marshall, Kayleigh Foland, Justine Caylor, Marisa Sevenski, Tandia Dudman, Shana Heinrich, Kyla Clarkston, Victoria Webb, Takecia Bright, Marisa Alsua, Kayla Hjelmstad, Tasha Jenkins, Megan Cristofaro, Courtney Stosser, Yaneth Aguirre, Brianne Glickman, Brynly Kapelanski, Bekah Abraham, Jenna Romano, Kristianna Weppler, Olivia Baumgartner, Mandy Carleton, Madi Healey, Alisa Tippin, Liz Adams, Le'Yema Walker, Lara Kine, Cheyenne Terry, Raqui Cobo-Flores, Nadia Larumbe, Alex Hawks, Krista (K.T.) Magrowski, Sarah Heifetz, Maria Schmelz, Evan Hathaway, Heather Aspero, and Zoë Osik. Thank you!

And you, yes you reading this. I am grateful.

Love,

Frankie

ALSO BY FRANKIE DIANE MALLIS

The Drowned Empire Series:

Daughter of the Drowned Empire, Drowned Empire #1

Guardian of the Drowned Empire, Drowned Empire #2

Solstice of the Drowned Empire, A Drowned Empire Novella #0.5

Lady of the Drowned Empire, Drowned Empire #3

ABOUT THE AUTHOR

Frankie Diane Mallis lives outside of Philadelphia where she is an award-winning university professor. When not writing or teaching, she practices yoga and belly dance and can usually be found baking gluten free desserts. The Drowned Empire Series is her fantasy romance debut series. Visit www.frankiedianemallis.com to learn more, and join the newsletter. Follow Frankie on Instagram @frankiediane, and on TikTok @frankiedianebooks.

LADY OF THE DROWNED EMPIRE: CHAPTER ONE

MORGANA

(One year earlier: the night of my Revelation Ceremony)

I thought I'd known pain before. I was wrong.

My knuckles matched the white of the marble banister beneath them. I stood at the edge of my balcony outside my bedroom. My shoulders were tense and my gaze unfocused on the crashing waves of the Lumerian Ocean. A full moon cast light on the fortress of Cresthaven, but the headache pounding through my skull blurred my vision, making the familiar towers appear foreign.

In the distance, a seraphim squawked, and the rolling sounds of waves rushed forward over the sand. I swayed, dizzy from the pain. Still, I gripped the banister. Harder. Harder.

The clocktower began screaming the new hour. Ashvan fled to the sky, riders on the backs of the jewel-toned horses scouting over Bamaria.

It's late. So fucking late.

When I'm done here, shit's going down!

Buy more rice tomorrow.

I slammed my hands on the railing. The Godsdamned voices. I couldn't escape. I'd been hearing them for hours now, ever since

Arkmage Kolaya had removed my Birth Bind. The blinding torment of the incessant thoughts had begun on the dais in the temple, and it was unrelenting. Nothing seemed to relieve the pain; nothing stopped the noise. I couldn't hide, couldn't find a moment of fucking silence. My own mind was no longer safe.

The backs of my eyes burned. Shit. Shit. The voices were coming faster now. Louder. Interrupting my own thoughts. The ashvan riders in the sky were too close for me to ignore.

Fucking Ka Batavia, stupid blue palace.

If I ever get to Lady Morgana...skirts going up....

I released the banister, pressing the heels of my palms into my eyes. I would not cry. I would not cry. Between my two sisters, enough tears had been shed tonight, enough tears for an Afeya's lifetime. I wouldn't add one single tear more. Tears didn't change shit. Tears didn't get you what you wanted. They made you weak. They forced you into a ball on your bed with your fingers digging into your belly as you sobbed in agony, crying like a child, waiting and waiting while no one came to help.

I've kept the secret this long....

The voices pounded through my thoughts.

They don't know she's a traitor. Soon they will.

Fly faster, you Moriel-horse. Fucking tired....

I covered my ears. It didn't help.

Shekar arkasva!

I pressed harder into my temples, pushing back the tears. I could see my father's dagger in my mind's eye, covered in my blood, in his blood, in the blood of my sisters.

Picking up the dagger and sliding the blade down the skin of my wrist—slicing off the scars of my second blood oath—had been on my mind all night. The thought overwhelmed me, its grip like a vice on my soul.

I hadn't done it. I wasn't stupid. The act would be nothing more than useless violence with no result. The magic my father had invoked ran far deeper. I could cut off my arm, and I'd still be bound for life.

Even without the oath in place, I would remain vorakh. I was doomed to this pain.

I shut my eyes, leaning forward against the cool stone of the banister, listening to the waves crash in the night.

Need a Godsdamned drink.

Final shift tonight. Thank fuck.

So many thoughts. All in my head. All at once.

Gods, I want....

Fucking gryphon-shit....

Emartis....

Releasing my grip, I stumbled backward. My back slammed into the wall, and I slid down to the ground, to my knees, with my head in my hands. A hammer pounding in my mind.

Why was it all so loud? Shut up! Shut up! Shut the fuck up!

The blue lights faded. The patrol was over. But the thoughts of the riders and every other person awake within the walls of the fortress continued.

One red, one blue....

Need to piss!

Hurts, doesn't it?

My fingers tangled in my hair as the new thought entered my mind. The voice was smoother and louder, standing out for just a moment before mixing and joining the thousands of others.

I groaned, wanting to slide a blade into the heart of whoever had thought that. Whatever they thought was hurting them, they had no idea. They didn't know pain.

You're wrong, said the voice again. *I know pain. I know it well.*

The thought rang so clearly in my mind, sweat beaded at my forehead, dampening the thick hair at the nape of my neck. An ashvan rider? A sentry on duty below? It sounded like they were responding to me. To my thoughts. But that...that wasn't possible.

Isn't it, though? Possible? Because here I am. Responding.

His voice felt like a shadowy fog, deep and smoky.

I stood up and rushed forward, searching beyond the balcony and fortress walls for him. But the grounds were empty, the neighboring balconies abandoned at this hour. I raced back inside where the torches were lit, fires crackling and spitting and dousing the room in a golden fiery glow. Not one soul was in sight. No escorts or sentries were allowed up here.

Don't try to look for me. You won't see my face. Not until I want you to.

I clutched my head. Was I farther than Lethea? Was this actually happening? Had the pain twisted and ruined my mind to play tricks on me?

How many times have you heard of Lumerians being arrested and taken away for vorakh? Taken to Lethea? Stripped? Or worse? You don't think it's possible that this is happening? Did you think that you were that special? That you were the only one? Your sister and cousin were cursed with the same affliction.

I shook my head. *No...no.* This wasn't real.

I assure you, this is very real, unfortunately for me and for you. I hear you quite clearly, just as I know you hear me. You're not the only mind reader in Bamaria. You're not the only one in the Empire. Not by a long shot.

I searched the shore for movement, for signs of life. But there was nothing more than a seraphim resting on her belly, her wings, bronzed beneath the moonlight, rustling against the sand and the water rushing back and forth across the shoreline. Not even a set of footsteps marred the beach.

How many are there? I asked.

Too many. Too many who found far worse fates than the pounding in your delicate noble skull.

I sucked in a breath, my chest rising and falling. *How are you doing this?*

How can I hear you? came the response. *Stupid question. We can both hear. Doesn't take much to focus. The same way you have a conversation in a crowded room and still hear the person you're speaking to.*

I could feel their vitriol and lack of patience in my mind.

So you really are like me? The moment I had the thought, I checked my wrist, expecting the scars of my blood oath to redden, to burn me.

You haven't broken your oath. And before you ask, I already knew. Knew the moment it happened. I knew about Meera. There was a long beat, and a shadow swept through my mind. *I know about Jules.*

My heart pounded, sweat dripping from my neck to my collarbone.

Who are you? I asked.

If I won't let you see me until I want you to, you won't know my name either. Until I want you to.

What will make you want to?

He was quiet as my mind raced.

How do you do that? I asked desperately. *Go silent. Stop thinking. Tell me.*

That wasn't what I came to teach you tonight. Nor was it my intention to see you. Or to tell you my name. You must learn patience first. For some time now I've been watching you, listening, and I know you have none, Morgana.

I shook my head. He'd been spying on me. How long? How many thoughts had he stolen from me? My family?

You go too far when you speak my name informally, I thought.

I didn't speak. And all things considered, I think we're far past formalities. Don't you?

What do you want? I asked.

He was silent again. I couldn't tell if he'd decided to end our conversation or was refusing to answer.

I bit my lip, fighting back the anger inside me. *I don't want to play games. Speak, or end this now. I see no point in you revealing this much of yourself if you don't intend to help me.*

You dismiss games too easily. Games can be fun. This is all so you know you're not alone.

Gryphon-shit! I stared again at the empty shore, the abandoned balconies. *I'm still alone!*

If a thought could translate into a shrug, he'd done just that.

You're powerful, he thought. *Perhaps more so than any other vorakh I've met.*

I sneered. *I wouldn't exactly call this a meeting. And I've been vorakh mere hours. How could you know anything of how powerful I am?*

Because of who you are.

Ka Batavia? So?

Your power comes from something far deeper than your bloodline and name.

I returned to the edge of my balcony, staring at the waterway beneath. A smooth sheet of glass covered the running water that fed magic from the Lumerian Ocean throughout Bamaria. I wasn't too high up. If I drank myself into unconsciousness, that would solve tonight. But tomorrow, I'd still be here. And hungover. I eyed the glass, calculating the distance below, my leg already lifting to straddle the ledge. Maybe it was far enough. I eyed my tower. Maybe I could climb until I inevitably slipped—

Stop! the voice shouted. *Put your Godsdamned foot back on the ground.*

Why? I shifted my weight back until both feet touched the floor. *I don't want this—this life, this pain, this whole conversation with you.*

You'd rather break all your bones? That's all that will happen if you jump. You won't die. I'm sure of it. If you think you're in pain now, just wait until you're healing every single broken bone in your body, feeling them mend and reshape, all while listening to the endlessly inane thoughts of the healers caring for you day and night.

Go away, I sniffled. It was too much. It was all too much.

I can take your pain away.

I froze.

But only briefly, he thought. *There are ways to manage vorakh. They don't want you to know, they don't want you to hide from them, to learn their secrets. I can help you. I don't mind, especially for someone with your...qualities.*

There was a seductive edge to his words.

Are you going to bring me a glass of wine to numb my pain?

You can drink yourself to oblivion if you want. Smoke moon-leaves until you're higher than a seraphim. I have another method to ease your suffering. His words were like a caress in my mind.

What method? I asked, my throat dry.

Let me come to you. Let me show you.

You said you wouldn't show yourself to me.

There was a smile in his words as he thought, *I won't. It's dark.*

How do I know you won't hurt me? I crossed my arms over my chest, a chill spreading across my body. The hairs on my arms stood on end.

If I wished you harm, I'd have let you be. Watched you climb to the top of your little tower and fall. You're the only one trying to hurt yourself tonight, acting out, imagining blades on your skin, falling, hiding from your fate. You're acting as scared as a helpless kitten.

I squeezed my eyes shut. I couldn't let him come to me alone, but what other option did I have? I couldn't explain this to an escort. Certainly not to Meera, definitely not Lyr. Not without them becoming suspicious and scared and hurting my head with their thoughts more than they already had.

This was a bad idea. Too dangerous. Too unknown.

And yet, as much as I was afraid, something inside me wanted to say yes.

If this was a trap, if he were to hurt me, to kill me…. I squeezed my hands into fists, my nails cutting into my palms. Lyr had things under control. She'd care for Meera—far better than I would. I wasn't necessary. I wasn't needed. And I couldn't take much more of this pain.

How will you get into the fortress? I asked. *We're surrounded by walls, guards. Only one entrance will open. The rest are warded and have been impenetrable for a thousand years.*

I'm aware of Cresthaven's protections.

Are you Ka Batavia? I asked.

I am beyond the Kavim.

Lumerian? I asked.

I consider myself beyond that as well.

I frowned. *Afeya?*

Don't insult me.

Then don't come.

I'm afraid it's far too late for that.

There was a knock on my door, the thud loud enough to steal my breath. I stepped back as wind gushed through the doors of my balcony, swirling my black gown against my bare feet.

"Lyr?" I called, my voice shaking. "Meera?"

You're vorakh. You'd have heard your sisters approach. You know Godsdamned well it's me.

I stepped back, shocked he was inside the fortress, shocked he'd gotten so close so quickly. *There are guards downstairs.*

A fine threat indeed. I walked right past them as I came inside your little fortress. I'll walk past them again when I leave.

The backs of my legs hit the bed. I stared down at my discarded diadem at the edge of the covers. Nothing else was in sight to use to fight—

I told you I wouldn't hurt you. But you're well on your way to doing that on your own.

I don't trust you, I thought, fear overriding my desperation.

That's good, came his response. *You shouldn't trust anyone. Men lie. Most often to themselves. Thoughts aren't truths. Just thoughts.*

I squeezed my eyes shut, grabbing the folds of my gown. I didn't know what to do, only that I'd been in pain for hours, and my future held more of it.

It's your choice, he thought. *Say yes, and I enter. Say no, I leave you to your suffering. But you will succumb to me sooner or later. One day, the pain will be too much. Too hard. Too blinding. You won't be able to take anymore. And on that day, you'll take things into your own hands. Or someone else will. Someone will notice. Vorakh hunters stalk your fortress; one is already too close. You know of whom I speak: the young Lord Grey. If you do not gain control, the secret will cease, and your greatest fear will come to pass—your sisters will be exposed.*

I stared at the door, the only thing separating him from me. It was unlocked. If he'd wanted to enter, he would have by now—with or without my permission.

Exactly, he confirmed. *You're showing a real talent for reading and discerning thoughts.*

Men lie, I thought.

They do. Now make your choice.

I squeezed my eyes shut, my chest heaving. *You can really help me?*

I don't allow other vorakh to suffer.

I could feel the truth resonating in his words, the thought carrying far more conviction than anything else he'd communicated. I nodded. *Come in.*

Turn off the lights. Use your stave, the one you left on your nightstand. Every single light. Don't just extinguish them, make it black. Call the darkness to you. You know the spell.

He not only knew my thoughts, but he could see through my eyes. He knew my name, my secrets, my fears….

And I knew nothing of him. Why couldn't I see through his eyes?

There was no answer from him. I was sure he'd heard me and was choosing not to reply, going silent like he had before, keeping me locked out of his mind.

My head was screaming, my heart hammering. But nothing could be worse than this. This pain, this agony.

My hands shaking, I walked alongside the bed and retrieved my stave, the twisting of moon and sun tree branches cool and smooth against my palm.

This was to be my first true show of magic. My first spell, my first act as a mage. Perhaps my last.

I lifted the stave and winced. Every movement worsened the pain in my head. I pointed at the first torch, the stave warming to my touch, the tip glowing with blue light.

"*Ani petrova lyla.*" A spark shot forth, smothering the flames. A hiss of smoke on a charred stick was all that remained. I turned, directing the stave's light to the next torch and the next, repeating the spell until I saw nothing but black and heard nothing but the sound of my heavy breaths against the whisper of extinguished flames and the wind hissing across the waves of the ocean.

Good, he thought. *Now I ask one last time. Are you sure?*

Yes.

Will you let me into your room, Morgana?

Yes.

The door creaked open, filling with his dark shadow.

My heart hammered even louder, as he stepped inside with another caress of his thoughts against my mind.

Hello, kitten.

Made in the USA
Coppell, TX
08 October 2023